FALLING BACKWARDS

Marti Leimbach was born in 1963 in Washington, DC. She is the author of three previous novels, including *Dying Young*, which served as the basis for a major motion picture released in 1991, and *Love and Houses*, published by Pan Books in 1997. She now lives in Berkshire.

books by Marti Leimbach

DYING YOUNG

SUN DIAL STREET

LOVE AND HOUSES

FALLING BACKWARDS

Marti Leimbach

PAN BOOKS

First published 2001 by Macmillan

This edition published 2002 by Pan Books
an imprint of Pan Macmillan Ltd
Pan Macmillan, 20 New Wharf Road, London N1 9RR
Basingstoke and Oxford
Associated companies throughout the world
www.panmacmillan.com

ISBN 0 330 37597 0

1 3 5 7 9 8 6 4 2

A CIP catalogue record for this book is available from
the British Library.

Typeset by SetSystems Ltd, Saffron Walden, Essex
Printed and bound in Great Britain by
Mackays of Chatham plc, Chatham, Kent

In memory of MacDonald Harris

1

The day before the end of our marriage, we'd been at a wedding. This is the sort of irony which, had it not been our Darkest Hour, might have sparked James into fits of laughter over the tragicomedy of it all, the emotional slapstick that had the effect of making our lives indeed imitate art, or not art exactly but a kind of sordid student production. Our lives with black-box staging and poorly constructed, borrowed props. If it weren't so serious an offence he'd have confessed it all to me just as we took our seats among the other wedding guests.

As it was he complained because his suit was too tight and asked if I thought he was getting a paunch. The idea of James with a paunch was ridiculous. The idea of James with any excess body fat at all was ridiculous. He seemed forever to radiate energy and this odd physical quirk had the effect of keeping him very thin despite a lack of formal exercise. He sat down, his curly hair catching the light from a spot lamp fixed to the wall behind him, and looked up at the vaulted ceiling, squinting at the Latin sculpted in chipped mortar above us. I watched as he drifted in thought, or rather as his mind launched him to a plane only he could inhabit, for he was in the incipient stages of a manic cycle, and was capable of thinking with lightning speed about the most obscure subjects: the numbers of days, hours, minutes until the next solar eclipse, what time it was – what time exactly – all over the world. He might state out loud some complicated mathematical theorem, as though reading it from a book, or recite pi to the 25th digit. I knew from experience that these flights of intellect did not yield perfect results, he was likely to run diverse and mutually exclusive ideas together in a hodgepodge that rendered them nonsensical, frustrating, impossible to communicate or even pin down for digestion by his own inexhaustible appetite for thought. One version of this phenomenon, this blending that punctured all order, was when he mixed languages into a cocktail – German with French, for example – so that a listener was at once perplexed and mesmerized. It was when he began such streams of infinite digression that I knew to take charge. And it was because I would take charge that he resented me utterly; resented the power that my steady but less capable mind granted me.

Who would speak about such a marriage? Who would dare tell?

On the way to the wedding he had complained of a migraine. He often complained of migraine. I cannot count how many weary days and weeks he has spent in the darkness of our bedroom, curtains drawn, silence his only possible companion, waiting like a prisoner to be released from the flooding of blood that turned normal speech into shouting, small movements into enormous, painful physical feats. 'I can't bear to hear my own piss hit the toilet,' he'd once told me during a particularly bad attack. When I voiced sympathy, he stiffened as though struck as my whispered, unfinished sentence halted to nothing. Afterwards, he often felt a residual pain, a kind of shadow pain, a liquid, mobile tenderness that circulated his skull. Sound seemed echoing and hostile; even the English sky, with its low clouds and weak, milky sun, would for days be too bright.

As often as not it faded away to a mere headache which any over-the-counter drug could quell. Ibuprofen might fend off another wasted day. He'd taken two the morning of the wedding and seemed fit enough for the journey, but as we sat down with the rest of the congregation I sensed a shift in his temperament. Occasionally a migraine precedes a stage of mania and I was on guard for the sort of bizarre, inexplicable collapsing of judgement that marked out his manic days. Sometimes it never happened. Like a storm which brews and then blows out across the ocean where it dissipates without consequence, there was always the likelihood that the mania would fail to converge into madness, and would simply pass us over.

You might think me lucky to lose such a man, for he was always both a prize and a burden, but there are attractions to those who are different from the common stream of humanity and James was capable of sustaining a level of passion and interest that made my friends envy me. Marriage is so deadening, my friend Claire once told me. I've heard others remark in the same manner. In my case my marriage was my life, and though people often felt sorry for me, felt obliged to stand in allegiance and hold me in my suffering, they often crowded there on the sidelines. And during better times they envied me utterly.

'He is sexy,' my sister once said. By which I think she meant danger has its allure.

'Come on, Rebecca, it's a wedding. Pay attention to the main attraction. Try and look happy,' James said.

I'd been watching him – James, of course – with what I'd hoped was a concealed measure of scrutiny and dread, but he'd caught me at it.

'I'm sorry,' I said, pushing my mouth up at the corners. Touchingly, for I knew that he was himself struggling with appearances right now, he put his hand protectively on my sleeve.

'Tic, toc,' he said, pointing to his temple. What he meant was that his head was like a bomb.

I've always hated weddings, hated getting dressed up during the day, standing in crowds, in unbreathable, gassy air, and moving as one with the crowd like a great lumbering animal. I find myself ready to do anything just to peel off my tights, pull off my cinched belt, my itchy hat, poke my fingers into my eyes and disengage the contact lenses I both loathe and insist upon. I have always felt uneasy at church – again, it's that dressing up in the middle of the day thing – and the few times I've attended mass have convinced me it is easier to pay eternally for my sins than visit with regularity a building that has the simultaneous effect of making me feel guilty and sinful but also angry and disgusted, not to mention physically uncomfortable.

'You are suspicious even of God,' James might say. In fact, he did say this once and my response (I can remember exactly) was, 'Oh, stop talking like he's a person in the next room.'

Godless and church-phobic, we nonetheless had a traditional wedding. James insisted on it. 'Everything in your life has been thrown together half assembled. Let's get married the *right way*,' he'd said. How had I interpreted that remark as his caring for me? I married him after my final year of university, my final because I dropped out, not because I graduated. I'd spent the early years of my life being very good at school and thinking – assuming – that I would be a great academic success and eventually go into medicine. I'd wanted to be a doctor since I first discovered there existed anything as magical and fearsome as hospitals. Something about their tidy systems, their stiff, dependable procedures, the schedules of shift work that transcend a normal day, the stocked closets of supplies, all labelled and accounted for, the sheer orderliness of life within the wide doors of a hospital, held for me a great attraction. Disease, itself, stands in compelling opposition to the logical harmony of a hospital, and I am luridly fascinated by the pathology of disease. How cancer manifests with spreading tentacles like a sinister plant from deep beneath the ocean, or as small discreet lesions which in autopsy can appear almost like a mould across the organ. I've seen a malignant growth shelled from a body cavity in one great lump as though the patient had swallowed it whole, melanoma appearing from nowhere beneath the skin of an otherwise healthy adult, whose life expectancy, with the discovery of that singular lump, would be cut in half. My clinical training is limited to volunteer work – I never became a doctor, not even close. But I worked in hospitals, in one capacity or another, for so many years that I became privy to matters which ordinarily would have been well off limits. There are stories to many people's lives that I've been party to, then lost halfway through: the sixteen-year-old with Hodgkin's Disease, too young to even understand why he was being asked to masturbate into a cup so the resulting sperm could be frozen for the future; the depressed recipient of a hysterectomy whose Latin husband had not understood what a hysterectomy was and now wanted to divorce her as she was sterile; the in vitro twins born after twenty-four weeks gestation and neither weighing a pound. Their mother had circled round and round the plastic incubators, then gone out to the corridor calling at the top of her voice to a passing doctor that the intubation procedure had been wrongly done. Shrieking between quick flights back to the incubator to check her twins were breathing, she berated the staff and then raced to stand in quiet attendance at her babies' sides. One spring a fledgling blackbird fell from its nest outside our kitchen window, and as I watched its mother flap and caw and dive-bomb the neighbours' cat away from her wayward baby I was reminded of that mother in the intensive care unit, who would not leave the building, the room, the five square feet surrounding her babies' tanks. She herself had ten hours previously undergone major surgery, the caesarean which saved her babies' lives and left her with a blood count so low that on the third day of vigilant watching over her infants, she collapsed to the floor.

My desire for medicine had pushed me beyond what really ought to have been my intellectual limits and I went to university to study biology, which I hoped would lead to a medical career of some sort, perhaps as a researcher. But in the end I could not cope. I spent my university days with my head swimming. My memory, which had once been my most reliable tool, went wonky on me the second I stepped into university.

James claimed it was his fault. 'I ruined you. Me and my spectacularly dysfunctional life. You should have stayed clear of me.'

This is what he says now, but when I finally decided to leave university the first person I told of my decision was James. And he'd said, 'Marry me.'

It was a Thursday, the day he proposed. Thursday, what an odd thing to recall. I'd been the day before to the registrar to end my official status as a student and was feeling unstrung and hopeless. For so many years my days had been marked by a highly structured frenzy of reading, attending lectures, working in hospitals. I'd been the sort of person who structured every second of the day and who economized greatly so that no moment of study was lost: lunch on the bus, text books while combing out my hair. With the close of student life came an endless stretch of time impossible to fill. I'd finally given up the one, singular direction I'd maintained since childhood, and the debilitating emptiness which set in moved me to the rim of a cavity of depression, a blue-black recess which seemed at the time as much an isolating split as a refuge. It was there, in that liminal space, where James found me, preoccupied and grieving, and pulled me away, back into the world of the living. Marry me, he'd said, extending his hand.

'Remember our wedding cake?' I asked James as we waited in the church. It had been a traditional three-tiered cake with royal icing, spidery skirts and yellow piping around sugar roses. The woman who made it, a friend of James's mother, had gone to elaborate efforts with spun sugar, constructing not only a bride and groom but a whole forest of white upon the topmost layer, the one which traditionally is to be saved for the christening of the couple's first child. She'd made hedgerows and a beech wood and a few tiny woodland animals, everything white, frozen and opaque, chilling in its effect.

'That lady was committed soon after that,' James said.

For years we'd kept the top layer wrapped in a linen tea towel inside a Cadbury's Roses tin on the top of a cabinet in the kitchen. One night, while chasing a wasp from the ceiling with a broom, I swiped the tin accidentally and sent it toppling to the floor. It clanged on the cork tile but stayed intact, probably because of the excess of masking tape I'd used to keep it within its tidy bowl. James came in and we both stared at the dented tin turned up on its side and decided we must open it to assess the damage. The procedure involved carefully cutting and unwrapping the tape, gently tapping the sides of the lid with a mixing spoon and finally, painstakingly, dislodging the two sides of the tin.

Inside, the cake seemed a smaller, slightly wizened version of itself. The hedgerows had come apart and some of the animals had been crushed or lost their legs, but what was amazing, beside the fact that it still looked not only like a cake, but quite a bit like the cake we remembered, was how the icing had stayed true to its whiteness, except for a slow-growing, lime-coloured fungus emanating from beneath the thick snowy layer of royal icing, not offensive in any way but almost as though spring had pushed itself into the middle of winter, upsetting the order of the seasons. James held the cake in both hands, rotating his vision to view it from different angles. I thought at first he was remembering our wedding, reaching back to the dreamy sentiment of that day, but I was wrong.

'I feel', James had said, controlling his voice so as not to break into laughter, 'like I am holding a shrunken head.'

'We have to keep it,' I said, remembering how that woman slaved away on the detail of her glorious woodland scene.

'Keep it? Either we have it embalmed or we donate it to science.'

'Well, what *do* we do? We can't just throw it in the bin.'

We paused, thinking about it. It did seem wrong, having kept it so securely all those years, to just chuck it out like ordinary rubbish. It was Tuesday and the rubbish collection wasn't until Friday, which meant for three days we'd be dumping all manner of potato peelings and empty milk cartons on top of our wedding cake – that felt to me too ominous. I am sure somewhere there is an old wives' tale that spells out explicitly the doom of a marriage in which the couple desecrate their own cake. I thought we might as well keep it, and was about to say as much when James jumped up, holding the cake under his arm like a book.

'We'll bury it,' he said, conclusively. 'It'll go under the cherry tree with the dead mouse.'

The mouse had been a household pest we killed in a trap. I'd found James hovering over the tiny broken body one morning, speechless with regret at what we'd done. We'd buried the mouse – it had only a small effect in assuaging our guilt – and we buried the wedding cake.

'It was the right thing to bury it,' James said now. How did he know what I was thinking about? How did he seem always to know *exactly*? 'Stop thinking so hard and watch your friend get married,' he said, gently.

He nodded at the front of the church and I turned my attention there. David, the groom, my last male friend to marry, was fidgeting nervously, casting searching glances for any sign of his bride. I remembered instantly two things about him: that he drank a litre of coffee right before going to bed and that he kissed so well you could go on kissing him for hours. James did not like David, not only because once upon a time – before my marriage – I had an affair with him, but because David made a great deal of money as a restaurauteur while James and I lived mostly off my salary. The only way James had been able to tolerate David was by reminding himself that David, at forty, was single, which he considered to be an indication of immaturity if not outright deviancy. Today all that was going to change and I got the sense James was only half pleased about it.

'Do you like the music?' I asked James. There was an ensemble of three violinists, a flautist, and a petite older woman with a piccolo. He looked in their direction and then – I saw this happen – his gaze stuck. His eyes locked and everything about him switched off. Just for an instant, but it was enough for me to detect – in a heart-sinking but familiar moment of humility and exposure – how her memory had absorbed him once more. There was a young girl playing the violin. She had the same lemon-coloured hair and the same white skin, the same bony nimble fingers and general beauty about her as Lea, James's first wife.

He knew at once that I had noticed, and that no measure of tact or retreat would shake us from that fact. There were times when we spoke openly of her, talking in circles about her memory, her life which was short, absurdly short, and about how both of us feel forever blessed and haunted by her. Talking like this, over a brandy or while holding each other's hands as we lay side by side naked in bed, smoothed away some of the hurt and confusion, some of the roomy pain which we inhabited constantly. I would say that I was more able than he to forget and go forward, but it is my sensitivity to his loss, to the whole way in which his mind since Lea's death heaves in waves of happiness and despair, that sends us constantly back, away from health and consolation, away from unity and love. If I could fail to notice his arrested gaze, if I could somehow dislodge the connection that makes me think immediately of Lea – because I know it is her memory which has struck him, there is no guesswork here – it would be easier. For him, especially. He could have a memory without audience. I'm sure he wishes for this, sometimes.

He said, 'They always play the same pieces.'

We were saved by my friend Claire. Her husband, Nigel, was away at a conference so she'd come on her own. I hadn't even noticed as she slid into the pew beside us. If she detected the rising tension between us, she did not show it. She kissed us both lightly, then turned her attention forward, to David. 'Eleanor is now ten minutes late,' she said about the bride.

I said, 'James has a headache. Are you sure your watch is right, Claire?'

'You didn't bring any aspirin, did you, Claire? What do you say I go get some aspirin? There's a Boots across the road, I could be back in ten minutes.' I gave James a sharp look. He squeezed my shoulder. 'Darling,' he said.

Claire said, 'What's the matter with you lot? Rebecca, my *father* gave me this watch. It is never wrong.'

'Oh, sorry.' Claire's father was a jeweller. I knew that, I don't know what made me ask if her watch was correct.

'James, I don't have aspirin. A long time ago I decided I didn't want to be the sort of person who carried aspirin. Sorry. You'd better go to the chemist. Unless of course this wedding actually *begins*.'

'You think it won't?' I asked.

'Fourteen minutes,' said Claire.

David was looking very uneasy, standing stiffly in morning dress. The masses of friends and relatives fidgeted in their pews, some of them sneaking glances to the back of the church, others studying the short order of service with the intensity you'd give a manual of instructions. I looked up at the ceiling to the stone roof that threatened to cave in as the wind howled in unseasonal storm conditions that rendered the May sky nearly black at one p.m.

'He's so worried,' I said. 'David.'

James said, 'He's forty years old. What kind of guy waits until he is forty to marry?'

'Scary weather and she's late,' Claire said. 'It's a bad omen.'

'She's supposed to be late,' I said.

'I don't know,' Claire said. 'Sixteen minutes.'

'I could have been back with that aspirin by now,' said James. He smiled, a mischievous grin, but beneath the smile I knew he was half serious.

'Be nice,' I said.

David was turning various shades of white now and kept licking his lips nervously. Once in a while he looked to the back of the church, searching for Eleanor. There was a buzz in the church, a low rumble of voices that dislodged the mood of the music, the solemnity of the gathering.

'Poor guy,' I said.

'Why poor him? It's his wedding day, for godsakes,' said James.

'It's about time he got married and joined the rest of us. He's been through so many women he could fill a football stadium with ex-lovers,' Claire said. 'Nigel is totally jealous of him.'

'It's a pathology,' I said, and it came out almost wistfully.

'Well, if it is, then Nigel wants to be that sick,' said Claire.

'Not me,' James said, and I laughed out loud. 'What?' he said, defensively. I laughed in part because I knew what a roaming eye James has – it's an inbred feature in him that he cannot control. And he's the sort of man who manages to convince women to do things he suggests, cook for him, for example. Claire, who is a wonderful cook, has spent whole Saturdays preparing meals for James. Something about his manner of appreciation, his meticulous, interested appraisal, his genuine gratitude, makes her do it. He gets women to wear certain clothes he finds attractive – these are his ordinary friends, not women he's involved with. 'I like you in that red dress,' he'll say to one of his female friends. 'You look so pretty in it.' Suddenly she wears the red dress all the time, buys a few more.

'Seventeen and a half minutes late,' Claire announced.

'God, I've got such a headache,' said James.

I felt like I had two impatient children with me, both wanting to get the task of a wedding ceremony behind them so they could escape to more interesting things. Besides the late bride, there was another factor which was contributing to the sense of dark anticipation that was gathering around us. A storm, which had originated somewhere in the Midlands and had been working its way south-east all morning, was raging outside in grand fashion. The wind was fierce, it felt like it could shove the stone church right off its consecrated foundations. We shivered in our summer dresses, listening to the ensemble, and turning to see who, if anyone, was coming in through the large oak-beamed door. We saw several of David's ex-girlfriends, some of them now with husbands who bore expressions of smugness and a certain evil glee, eyebrows pitched up, smiles cocked to one side, as though they had never quite believed David was going to get married, and now – given the bride's apparent disappearance – it was clear he would not.

'I *am* going to get some pills,' James said, on his feet suddenly and pushing me aside to get past in the pew.

'You can't leave now!' I said – just a little too loudly. The couple behind us baulked, then gave each other a look.

'It would be awful,' whispered Claire. 'It would look like the guests had given up and the wedding was a no-show.'

'Well,' said James.

'I am not letting you past me,' I said.

'My head is like a pressure cooker. All I want is some aspirin,' James said.

'You'll have to wait,' I said.

'Wait for what? Nothing is *happening*.'

Out of nowhere a hand appeared holding two white pills nestling inside a sterling silver pillbox. It was Eleanor's mother. She stood nimbly in a green and white raw silk suit, her white purse clutched to her side, her pillbox extended as though it were an hors d'oeuvre at a cocktail party. She wore an expression of extreme efficiency and mild irritation, and when James hesitated to pluck from her palm the two delicate pills she shook them to emphasize they were meant to be taken immediately. I could only surmise that she'd heard James's complaints on her way to the back of the church to find out what had happened to her daughter and had decided to extinguish the flame before it became a roaring fire.

James put the aspirin on his tongue. 'Thank you,' he managed, as she snapped the pillbox shut.

Suddenly the door flew shut, sending a cloud of cold air across the threshold of the church and causing the congregation to jump and turn as though the ghost of Macbeth had just walked in. The vestry clerk, a nervous man in an ill-fitting suit, shoes shined to gleaming and way too much hair on his neck, flitted about the back of the church making sure nothing had broken with the grand slamming of that heavy door. Meanwhile, the bride had, finally, arrived.

'Twenty and a half minutes late,' said Claire. 'What could possibly happen to make a woman that *late* for her own wedding? Does she lead such an interesting life that she forgot this was her wedding day?'

'A tree across the road,' I offered, 'an injury to the eye, the death of a pet?'

'Second thoughts,' said Claire.

'Quiet,' James said. 'My *head*.'

Claire cannot stand to be told to be quiet. So she said, 'The last wedding I went to in foul conditions like these, the couple lost all their luggage on the honeymoon, then had their passports stolen. The rental car got a flat tyre somewhere outside Faro and the groom had to sell the bride to a camel merchant in order to get a lift back to civilization or what passed for it – a delapidated city with a half-built airport. She escaped the camel man but never forgave the husband for selling her in the first place.'

There was silence. Then the organ began, levelling our conversation. We smiled, glancing around us. The great boom of the wedding march filled the church.

'Well, David has booked a holiday at some Swiss health farm so there's no chance of misadventures, unless they sauna themselves to death,' I said in a whisper.

'This noise is killing me.' James shielded his eyes. 'I wish the aspirin would kick in.'

Claire said, 'They're doomed. Have you ever seen so much hail in May? Their lives together will be cursed with babysitter cancellations, houses with mysterious damp walls, exploding microwave ovens, faulty birth control and poor train connections. The sheer frustration of it all will bring upon their end.'

Eleanor passed by us, looking beautiful and slightly stressed, her smile fixed across her face. She wore a floor-length evening dress that just happened to be white – it was the only wedding dress I'd ever seen that had that much style – and she was dynamite in it. She reached David's side, finally, and I puffed out a little breath of relief.

The organ music paused again, and now the vicar, in a decorated cassock, raised his hands in welcome.

'So what was wrong with the camel guy?' I whispered.

'Who knows?' Claire said. 'She didn't fancy him.'

Then began the formal sermon, the whispered recital of the Lord's Prayer, the heavy action of the organ and everybody piping up to sing hymns they only half knew. Suddenly it was me who couldn't stand to remain seated, to remain in the church. The whole church *effect* that always fills me with the uncontrollable desire to shock, to light up a cigarette mid-pew or make a call on my cellphone, kicked in mightily. Through sheer force of will I managed to stop myself from doing anything too terrible, but perhaps the ruination of the wedding was inevitable because James simply could not behave. He sat beside me grimacing, his skin was flushed, his eyes dried to a marbled, sore-red colour. He looked like a junkie or a murderer. I wished I'd let him escape to get the aspirin. With any luck they'd not have let him back in.

'It's splitting in *two*!' James cried, grasping his own head, one palm at the brow, the other at the base of his skull, and pushing together. This action, as well as his heavy, laboured breathing, drew the attention of the people seated near us. The couple who had baulked previously now scowled, and another woman, a silver-haired lady in a pink linen jacket, drew a finger to her lips. There was a moment when I thought I might have to somehow drag James out of the church altogether, whatever scene it might cause. But the thought of confronting Eleanor's mother, who had a headmistress's air of authority, stopped me. Suddenly a loud clap of thunder deafened the ceremony and sent James to the floor, holding his head, and I thought fuck it, we really must go now. It might have been even more embarrassing – for I would have had to enlist help in removing him – but a new bang outdid the first, and there were gasps all around. Nobody noticed James, clutching his head on the church's stone floor, so I decided to sit upright, smile and pretend that I didn't notice him either. Claire caught my eye to indicate that James was writhing on the floor like a possessed man. But I shook my head delicately, rekindled my stiff, bogus smile, and watched as David and Eleanor stood bravely through several eruptions from the sky. The vicar began the wedding sermon proper.

At which point a crash of lightning erupted above us and an oak tree – one of the giant Elizabethan oak trees that surrounded the churchyard – let go a mighty branch, which fell upon the roof with an immense boom, like a bomb going off. Looking up, I expected to see a great gaping hole and the whole of the stormy sky above us, but the old roof held despite the great showering of ancient mortar which fell like snow upon us.

For a moment there was a relieved silence, then a chorus of voices which rose up like a wave. We all kept looking up, expecting the roof to collapse. We could see a huge arm of the immense tree lurking outside the coloured glass in the window beside the ladies chapel. The wedding was momentarily forgotten. We were all stunned by what had happened; I am sure it was as close a thing to a religious experience as any of us had encountered. The vicar stood, his hands outstretched, his mouth open, and grunted loudly as he exhaled. We took that moment to breathe a deep, relieved sigh. James continued to hold his head, but behind his suffering there had erupted unexpectedly a kind of joyfulness and humour.

'We're all going to die,' he said, laughing.

And then the rain began.

2

At two a.m. I woke to find the bed beside me empty, its white sheet entirely filled by moonlight. It is not unusual for James to work very late into the night, and at first I listened for the sound of his fingers scrambling across the keypad of his computer. He is a novelist – he cannot stand this fact about himself, he thinks it makes him like Peter Pan, not quite grown up, not doing anything 'serious' with his life. When I tell him there can be no more serious work than what lightens the world – art, creation, products of the mind – he laughs rudely, a scoffing laugh, and says what he brings is worthless. 'My art is a dead, dead rose,' he pronounces. And again the gloomy laughter.

I know that secretly his writing means everything to him, which is why he berates himself, mocking his books, shaming himself, and why nothing is ever good enough. He is a hypocrite, for he could never align himself with more ordinary work, which he thinks – he would never admit this – is beneath him. To write, he has explained, to write well, requires a sense of timelessness, a solitary mind that can sweep from one end of itself to another, on and on like a pendulum swinging. The process is disturbed by the buzz of ordinary life, by ringing doorbells, housekeeping, voices which plug inside his ear and require action. The sheer energy of so many waking bodies stops him from writing in the day. For him it is a night-time affair. Night releases his mind from its usual absorption with the regular, pedestrian concerns of living and offers him a sense of inexhaustive time. It gives him a dense string of empty hours, a featureless landscape onto which he can create something new. There are people who write by pulling ideas from newspapers, by listening to their friends' real-life stories and embellishing from there. They have minds far less cluttered than James's; for him writing becomes a case of clearing away words, of discarding and culling, of simple erasure. Anything can disrupt him.

I stayed still, listening for him, and hearing instead only the sounds from the street, the rustling of rose branches across the window, the play of wind through the oak trees that line our road. We live in Buckinghamshire, as far from our beginnings in south-east London as possible while still remaining near the capital, and we have been happy here. I think so.

Last night, despite his headache, we'd made love frantically, unexpectedly, and he'd fallen asleep so quickly afterwards that his body was still sweating.

'Don't worry,' were his last, sleep-filled words. I have no idea why he said this.

I waited for the sound of the kettle, for a toilet to flush, for his footsteps across the squeaky planked floor of our hallway, but there was no sound. Moving from the bed I brought with me the corner of the sheet so that I could wrap a cover around myself as the windows and curtains were all open. James maintained that the pressure of a house closed off from the air outside made his head sing with pain. Open the windows, open the doors, he'd cried once we'd arrived back from the wedding, pushing up the windows so that they sprang on their sashes. We'd made love with the wind bringing rain across our backs, on sheets that had been showered and dried so that they smelled like wet leaves.

I stepped across the room and out into the hallway, turned on the light then winced at its brightness. His office door was closed but a wedge of light beneath the door told me he'd been working. Opening the door I saw the computer screen filled with words, his coffee cup, his array of books and notepads. When he writes he surrounds himself with books he loves, like amulets, like lucky charms. He has explained many times to me the importance of voice, of the sense of a presence behind every story. Without voice, he says, even the most interesting storyline reads like the six o'clock news. Certain books have such profound voices that you cannot recall what the actual stories were, what happened to whom and why, only the sense of being told a great tale, of sitting solidly in the presence of the teller with absolute connection. Books like those are the ones he picks off the shelves to accompany him late at night, when insomnia or boredom send him to his desk. Walking to the computer, to his chair angled exactly as though he were sitting there still, I looked down at the screen:

> *my headache sits on top of me, pressing so that I hunch my shoulders up, dip my chin to my neck. Do you have pain like this ever? Across the back of your knee is a blue mark, like an ink spot or a bruise. You said it was where a needle was once inserted for a childhood illness. What illness? Who hurt you? Across the base of my skull is a rattling, when I move my neck I can hear it, the sound of a nail head trailing against rusted iron. Sometimes I think that is what is wrong with me, a mechanical dislodgement, a foreign body in the grey matter. Have I mentioned your knee? What happened there?*

It did not occur to me this was anything other than his normal work, as he told most of his stories in the first person and was given to broad dialogues concerning his real-life physical and psychological troubles. I pressed ctrl-s to save the work, then went downstairs trailing my sheet-gown to find him sitting cross-legged in a wooden chair, staring into his fish tanks in the utility room. He does not keep fish, but various other exotic creatures – a tarantula, a pair of tree frogs, sometimes a few insects he's collected in the garden. It's an odd menagerie, one I find embarrassing and exhilarating and highly idiosyncratic.

'What are you doing?' I asked.

'I thought the tortoises were hatching,' he said, looking into the infrared glow of a tank in which, on a grid of metal, sat three leather-like tortoise eggs. The parents were in our garden wandering around eating strawberry plants and loganberries, fallen apples, all manner of insects, including the grub worms James supplied for them. As a child, James had captured the male tortoise when out on a golf course searching for a ball his father had sliced badly into a thick wedge of marsh. The female had come along two decades later, a gift from a couple who thought her lonely. This was their second clutch of eggs; the first, which he'd allowed the tortoises to sort out themselves, had never hatched.

'What made you think they were hatching?'

'They should have been born yesterday. I thought about calling a vet but I guess there's nothing a vet can do until after the hatching. I mean, I doubt vets treat *eggs*.'

'Well, are they?'

'What?'

'Hatching.'

He peered closely at the three still eggs, more round than oval and the size of ping-pong balls. They looked no more alive than Easter eggs or papier mâché balls. 'Not at present,' he said.

'Are you coming to bed?'

'Yeah, yeah.' He fussed now with the dial which controlled the lamp heat, searching for something among his jam jars and plastic tubs.

'Nice work on your computer,' I said. He stopped rummaging and looked up, as though I'd made a shocking, important statement.

'Oh, yes. Good,' he said. 'Thank you. It's all rubbish anyway.'

'Come to bed,' I said, smiling.

He did not come to bed. I shut the windows and put on some pyjamas, then knocked on the floor with the spine of a hardback book.

'Sleep!' I called down to him. He could go like this for nights on end. Having written successfully for a short while, he suffers the remaining hours until dawn with fitful awakenings, so many that he feels as though the days are strung together with an exhaustive connection. During times of sleeplessness he never lies in bed staring at the ceiling as some do but instead sets himself upon a task. I have found him at various times asleep at his desk with his cheek flat against the keyboard of his computer, or lying fully clothed on the couch, his wallet making an uncomfortable lump in his jeans pocket, his shoes still on, positioned just as he would have fallen with his feet almost touching the floor. I've discovered him in the front seat of the car, his head lolled back against the headrest, on the bench in his garden shed, on the window seat in our living room with his shoulder huddled against the icy pane. He is too big for me to move. All I can do is try to adjust his limbs into a comfortable position and wrap a blanket around him.

I banged the book once again on the floor. '*Upstairs!*' I yelled, and this time I heard a response, a single shouted word I could not clearly decipher. After a few minutes I gave up and went to sleep myself, part of me still straining to hear his footsteps coming up the stairs.

3

I come from a family of spinsters. All around my family tree are lone fragments of the branches that did not blossom further but stopped without explanation. Helen Mary Penn, Angela Violet Penn, Josephine Preston, Catherine Elizabeth Preston. These names and others hang in solitude without descendants. I do not know the histories of each, but my grandmother's three sisters, Margaret, Elizabeth and Rose, spent the last part of their lives inhabiting the house their parents had left them, complete with the very furniture they'd grown up with, without, to my knowledge, ever alluding to past love affairs or complaining of the bizarre, sterile life of sisters. They collected damask linen, unhemmed, enough for a banquet table, jewellery prized for its pale gold, silk scarves always too good to wear, white kid gloves with pearl fastenings stored in plastic wrapping and saved for best, monogrammed silver ladles and so many lace tablecloths an entire tallboy was given over to their storage. Margaret was an organizer, drawers of folded paper, balled string, an immaculately packed embroidered sewing kit with wooden cotton reels of thread so old that when I discovered the kit after her death I found the thread pulled apart like lint. Elizabeth's religion sent her to her knees every morning in the room that had been her father's study. Centred on the oval carpet that hid the sagging middle of the rotting planks below, she dropped in slow, laboured movements to the ground, pushing her arms out like Christ on the cross, before drawing her palms together in prayer.

They dressed in thick woollen skirts in winter, dark hats decorated with brooches, their square handbags hanging on their elbows like awkward fruit upon spindly leafless trees. Summer saw them on the patio early in the morning, fully dressed as though they were planning an outing, then back upstairs by eleven to rest until the heat lifted. Mother called them the Sisters, with the full monastic allusion that the term suggested, and cosseted them in a maternal, protective fashion I never understood, as she was not terribly maternal, my mother. They were so opposite Mother, whose passion for life was so fully exercised she risked offending them at every turn. Mother was a career woman and an incorrigible flirt. She smoked and drank Scotch by herself in the kitchen, sang to the radio and danced across the floor like a clumsy ballerina. After my father left she had boyfriends, never any one long enough to make a difference in our lives. The Sisters were not often exposed to this side of Mother – they lived in London while we lived in sunny California – but there had been summer visits in which they got a truer sense of their niece, her high moods, her infinite speech and quick movements, which were more like those of a man's. Rose seemed amused, puzzled, curious, but Margaret and Elizabeth held frozen, nervous smiles and shuffled away, presumably to discuss Mother in private. They were kind aunties for me – like three extra grandmothers. They died in their seventies, one after the other in the order of their birth.

'Don't run after the first man who says he loves you,' my mother warned me at Rose's funeral. 'But don't go years without one either.'

In the mornings I walk our dog, an ancient greyhound with a limp like a sea captain, who brings to my attention all that is hidden in the woods, a deer, a fox, a pheasant whose fear suspends him motionless in the hedgerow. Just about the time the dog arches his neck and takes in the smell, chewing it in his moving jaws, feeling its direction in the quivering muscle of his thigh, I catch sight of what has hooked his attention and realize how close I am to this living, invisible thing, this hare, this squirrel, this man who if he had a pistol could shoot me dead. The morning after David's wedding I felt just such a presence, a murky outline on the horizon, an unseen creature with a heartbeat. It felt as though I were being followed, as though a being separate from myself was shadowing my footsteps. If I were more given to intuition, I'd have said that there with me in the cowfield behind our house I felt the presence of the woman who would lead James off. I had no specific thoughts of another woman, only this unaccountable feeling, which by its very anonymity lost the power to alert me fully, and brought me instead to stand there both knowing and not knowing.

I called the dog back and turned homewards before crossing the stile that leads into the woods, which is my usual route. The woods is an expanse of old oak trees and coppiced beech, banks of barren mud where the kids ride mountain bikes over the rim of a bowl of scooped-out earth. Either side are grazing pastures, barely used by the farmer who sold off most of his land to our developing London suburb and no longer even makes a show of farming for a living. I like the woods in all weathers, the earlier in the morning the better. I've seen foxes as big as spaniels, their russet coats gleaming as they sink down, running flat against the ground to cover, hares gliding effortlessly, springing in silent slow motion on a path above me, ordinary house cats practising their hunting. Passing the messy expanse of an owl's nest, it is hard to believe our proximity to London. The woods allow me sanction against the stresses of this city's life; I leave them usually with reluctance. That day, however, I turned back, my mood like a filter of mild despair around me. I did not connect this feeling to James but wondered instead if I were ill. I am the type of person who does not at first notice my own physical weakening. I can have a fever for a day before it occurs to me to take my temperature, stay up all night being sick without considering that I might need to take a day off work to recover. I walk the dog when I have a sore throat or an ear infection. I do not like to bow down to illness or even to acknowledge it.

'You're back early,' James said, standing in the threshold of the garden shed. He'd tucked in his shirt, fixed his cuffs so they hung at his wrists, pushed his fingers through his hair to tame the curls, but I could tell he'd just woken. In the shed is his collection of spiders and beetles, mantids and odd flying insects – all the creatures I prohibit from the house because of their likely escape. I wouldn't mind the tarantula being added to this category but he refuses on the grounds that tarantulas are slow creatures with movements a greyhound would find irresistible. The dog would kill it, he reasoned, should it escape. As it was one of his favourite possessions, I was convinced he would not risk this morbid end to its life. So the tarantula – whom he'd named Lucy – remained in the utility room. The shed is a territory marked out by spider webs and crickets, beetles and the occasional visiting family of mice. I won't pass through its threshold, though James apparently feels happy to sleep in it.

'We have to get ready if we're going to this party,' I said. The disaster of yesterday's wedding had yielded an unusual outcome. David and Eleanor had managed to marry, but the reception was cancelled due to heavy winds that dismantled the reception marquee and caused an electrical problem which meant the food could not be cooked properly. The advancing flood conditions in the garden where the party was to be held meant we'd all be standing in four inches of water anyway, so the whole thing had been postponed until today. It had been decided that we would all assemble for an ad-hoc breakfast this morning, before the couple flew to Switzerland for their honeymoon. 'You slept on that bench again?' I asked James.

'On the floor. My head hurts, I can't sleep anywhere.'

'I'll get you an aspirin.'

'I don't like this book I'm writing. It's not coming together, there's no cohesion to the plot, no definite structure. I feel like I'm picking up random pages and scribbling on the backs of them, that sentences are in disarray. In my head, the reviewers' voices rule,' he said.

'Write that down, all that hangs together pretty tight.'

'It's easy for you, you're one of them,' he said.

'I'm not a reviewer.'

'Same thing, editor. One set of noises precedes publication, one set after.'

'Stop it, you're acting crazy.'

'Crazy,' he repeated. Then, turning back into the dark mouth of the shed's open door. 'I want to kill those voices dead.'

'I'll make us some tea.' I turned, folding the dog leash in my palm as I went towards the house to do what I did every morning.

'I don't want a goddamned cup of tea,' I heard from behind me.

I should have kept walking. I know better than to engage in any sort of argument when James hasn't slept. But suddenly I found my steps impossible, it was as though I were locked in place with a powerful magnet pulling me around to face him.

'Don't be cross with me,' I said, 'just because you wasted a night not sleeping and not working.'

'Is that some sort of reprimand? Is the teacher slapping her pupil's wrist?'

He wins every argument, by the sheer power of his unpleasantness. Knowing this, I tried another tack.

'You might feel better if you sat in a comfortable chair and had a cup of tea and some pills for your headache. You might recover yourself enough to enjoy a fraction of the day. That's all I'm saying.'

I might have said this in a perfunctory manner. It may be that there was too much instruction, that it was a patronizing suggestion – *for his own good he ought* – but however the words were spoken, I did not expect the explosion that followed.

'It's ruining me,' he said, his voice a growl, his chest heaving. I watched his set jaw, his intense eyes, his hands which were literally shaking. 'Your lifestyle, your regular hours, your cups of tea! I am *disgusted*,' he pronounced. 'You disgust me.'

'I am not going to be spoken to like that,' I said, sternly. 'I am not going to stand in the garden, flanked by our neighbours, and have you calling me names.'

'Oh, no, that would be terrible. If the neighbours heard. That would be just awful!'

He kept calling to me as I walked away, then he ran after me, his body turned sideways, his face popping at me like a puppet on a stick.

'You'd just hate that, wouldn't you? Because to you, all that matters is that everything goes along smoothly, that nobody breaks the silence!'

'What silence? Stop being such a bully,' I said. 'Stop barking like some dog at my heels.'

With that he suddenly stopped, stood stock still and raised his chin to the sky, letting out a long howl. 'Rroooooooo,' he called. 'Rrooooo!'

'Stop that,' I said.

He put his hands up to his chest and began panting, his tongue lolling, his eyes wide. 'Rruuff, Rrrufff.'

'It's not funny, James. Stop it. Stop it now.'

But he would not. He barked and panted, then ran in circles. He whined and fretted and yapped at my leg. It went on for minutes, and whenever I moved he came at me again just like some huge, demented dog. I couldn't stand it. I rushed inside the house, pushing the door behind me. He pushed back and a moment of tug of war took place with him finally crashing in behind me. I ran down the hall, and James sped after me, yowling and howling and making a sound like someone coughing up a chunk of food they were choking on. He was everywhere, four limbs in four different directions, the dreadful sounds calling after me. It was like a horror movie with me running away from a werewolf. I ran upstairs and he grabbed my ankle and almost knocked me down. Scrambling back up I managed to get inside our bedroom and shut our door. He pushed his hand through and I bit it. This was madness, I know, but there was no place to run if he got inside, and I just couldn't bear having him near me, clawing at me, drooling on me, making those howling noises.

I bit down and he yelped, first like a man in pain, then like a canine. His hand went limp. I disengaged my teeth long enough for him to pull his fingers back from the door, then pushed the door shut and pulled the bed in front of it. He scratched at the door, just like a dog, whimpering.

'Go away!' I yelled. There was no sound from him. 'Get out!' I said. For a few minutes there was quiet. I went to the furthest corner of the room, sank down into the corner and wept, trying not to make any noise as I did it. I heard nothing from James. Then I heard a noise that sounded immediately familiar but which I could not name. Twenty minutes later, when I was sure that James had gone, that this fight, this game, this mood, this torture had passed, I opened the door to discover that he'd peed all down the wood.

You see how crazy it is – why can't we argue like a normal couple?

I went to the kitchen, put on the kettle, found the tea bags, put cups and saucers on to a black lacquered tray, warmed the teapot. All this I did to make myself feel better, regular domestic acts that pushed back the extravagance of that horrible fight and brought me back to a world of normal everyday life.

I extracted two ibuprofen tablets from the blister pack on the ledge above the sink and arranged them on a small plate with biscuits. I gave the real dog his breakfast and, in slippered feet, went to the garden to find James in exactly the place I knew I'd find him, lying on the hammock, a canvas draped between metal rods that kept it suspended above the air. He did not call to me but when he heard my footsteps he lifted his arm so it appeared above the canvas like a puppet above a stage.

'I'm here,' he said. 'I'm sorry. It's my head, it's killing me.'

'I've left the door for you to clean up,' I said.

'Good. I will.'

'Yes, you will.'

'I'm sorry. I got carried away.'

'*Carried away?* Is that what you call it?'

He laughed.

'Don't,' I said. 'It just isn't funny.'

There was a weighty moment of silence. He reached out and gently touched my thigh.

'Please, sit down. My head is on fire. I know I shouldn't even ask, but can you massage my temples?'

I set the tray flat on the grass and in nurse-like fashion dropped the two pills into James's mouth. He drew his knees up and pushed into the hammock with his shoe heels, bringing himself up higher on one side so he was angled almost to sitting. He left the saucer in my hand as he took the teacup, enveloping it in both palms. He drank the tea like it held medicinal value, as though I were a shaman delivering a solemn promise of recovery from this sacred offering. I wedged myself on the outer edge of the hammock and waited for him to finish, then took his head in my hands in a manner similar to how he'd clasped the teacup. I knew where to start, the valley that sits above the cheekbone, from the rim of the ear to the peak of the brow. In that familiar recess I pushed with the seat of my palm into the gentle slope of his skull.

'If you don't sleep you know what will happen to you,' I said.

'Please,' he said. 'Whisper.'

I leaned down towards him. 'You *know*.' I breathed into his ear.

'I promise to sleep, but you mustn't say a word. It's like hearing ice break from the top of my skull. Even my own voice sounds like a cave full of echoes.'

It was probably too late to save him from what I knew was coming. Sometimes a manic turn could be staved off by the same simple logic any layman would recommend, plenty of sleep, good food, the close physical comfort of a friend. But sleep was the main ingredient to health, without sleep the mania was inevitable. If you think about it, insomnia brings on a lapse in judgement to even the most reliable of minds, so the likeliness it will create even more havoc for a manic-depressive is understandably higher.

For James insomnia has catastrophic results so it is especially unfortunate that he suffers from migraines. If he could stop the headaches that keep him awake he might stave off the manic attacks that follow. The pattern is not always the same but usually his head pounds for days and keeps him awake. He fidgets and groans his way through hours until phoenix-like he rises and furthers the trauma by a staggering physical unrest that catches him like a great wave and carries him off. During this time the headache will drift off, forgotten in the wake of new, dynamic energy, and he goes into a new episode of mental elevation that he actually enjoys.

He will sleep for only a few hours a night, juiced up on his own biochemistry, a cocktail of hormones and enzymes, adrenalin and epinephrine, a whole gamut of brain food that feeds him in this golden moment of his supercharged cortex and fixes him on a course of behaviour – reckless, persuasive, creative. At these times he can be unimaginably intoxicating, not only to himself but to those around him. I have been woken at three in the morning to a room lit up by candles so that it feels like sitting inside a glowing jack-o-lantern on a starry October night. On a trip to Safeway I've diverted my attention long enough to let him cruise off in the direction of the motorway and found myself hostage on a trip to Edinburgh with little more than my handbag. We've made love in sand dunes on winter nights, our torsos sweating while our fingers turned blue with cold, marched from Trafalgar Square south across the river and circled the Thames, talking between ourselves for so long it took a policeman's question to make us think about the time and where we were, Bermondsey at four a.m. At home, his mood finds practical use. He lunges from one activity to the next, reordering all his books, taking the furniture from one room to another, cooking lasagna at two a.m., spinning records and dancing. 'Come dance with me,' he'll say, his arms outstretched, his mouth soft, his body already bending to embrace me. And I allow myself once more to be swept into his mood, its riveting electricity, its delicious precariousness. His best writing comes when he is manic, sitting hunched in front of his computer, typing furiously one sentence after another without so much as a paragraph break.

'It's happening!' he'll say, smiling into the ghost-grey screen in triumph. Once upon a time I enjoyed the effortlessness of his creativity, the surprising upsweep of his mood, but now I am a veteran to the disaster that it causes. Even when he is enjoying his manic highs – and occasionally they are enjoyable – I anticipate their stinging reality and dread the inevitable. For it is always inevitable that he will drop into a stream of sad, inward, wasted weeks which will make him suffer and which I will suffer with him.

The only time he is happy as a novelist is when this demon energy makes good use of a mind for which words are the most comforting, familiar mirrors of thought. James can do anything with words; push you in directions you cannot imagine going, so that you end up at an airport in Lisbon arguing for a rental car when you were meant to be at a nine a.m. meeting, or swimming at midnight in a dark, icy ocean, naked because you don't have anything but the clothes you left home in hours previously. With words he's seared a few relationships to chalk, but also broken down the normal barriers of social discourse, so that he's made more friends in his short life than most of us do in a century. He is handsome in a particular way but that is not his appeal. It's the way he talks, how he connects – everything. In a letter he can seduce you blind.

The onset of mania is hugely predictable. First the insomnia, then a painful heightening of the senses. Colours swim at the corners of his vision, music contains a new, fuller experience so that he seems to float away with sound. But then it all becomes too much. I can arrive home to find a dark house with him knocking around inside, refusing anything more than candle-light; or with every lamp draped in pillow cases and T-shirts, anything to temper the brightness, to dull the assault on his raw eyeballs. His mouth becomes a den of evil tastes. He drinks and spits, scrapes his tongue against his teeth and spits again. Sound is amplified along with all his other senses. His shoes over frozen grass resonate like crunching over balled aluminium foil. The cork from a wine bottle squeaks and rubs, making a sound which riles him so that he bites it in half with his teeth, then recoils from the noise this in turn emits. Even the most bland food seems too salty or sickly sweet. He toasts white bread, boils potatoes. The pasta is too filmy for him, the apple makes that thundering crunch. Making love is a tortuous affair, he wants it so badly, he is like a high-school boy, newly erect and uncontainable. But the act brings on a pleasure too excruciating, his body becomes raw to its own pleasure, so that continuing becomes as impossible as not.

The wave that strikes him and pulls him away forces him first through these initial sensual explosions, then on to the true mania with all its lofty imbalance and advantages, then out to a murky sea of new physical quirks. His movements become clumsy, all day there are missed stairs, doorjambs that seem to jump at his shoulder as he passes, paper cuts and steam burns. His hands become mapped with small incisions from all the accidents of the day, older injuries show a healing of horny skin over the inflamed red centres. Across his legs are bruises from walking headlong into chairs and radiators, a line of rubbed-off skin along his shin bone marks the moment he stepped wrongly from the car so that his leg scraped against the edge of the door. At times like these I hide his razors, put the sharp knives away, check every night that the burners are off on the cooker, drop his car keys in my purse.

The aftermath continues, a long dull road that isolates him into the locked room of his overwrought brain.

'I'm hurting,' he'll whisper, thinking he's said this in a normal voice. 'I'm so tired,' he'll comment, after ten hours of sleep.

He has been diagnosed as a manic-depressive and we know – both of us – that lithium would iron out the wrinkles in his moods, end the fractious, riveting manias and temper the warped purposeless depressions. In the doctor's office the prescription was pressed into his hand, and he was urged to get it filled immediately. The psychiatrist is a heavyweight in his field. He is smart and kind, not at all judgemental, perhaps the only person I could have trusted with James's illness. I warned him that James was decidedly against medication, specifically lithium which has side effects that blur vision, so that the ordinary practice of reading a newspaper becomes impossible, and that it would be difficult to keep him on it.

'So I take the pills. Then what?' James asked the doctor. He spoke this sentence in the slow, halted manner of a hopeless soul, as though the possibility of a cure for his condition was more a closing to his life than a balancing.

The doctor shrugged and held out his hands, then clasped them together slowly. 'And then you'll be like the rest of us,' he said, smiling as James turned away.

In the garden now, with James's head in my hands, I moved my fingers over the points of his skull, down the stem of his neck, and up again to the soft inroads of his temples. His skin was flushed, sticky, his pulse so strong you could see his heart-beat against the fabric of his shirt. His body became a booming rocket of energy, so keyed up and vital, so unrelentingly active, that even now he was stiff with anticipated movement, though his eyes were closed, his breath rhythmic.

'Go put on a beautiful dress,' he whispered.

'James, we certainly can't go anywhere with you like this,' I said. 'Of course we won't.'

He reached his hand up and touched my face.

He was asleep when I left him there; I wrote a note apologizing for our absence from the breakfast. I went out to buy some groceries, to put some petrol in the car. When I returned the hammock was empty; he was not inside the house. There was a note explaining that he'd left and asking me to ring a phone number, which I did not find for several hours because I did not look. He hadn't taken anything with him, not even a change of clothing. It was hard, therefore, for me to realize what had happened, that I'd been left. That my husband had left me.

I don't know exactly what I would expect to happen when a husband leaves, I guess I'd expect a warning, at least, a stream of horrendous fights, a packed suitcase, for example. But I had grown so accustomed to overlooking James's behaviour. Even his acting like a dog was not all that unusual in the scheme of things. Aside from that particular, memorable fight, I don't think we were arguing any more than usual. Yes, he'd been more distant. For some time he'd been less likely to come down from his office when I arrived home from work. I'd go upstairs to find him, hidden away behind a closed door and not wanting to be disturbed, but that is not so unusual for a writer. There were, however, other things. He'd made plans for the weekend which did not include me, he kept quiet when usually he always talked, and he'd taken to visiting Dartmouth Row, the house which we owned but would not live in, nor would sell.

Fighting was a normal part of life with James. Odd behaviour was the norm. How was I to know when he left that he meant it anyway? After all, he'd tidied the bedroom, I noticed, and he'd cleaned the door.

4

Can manic depression be triggered by a single incident? Medical opinion would state not. The problems James has must always have been there, dormant – it is a physiological disease, after all. Ordinary depression, by which I mean the more common form of depression, sometimes originates with a particular grief, a traumatic event, or in something as banal and inevitable as old age. Manic depression usually begins in adolescence and escalates from there. I have asked James whether he has any memories of mania, of the same soaring energy, the crashing bleakness that follows. What do you remember, what exactly? I've asked. He claims he was relatively all right – temperamental and with a tendency to overfocus, to be compulsive and demanding of his body. But he was not manic, and he had no crushing grief.

'If I'd known I was suffering from manic depression do you think I'd have married Lea?' he says. 'I mean, would that have been *wise*?'

I agree that it would not have been. 'But people don't marry out of wisdom, do they?' I say.

'No,' he says, hurt, thinking I mean him. 'You certainly didn't.'

So it started with her death. This is what we conclude.

I married James when I left university, but this was not when I met him. I met him as a child of sixteen and when I look back on that time I see in my mind's eye two people who might as well be strangers from another era. When my great aunts died my mother inherited a trunk full of photographs; albums stocked with family portraits, with black and white photographs of hotels and houses I'd never seen but which had been the seat of holidays and family events. James and I might well have been any of the characters in those photos, whose dark eyes and over-pale faces had looked up to the lens as though whoever held the camera – probably one of my aunts – were some great friend. Every photographed face conveys a simple message of familiarity, of trust and ease, and yet when I look at these photos of my relations, they are strangers with eerily familiar features. I ought to know them, and yet I do not.

That is how it feels when I think back to James and myself living on Dartmouth Row in Lewisham, the south-east suburb of London where my mother, sister and myself settled when we first came to England. After Margaret and Elizabeth died, my grandmother's youngest sister, Rose, continued to live in that house, the very one in which they'd been raised. It was situated on a rather grand street in an otherwise unimpressive part of London, and was too big a house for Rose to occupy alone. She complained in a miserable, small voice over the dizzying miles of phone line that she did not like to be in such an enormous echoing house without company. So after a harried visit to England, my mother arranged that the house would be divided in half. Rose would occupy one side, and the other would be sold. The proceeds would be put into an investment account for Rose. The arrangement might have been suitable, except Rose then called saying she did not like living in one half of her house alone, as it still was too much and could Mother come out and sell another quarter of the house so Rose did not feel the walls vibrating with emptiness?

Mother was an estate agent for Century 21, buying and selling houses was something she did with great ease. But dividing up dilapidated Georgian properties into habitable quarters required vast amounts of money and time, not to mention planning permission, none of which she had. Besides which, from what

Mother could tell, she might fly to England and divide the old house a hundred times and still hear the same sad complaint from her aunt, one of isolation and loss. My great aunt had never lived alone and now, suddenly, two dead sisters and a house with wall vibration.

After a few more desolate phone calls from Rose, whose general sadness penetrated every time zone from England to California, it was decided Rose would come to live with us. My father is American and Mother often said that the only good thing about marrying him was that he provided a nice passport. My sister and I certainly considered ourselves American, despite having been born in London, but we liked the idea of our English great-aunt coming to live with us. It added a little cachet to our dreary lives and, besides that, we had no choice. Aunt Rose, however, found it too difficult an adjustment. We lived in a 1960s colonial-style split-level with a bay-windowed living room, a small nook which in estate-agent parlance is called the dining area, three tiny bedrooms upstairs and a converted porch that housed the television and all the furniture not good enough for guests. Aunt Rose arrived to occupy this porch area and over the next few months, robbed of the familiarity of England, her family home, all the precious objects that had reminded her of who she was, she gradually began acting senile. I say acting because we were never sure whether she was in fact senile or just pretending. She had a remarkable recovery, we all noticed, about the same time she stepped foot once more on British soil. But in California she took to being a real old lady, telling the same story twice in one day, mistaking people's identity, that sort of thing.

'Elizabeth,' she'd say, addressing me as her own dead sister, 'is tomorrow market day? Really, I cannot remember.'

We were in her room because it was the only place with a television aerial socket. I was reading over my science lab report, Isobel and Rose were playing draughts. Mother was in her chair, feet tucked under her, reading the newspaper. We were watching a wildlife programme, the American equivalent of David

Attenborough, called *Mutual of Omaha's Wild Kingdom*, in which a troop of baboons featured.

I said, 'I'm not Elizabeth, do I look like Elizabeth? Do I have lipstick on my teeth?'

'Reb*ecca*,' Mother said, 'that was unnecessary.'

'I meant Rebecca, I had it on my mind to say Rebecca,' Rose said.

'That's okay, Aunt Rose. Anyway, here in the New World every day is market day. What do you want?'

'Caster sugar, lemon curd, Crosse and Blackwell marmalade, granary bread, oatcakes and Wensleydale cheese.' She thought for awhile. 'Can you buy cat food?'

'Yes, you *can* buy cat food,' I said. 'You can't buy any of the other stuff you mentioned, but cat food, yes.'

Mother looked up from the *Register*, her hair locked into curlers she'd heated in a plastic steamer on the floor. She had a date that night and was wearing her satin peach dressing gown, a garment so slippery and shiny it looked like something you'd pour, not wear. Upstairs in her bedroom her make-up sat on a gold tray, poised at the vanity mirror like a plate of food readied for a banquet. She smelled of Noelle and freshly applied nail varnish and when she looked up she also waved the back of her hand, fingers separated, in an attempt to dry the varnish which had an oyster-like glow. Normally getting ready for dates put her in a good mood, but she threw me a warning glance, keeping her eyes on me as she turned the newspaper page.

'Then some cat food,' said Aunt Rose.

'For the cat?' I asked, trying not to laugh. We hadn't any cat, of course. The cat she was remembering, probably one of the hairy flat-faced Persians she'd kept with her sisters in the house on Dartmouth Row, must have been dead for years.

'*Rebecca*,' began Mother, from behind the paper.

'Never mind,' Aunt Rose said, leaning forwards in her chair. 'I just recalled the cat isn't here.'

'Rebecca will feed the cat,' said Mother.

I rolled my eyes.

'Go feed the cat,' Mother instructed in a serious voice as though for that instant she, too, believed this long-dead foreign-living cat was waiting in our kitchen for his Tender Vittles.

'Oh, sure,' I said. 'Meow, meow.'

Later, when Aunt Rose was taking her afternoon nap, Mother said, 'I won't have you teasing your great-aunt.'

'I wasn't teasing.'

'That's the *least* you were doing.'

'Isobel teases her and you let her get away with it,' I said.

'I don't tease,' defended Isobel. She'd been playing a game of jacks on the kitchen floor and when I said her name she caught the neon rubber ball in her palm and stared up at me. 'I *play* with Auntie. We pretend to be people,' said the sister, who was ten.

'That's what I was doing, too,' I said, facing Mother full on so as to make my lie more believable. 'Just playing along, like you say to.'

Mother had replaced her dressing gown with a glittering blue-grey pantsuit in stretchy material with spidery silver threads woven into the fabric. Her hair was curled into an exaggerated pageboy and she had false eyelashes that floated above her eyes so thick they gave her a dreamy look. This close to zero-hour, when He was due to arrive, I knew she'd be a pushover.

'Bullshitteth not thy mother,' she said, holding up a finger.

'Accuse not the daughter on whom you rely to babysit,' I warned back.

'I don't need a babysitter,' sang Isobel from the floor. 'All I need is a big mean dog that chases away burglars.'

'But that is impossible,' I said, looking straight at my mother. 'It would eat Rose's cat.'

'*Aunt* Rose,' said Mother, taking her keys from the table.

From that point it was only a matter of time before Aunt Rose went further gaga and began roaming the house searching for the cat. One day we found her scuttling behind the sofa, her big haunches in the air, calling, 'Pretty, pretty, kitty, kitty.' Later she went up a ladder, looking to see if the cat was by any chance perched on top of a kitchen cabinet, at night she waded outside in the bushes, aiming the high beam of her flashlight into the bougainvillea. She left bowls of milk in all manner of places, in the kitchen where I stepped in it or kicked it or poured it out with a huff, beside the welcome mat outside our front door, where Mother laid down the groceries on it, yelling 'Fucking cat!' as she did so, like there really were such a cat. The dead cat's name was Stanley and for a time we considered actually buying a Persian cat and calling it Stanley in an effort to stop Rose from carrying on: bending down to peer under parked cars and questioning the neighbours, had they seen her cat? She thought the Mexican gardeners who tended next door's garden had stolen her cat for breeding purposes. She was sure she'd taken the thing with her to the airport. She thought the cat was starving to death and worried herself late into the night. She called long distance to the RSPCA in London to report the missing cat. She called a local newspaper in her old neighbourhood and tried to persuade them to run an ad in the lost and found section. Sometimes she thought the cat was in Orange County but was afraid to come to our house because it had never, before coming to America, lived with children.

'You mean your cat doesn't *like* me,' said Isobel, heartbroken.

'It isn't a case of *like*,' said Rose. 'He isn't used to young children.' She put her hand on Isobel's, and said these words as kindly as she could.

'Damned cat,' Mother whispered when she thought Rose couldn't hear. 'Maybe we could dig up some old cat carcass and show it to her. Stop all this nonsense.'

'Oh, *that* would be kind,' I said.

'Put her out of her misery,' said mother, bracing herself at the kitchen sink. She'd had a bad time with a man she'd been seeing who turned out to be separated, not divorced, and who had, during the weeks he'd been dating Mother, managed somehow to reconcile with his estranged wife. He told Mother she had been a 'helping hand' that pulled him out of this troubled time in his marriage. He'd even given her a present to emphasize his point, a little pin in the shape of a gold hand holding a flower. 'Sick, isn't it?' Mother had said when she showed me that hand.

'Fake,' I'd said, examining it for a carat mark.

'Helen, have you seen his little plastic brush?' called Rose from her bedroom beside the kitchen.

'What's that, Rose?' Mother said, tilting her chin up as though to call back behind her, her voice booming much louder than needed in our small house. 'A *kitty* brush?'

'Yes, darling,' came Rose's small, apologetic reply. 'I'm sure it was I who left it somewhere.'

'We're going to brush Stanley!' said Isobel, animated at the thought of grooming the ghost cat who, if it existed in the first place, would have apparently hated her.

Mother decided the cat was an early sign, a warning to get out before Rose began bedwetting and drooling. Before the retirement communities wouldn't take her, in other words. My project that spring was to look into residential homes for Rose. 'Get her one of those places that looks normal except the sidewalks are extra wide and there's an ambulance on site,' Mother instructed. 'Don't let it be too far a drive.'

'Make sure it takes pets,' Isobel said, helpfully.

'And not too expensive,' said Mother.

'What about waiting lists?' I said.

'Bribe all necessary powers,' said Mother.

'May I put your name down while I'm at it?' I said.

'Don't be so smart,' said Mother. 'On second thoughts, yes.'

I researched available retirement communities using my high-school library, the Index to Periodic Literature and the Yellow Pages, recording my findings in a blue spiral-bound notebook. Over the next few months, on Saturdays, we all piled into Mother's Cadillac Seville. Mother always drove a Cadillac. She said she needed such a car for taking clients to see houses, but really it was vanity that kept her in Cadillacs. She was born in Essex but upon arriving in America as a young woman had embraced all that which spoke America to her. Cadillacs spoke it real loudly apparently, in eight years she'd had four different cars. Mother put on her horn-rimmed sunglasses, tied her hair in a scarf and smoked furiously as we drove up and down Route 1 looking at *leisure communities*, as they were called.

'Where are we going?' Aunt Rose always asked. When we told her we were looking for a bungalow in a leisure community, she'd say, 'What's the matter with the house you have, then, Helen?' Rose always brought a picnic: coffee in a thermos, crustless cheese sandwiches wrapped in a napkin, a tin painted with pictures of fruit with half a dozen biscuits inside. The thermos and the tin she'd brought with her from England, having made herself a picnic for the flight. Like most people who lived through the war, she'd never fully recovered from the idea of rationing. We'd find her bent over a crisper full of old vegetables, pondering what kind of soup to make with four carrots, three new potatoes and a quarter head of cabbage, or engaged in her own form of alchemy in the laundry room, combining the last ounce of Tide with a few tablespoons of leftover Cheer from the plastic gallon tubs she tipped upside down overnight so that they would give forth the last of their precious fluid. She was forever dividing up goodies, a single bar of chocolate would be sliced into pieces with her paring knife, to be enjoyed, square for separate square, each night for a week after dinner. If she saw us tear into a box of cookies, scraping the gooey centres out with our teeth and discarding outright the ones we didn't like, the expression on her face was more one of confusion than disapproval. 'What's this?' she'd say, looking into the cookie box with its broken halves, rejected fillings, all rifled through so a thick layer of crumbs lined the box like a carpet. She'd take the box away, not to punish us, but to find use for the crumbs in a pie crust.

All you needed to do was mention a car journey and she packed a picnic. Same thermos, with a broken pouring spout so you had to steady it at an angle, same triangles of plain cheese on buttered crustless bread without so much as a leaf of lettuce to help with the chewing, same tin for biscuits. She kept a

Brownie box camera in a canvas bag alongside the picnic, and a square rug of rough wool we were meant to sit on. These objects I ridiculed in secret for being dowdy. In an age of crazy straws, jawbreakers and disposable everything, they seemed unimaginably boring. There was also the issue of hygiene, as an American I found Rose's method of washing the thermos faintly repulsive (my expression at that time would have been 'gross') as she did not put it in the dishwasher but instead poured hot water on it for a few minutes then let it dry on the rack by the sink before sealing it up for the next outing. Many years later I found myself storing these items in my own kitchen cupboard – the thermos and tin, the Brownie camera and worn canvas bag – these keepsakes from another era. They had become treasures by which to remember my great-aunt, who would never have understood why, if I had a decent tin, a workable thermos, a tartan rug, I didn't make use of them rather than leave them sitting like museum pieces.

'I don't like this place,' Isobel said the minute we entered the driveway of a retirement community, *any* retirement community. The Evergreen Mansions, with its four-figure monthly bill, Olympic-sized swimming pool and waiting list that grew every year like bindweed, was rejected outright just the same as the desolate Carleton Oak Towers with its pair of tall, cement buildings like two tombstones jutting from a cliff. She twisted in her seat so her nose touched the window, her breath making a cloudy o on the glass. 'It looks ghostly.'

'You haven't even seen it yet!' said Mother.

'We can't leave Granny Rose in a place like this!'

'You're not leaving me anywhere,' said Rose, patting Isobel's arm reassuringly. 'Honestly, Isobel, where do you get such notions?'

'The hell we aren't,' Mother whispered under her breath.

In the end, Isobel was right. We couldn't leave Rose. The decent places had long waiting lists and cost the earth, and the ones without waiting lists were dreary establishments Mother said she couldn't with good faith put the pretend cat in, let alone

Aunt Rose. We spent the summer looking at retirement homes and the autumn enduring Rose's grief over the cat. By Halloween the man who'd given Mother the detested hand pin sent her a card on which a picture of roses sat below a banner of gold-embossed letters. 'Thank you', it read. Inside, below the Hallmark message, Mother learned he was now living with his wife and they were expecting a baby. 'No, thank *you*,' she said, punctuating her sentence with the stub of her cigarette smack into the card's blossoms.

After that, Mother went into one of her bouts of heartsickness. Mother's heartsickness was not a depression as such. I've seen enough of real depression to know that hers was just ordinary self-pity. She used to lie in bed, an ashtray of cigarette butts beside her, watching television and reading daytime soap magazines during the commercials. A depressing sight to behold, but I believe such behaviour had more to do with anger at how the world had so far failed to value her, than any oblique sadness. She did not come downstairs during these times and when you asked how she was, she looked at you through television-fatigued, red-rimmed eyes and spoke in a dramatic, whispering manner. 'I'll be all right,' she said. 'Give Isobel some dinner, would you?'

I brought her trays, watched that she ate, cleaned the downstairs of the house because I could do that without making too much noise and bothering her. I took myself and Isobel to school, handing Isobel her packed lunch and telling her Mother made it for her during the night, which was not true. Mother rarely slept at night, but she did not put herself to any useful task either. She treated her lovesickness like an illness, and in accordance with this diagnosis, took to her bed. It was a spooky, confusing time for all of us when she became like this – she might go for three weeks or so before returning, gradually, to her old self, like snow melting back to river water. But Mother's disappointments in love had far more effect on Isobel than myself. Isobel was young enough to believe that Mother really was ill and she lived through each laboured minute of Mother's unhappiness, her face crunched into worry, her eyes hooded with the fear that this time she might not get better. During this particular bout, Isobel clung to Aunt Rose, playing gin rummy with her in the evenings, sitting on her bed while Rose darned socks by the window.

'Granny Rose, can you teach me to talk like you?' Isobel asked.

'Like me, how do you mean?'

'With an accent,' said Isobel. 'I want an accent.'

'You have an accent.'

'No, I don't,' insisted Isobel, 'I'm American.'

'Half,' I corrected. 'And you have an American accent.'

'Americans don't have accents,' she said, crinkling her nose as though she'd smelt something foul. 'They have the sound you get before you get an accent.'

'Oh, *really*, Isobel,' said Aunt Rose.

'Please, Granny Rose, teach me.' And so Rose would recite a list of words like 'can't' and 'thought' and 'tune' and 'kitten', emphasizing the vowel sounds and snapping out the ts so they didn't sound like ds, until Isobel laughed and thought she sounded as English as the queen, which she did not. When she practised her English accent she sounded the way most Americans do when they put on such a voice, like a drag queen on Quaaludes, and an American one at that.

As usual, after a few weeks Mother ventured downstairs in her shoddy tartan bathrobe, the one she wore when she was feeling bad and which contrasted her shiny peach one in both texture and abundance. The peach floated away from her so that very little on her person, from collar bone to knee, was kept entirely hidden. The tartan was flannel, and wrapped around her all the way up to her chin. Cossetted in this fashion we discovered her one day retrieving a cup of coffee, a fresh matchbook. Soon she was regularly downstairs once more, making herself some toast, glancing impatiently over the piled stock of mail, enquiring as to whether anyone (meaning me) had put gas in the car. A few days later she was standing with her leg propped on a chair, rifling through the bills and using the sink as an ashtray.

'Lord and fucking Taylor. I'm going to put that credit card through the garbage disposal before we have to pawn the silver to pay their bills.'

'We don't have any silver,' I reminded her.

'I mean the silver-*effect* cutlery,' she said. 'And what is this oil bill? Have we been heating half the neighbourhood?'

'It's good to see you in such high spirits again,' I said. I meant it as a tease, but honestly it was beautiful to see her full of fire and bile again. When she was angry over love she simply did not engage in the rest of life. She collected herself – that is how she described it – while the rest of us waited. And then walked back into the world.

'It's good to be back,' Mother joked, 'in the kitchen.'

'It's not just the kitchen,' I said. '*All* the rooms missed you.'

The blackness of November faded and with her renewed spirit came a longing for adventure. One morning, watching Isobel and Aunt Rose in pursuit of the elliptical cat, she had a turn of heart which changed the course of our lives.

'We'll move back instead,' she said, as though within the middle of a discussion. 'We'll go back together, as a family.'

'To where?' I asked.

'To London.'

'To *where*?'

'*You*', she said, eyes fixed on my own now, 'will *love* London.'

'*I*', I said, in the same punctuated manner, 'will *not* go.'

It was for Isobel's sake that she did it. She realized that her black moods played hard on Isobel's sense of security and she worried that Isobel was like her in being 'sensitive' and 'changeable'. Aunt Rose cushioned the effect of Mother's occasional emotional absences and it was for this reason, I believe, that we all ended up back in Rose's old house, or the half of it that had not been sold.

Three weeks later we flew from LAX to Gatwick, ten suitcases between us plus all of Mother's stainless-steel kitchen pans as she didn't trust Rose to have anything more modern than an iron skillet. We took a train up to London and arrived on New Year's Day. The house stood, an imposing three storey Georgian structure, flanked by an abundance of overgrown hedges and fronted by a long stretch of intricate iron railings. There was a series of stone steps leading to the front porch with a door wide enough to drive a car through. From as far back as the street came the sound of a violin. I can tell you now what it was, Tartini's Sonata in G minor, though I did not have any idea at the time. We rang the buzzer and waited, hearing the violin stop abruptly, and then from the top of the house a window shutting. At that moment Rose suddenly remembered she had a key and asked me to look through her bag for it as she didn't have her reading glasses on. I didn't have to look for more than about two seconds. The door key, an ancient iron shank the colour of charcoal, was a hard item to miss. It sat on its own at the bottom of the purse and was easily six inches long.

Rose nodded approvingly. 'Try that,' she said. I stepped up on to the stone porch of Aunt Rose's house, bent over and on an impulse looked through the keyhole before trying the key. I don't know what inspired me to do this, except that the keyhole was so large, inviting one to peer through. I'd never seen anything like it in America, and when I put my eye to it I saw as clearly as though I were looking through a window. A man and a woman were standing together, the woman holding a violin, both staring with confusion at the door.

'Why don't you let us in?' I said through the keyhole.

'Is there somebody there?' asked Rose. 'Inside the house?'

Mother, who had finished paying the taxi driver and was now stepping along the paving stones in the front garden, assessing the proportions of our new home, came suddenly to the door.

'It might be the people who own upstairs,' Mother said, impatiently. Then to me, 'Use the bloody key.'

'Why are you two standing there?' I asked the figures inside the door. The woman inside raised an eyebrow at the man, who shrugged his shoulders. Then everything went black in my tiny diorama of vision as the man stepped forward blocking my view with the breadth of his torso. The door opened with a series of clanging locks and a great creaking, like a sound effect in a horror movie, and from the inside of the entrance hall, itself bigger than our entire upstairs back home, came a cloud of warm air from the fireplace, which was so large I'd thought for a split second that these two strange people had made a bonfire in Rose's old home.

'Hello,' I said.

'We're sorry to intrude,' Aunt Rose began. 'I hope you got my letter explaining our return. It wasn't possible to give an exact time, of course, and I realize it is very early to be—'

'Rose, it's your house,' said Mother, her arms laden with suitcases. 'Go inside.'

The man stepped aside, opening his arm to welcome us through. The woman retreated in the manner of a cautious deer to the bottom of the staircase with her violin. I saw now that she was wearing a thin cotton gown that fell to her ankles and no shoes at all on the tiled floor. She had blonde hair, wispy and uncombed, pushed aside as though she'd just woken (which very well might have been the case) and cheekbones so high they jutted catlike from her face. I thought she was perhaps the most beautiful woman I'd ever seen in my life, with exactly the sort of looks I'd always dreamed of. I admired her long hands, her pale complexion which was in contrast to the bronzed overly tanned skin which was fashionable just then in America. She had a small shy mouth, crimson lips, a long slender neck. She ran her fingers over the violin in a repeated fluttery motion, the way some women finger a necklace. She smiled at me, bewildered, amused. She would soon be my best – my only – friend. The man, who I'd hardly noticed except that he took up a chunk of space to my right as we came through the door, was James.

5

It was not the first time I'd been to my Aunt Rose's house. We had visited the house before as very young children, on what Mother had called a 'duty holiday', which meant the holiday was born out of familial necessity and wasn't going to be any fun at all. Then, it had been a single family house with the three sisters fluttering about, forever washing floors, scrubbing potatoes, and attending to the small ornaments that graced every surface in a composite of organized clutter that Mother scorned. We'd stayed in a pair of rooms separated by folding doors on the first floor, Isobel and I shared a bed with heavy drapery around it. The bed was lumpy and so soft it gave way beneath our backs so we had to strain to see each other when we lay in it. Isobel, who was only four, peed in it twice and after that I refused to sleep with her so she went to Mother's room, which had a brass bed that bowed in the middle, and a dark splintered floor. I remember there were peacocks on the wallpaper and the fireplace had a clip rug Mother stuffed into a wardrobe. The mantel was studded with dozens of ceramic roses and porcelain Royal Doulton maidens in flowing china dresses. These things I adored. Mother shook her head as I held each beautiful doll up to the window. She didn't stop me admiring them but she said, 'Don't get your heart set on one of those for Christmas.'

The bathroom was across the hall and so big there was an armchair in one corner and a reading lamp, too, which Mother informed me was against fire regulations. She disapproved of the standing lamp so close to the bath like that, but she made a lot of use of the armchair, where she sat with her chin on her hand, dreaming out the window as Isobel took her evening bath. The bath was a long narrow one of cold white porcelain with two taps, one for hot and one for cold and no overhead shower. The absence of a shower did not bother Isobel at all, who likened the bath to a small swimming pool and floated on her stomach, flailing her legs and arms in an attempt at freestyle. For me the idea that a house, any house, let alone a big one like this with a half-dozen people in it, did not possess something as banal and necessary as a shower was acutely misguided planning.

'Where is the shower?' I had asked with indignity.

'With the fridge-freezer,' said Mother, meaning nowhere.

Six years later with the house now divided we still had a bath without a shower, but this one was a converted pantry which had been rushed into a make-do bathroom when Aunt Rose sold the rest of the house. Though the house was large, a great deal of its vastness was in the form of public spaces, corridors and entrance halls, landings and porches. The grand reception hall with its sweeping, elegant staircase and towering ceiling, vast and white like a huge ice rink over our heads, served as the centre to the house, but was of no practical use other than sheer impressiveness and consumption of space. The upstairs rooms we'd occupied on that previous visit were no longer accessible, as they'd been sold along with the grand bathroom and the bedrooms above. The rooms Rose had retained were all on the ground floor, a decision which made infinite sense at the time of the sale, as Rose would not always be able to negotiate the stairs and certainly had no need for so much space. But these rooms, some of them quite nice, were regarded by my mother as no better than servants' quarters, although, frankly, the real servants' quarters – what once were servants' quarters – were up a rickety back staircase off the kitchen. There was a drawing room, so cluttered with possessions and tapestries, with small oil paintings of countryside scenes and framed china plates that it looked smaller than it really was. The room contained a horsehair sofa and chairs with carved mahogany frames, a dull green marble mantel with a brass clock beneath a halo of thin glass, a pair of candlesticks and two porcelain shepherd boys one for each side of the mantel. A mirror was set here, of course, framed in laboriously carved ebony wood. Everywhere you looked there was some sort of decoration, a set of four connected satin-framed photographs, or ornamental vase of roses, tiny ceramic figurines, an ivory owl no bigger than a shotglass, a tortoise made of jade. There was a hearth rug, a matted, threadbare Persian rug, and a lambskin laid out over floorboards that had long ago been painted black. The television, which had always occupied centre stage in our living room at home, was tucked away beside a cupboard of tea-making things. Mother, who said the room was a mausoleum, regularly reiterated what she would one day do to the room (one day meaning, I suppose, when Rose was dead), which was to 'clear out all this junk'.

Meanwhile, it served as a bedroom for Rose, who felt it rather strange to sleep in the parlour but did not object. We moved in her bed and she instructed us as to how to angle it. She then went to fetch something from another room and returned with a wooden cross with a figure of Jesus on it.

'There's a hammer in the garden shed, Rebecca,' she said, holding the crucifix in her hand. 'I'm not sure where we'll find a nail.'

She indicated a spot on the wall above her head. 'Just there,' she said, tapping at the air.

How one sleeps beneath such a thing is still a mystery to me, at the time I was horrified at the thought of looking up to see a crucifix, the lolling head, the half-closed eyes, the spindly body thinly covered by a loincloth. But I did as she said and we fixed Jesus where she wanted. Isobel, who had by now adopted Aunt Rose as her own grandmother and could not be separated from her except by means of a crowbar, moved her own folding cot into this room and set her clothes beneath it in careful piles.

That left one room for Mother and myself. It was a large rectangular room with a pair of French windows that opened on to the front garden, floorboards thick with varnish that gave an icy feel to your bare feet, a fireplace so large you could stand inside it, and which emitted great gusty drafts so that the first order of business was to board it up. The room had been used as the dining room long ago, when the house was whole, and contained, among countless keepsakes and other useless artefacts, a gateleg table, a half-dozen heavy neo-Georgian dining chairs, a china cupboard, a set of nesting tables and a rather sumptuous chaise longue, which was the only piece of furniture Mother retained.

We hadn't owned anything good enough to sell in Orange County, even Mother's Cadillac had been rented, and we were now living, literally, on the meagre rent our old house was fetching. Despite this Mother insisted on going to John Lewis and ordering an expensive queen-sized bed, the innards of which the salesman explained in detail using a model that showed a cross-section of pocket springs, horsehair, battened cotton and wool, all of which combined to provide her an ample bed of spectacular comfort. This, she claimed, was the least she could have, considering she was now living in a tiny section of what by right ought to be her ancestral home. She offered to get me a single bed of the same quality, and said it could be angled away from the fireplace, which I'd taken a dislike to, but at sixteen I was not willing to share a room with my mother. Not even a room so large you could have parked her Cadillac at one end and still had room for the queen-sized bed and the cherrywood chest of drawers (which she'd fished out of the cellar and had hauled up by a pair of window cleaners who'd called upon us in search of work).

That meant I had only one option. I slept in a box bed next to the range in the kitchen. For 'privacy' we hooked a clothes line on the wall and ran a pair of curtains across it. Mother, in an unusual moment of domesticity and parental guilt, set up a second line with curtains that ran down the side of the bed and hid my pyjamas and shoes beneath. Although it was not what I was used to – and when I woke up the first thing I saw each morning was clothes hanging off the sheila maid above me – living in the kitchen was not so bad as it first sounds. The kitchen was not a single room as such. There were numerous ancillary rooms, the pantry which had been converted into a bathroom but still retained its bellboard and telephone exchange, also a larder in which we stocked all our canned goods, coats and hats, Isobel's paints and crayons, a box of her toys. There was a scullery with walls of plate racks and a six-foot oak refectory table which we now used as a dining area, and a long corridor in which we set up cupboards, and chests of drawers we fished out from the cellar and kept our clothes in. The floor was slate, the walls a smooth stone, painted white, and the whole area was lit by glass lanterns hanging from a lofty ceiling with a set of windows so high you saw only the tops of trees and the sky beyond. Far from feeling sorry for myself, I liked living in the kitchen, for after nine o'clock or so it was a grand area occupied only by myself. I set to work figuring out how to use the extraordinary and complicated range, and lined up glass bowls along the oak table in which I conducted chemistry experiments from a book I bought on how to conduct real experiments in a home laboratory. Late at night I could hear the faint melody of a violin above me.

'What sort of music is that coming from upstairs?' asked Aunt Rose at breakfast the Monday after we moved in.

Mother was scraping the burn off a piece of toast she left too long under the grill. She didn't say as much but I could hear her mind working. Get a toaster, it said. To Rose she said, 'What music?'

'Violin,' I cut in. Rose squinted her eyes. 'Lea is a violinist.'

Rose still looked a bit puzzled, so I said, 'The couple upstairs, she's a musician.'

'They seem far too young to own a whole house,' said Rose. 'I assumed they were the *children* of the people who own the house.'

'They don't own the *whole* house,' I corrected.

'A bloody great chunk of it,' said Mother. Therein followed a conversation about the tragedy of selling the greater part of the house and how if Mother had known she'd end up living in it, in this relatively tiny portion with her whole family, she'd never have facilitated the sale. Rose shuffled around looking guilty and agreeing wholly with Mother who went on and on about recent market trends and how the house, had they held on to it, would be worth twenty per cent more than it had been when they sold it, almost a year ago.

'How old is she?' I asked, still thinking about Lea. Lea had been a name I found particularly ugly, perhaps the ugliest name in the universe. Since I'd found it attached to this very beautiful young woman, however, I'd suddenly taken a fancy to it. There was a shimmer of electricity around the name, a lightness. My own name, with its three syllables and staccato ending, sounded abruptly pretentious. A loud name, an American name. I wanted the simplicity of a single word, the softness of what I suddenly thought of as a whispery, sexy word. Lea.

'What dreamland are you in, Rebecca?' Mother asked.

Nobody answered my question but I found out later she was twenty-six.

That morning my duties were to wipe every wall and surface in our part of the house, including the entrance hall which we shared with upstairs, with a mixture of soda crystals and water. Aunt Rose made up the mixture, which she lifted from the sink in a little grey bucket with a plastic handle. Isobel was given a bussell, which she ran at speed over the carpets, making a terrific noise and doing no good at all. It would be some weeks before we started school and Rose wanted us not to be idle. For a woman who was meant to be losing her marbles she seemed, now that she was back on her home soil, remarkably lucid and commanding. She was a serious housekeeper who did not allow for splotched floors or watermarks on mirrors, who oiled the furniture on a weekly basis and wiped off the condensation that settled on the window frames every morning at the same hour to ensure that mildew did not set in. Dust defied her, she could no longer see it, but wielded an old feather duster like a sword.

'We need a painter,' Rose said, dabbing at the lower corner of the window where mildew peppered the woodwork.

'We need a *man*,' Mother corrected. She'd been to the letter box in her silky dressing gown and shuffled through a few brown envelopes looking for her name, then dropped them like flower petals back to the floor. Like an actress playing a distressed, isolated beauty, in a movie that Hollywood would describe as Rapunzel meets *Room with a View*, she'd decided that the landscape of men in south-east London was an arid desert devoid of beauty. The shimmery dressing gown revealed she held some small hope, however, of being discovered by an unlikely but dashing suitor with whom love would flourish. Returning, she declared, 'Nothing for me today. But there's always tomorrow. I'm going to get dressed.'

'Rebecca, the point is *not* to drench the walls,' Aunt Rose said, assessing my work, 'but to run the cloth over the surface *lightly*.'

To Isobel she said, 'Slow down or relinquish your appliance!' which made Mother laugh. After a time Isobel contrived to watch television in Rose's room while I went to the entrance hall with my bucket of soda crystals. I started on the fireplace mantel, which was so littered with ash and dirt I had first to get a dustpan and brush to clear it. I then made the mistake of sweeping the ashes forward and caught an eyeful of grit that blinded me. I tried again, sweeping to the side. I did not mind the work; I am the sort of person who enjoys performing a job that is easy to assess and that I am fully competent to do. Also, I loved having a reason to be in the entrance hall, which was vast and airy, with light pouring in from the windows as tall as myself and an echo that rose against the ornate ceiling. In America our front door had opened into a reception area not big enough to put a chair. The one window it had was crowded by a rubber tree that Mother had been given by some man, and which flourished spectacularly while the relationship went down the natural road to extinction that marked all of Mother's love life. But here the hall was of a new order altogether. It felt like the entrance to a palace. I was kneeling at the tiled surround, deriving a measure of satisfaction from my work, when James came through the front door, startling me so that I jumped.

'Oh, hi,' I said, trying to appear natural. My only surprise was that he'd entered from the outside, as I'd been hoping, of course, that either he or Lea would come down the stairs so I could get a glimpse of them. My fascination for the couple had begun at once, the minute we first entered the house and saw them standing together wondering who was coming through their front door with a key. That morning, as we lugged in our baggage and set upon making a home for ourselves, they'd only said, 'We'll let you get on.' This was meant to be polite, I was sure, but Mother informed me that the translation of this sentence into Americanese was 'We are going to get as far away from you as possible.' Later, Lea appeared with a tray of tea, which Aunt Rose made a fuss over and said was very kind, but Lea did not stay to have it with us. This fact was of great significance, I discovered. Aunt Rose, who was not given to translating English into American, perhaps because her short stay in the USA was marked mostly by journeys to rejected nursing homes so she was not capable of transatlantic parlance, sniffed at the abandoned tray.

'She must be a very busy young lady,' Rose said.

'Translation, Mother?' I said.

'What a bitch,' answered Mother. 'If that girl had wanted to be friendly she'd have invited us into her *home*.'

'What does it mean that she left the tray with us, then?'

'It means, we will tolerate living under the same roof as you as long as the only time we see you is in case of fire.'

I was half English, had been to England twice and lived there as a baby, which in America had made me exotic and interesting. Now I saw that I had a great deal to learn if I were ever to understand this country and its subtle, yet penetratingly communicative language. Despite the fact that Lea and James had clearly rejected me along with the rest of my misbegotten family,

I was determined for them to like me. I smiled now at James in a manner I hoped was friendly but not overt or insincere. A polite, morning smile was what I attempted to effect.

James said, 'I'm sorry to startle you. I guess . . .' He stumbled on his words. He looked half awake and somewhat drunk, though in my naivety I assumed he was merely preoccupied. In his hand was a parcel from the bookshop, wrapped in grey and white candy-striped paper and fastened by tape as though it were a gift. Across one side, in marker pen, was written Hatfield, his surname. He'd obviously ordered the book and rushed out when the call from the shop announced it had arrived. He went swiftly to the bottom of the stairway and leaned on the banister. 'I guess we'll all have to get used to each other's comings and goings,' he said.

His apology had been spoken as though he were not in the least bit sorry about startling me, but about me being there in the first place. And the second part of his comment, the bit about 'comings and goings', was, I am sure, in respect of his wife's unusual musical practice. Lea was given to practice sessions lasting three hours which she began well after midnight. Mother drank enough Scotch before bedtime that she was unaware as yet that we'd moved to a house with night owls who played Mozart while the rest of the world was sleeping. I, however, was very much aware of Lea's hours. I found James's lack of apology for it, and his sly way of telling me he found me inconvenient, a direct insult. I might have hated him on the spot, but I was so pleased I'd managed to distil through the camouflage of language what he really meant to say that I couldn't help but feel utterly pleased.

'Your wife plays beautifully,' I said, and watched with relief as the tension drained from his face.

He took a step towards me, pulling his gloves off slowly.

'I'm the only one who hears her – the rest of my family are heavy sleepers – it's like waking to a dream when she plays.'

A smile curled on his face, exposing a gap between his incisors and a rather fetching dimple on his left cheek. 'I hope she doesn't wake you too much,' he said, again in a way that meant something else completely. He was saying, I hope you are delighted by her music.

'Not at all, it's lovely.'

'Thank you,' he said softly, as though it had been him I complimented. He extended his hand. I believe it was the first grown-up handshake I'd ever performed. He shook my hand without any comment on the fact it was wet with scrubbing water and probably cold to the touch. In America there would have been a moment of revulsion masked by humourless laughter, but in England if a man shook a woman's hand while she was scrubbing furniture, he didn't act surprised at the fact it might be wet. He said my name, he nodded, then backed away to the staircase that led up to the many rooms above. He turned back to me at the landing and said, 'Lea will be thrilled.'

There was a great deal of settling in to be done. We'd moved from southern California, where mid-January you might sport a light jacket in the evening, to a climate in which boots and hats, underclothes and long, water-resistant coats were required half the year. We spent the first few days of our arrival scarcely leaving the house, focusing all our attention on the innumerable cleaning chores Aunt Rose set out for us, so when it finally came time to go outside, into the rest of London, we discovered we did not have a single coat among us that was adequate to withstand the winter temperature. I didn't mind, it was a good excuse to stay home. I'd fallen in love with the house. Never in my life had I lived in such a grand, idiosyncratic structure. I liked the cellar steps, smooth stone slabs worn down by thousands of footfalls with a shine as though they'd been waxed, the sash windows that rumbled as they glided along a system of pulleys and counterweights which I'd never known of before, all the decorative mouldings and embellishments across the vast ceilings, the austere grandiosity of the kitchen, the cosy hidden den of my bed. In the garden Isobel and I had unearthed several unusual (we thought) objects, including a Victorian mud scraper, rusted but still functional, a brass doorknob, a china bowl. It was a little like living on an architectural site.

'Why are they digging up all this old garbage?' Aunt Rose asked Mother.

'I couldn't say. Come inside, girls, before you die of cold.'

It was probably the sight of us rushing around the frosted grass in tennis shoes and thin jumpers that brought Mother to take us shopping the following afternoon. For the expedition, and that is what she called it, a shopping expedition, as though we were going through a jungle to find suitable attire, we wore two jumpers, tights and our heaviest jackets – which in my case was a windbreaker – and huddled together on the ten-minute walk to the railway station.

'Will we see any castles?' asked Isobel.

'Just because it's England does not mean you see castles every time you leave your front door,' I said. Secretly, I had a tourist map in my pocket and I'd already searched it for castles and had discovered there would be none en route to Oxford Street. My disappointment in this I took out on Isobel, who glowered at me.

We rode a train that seemed to cut a line directly through the ugliest back sections of Lewisham and Southwark. It featured abandoned warehouses, roofless and gutted, with banks of windows lying shattered below gaping holes in the brickwork, a dump piled with the rusted frames of cars smashed flat, and the same slabs of concrete system-built highrises arranged domino-fashion that you find all over south London. There were rows of Victorian houses, backed on to one another, others with narrow gardens with clothing drying on umbrella-shaped washing lines. If you looked for them, you could find landmarks of spectacular beauty, Southwark Cathedral somehow held its allure despite being steeped in the grim panorama, for example. But even as I clutched my guidebook, busily trying to match the shape of the buildings in the distance with the silhouettes across the page, I saw that it was a futile and hopelessly optimistic exercise. I was better off closing my eyes as the other passengers had. Isobel, by contrast, was enthralled with the train and particularly with our wood-panelled compartment with plush crimson seats patterned in paisley and a window she could raise and lower by means of a catch at its centre, but Mother's face mirrored the desolation of south London. Her hands clutched her pocketbook and she licked her lips over and over. I knew she was thinking she'd made a terrible mistake in coming back to England. She'd loved California, with its eternal summer, its proximity to the ocean, which was always with you, just ahead where it looked like a saucer of blue you could fall into, or flanking your side, or sparkling in your rear-view mirror. The palm trees with their shaggy heads were mysterious and paradisical. The rows of neat, little houses in our suburb were completely devoid of character, but aligned cleanly and bordered by cream-coloured sidewalks neatly swept by a team of local government workers who beautified with great skill every square inch of that county. Here, the city seemed ad hoc and random, and extremely dirty. When we'd passed the Houses of Parliament on our journey from the airport, they'd looked grey and dull like a book of spent matches. But today, as we passed over the railway bridge that links Waterloo to Charing Cross, along with the grimness of South London, I also got a sense of the city's vast possibilities. With the suddenness of all English weather, the clouds separated and a shaft of sunlight fell around us. Now the Thames was sparkling blue, the river boats filling its centre in a slow procession up and down stream. The flags at the South Bank waved in a cheerful array and, from this distance, the Houses of Parliament and Westminster Abbey beyond did not look so much dirty as graciously old.

At Charing Cross we rode the number 13 bus up to Oxford Street where Mother went directly to the third floor of John Lewis and purchased her queenly bed. Isobel and I got a kick out of being allowed to stretch out on a mattress in full view of the public. We watched as the salesman guided Mother from bed to bed, encouraging her to try out all the different makes. Mother hardly needed to be encouraged, of course. She made a show of feeling embarrassed as she stretched out, arms akimbo on the pristine surface of each, but secretly I could see she was loving the experience. She looked up at the salesman, a man probably not much older than James, and said coyly, 'This is gorgeous. Have you tried it? Go on, you have a turn.' Somehow she got the man to lie on the bed after her and they went on like that from bed to bed, as though he were intending to share her new purchase and needed to try it out for size. Finally, when she got to the most expensive and enormous model, the one which had more horsehair and more batting and more pocket springs than any of the others, she moved over, making room for the salesman to lie beside her and announced, 'Mmm, this is it. I think this is the one. What do you think? Is it all right?' The salesman, looking down on her lying like an empress in her colossal bed, must have suddenly remembered who he was and where he was, because he did not seat himself on the part of empty mattress she'd designated for him. He stood quite straight, put one hand in his pocket, and nodded furiously without a word.

The next thing I knew we were being ushered down the escalator to children's clothing, where Mother shelled out the equivalent of a month's rent on forest-green school coats with wooden tassel buttons and ridiculous hoods that flopped behind. Ordinarily, I would never have contemplated wearing such a coat. In America there hadn't been anything as outrageous as a school uniform and the idea of one at my age seemed absurd, if not personally damaging. The only reason I tolerated it was that Mother made such an issue of pride about buying them new, not second-hand the way all her own school uniforms had been purchased, that I felt obligated to put the thing on and pretend I actually liked it. Isobel, as usual, found reason to celebrate.

'It's lovely,' she said, imitating Aunt Rose in a manner which, for the first time ever, sounded vaguely accurate.

Luckily we also got woollen hats and pairs of gloves, for when we emerged onto the street again the wind was blowing hard and it had begun to snow. The traffic was stopped and all around us taxis filled, their lamps dimmed to indicate they were already hired. The queue at the bus stop told us that we were in for a long ride home. At this point, Mother cursed and let it be known that we could have gone to the shopping centre in Lewisham for our coats, which in all likelihood would have been a pound or two cheaper, but she refused to set foot in Lewisham, which she called a dump. This speech was followed by one regarding the general maladies of English life, which focused mostly on the influx of foreigners to a nation which was geographically and economically limited. She went on for some time, apparently unaware that she'd added two (half) foreigners to the heaps of others just days previously. Finally, a number 12 bus came, which Mother said would do, and we were told as we boarded that there were seats on the upper deck only. This suited Isobel and I fine as we loved to ride on the top of double-decker buses. While Mother sighed and huffed and fidgeted in the crowded seat, the enormous heaving bus waded through a crushing line of traffic. Isobel and I wiped the condensation off the windows and delighted in the elevation of our vision. It didn't matter that we were moving slower than one would on foot, we felt as though we were on a giant float in a teeming, mid-town parade. I don't remember what time we got home but it was way past dark and Mother claimed to be too tired to eat any of the pie Rose had made for us. She poured herself a tall Scotch and headed for the bathroom where she shut herself in so long we had to find a make-do chamber pot for Isobel. Rose fussed over our new coats and told us how marvellous we looked in them, then checked our hats for thickness and declared them 'top notch' as well. *Where did you go? John Lewis, oh well, that's the place, isn't it. Aren't you girls lucky. I say . . .*

There was a general sense of celebration after our day in London and, though Mother seemed wrung out from it all, I remember going to bed that night feeling genuinely happy to be in England. By the time Lea's violin started I'd slept long and felt rested enough to sit up in my bed and listen as though to a private recital. There is something about the flight of notes from a violin that brings light to the mind and allows it to follow thoughts anchorless and free. I remember sitting in bed, thinking that this was why people listened to music, for this feeling, richer and deeper than any I'd ever known, that had nothing whatsoever to do with ordinary life. Sometimes when I woke to Lea's violin, it seemed in my dreamy state as though the house itself were singing, and that all of us – myself, Mother, Rose and Isobel, even James and Lea upstairs, who in my imagination had already become our close friends even if they felt they couldn't stand us – had entered a new world in which anything could happen. Houses could sing, children could find treasure in their back garden. Rose's cat, Stanley, the one we had believed to be a figment of her imagination, had returned to the house a few days previously. A wanderlust tom, he wasn't quite as sure as Rose that he was her cat and had been otherwise engaged at the time Rose had left for America. He strode through the catflap in the back door, meowed deeply for his dinner and Rose said, 'Oh, *there* you are,' and got out a can of food as though she'd only just seen him yesterday. So cats could be brought straight out of the imagination, conjured and then seen, as palpable and real as the iron-handled range I could reach from my bed to touch. I was thinking all this, my hand outstretched and clasping the cold metal, when suddenly the music from upstairs came to an abrupt halt. It seemed to have stopped just as it had reached what seemed to my uneducated ear as a pivotal and moving moment. Then I heard the sound of footsteps and laughter, James's and Lea's. And then there was quiet.

I could not keep myself from them. The truth was I'd fallen into a fascination that would not be moderated, much less stopped. The more I found out about either one of the two people living a floor above me, the more my curiosity fixed on them, like a sight glass on a periscope – which if I could have used, I would have – that angled constantly for a better view. I had gathered from the times I'd seen James with those grey and white striped packages from the bookshop, plus all the punching of typewriter keys in the evening, that he was involved in some sort of writing. Because of the way he dressed, in broad ribbed corduroys and jumpers worn at the elbows, I'd figured him to be an academic. In fact, I was not far wrong as he had originally wanted to be an academic. He comes from a complicated heritage of university professors and slightly insane biologists (his father was a renowned expert on the evolution of fish and was considered at his death to be the authority on metabolic variation in skate, for whatever that's worth). His mother studied art. All over the walls of my great-grandfather's house were solid, elaborate gilt frames, draped in heavy burlap to protect the paintings within from light. I'd noticed one on the landing at the top of the stairs and had figured it for a hole in the wall they'd wanted to cover until, one afternoon when nobody was home, I summoned the courage to go up the stairs that led to Lea and James's rooms, and look beneath the curtain of fabric. It was a painting of a little boy in a soldier's costume sitting on a planked floor with a toy dog beside him. It looked impressively old, but because I could not see any signature in the corner I reckoned it to be of no particular value. Later I learned that the little watercolour could have bought a car. Since arriving in England Mother had been hankering for her Cadillac and was busy flipping through Rover brochures, dreaming of the day she could purchase England's version of a Sedan de Ville – which given our complete lack of income was never. The soldier boy could have bought a Rover with change to spare, but I didn't know that then.

The paintings were among the innumerable subjects James and Lea fought over. Lea did not like the idea of 'paintings in purdah' which was how she described the dozens of paintings covered in burlap around their home. I have to admit I don't much see the point in hanging a picture and then hiding it so you can't see it anyway, but this is how James dealt with the two contrary wishes of his dead mother. *Show the work.* You must show the work. But then, *Preserve the work.* You must at all costs maintain these important pieces. James's compromise, which was to staple tiny burlap curtains to the backs of the paintings' frames which he drew closed during the day when the damage of the sun's rays might adversely affect the colours, made Lea crazy.

'I'm tired of playing peek-a-boo with your mother's paintings,' she said, her voice booming as they came down the stairs together. 'Either they are shown or they are stored *elsewhere*. I'd rather have a few posters, which were able to see the light of day, than live with cloth sacks covering your mother's precious art.'

'This is not about the art, it's about my mother, isn't it?' James said.

'Fighting about a dead woman would be about as absurd as hanging paintings one cannot actually look at. I'm opposed to both,' said Lea.

'We can look at them at night,' James said, referring to the practice he had, once the sun had gone down, of flipping back the burlap.

'Yes, but I'm not often home at night, am I?' said Lea, in response to which James grumbled something about no, she bloody well wasn't. She was always playing in concerts, and this fact disturbed James, who had long ago tired of traipsing around after her and feeling like a useless appendage.

There was another problem with the paintings. Although the paintings were invaluable, and selling even half the collection would make James a fairly rich man, the bulk of James's inheritance had gone into purchasing the house (he did this, I learned later, so he could not squander the money) and there was not a great deal of ready cash left. That meant James and Lea lived on a shoestring budget, yet in a large house and surrounded by great art. At times this caused tension. Lea wanted a particular violin, which cost the earth and which she could not have – unless one of the paintings were sold. James and she had no car; their only means of transport were the two rickety bicycles they chained outside and covered in a blue tarpaulin in the winter. Occasionally they splurged on a taxi, but that meant doing without some other necessary thing. They lived with hardly any furniture and their bathroom had rotting tiles that stank and fell off the walls, shattering in the bath. Lea came away one morning with tiny shards of painted clay stuck into her bleeding feet; James had to pick them out with a sewing pin he borrowed from Rose. James and Lea were often invited to fancy dinner parties, receptions and teas connected to Lea's work, and Lea complained about not having enough different dresses.

'I'm seen in the same old frock,' she pouted one evening as they went through the front door.

'You look beautiful,' said James, a bit too perfunctorily to be believed.

'Oh, shut up, It's all right for you. Men are meant to wear the same thing.'

She was right, of course, and now I would have some sympathy for her as it is strangely galling to a woman to be seen in the same dress over and over again. At the time, however, I envied her clothes and thought her too much like my mother, who seemed to me to have hundreds of clothes she never wore and yet was always searching for more. Also, she was so lucky to be going out at all, in my opinion. I was sixteen at a time when being sixteen meant you did not go out, at least not very often, and certainly not to anything that would require smart dress.

But the worst aspect of the paintings was the problem of their being stolen. This had happened before, not when James was in charge of the paintings' welfare, but when they belonged to his parents properly. A half dozen paintings were removed from the downstairs of their home while they were away at a family christening. The story goes that the nephew of his father had insisted they all come to his baby son's christening in Milton Keynes. Milton Keynes was not terribly far from where they lived at that time, when his father was still teaching in Cambridge, but without a car the train connections to Milton Keynes were complicated. They'd had to take a train from Cambridge to King's Cross, then a taxi to Marylebone, and from there connect to another train which took them through the Chilterns to Milton

Keynes. The fact that it was a Sunday meant they had to wait for each connection on the many legs of their journey. 'We could have gone to New York in less time,' James joked later, telling me the tale. The christening had gone on forever and was followed by both a reception at the church where it was held and at James's cousin's home. They ended up missing the one evening train back to London and had to go to a hotel for the night. The next day, arriving weary back at Cambridge, they discovered the paintings had been stolen. The places where paintings had been were pale squares on the otherwise blank walls.

When James moved into the house on Dartmouth Row, he installed an alarm system to protect the works, which he could never have afforded to insure. But spiders were forever alerting the infrared detectors that an intruder had entered, and inexplicable false alarms made him question the system's efficacy. Besides which, the alarm itself would not deter a serious thief, who would grab a half-dozen paintings and flee before so much as a call to the police would be made. So James tried not to make it a habit to be away from home for long stretches of time. This proved a sore point in his relationship with his wife, for Lea was not only a concert violinist, but first string of an orchestra. She spent a good deal of time on tour. James might have been able to come with her some of the time, but he would not leave his paintings. The resulting battles, over tour dates and burdensome legacies, shortness of funds and general frustration, I was mostly privy to by means of the kitchen flue.

The house was large enough that I doubt I'd have heard much that went on upstairs had that flue not been there, precisely three feet from the bed where I slept. But with the help of this modern convenience I hardly needed to eavesdrop. Whatever transpired in their part of the house was brought with shimmering clarity directly to my bedside.

'There is no way to have a discussion with you,' he told Lea, and stomped around loudly.

Lea was no slouch at argument, and held her own with James quite nicely. 'It's fine being married to a musician when you can tell all your friends about her, the big prize you won, but when it comes to actually letting the woman go to work and do her job – yes, James, playing in an orchestra is my *job* – then suddenly it is altogether too inconvenient!' she shot back.

'I am not asking you to quit the orchestra—'

'I should hope not! I should bloody well hope not because if you want to make that sort of ultimatum, I can tell you now that the result might not be to your liking!'

'I've made no ultimatum. You needn't act as though I have!'

'What exactly are you asking for, then? Do you see my point, James?'

'Birmingham, Manchester, Edinburgh, then three different cities in Spain and a trip to wherever the fuck this is – *Baltimore*?'

Maryland, I said out loud. Sitting up in bed, knees to chin.

Lea said, 'The United States would be the fuck where that is.'

'Do you see *my* point?'

'No.'

They banged around upstairs and then, usually, she came storming downstairs with him trailing after her. Carefully, and I had to be utterly careful in this, I would move a stool to the kitchen wall and stand upon it, one eye to the window where I watched as she walked straight out into the night, without so much as a coat. James, thinking no doubt of his mother's art collection, fumbled with a great hunk of keys, trying to lock up before losing sight of her. No doubt he sometimes cursed his wife's athletic gait; she had an alarmingly swift walk for such a small woman and was of so fierce a nature she'd rather go out in her pyjamas, without her purse or anything else, just to make a point. I watched as he fled to find her, racing down Dartmouth Row, the flaps of his greatcoat butting his knees. I was usually asleep when they returned, that same coat draped over Lea's shoulders, him with one arm pinched to his body, balancing takeaway cartons, the other around his wife. They laughed and kissed, sometimes he dropped everything by the door and carried her upstairs.

They did not always fight, but when they did it was James who recovered the situation. James was always the one to apologize, to make amends, to beg forgiveness. Many years later, when I'd replaced Lea as his wife, I appreciated this aspect of his personality even more, as I discovered like many married people how hard it can be to concede blame, or accept one's faults, and yet how impossible it is to proceed in a marriage without those two skills. James, for all his troubles, was a peace-maker, and this one, humble quality of his, made him terribly loveable.

He was humble in other ways as well. For example he lacked any sense of vanity. By this, I do not mean he did not wash, only that he was not interested in his appearance and regarded everything about his physical person to be of no importance. The central heating in that big house was not particularly effective. There were just too many large, draughty windows, uncovered floorboards and lofty ceilings into which the heat vanished, to allow for continual warmth through winter. Down-stairs, we managed with space heaters and electric blankets, ours was such a small space that it was possible, just about, to keep an average temperature of sixty-five degrees. But James and Lea, who had many more rooms and all of them boasting large, draughty windows, suffered much more, even though in theory their place on the first floor ought to have been warmer. For this reason, James had taken to sleeping in a battered, grey woollen watch cap. I knew this only because Lea was given to divulging intimate and usually embarrassing (to James) details about her husband. Also, because the hat flattened his curly hair into an odd, displeasing shape so that he appeared to have suffered a particularly damaging bit of topiary atop his head. Because he worked at night, when the house was especially cold, he wore the cap then as well. If you happened to catch sight of him at his typewriter what you saw was a thin form in a wide-necked sweater jacket, woolly cap and flannel longjohns, old-fashioned bed socks and fingerless gloves, typing furiously with a cigarette dangling from his lips.

He looked ridiculous. And his concern over his ridiculous appearance registered a definitive zero. Any other man would have, at least, wet-combed the hair out and relaid it every morning, or possibly found a suitable heating device that reduced the number of nights spent wearing such a costume. But James seemed not to care at all. Lea, who was very much aware of physical appearance and who was a beauty herself, felt this trait of James's was selfish.

'It's *me* who has to look at *you*!' she'd say, disgusted.

'But I'm not asking anyone to look at me. See these thermal leggings? These suede indian-like moccasins, this doghair jumper? All of these items have a message for you and everyone else in the world and that message is *Avert Your Eyes*.'

'But I can't, my eyes are drawn to atrocities. Whenever I see a clump in the road I look to see if it's an animal carcass. It's a defect in my personality I can't help.'

'I'm the same,' I said. 'The other day I saw a dead squirrel.'

'*Eeew*,' Lea said. 'But you had to look, right?'

'Had to,' I verified.

'See how it is, James? See why you have to have consideration for others?'

'But I'm not a squirrel carcass.'

'Okay, okay,' Lea said. 'Another example. Think if someone painted their house neon orange, they don't have to suffer because they are *inside* the house, but think of what it would be like to live opposite. You get me?'

'But these clothes are the colour of porridge, they don't exactly draw the eye.'

'James, I sleep next to you.'

He reached over and covered my ears with his gloved hands. He said, 'Not in front of the child.'

'But she knows! Everyone knows. The fact that there is a Mrs in front of my name declares to the world, to perfect strangers, that I sleep with a man who looks like a woollen mummy with hedge hair!'

I laughed at that, and again at James's expression when he turned to me, making a pretence of being hurt by such an assault on his appearance. The truth is that I felt strangely comforted by James's lack of vanity. The more slovenly he became and the more uncaring he was of what others – even his wife – might think about it, the better I felt. In the space of a few short months I'd seemed to grow several feet, and my hair had thickened so that it stood away from my shoulders in a heavy, lampshade fashion. I'd been drinking too much coffee (in an effort to stave off my appetite, which had grown along with my hair and bones) and my skin had gone livery. I suppose I was undergoing a normal adolescent shift, but to me it was a huge problem. Everywhere I went I saw girls my age in tiny skirts and long, smooth unblemished legs. They had slim ankles and tiny bird-boned hands, big eyes and neat, shining hair that did as it was told. By comparison I was a hulking dinosaur, a large-boned heavy-shouldered creature with fleshy kneecaps and a boxy shape, and no style at all. Every morning I went out into this new, foreign, English world to be ridiculed by the teenage natives who, despite diets of cheese sandwiches and sausages, seemed to maintain figures of model-like proportions. The girls looked at me sideways and indicated to their friends that there was something slightly askew, slightly embarrassing in my very presence. The boys called at me – they were horrible – and my sleep was plagued with images of them shouting at me on the street. Even in my dreams I could not bring myself to say much back.

But Lea and James made me feel better. If I could be their friend then there was something special about me after all. And when Lea colluded with me over James's appearance, when she included me in on the joke, I felt released from my burden of ugliness. This, to a teenager such as myself, was perhaps the greatest gift imaginable.

'You are so terribly nice to look after our paintings when you could be out on the town with your friends,' James would say to me on Saturday nights when I 'babysat' the paintings. His implication, that I did have friends, that I would have somewhere to go, made me feel a sense of relief, of potential, of belonging. He and Lea came downstairs, all dressed up and looking wonderful, and thanked me for looking after the paintings while they were away, as though this mild chore which involved nothing more than me staying at home (where I would be anyway) were a great kindness, and it was the vision of them so ready for their night out that stayed with me all evening. In return they allowed me to accompany them every so often and it was on those occasions that I felt truly alive, as though my life had finally begun and was my own. Little things, like when James opened a door for me, or helped me into my coat, or when Lea made some funny comment into my ear and refused to share the joke with James, or when we all laughed together at some silly, unimportant thing. To have friends such as these, I often thought, was better than a hundred school friends, and I would not have traded places with anyone in the world.

6

Mother found work at an estate agency in the village. She came home, her cheeks full of roses from walking across the heath and I could tell she was in the house even before I heard her, just from the energy she brought. She stepped into the kitchen as though into a party, grabbed the neck of a wine bottle and tipped it into a tumbler, drinking the wine like it was lemonade.

'The shop on the corner next to the office supply store, the one with the green sign, not the one with the gothic lettering. That's a rental agency, this is residential sales,' she told Isobel and myself, who sat opposite each other doing our homework at the kitchen table. 'It's a small agency – Oops, there are no small agencies, only *independent* ones,' she laughed.

Isobel giggled along with her, then said, 'I don't get it.'

'Estate-agent humour,' I said.

'But I still don't get it.'

'Well done, dear,' said Rose, from her own seat. She was admiring Isobel's spelling report, which had come back all correct except where the word 'spectre' had been Americanized into 'specter'. Rose said it wasn't really a mistake as Isobel was half American and therefore had the right to spell spectre either way, and the score should have been one hundred per cent. Rose was always looking through our papers, where she invariably found something to admire. Isobel's handwriting or my biology drawings in which the alimentary canal of a worm or frog was infinitely detailed in coloured pencil. *How marvellous*, she would say about such a thing, *now I can see exactly the division between the oesophagus and the . . . er . . . bronchia. Isn't that splendid?*

'Isn't that splendid!' she was saying now about Mother's new job. 'I do admire you girls, how you can do just anything. It didn't used to be like that, I promise you. In my day we were either nurses or teachers, and very often neither.'

'Rebecca wants to be a nurse,' said Isobel.

'Doctor,' I said, singing the word, 'or perhaps medical researcher.'

'Were you a teacher?' she asked Rose.

'I taught French,' said Rose proudly.

Isobel made a face. 'I don't like French.'

'Just as well, because I can't remember any of it,' said Rose, and they laughed together.

Mother said, 'Stephen – the man who owns the agency – is so nice. When I brought in my CV he put it aside, not because he intended to ignore it, of course, it was clear he'd get to that later, but *first* he wanted to interview the person in front of him. And it wasn't like an interview at all. He just talked to me, I mean really talked. He wanted to know everything about what had brought us to America and how we'd decided to return to London, and how we were getting on. Not just how many properties did you shift in a month, but what kind of *person* I was.'

Rose nodded her head, listening. 'He sounds like a very nice man.'

'He's like that, you see, he wants to know personally every member of staff.'

'That's nice. That's the way it ought to be,' said Rose.

'It's not what would happen in America. In America they have no interest in the individual behind the CV. Everything is bottom line there with no humanity –' she took a big gulp of wine '– whatsoever.'

Mother was ambivalent about both America and England. When the weather was piss poor, or a bomb scare sent us marching out of Marks and Spencer just as we were next in line for the till, or the quiet judgemental nature of our suburban neighbours annoyed her so much she felt like shooting the moon through the window, she claimed England was a country full of incompetents, pendants and freaks. But when it behoved her to scorn America she did it with great skill. A violent country full of loud, uncouth, vain citizens obsessed with money and largesse. And fat, too. Families so fat they couldn't all go up in a lift at the same time.

'When do you start?' I asked.

'Next Monday. Stephen said he wanted me immediately, of course, but I told him I couldn't. Take a leaf from my book, Rebecca, always let a man wait. Besides, I had to tell him I owned a car, which means I have to come up with a car somehow within the next five days. And a wardrobe! I can't show houses in ten-year-old suits. Luckily there is a shop in town that sells designer clothes at discount prices. Otherwise, we'd be in the poorhouse.'

She described this particular 'designer' shop in which she'd had time to browse on her way back from the interview. I didn't hear anything she said on the matter. I was still reeling from what she had said about a car, which evidently she'd told this Stephen person she owned.

I looked at Mother. 'How exactly are you planning to buy a car?' I knew how much rent we received from our house in Orange County and I knew how much food cost each month. The two were virtually the same number. Mother was still paying off the debt from our school coats and her outlandish bed, whatever salary she was hoping to get from this estate agent would undoubtedly be commission-based, which meant that even if she sold a house right away she wouldn't see a sizeable chunk of cash for several months. Unless she was planning to make Rose take in laundry, I couldn't see how we were going to both buy a car and eat for the foreseeable future.

'I've just gotten a job, Rebecca,' Mother said, sternly. 'Can't you be happy for one minute for me? Must you always criticize? Really, one would think you were running this household!'

'I am just asking how it is we are going to pay for a car.'

'*We* are not going to pay for it. *I* am going to pay for it, and that is all I need to discuss with *you*!'

When she spoke like this there was no point in continuing, but I had a suspicion about how Mother planned to buy the car. Rose still had the money from the sale of half of Grandfather's house. It was held in a fund and tended to by a man named Simon Walters who wrote quarterly reports for his clients, giving figures on gross and yields and describing risk strategies and inflation adjustments. Rose had brought one such report to me and asked me to explain it to her, which I could not. I studied the document, gave up in the first five minutes, and tried to reassure her that the tone of the letter suggested a fair-sized profit. Since then, whenever any document came from Simon Walters' office, Rose opened it, flattened the creases and, without so much as pretending to read it, laid it in a pile of others so that a small, tidy stack grew in her bureau drawer. The principal was not enormous, but you could buy a car out of it. I reckoned Mother had Rose in mind when she promised this Stephen Price character that she had her own transport.

A few days later I came in the house and heard Rose and Mother talking in Rose's bedroom. I hardly needed to listen to the conversation to know what was transpiring. Mother had never before stepped into Rose's room except to dump Isobel's clothes on the bed, and I was sure the closed door – I'd never seen the door closed even once – meant Mother had a specific task in mind. She was using her optimistic, sing-song voice, but inflected at times with a serious, almost manly tone that spoke of monthly earnings and expenditures, quarterly taxes, and a schedule of payments, which I heard her say, 'will be my highest priority after feeding and clothing the children'. Rose's voice was quieter and I could not make out specific words, but I could tell Mother had convinced her to give her the money and that what remained was Rose's general confusion about how to extract her money from Simon Walters' fund and put it into Mother's bank account.

'I can do all that for you,' Mother assured her. 'And I'll work with Mr Walters to repay the loan as well. It's easier that way, a direct debit into your account so you don't have to go asking me for the money.'

Rose made a remark I could not hear, and then Mother said, 'I know you don't mind, but it matters to me.'

Everything went quiet and then Mother said, 'Thank you, Rose. This means so much to all of us.'

The door opened and Mother strode out of Rose's room. When she caught sight of me she stopped abruptly. 'What's the matter with you?' she asked.

Of course, she knew exactly what was the matter. 'Nothing,' I said.

'I cannot work without a car. No car, no job. This is only a loan.'

'I didn't say anything.'

'And she is *glad* to give it. Do you understand me?' She shot me a look. I can picture it in my mind perfectly, an expression of frozen anger, a wall of threat and defiance. Don't you dare, the look said. Don't you dare go any further. 'The old lady is grateful to help us after everything we've done to help her.'

'I'm sure she is,' I said, miserably.

'What would you have me do? Beg on the street? I need a car to do my job. You're old enough, you could do a few hours at a shop to help pay the rent around here.'

She turned, walking to her own bedroom, her heels clapping the ground in a manner that punctuated her importance.

'There is no rent around here,' I said. I could not believe my bravery, my idiocy in speaking like this. It was not like me to challenge my mother, but something about the way she'd called Rose *the old lady* made a well of raw anger churn in my chest. 'Rose owns the house,' I said.

This ignited a new fury in Mother. She'd given me the *do not go there* look and I had gone ahead anyway. She turned so fast it was like watching a swimmer ricochet off the side of a pool.

'And I own my house, but I had to give it up to look after her, didn't I?' She said, her voice a whisper. 'Didn't I?'

'Yes. Yes, you did.'

'So you can step right off the moral highground, missy. You think you're so good and kind, but I don't notice you bringing home any groceries.'

'I'll get a job,' I said.

She sniffed and turned again away from me. 'Yes, you do that,' she said, as though it were a laughable notion.

What was bothering me really was not the idea that Rose was giving money to Mother to buy a car. And I mean *giving*, Mother would never pay a dot on that loan. The galling aspect of the exchange was that Mother had planned the whole thing from start to finish. She'd sent off for the Rover brochure almost upon setting foot in London. I'd seen her pore over pictures of cars and circle the colours she preferred. Apparently, when Isobel and I were at school, she'd even visited a few dealerships. All of this happened long before the prospect of a job came up. She needed a car – I was sure of that – but she did not need a brand-new executive saloon with leather seats, a moon roof, and a seven-speaker sound system. She did not need to spend that much money, all at once, and then to act as though she was entitled to it. Such behaviour made me think of her as mean-minded and selfish, and I did not like to consider her so. Her indulgences were legion, but like most daughters I enjoyed seeing my mother do things for herself. When at night she sat stiffly at her vanity, dabbing with the third finger of her hand a face-firming cream that promised to condition her skin while she slept, I was glad that she held herself in enough esteem to spend the twenty-five pounds the cream cost. I had been with her one afternoon when she bought a bottle that looked like something I might use in chemistry class, with clear laboratory glass and a stopper top with an eyedropper inside. The saleslady told her this 'repairing liquid' would eliminate fine lines near her eyes. It was thirty-nine pounds and I was happy she bought it. Happier still when she got a pair of dress shoes and a winter hat with a feathery brim that made her look like one of the cover models for *Harpers and Queen*. But there is a big difference between that and buying a swanky new car, which she drove home one Saturday, parking in a bay outside the house so its shimmering enormity was immediately evident through all our windows.

'Anybody need a lift?' she'd cooed from the doorway.

We all dutifully assembled outside, Isobel and me in our forest-green school coats, Rose in her old Danimac parka and her pillbox hat, Mother in one of her new 'designer' outfits, which included an ankle-length leather coat that creaked when she walked. She'd taken on a whole new appearance since getting her job with Stephen Price, bright suits with fitted bodices pinched in at the waist, spiky heeled shoes and 'nude' hose which showed off her good legs. She'd dropped the false eyelashes but taken up nail varnish and bangles that glided up and down her arm every time she moved. Her earrings, a pair of which she bought to match perfectly each of her new outfits, were so chunky she had to unclip one to talk on the phone. And when she dialled, she had to use a pen.

'Becca, darling, did you colour your hair?' she asked me as I stood in attendance while she showed off her new car.

'No.'

'Because I love it. You are so lucky with your hair.'

The car awaited us on the street like an unopened present, the chrome shining, the paintwork waxed to perfection. Mother showed us the boot, which was carpeted and so clean and vast you felt you could curl up and sleep in it. When she closed it the sound was like a football being kicked directly in the sweet spot. The back seat was divided into three areas, each with a safety belt and headrest and when we sat inside the hide cushions sank down with a slow sigh.

'You sit in front,' Mother told Rose, patting the seat beside her. 'This is your place.'

Rose said she preferred the back but Mother insisted. She talked to Rose all the while she drove, showing her how easily the car stopped and how quickly it accelerated without even a sound from its enormous, purring engine. We drove across the heath towards the Hare and Billet, then down into the village, lit up in gold street lights already, at only four in the afternoon. The car was wonderful, and watching the winter sky through its spotless windows felt like driving through a movie. The village lights showed off its frosted paintwork, which was in a colour called verdigris. 'I love this car,' Mother said, gliding to a halt. She turned into the railway station and Rose sat bolt straight, holding the inside of the door as Mother wheeled the car in slow circles in the station car park. 'The turning radius is spectacular,' Mother said, quoting – I am sure – the salesman who sold it to her. Isobel asked questions about all the glowing dials across the dashboard and I sat quietly, trying not to appear to be pulling a face, which is what Mother would accuse me of unless I mustered up some enthusiasm in short order.

'I love that new car smell,' Mother said, breathing purposefully through her nose. 'Don't you, Rose? I suppose you know exactly what makes a new car smell like this, Rebecca. What is it, a special shampoo?'

I cleared my throat. 'It's a chemical in the, uh, fixative,' I said.

'What, like rubber cement? It doesn't smell like rubber cement.'

'Formaldehyde,' I said.

'Oh, right,' Mother said, and laughed nervously. 'Hey, Rose, what do you think of the glove compartment? Go ahead, open it right up. There's enough room in there to store your picnics on our days out! Enough room and more to spare! We will drive into the country the minute we see a sign of spring.'

'Oh, that would be nice,' said Rose.

'Bluebell woodlands, Sissinghurst. We're just a stone's throw from Kent, really, and it's all accessible once you have your own transport,' said Mother. Then, in a different voice, she added, 'Formaldehyde, really, Rebecca, I don't know where you dream these things up. There's nothing like that in this car.'

We drove down the hill through Greenwich Park along an

avenue of ancient oak trees, leafless now in winter, then around the one-way system and back up Lewisham Road towards home. The Rover came to a stop on the pavement outside our house, and I punched the red button on my seat belt and got out, careful not to slam the door and upset Mother. She was in one of her high moods, but these moods were always precariously balanced, easily tipping into anger. We arrived back just as Lea and James were coming up the road. When they saw all of us piling out of the car, they stopped. Lea was wearing a black cape with the hood drawn up around her face, woollen tights and Chelsea boots. Her legs were long and thin, with an acrobatic quality to them. I half expected her to come to a halt and execute a series of back flips right there on the pavement. She cocked her head to one side, in all likelihood trying to imagine how exactly we'd come upon such an extravagant car, as James came striding forward, saying, 'Is this *yours*, Helen? My God, what an excellent car. You just got it? Do you mind if I look inside?'

Mother went through the same general tour of the Rover she'd given us, injecting a smidgen of modesty. Rather than gloat over the smooth leather interior, she merely indicated that she'd chosen hide because it was easier to maintain. James couldn't stop himself, he was inside the car within minutes, sitting right behind the driver's wheel, examining the computer-based sound system.

'Darling, you would love this,' he said out the door to Lea, who had not moved.

'I'm sure I would,' she said, evenly.

James said, 'I can't remember the last time I was in a new car. Isn't that a great smell?'

'Rebecca says it's formaldehyde,' Mother said, and I felt myself blush all the way to my shoes. 'But I say it can't possibly be.'

'Who gives a damn, it's The Smell. The Smell we'd all pay for if we could have it. Lea, come sit in this thing.'

'I couldn't,' Lea said.

'Go on,' Mother insisted.

'Thank you, but I won't.'

'You must. It won't bite you,' James said.

'James, we're going to be late.'

'One more minute.' He closed the door and we all watched as he unabashedly fell trance-like into his daydream of driving Mother's new Rover. He put his palms on the steering wheel, looked up at the rear-view mirror, then cast a glance both right and left. He studied the dashboard, tapped the glass above the many dials, then peered straight through the windscreen where his attention fixed on some faraway place he occupied utterly for the duration of one minute, just as he'd promised his wife.

'Well,' he said, climbing out of the car, 'that's impressive.'

He and Lea walked back into the house, she was well ahead of him.

'Talk about icy,' said Mother. 'I mean *her*, of course. *He's* delightful.'

'They're married,' I reminded Mother. The tone of my voice took her aback.

'I know that. Good lord, Rebecca. I might look young, but I'm nowhere near that boy's age. Oh, I get it,' she said. She stretched up, tucked her chin to her chest, and smiled. She nodded her head slowly as though she'd just been let in on a secret.

It was too much for me to bear, her standing beside her new car, her varnished nails spanning her hips, looking down at me with that knowing expression. Besides that, she'd pronounced Lea icy without knowing, as I did, that Lea herself would love such a car – any car really – but James would not part with a single one of his mother's paintings so that they could buy a car, or at least so they could afford to take taxis, Lea's favourite luxury, when they went out.

I went to bed that night feeling as though my mother had turned against me, which is exactly what she probably would have said about me. That I'd turned against her in a fit of ingratitude and adolescent angst. I don't know how it was our relationship deteriorated quite, but there it was, a ragged scrap of what it had once been, when I nursed her through various broken hearts and moments of bruised spirit. I suppose she'd allowed me to look after her then because she imagined, hoped even, that one day she would be the wise, veteran woman who counselled me in my own hopeless pursuit of love. She once told me that when the midwife held me up to the light at Guy's Hospital, announcing that a daughter had been born, she had a momentary vision of her own, true best friend, her daughter. I was meant to be her one great confidante, the player always on her side. For a time it might have been like that, all children idolize their parents, but as I grew up, as I grew into myself, it was apparent that in no way would I be my mother's soulmate. We were as dissimilar as we could be, and it was not just that she wore plunge necklines while I went around in cable knit jumpers. The way our minds worked, the habits of our conversation, the very mechanics of our thinking, were unalike. I would say I was like my father, but this is not true either. One day around the time we acquired that beautiful, horrendous car, and Mother began her job – and her affair – with Stephen Price, she said something which was perhaps as sad and true a statement as can ever be told to a child. She said, 'Sometimes a family just gets one member who is from the outside, and we got you.'

She said it within earshot of Aunt Rose who shot up from her chair as though she'd sat on a pin. 'Helen, *really*,' she said, in what was the first and only time she took a tone with Mother.

'It doesn't bother me,' I lied.

'It does, dear. Of course it does. Helen, please tell the child you didn't mean it. Tell her!'

And here is where the thing goes from bad to much worse. I might have been able to forgive, if not forget entirely, a randomly cast-off comment from Mother. She was capable of the most silly, grand statements which bore little relation to what she felt inside. The way she swung wildly in her opinion about England, for example, calling it at times the last civilized nation and at others a country which was past its sell-by-date, was enough to keep me from taking too seriously any single remark she might make. But when Rose asked her to take that comment back, and Mother sat there, staring fixedly at me, unable or unwilling to utter a syllable, I was stunned and humiliated. The silence went on forever and finally, because I truly could stand it no longer, I got up and left the room.

I walked out into the hall and I heard Lea's violin. She was playing the slow movement of Mozart's Sinfonia Concertante and the sound held a melancholy air of such precise beauty that it swept me up into it.

In part, it swept me up. But another reason I stood at the bottom of the staircase, pausing in my flight from my mother, was that I'd left my shoes behind. Though I might have liked to storm out into the night like Lea, she was always followed by James who brought her a coat. I hadn't anyone to come stumbling after me with my shoes. So I stood at the bottom of the staircase, listening with great admiration as Lea wrung note after note of a particularly beautiful piece of Mozart. For one moment the leaning voice of my mother, the sound of her contempt, of what had become her dull, sorrowful love, lifted and fled like some spirit that had been exorcized through the very beauty, the clarity, of Lea's playing. I went up the stairs, picking my way delicately over the uneven floorboards, watching from the corner of my eye as the hallway disappeared beneath me and the white ceiling of the first floor came into view. I passed the painting of the soldier boy – what I knew to be the soldier boy, because of course it was covered by a wine-coloured rag – and turned to face the wide upper hall that I remembered all at once from those many years ago when I'd come with Mother and Isobel and stayed in the first two rooms, the doors of which I could see now. I don't know how I mustered up the courage to ascend those stairs, but of course I hadn't thought about it. I needed a place to escape my mother and that is why I found myself standing outside the sitting room, listening to Lea's violin.

The door was half open and I could see her by the window, curled over the instrument, her fingers arched above the fingerboard, her lips turned down to meet her chin, which was slightly squashed against the chin rest. One leg was positioned ahead of the other and she moved into the extended leg, her hips reaching upwards, following the violin, which seemed like a living thing, moving in her hands. There was a chrome music stand set to catch the light from the window and however she moved with the violin her gaze was fixed on the page on that stand. She played and I watched her playing, then all at once her fingering caught upon a tricky run of notes and she hesitated, tried again, then stopped so abruptly it made me jump.

'God damn it!' she said.

She stamped her foot, then wiped her mouth on her sleeve, pushed her hair out of her eyes and started again. It always made me laugh to hear her swear. You could tell she was a girl who grew up in a family whose language was clean, because swearing was not second nature to her. She had to think about it, and she often got things ever so slightly wrong. 'Oh, titties,' she said, making another error.

She tried once more and this time she got the fingering right and she continued the concertante with what, to my very untrained ear, sounded like perfection itself. Then she propped her violin against the music stand, and turned to look at me. I could tell from her eyes she'd known all along I was standing there.

'What's wrong, darling?' she said, surprising me.

'Nothing. I heard you playing.'

'It's your mother, isn't it? I don't know why she's so horrible to you.'

'Is she mean to me?'

'Of course she is,' she said in a perfunctory manner, as though this were obvious. 'Don't tell me you haven't noticed.'

'I have. I mean, I think she is sometimes, you know, quite unkind. But then, aren't all mothers occasionally like that?'

'I'm sure they are. Anyway, you mustn't worry about it. Come with me to James's do. It's his publication day – whoopee, ding-dong – we're celebrating.' She marched from the window and moved past me, wheeling me by the elbow so that I had to follow her. She went directly into James's and her bedroom, which was the room Mother had occupied during our brief stay years ago. The wallpaper was the same, peacocks and some other obscure crested bird, but the brass bed was gone, replaced by a slipper bed, smaller than I thought was right for a couple, and almost totally hidden by clothes. There were clothes everywhere, in stacks at the corners of the room, layered atop the chest of drawers, stuffed in the tiny, 1930s wardrobe which was not deep enough to hold James's jackets so that the shoulders pushed through the door, which could not shut properly as a result.

Lea was, if anything, unselfconscious, and brought me directly into the most private quarters of her house without a thought. There was a black negligee on the floor, within approximate throwing distance from the bed, and a packet of condoms which had been left on the nightstand, a quarter bottle of red wine and a dozen spent candles. None of which I failed to notice and all of which embarrassed me utterly as I gaped and dragged my eyes away, trying to appear nonchalant and sophisticated in the presence of the one woman in the world who I'd gnaw off my own wrist to be friends with.

Lea unhooked the back of her dress and let it drop to the floor in a puddle from which she stepped, flicking the garment up with her big toe and catching it with her hand as it rocketed skywards.

'Put on this. I'm wearing red tonight; a dress James likes me in. It's just . . .' She faltered, snapping her fingers in the air as she finally conjured up the words. '. . . I can't find the thing.'

I looked at Lea who stood naked except for her underpants in front of me. She had tiny breasts with large nipples like the faces of two clocks across her chest. I was a 36D and wore an underwire so I didn't wobble. She had a wasp waist and a bottom that scooted under her, hardly noticeable, while I squeezed into jeans feeling like there was a good bit behind me that needed securing.

I could not reject her dress. The offering had a special meaning,

I knew that. But I could not imagine how anything that fit the lithe, sinewy shape before me could possibly cover more than half of one of my own fleshy thighs. Nonetheless, I tried.

I unbuttoned the waistband of my skirt and let it slide to the floor as Lea had done. My blouse had a million tiny buttons, every one of which I cursed as I pushed them through their holes. When finally the blouse was done there was my elaborate M&S bra with its crossplate of elasticated support bands and the humiliating vest, which I realized all at once was an absurd garment for anybody over the age of ten.

When Lea handed me the dress she acted as though she hadn't noticed the size of me, nor the vest, nor anything else apart from the need to drape me in her stylish clothes. But deep inside my stomach a panic had set in about what would happen – *what on earth* – to the demure shape of Lea's lovely dress when I attempted to put it on. Would it clasp me around my hips demarcating every fold of fat from pubic bone to bottom cheek? Would it flatten my breasts so that they looked like two cushions swaddled in velvet? Would the seams split apart entirely?

I took the dress over my head and felt – this seems silly now – as Joan of Arc must have felt walking to the stake. I'd had my moment of heroism, but now things were decidedly not going my way and it would take a miracle – and I mean by this a definitive act of God – to save me. Once I was found to look ridiculous in the dress, my stint as Lea's friend would end, just as abruptly as the Mozart piece had ended, without so much as an echo. Indeed there was the question as to whether I could even get into the dress, and I had in my mind the horrid vision of me standing, arms above my head, with my face, neck and shoulders covered in dark velvet, while the rest of me remained bare and exposed, too fat to push through the dress bodice. This vision, of me being literally *stuck* in Lea's dress and unable to move, caused me a moment of profound panic at the idea of Lea herself having to come to my aid and with her thin, capable fingers peel away the fabric. My only thought was that if such a thing occurred, I would, once finally I managed to get my head back out of the neckhole, run naked out of the room, down to the maisonette and into the bathroom, where I would drown myself.

In fact, none of this happened. I should have known that Lea would have already assessed my shape and height, my relative girth and meaty bottom, and figured that the dress would fit, if only just. I slipped it on, watching how the dress now popped out in new places, in the chest area where the neckline pulled away from my body, showing a line of cleavage as long as my thumb, at the hips where the velvet, elasticated fabric stretched to accommodate its unusual load. It was a three-quarter-length cocktail dress, with a cut so flattering you could not detect the extent of my thighs, and when I put it on Lea gasped with delight.

'You are *fetching*,' she said, emphasizing the point with an open-mouthed 'Ha!'

'It's a fabulous dress,' I said.

'You'll need shoes.' She grabbed at a pair that appeared as though by magic from beneath the bed. 'Let's go. James is terrified so we mustn't be late.'

I had never before been to an adult party except during the Christmas season back in California, when our neighbours would invite everyone on the street for eggnog and canapes, Christmas cookies and mulled wine. Those brief affairs were marked primarily by Mother's astounding gaiety the minute she walked through the door, no matter how black her mood had been minutes previously. She'd trudge out our front door and across the lawn, tugging Isobel by the hand, her face frozen in expression, her eyes dead angry at some minor behavioural infringement on our part – a broken vase, tipped during a forbidden indoor ball game, too much noise while she was trying to watch her evening soap, the house a mess, paint from Isobel's watercolours on the carpet. But the minute she set foot on the paving stones leading to the house where the party was to be held, her step quickened, her face shed its glowering expression, she even began smiling a bit as though in practice for all the smiling that was about to take place. She punched the doorbell and said softly, 'Now, let's all try and have a nice time,' as though it had been Isobel and myself who'd been walking with the hostile expression of a prison matron all the way down the road.

'Oh, hello!' she'd call when the hostess answered the door. She'd tilt her head in at a particular angle and smile, her hands raised wide for an embrace. She was not a shy woman, and did not have an ounce of what is called 'English reserve'. I stood by her side like a stuffed dog, half proud of her amazing dexterity in the area of chit-chat and her ability to 'work a room' as she put it, and half cringing at the elaborate construction she put on even the most basic social exchange. 'How *are* you? I'm *so* glad! It is *lovely* to see you!' she'd say when the other person had only said, 'Fine, thank you.'

Being with Mother at a party had the advantage that one never had to actually initiate a single conversation oneself. She was the icebreaker, she was the angler for topics that interested the small groups, that huddle together clutching their drinks. I'd never had to make conversation myself and I had never, ever, been to a party held anywhere public, like in a bookshop which was where James's launch was held, just off Tottenham Court Road.

A book launch is the inaptly named party that a publisher sometimes hosts for an author when his book finally – after months and months of revision and copy-editing, galley corrections and empty waiting – is released with a startling anticlimax to the general public. The party is meant to attract media attention, as well as alert booksellers to the fact that this long awaited for addition to the published works of so-and-so is now available. When they go well the author sometimes receives an invitation to do a signing or reading, which makes the publicist jump up and down with excitement, and initiate a discussion about an author 'tour', which is an exercise in humbling all but the few celebrity authors whose names are household words. In the best of all worlds, the launch gives a reassuring feeling to the publisher and a warm, fuzzy feeling to the author, a few notices are printed in papers that would otherwise have ignored altogether this microscopic moment in book publishing that is, for the author, a huge and momentous occasion. When the launch goes badly, few people other than the assembled crew from the publishing house show up and the author, completely mortified by the lack of interest in him, his book, or even the free food and drinks the publisher supplies, goes home in a state of despair. He knows, with a certain amount of accuracy, just how little impact his contribution to contemporary literature will make on the book trade, let alone any member of the public who may never see the book at all except if he is searching for a different title altogether in the stacks of books arranged alphabetically in the far reaches of the shop floor.

We took the tube from Charing Cross and emerged into the icy night with its usual London halo of orange. My brief explanation to my mother as to where I was going did not include mention of a trip into the city; I'd only called from the door that I was going out. But once we were on Tottenham Court Road, ploughing through the crowds in our thin dresses with our coats open (me in my school coat, Lea in a leather Mac) and our bags flapping against us, I felt a new lightness. I felt as though I'd been waiting for a night like this all of my life, ever since childhood folded up behind me and the long stretch to adult life loomed ahead. I followed Lea, who darted and skipped, and generally raced to the bookshop, which I did not see until we were practically on the doorstep, being ushered inside by a man in a duck-down coat who held open the door.

'Oh, good, it's packed,' Lea said.

She was right, judging from the number of bodies inside the shop James could count himself among the lucky authors whose launches are a success. It helped that the shop was small to begin with and that the many tables and display racks of novels, travel guides, Penguin Classics and bestseller dumpbins meant available floorspace was at a premium. There was a sense of this being a party in transition, the champagne came in plastic glasses and not a single guest removed his overcoat. Some even held on to their satchels or maintained throughout the evening a copy of the *Guardian* pinched between elbow and rib, but the faces were enthusiastic and young, remarkably young. The men wore rimless spectacles and cotton shirts with grandfather collars, Doc Martens and faded jeans. The women were either in tight jeans and boots with heels or dresses of the sort that Lea – and for tonight, myself – might wear. I don't suspect anybody was as young as seventeen, or showed up in their school coat as I did, but it was nothing like the Christmas parties I'd been to with Mother. Nobody wore a corsage, for instance. And the ambience had not been attended to. There'd been no concern over the right lighting, the perfect not-too-intrusive music, the strategic placement of chairs and sofas. The launch was a crowd of people beneath fluorescent strip lights, talking at each other over their flimsy, plastic drink glasses, their skin flushed with the heat of standing so close together in winter gear.

There was a cloud of cigarette smoke thick as butter, no place to sit or even lean, the windows had long since steamed up and were now dripping with the moisture of so many exhaling humans in a building that originated long before ventilation systems had been dreamt of. Someone figured out to open a few of those windows, and then the door was propped open with a box of hardbacks. It was a great relief to breathe in air from the street, because the cigarette smoke was making me feel lightheaded and I'd begun to find it difficult to focus with clarity on the guy I was talking with – he seemed terribly sophisticated to me, but he was probably twenty-three – whose curly head bobbed in front of me as he described something about the college he'd been to or perhaps it was the surroundings of the college, a plain or moor or vale that was quite famous. He mumbled and spoke into his drink, while I smiled and nodded and tried, without making it appear I was doing so, to catch sight of Lea or James. 'Phenomenal aftertaste, almost like sulphur,' he said, another mystery sentence that I could pin to no specific topic, then he pointed over my shoulder and disappeared abruptly, I had no idea where.

I finally caught sight of James, who was wearing a tweed jacket and jeans and standing about ten yards and dozens of people away from me. I called his name but my voice sunk into the din of the party. He might as well have been on the other side of the country, there was no getting near him. I did not know that it was unusual – if not impossible – for a writer's first novel to get the kind of attention that James's was apparently revelling in, so I did not question why so many people were there. Only later did I discover that Lea had convinced her entire orchestra, and two other orchestras with which she had some small connection to appear that night in honour of James's book. If I'd been able to hear any of the conversations around me I might have noticed that the topics did not so much focus on who was doing what paperback, the impact of a Booker nomination on a particular title's sales, or when a much-hyped anthology was due to be published, but on that latest, best, or most collectible rendition of Mahler's Fifth.

I was surrounded by musicians but could not have taken in this information, anymore than I could understand what the hell my young man with the curls was talking about. He returned – apparently he'd only ventured away to bring me a drink, which I downed in short order out of a combination of thirst and nervousness – and sent him packing off through the crowd to get another. When he returned for the third time I knew his name – Geoff – but with the infusion of alcohol and the continuing noise of the party, I still could not follow his conversation. 'Absolutely top rate but you must get there early,' he said, about what I could not guess. It did not matter. I was standing among adults at a party talking to a man – that was all that mattered. Finally the guests thinned, Lea appeared and hooked her elbow through mine, telling Geoff she needed to borrow me for a moment, and I nearly floated beside her on a tide of euphoria.

'His name is Geoff,' I giggled.

'I know, I know, second desk clarinet. Mumbles and stutters a little but v-v-v-very nice. He'll call you every day until you agree to see him.'

'Oh, I doubt it,' I said, not because I was being modest, but because he'd failed to ask for my phone number.

She led me over to James who was standing before a table with a small stack of his books on it. His novel was called *The Card Thief* and was about a man who teaches a group of attractive women how to cheat at cards, win lots of money and leave their boring lives as housewives behind to join his band of grifters. I can't imagine what made him write such a novel, except that he was given to magic tricks and sleights of hand. He likes to gamble and has a mathematical mind that can remember sequences of numbers with an ease that makes ordinary people feel uncomfortably dumb. The novel was illustrated with a playing card torn in five pieces and pushed back together puzzle-like. His name was printed in blocked, small lettering across the bottom and a photo graced the inside flap.

'It's so exciting,' I said to him.

'Tonight's his night,' said the woman beside him, his publisher, an efficient, attractive, chain-smoking blonde in a lemon-coloured suit with great moons of purple beneath her eyes. She was so exhausted she might have teetered off her heels and fallen headfirst on to the table of food, now just plates of crumbs, except that her determined will and a steely professionalism forced her to stand erect and smile. Her name was Sarah Nieson and she read a manuscript a night after working all day, had two children and a complicated system of child care, involving nannies, neighbours, nurseries and, only occasionally, herself. She was very good at her job and the fact that the book had been her acquisition, that it was *her* book, had itself added thirty-odd guests to the party.

'Can I go yet?' James asked.

'In a minute. You've got to sign all these first,' she said, producing a pen out of the air.

'Nice crowd,' I said.

'It's his night,' Sarah repeated.

Eventually we ended up at a café on St Martin's Lane. Lea, James, myself and Sarah, who sat perfectly straight with her Coach bag across her lap, a leather case of loose papers beside her chair, and two packs of Rothman's red on the table by her fork. She smoked and took a couple of aspirin from her purse, checked her watch a few times, and then affected a half grin that helped to keep her eyes open.

'Go home,' James said, 'before you collapse.'

'Me? Oh, I wouldn't dream of it. No, no. I'm thrilled to be here. Don't be silly. Waiter, can I have a bottle of fizzy water, please? I'll be fine. It's just my head, but nothing a couple of paracetamols won't take care of.'

'You have a headache,' James said. 'For god sakes, Sarah, I'll get you a taxi.'

'No chance. I'm fine. Look, here's the waiter with my water.' She cupped the pills in her palm, then frowned at them. 'On second thought, it might be wiser to go straight for the ibuprofen,' she said and dumped the contents of her hand into the ashtray. She plopped her purse on to the white tablecloth in front of us and fished around in it until she came up with a blister pack of slim, white capsules.

'Sarah,' James began.

'I'll be fine!' she sang. We tried not to watch as she downed the pills, which were cumbersome and not easily swallowed.

The waiter came to take our order, but the champagne had made me woozy, and my stomach felt bloated. I asked for coffee, explaining that I'd eaten before the party, which was not true. James ordered a bottle of red wine and poured out three glasses, one for himself, Lea, and one for Sarah, who sipped at the wine for a few minutes and then fell asleep with her head on her handbag. He and Lea drank the rest while waiting for their pasta, then ordered another bottle. I stirred my spoon around my coffee and watched these two people, who I adored, who I'd have done anything for – swallowed fire, tap-danced on the table, tattooed Noddy across my buttocks. Tonight I'd worn a dress I loved, I'd been to a party, I'd talked to a man. I was sitting at a table in an Italian restaurant in London with the two most fascinating people I'd ever met, and one who had been interesting before she'd fallen asleep. For the first time ever I got a sense of what it must be like to be one of the in-crowd, of the trendy, popular, talented few. To be special and wanted and exquisitely, vividly alive. I was aware of the passing of time, not because I gave a damn what my fate would be when I came home, but because it meant that at some point the evening would end.

'Is señora all right?' the waiter asked cautiously, standing behind Sarah who was emitting small wheezing sounds. She slept with one hand demurely in her lap, the other resting across her cigarettes. James had taken a dinner napkin and draped it over her shoulders. I suspected she might kill him for it when she woke.

'Fine,' James answered, 'a little tired.'

At one point the subject of Mother came up. Lea said, 'Jealous of you. That's my diagnosis. *My* mother would never be jealous of me because she has always been much better at everything than I am. Oboe player, Mother. Horrible reeded instrument you have to soak in your mouth. True, don't laugh. She used to go around with this bit of reed stuffed in her cheek like a wad of tobacco. Muscles everywhere on her face – embouchure, you know, is everything to an oboist. But the simple truth is that little is written for the oboe, so Father's viola was all we ever heard in concert. She was jealous of that. Hah! She sure was. But not of me. She put the violin in my hand, sucked that puny reed, and conjured out of nowhere a duet. "We'll play this together when you've practised," she said. I was, hmmmm,' she thought for a moment, laid her hand on her cheek, 'three.'

'Start 'em young,' said James.

'But no pressure. Just play. Play like you play with dolls. Play like you pretend to be Peter Pan. Play and let the music come. Father was all books and counting measures and training the ear and memorizing. Father was a—'

'Great big bore,' James said loudly, then finished off a glass of wine.

'No, James. Unfair, not once have you had a normal conversation with Father, who is not a bore at all but a worldly man with a very large—'

'Gut,' announced James, then kissed Lea's bare arm.

'I was going to say *heart*. You are drunk, James. Stop nipping at me like that. It's gruesome.'

She swatted him with her palm, then blushed rose, which made her so beautiful I felt like a pig next to her. I loved how thin she was, with her long waist, her intricately muscled forearms, her articulated spine. She had that unusual, clipped manner of speech, with peculiar truncated sentences that always made me laugh even when she was being serious.

'It could have been worse. It could have been bassoon. Absolutely nothing is written for the bassoon. My brother is totally unmusical. "Bassoon," Father concluded after hearing Charles's desperate attempt at piano. "It will be safer."'

'How old was Charles then?' asked James, who clearly thought he knew the answer.

'Oh, I don't know,' Lea said, and chewed thoughtfully at her linguini. 'Six.'

'Six years old and his father declares him hopeless.'

'Not hopeless, just not terribly gifted. One can tell by then.'

'At six years old!'

'You're forgetting, darling, that Charles did learn the piano. Not very well, of course. Father didn't force the bassoon on him, though the bassoon became a kind of family joke.'

'Ha, ha,' James said flatly. 'I don't get it.'

'Well, you wouldn't,' Lea said, in a mock-scolding manner. She turned to me, 'Do you play . . . anything?'

I had a sudden, desperate feeling of remorse that I'd never once taken up music. When the school band back in California had marched across the playing fields with their trumpeting, shiny brass instruments I'd not only been unimpressed, I'd averted my eyes as though at the spectacle of sudden nudity.

Their cumbersome horns and drums, their absurd uniforms which included headdresses and epaulettes and narrow trousers with ribbons down the outside of the leg, their slow, booming procession from one goalpost to the other, then down an edge of the field and back into the school, a total of ten minutes in front of an audience who considered them a time-filler, embarrassed me almost as much as football itself did. I'd only attended the games because Mother made me babysit Isobel on Saturday mornings so she could rest, and it was easier to take her to the ball game than keep her amused at home.

Now, of course, I not only wished I'd had more regard for the pathetic junior-high band, I wished I'd been part of it. To say I could play an instrument, any at all, even the bassoon – an instrument I could barely picture in my mind – might elevate me in Lea's eyes, which was my certain and only ambition at that time.

'I'm afraid not,' I said, lamely.

'Rebecca is going to be a doctor,' James said. I don't know how he knew that I wanted to go into medicine, but the way he said it – not that I wanted to be a doctor but that I was going to be one – lit a beam of pride inside my chest, which, of course, I tried not to show.

'Oh, good,' said Lea. And then, in a voice that penetrated the carefree, festive air that had been with us the entire evening, she said heavily, 'Being a musician is hell.'

James did not speak, but he looked at her cautiously and said, in a light manner. 'Come on, Lea.'

'No, it is!' she said, and her small hand made a fist in front of her. 'You move around from place to place like a bunch of dumb cattle. Years and years of hope and striving and practice. How many hours have I sat by myself in a room and played to the walls? And then you realize, too late to do anything else with your life, that you spend every waking moment with a bunch of misfits and the whole thing is remarkably boring.'

She was the first violinist with a well-regarded London orchestra. She had every reason to be happy with herself, but she was miserable. The sudden collapse from cheerfulness to this black well of anger and frustration was not the first, not unusual, and not anything that she could easily shake off.

'I'm sorry,' she said. 'I'll stop now.'

She brightened her face with an attempted smile, but her eyes stayed heavy and preoccupied. The evening rounded off, quickly and without a great deal more laughter, except when Sarah woke up and said, in a clear voice that was convincingly alert, 'Wonderful evening!' as though she hadn't missed a thing. We filed out of the restaurant, Lea at the front, Sarah wobbling on her spindly heels, with a mark across her face from the buckle of the handbag she'd used as a pillow. James followed behind with one hand thrust deep in his pocket, the other holding his wine glass, which he parked beside the reservations desk on his way out.

We arrived home near midnight and I did my best to sneak noiselessly into our family's side of the house while James and Lea stumbled up the staircase, half drunk and laughing over James's imitation of Lea's father, who, if we are to believe James, spoke with a gruff, pompous accent and moved with a leaning, slow marching step that his great stomach required for its transport. I smiled and whispered goodnight. I did not want to wake Mother and so I waited until they were at the top of the stairs before opening our door. I was still wearing Lea's dress and had no idea what Mother's reaction to such a frock might be. She was forever haranguing me about my appearance: that I did not show myself off at all; that I had no 'beauty routine', by which she meant I did not engage in the three-step process she underwent twice daily to cleanse, tone and moisturize the skin; that I showed no apparent interest in boys. This, more than anything else, galled her. She'd never been out of a love affair for more than a few months at a time and if she were to find herself without a boyfriend for any period at all, she cried, 'And me here, living like a nun!' and swept dramatically into her bedroom where she rummaged through her wardrobe in search of an article of clothing so dramatic and deeply sexy that a nun would consider it outlandish if not downright sinful.

'You know, Rebecca,' she'd said when I turned seventeen, 'by the time I was your age I was practically engaged.'

'I think I knew that, Mother.'

'And not to your father, either. He came later.'

'Yes, well.'

'You aren't unattractive, you know. You have wonderful hair. I know women who'd pay a great deal for hair like yours.'

In early childhood my hair had been a terrible carroty colour, but over the years it had softened to a gentle chestnut. It was long and crinkled into uneven curls, which I found unruly and forever in the way, so I usually wound it into a single plait down my back.

'Let me undo it,' she said, reaching for the elastic which held the plait together at the end. 'We'll roll it and get a little spray—'

'Mother, please!'

'I only thought to roll the ends, so it has a shape, that's all.'

'It's fine like it is.'

'Some softness around your face. You need a change—'

Now, as I turned the door knob, searching with stockinged feet for the floorboards that were still sturdy and would not creak, holding my hand up to the dark wall of the corridor and guiding myself blindly down the stretch of hallway that lead to the kitchen, I was aware that I embodied finally all the aspirations Mother had pinned on me. A flattering dress that smelled of a mixture of wine and cigarettes and Lea's perfume, hair that had been combed out and spanned my back in loose spirals, lipstick I'd borrowed from Lea when she uncovered a tube from her bag. I did not look like myself at all but like a much younger version of the woman I would become. And exactly, I imagine, as Mother wanted me to be. But for some reason, I had the profound desire for her not to see me, not to assess my newly developed figure in Lea's dress, not to calculate the way in which the bones in my face would one day be delineated as the baby fat melted from my cheeks and chin. I crept silently, deftly avoiding Isobel's book bag, a basket of folded laundry, an umbrella that had been left open to dry, the assembly of wellies and shoes that lined that end of the house, until finally I reached the kitchen where a table lamp had been left on for me. I unzipped my dress and let it drop all at once, just as I'd seen Lea do at the start of the evening, then tried to hook it with my toe and bring it up into my hand. My effort managed only to kick it along so it slid half under my bed, so I fished it out and tried again, and about the third time I managed the feat Lea had performed effortlessly, spontaneously, in the dance-like fashion that marked most of her movements.

The house's thin windows let in the cold. The doors, raised too far up from the kitchen's stone floor, allowed for a sweeping draft, so that even in bed I shivered and found it difficult to sleep. Besides, my head was swimming, my ears popped and invented a buzzing sound that I knew did not exist in the enormous, silent house. Finally, when I was just about asleep, I heard the door open and knew – without looking – that Mother was standing at the foot of my bed, just beside the Welsh cupboard that held our dinner plates and cutlery, making sure that finally I was in bed.

'Rebecca, are you asleep?' she asked, softly. I pretended that I was. I did not want to answer any questions, to discuss the long, magical evening, or indeed to sully its perfection with a conversation with my mother. I kept my eyes closed, my face buried in the pillow, and was careful not to move a fraction for the time Mother stood watching me, which was a good five minutes.

When finally she turned to go, closing the door behind her, I let out a long breath and felt a mixture of guilt and relief. Now, however, I found myself suddenly very awake, keyed up from all that feigning sleep. It occurred to me that Mother might have known I was pretending and that is why she stood for so long, to see if I would give up the pretence and greet her civilly. That I did not was as clear a message as I could have given – I might as well have sat up in bed and told her to leave me alone.

When I think about the years our family lived on Dartmouth Row, I remember a most odd torment, self-inflicted and almost maniacal in its containment, in which I held my secrets close to me and watched as Mother despaired over lost opportunities, lost loves, a lost daughter, me, who she looked upon with fascinated contempt. I am sure she loved me, but I disappointed her in a thousand ways. That I was so studious made her feel uneducated. That I loved to read made her think I considered myself above her. This is what she often said, 'You think you're above us all, don't you, Rebecca? Above *everything*.' She would be wrong to imagine that I thought her stupid or myself in any way 'above' her. For she was among the most craftily imaginative women I've ever known.

That night, after she'd seemed to give up and leave the room, I had the thought that she might be standing on the other side of the door listening for a sign that I was awake. I don't know if this is the case or not, but it would be like her. She was determined and fearless and not in the least bit concerned about embarrassing herself – and anyone else along with her – in whatever pursuit grabbed her heart. This, to a teenage girl, is a disarming combination in a parent. Ironically, because she is a more gentle woman than my reflections allow for, I was afraid of her.

7

Sometimes Lea sat with me in her music room and told me her dreams. Of a black poodle dog that had somehow come to be hers, of an aeroplane she's in and has no idea where it is taking her, of a romantic walk along the Thames with a man, not James. Who was it, then, I wanted desperately to know? Just a face I cannot recognize, says Lea. But much different than James, taller and more thickly set, but she cannot remember because the dream seems dimly lit, everything takes place in a filmy dusk and all she can remember is the man's sleeves are rolled up, and his forearms are both powerful and soothing. You mustn't tell James, I say, open-mouthed, my spine tingling. I know nothing of the way men and women operate, of what passes between husbands and wives. In my mind I envision a dramatic, violent fight between them at the prospect of this phantom lover. Threats and attacks of the most gruesome and unforgivable nature. But all she can do when I voice my concerns is laugh, holding her shoulders as she falls back against the chair. He wouldn't give a *damn*, she assures me, he'd think it was *funny*.

Mostly, Lea dreams of music. At night, when her busy, endlessly mobile body finally relinquishes itself to sleep, her mind comes alert, conjuring music, inventing music. In her dreams she can compose the most exquisite pieces. To compose music is her greatest ambition and the one which escapes her utterly. She declares herself empty of creativity, and a master solely of the art of interpretation and, more successfully, memorization. She can predictably deliver the same performance, and by this she does not only mean note for note – of course that – but also the exact same mood and emphasis, which makes her a useful orchestral player. Useful is her word, and when she says it, the word is spoken in a dreadful manner that makes it seem the opposite of what it means.

'I would love to compose music,' she tells me one afternoon, 'but when I wake the glorious orchestral song that sounded in my mind, which in my dream I actually transcribed into notation across some mental sheet of paper, escapes me. It is absorbed into the air like perfume. I remember fragments, moods, the occasional sequence of notes, but the heart of the piece is gone. When I try to write music, what comes out is paltry and derivative, embarrassing and perhaps even corrupting to my technique. I am ashamed of this. I feel like a fraud, like a talentless recorder of sounds.'

I tell her this cannot be true. Talentless, is she joking?

'Okay, not talented *enough*.'

We are sitting in the music room, the very place from which I have heard the most beautiful lyrical songs of a type that I never before knew existed, played by Lea's hand. Surely, that counts for something, I tell her.

'They are beautiful pieces and I deliver them to you as such. But they are not mine,' she emphasizes. 'Nothing I play is mine.'

It is February and the days are so short they curl up into evening by four o'clock. As we sit by the window we watch as a normal winter afternoon sky goes purple, before descending into the darkest blue imaginable, and it seems this happens in a matter of minutes.

'My father composed,' Lea tells me. She describes her father for me, not as the pompous toady man James makes him out as but as a bewitching sorcerer of enviable musicality. She says: 'I was his scribe. He played the music and I wrote it down note for note in number two pencil on the composition sheets we kept inside the piano stool. I thought if I wrote it down as it was played, if I ticked off the notes that I knew by heart, I might learn to write myself. For years I did this. I believed that if I waited long enough the knack would come to me, like a sort of religious salvation that could be had simply by maintaining faith.'

She pauses now and catches her breath, holding at bay a painful memory. Then she says, 'James told me of a writer friend of his who could not manage a novel. He'd written many short pieces but nothing over thirty pages, so he got a copy of Evelyn Waugh's *Decline and Fall* and typed it out verbatim, night after night, until he held a transcribed manuscript in his hands. He thought by doing this he would learn what it felt like to write a novel. James laughed when he told me this, laughed in a kind of pitying manner, and I thought – though I did not say – that this was me he was describing. I wrote out my father's work in the hope that I would understand how on earth it came to him as it did. Of course, this was a useless exercise.'

She says nothing for a few minutes. Then she says, 'I wish I could do something else, anything else. I wish I had a different skill, a different way of seeing the world. You don't get along with your mother, and that is too bad, I suppose. But at least you will never look back and think that you were given every advantage and yet, somehow, you remained little better than competent. The world is full of dazzling stories of people who, despite hardship – poverty, nasty upbringings, physical problems, complicated political situations that ensnare them – manage somehow to triumph, to excel, to become *somebody*. Writers, musicians, artists. I was given every opportunity to be a first-rate musician, to be more than just a reliable orchestral player, and I failed. I failed utterly and my damnation is that I must continue to live in the world that shows me as a failure.'

The sky is almost black and the branches of the oak tree outside the window scratch against the glass. I make Lea a cup of tea and she shows me her father's compositions, which are faint pencil markings across ragged, yellowing paper. She sets them on her music stand and takes up her violin, her rasping, delicate bow, and sounds out the notes of what is an exuberant melody full of flight and grace, that she executes in a soaring, intoxicating manner. She fairly dances to it and I look at her in wonder, in awe, as she sets about demonstrating the genius of her father and allows her tea to go cold.

The first months we lived in London, I mapped out the city by its important historical monuments. At the kitchen table, with a map I'd photocopied and enlarged, and with Isobel as my assistant, I stuck red tags where one would find Buckingham Palace, the Tower of London, the *Cutty Sark*, the Houses of Parliament, the Royal Albert Hall. I memorized the major throughroads and tried to piece together in my mind exactly which of them met at the dizzying knots of roundabouts – Piccadilly Circus, Oxford Circus, the roundabout at Westminster, at Shepherd's Bush, at Waterloo – that stud the city. As I rode the number 54 bus down the hill from Blackheath and across the grim landscape of south London I quizzed myself for the names of each successive stop on the circle line. Though no definite time limit had been placed on our life in London, I had gleaned that it was to be a brief lapse away from America, and so I felt the need to fill my days as productively as possible and soak up as much of London living as I could.

My coursework managed to sap a great deal of my energy, but on weekends I could sometimes, through a combination of nagging and sulking, manage to get Mother to take us out, to see the changing of the guard or roam the many halls of the Victoria and Albert Museum or perhaps peer at the Crown jewels. The effort required to get Mother to accompany us to any of these venues proved disabling. The day she spent two hours in the main lobby of the Museum of Natural History, chain-smoking on a bench outside the loos and waiting for Isobel and myself to finish our tour, I knew it was pointless to ask her to go anywhere with us. Later, even Isobel lost interest. It turned out Isobel was exceedingly popular at her new school so she soon preferred hanging out watching television at one of her new friend's houses to venturing out with me. So on Saturday mornings I went out on my own. I was allowed to go by myself into London during the day, as long as I returned before dark, so I set out early with a lunch that Rose always packed for me (jam sandwich, sliced apple, a wedge of cheddar cheese and biscuits, sometimes a bit of chocolate), in order to take in Keats's House and Highgate Cemetery on one trip, the Imperial War Museum on another.

It was perhaps because I was so frequently seen leaving the house on my own, with my shopping bag filled with Rose's picnic and my assorted maps, my coat bulging with a pocket umbrella, purse, wool hat and gloves, that Lea and James thought to ask me if I'd like to go out with them. They were always going somewhere, to a pub lunch or a concert given in some obscure chapel I'd never heard of. They were keen walkers and Lea often took the bus across Shooter's Hill to Oxeas Woods, where she walked for hours by herself. She preferred walking in winter because it guaranteed a certain amount of solitude. I was privileged to walk with her, and on those days, when we passed hours in near silence, the frozen ground crunching beneath our boots. I shared my packed lunch with her and she offered her flask of steaming tea. She was a delicate-looking girl but had a tensile strength and tremendous stamina.

'Did you ever walk in Yosemite?' she asked, supposing, I imagine, that because I had lived in California, I would probably have visited that particular national treasure.

'Well, no. Mother isn't big on . . . uh . . . nature. She prefers car parks,' I said, which made Lea laugh. 'Anyway, Yosemite is as far away from Orange County as we are from Dusseldorf.'

'Really?'

'Well, no. I don't know how far away Dusseldorf is, but Yosemite is very far away from Orange County. Orange County is where Disneyland is.'

'Have you been to Disneyland?' Lea asked, her eyes suddenly saucer-sized, with a child-like gleam to them.

'No,' I said, looking out over the sky, which was studded with the moon on one side and a faint glow of sun on the other.

'Oh, well.'

'I'm surprised we didn't go to Disneyland,' I said. 'It seems odd on reflection because Disneyland has some very impressive car parks.'

She smiled. We were sitting at the top of a hill on a clear winter morning and we could see across Kent, which made me feel we were deep in the country. But Lea looked into the horizon and almost recoiled from it. 'James and I went to Scotland on our honeymoon on a walking holiday,' she said. 'You should go sometime, it's so different from here. It's so beautiful and wild.'

She must have seen in my face how unlikely I would be to go to Scotland any time soon, and in any case how empty a trip like that would be if made on one's own, because she said right away, 'Next time James and I go to Edinburgh, you're coming with us.'

'Do you go often?'

'I play there sometimes. You ask your mother and we'll arrange it. We'll take the train up and you'll see the countryside, which is marvellous.'

'Deal,' I said.

'What?' She looked at me for explanation.

'That would be lovely,' I said.

Though Lea was the one who enchanted me, I was more often with James. Lea was involved in music recitals, concerts, endless rehearsals and musical favours she did for friends by playing with them at particular events, parties or weddings or minor recordings done on four tracks in a rented studio. James and I became a kind of fan club and followed her to various concert halls across London, to the Barbican Centre and Wigmore Hall, to St John's Smith Square where we had a light supper in the crypt of a deconsecrated church and then went upstairs to the concert which was so packed there were people standing along the walls. It is odd to me now to think I spent so many hours with him, standing in front of him in a queue, sitting in the next seat. Anyone would have thought we were a couple, the manner between us was exactly the slightly bored, easy comfort of a long-standing relationship. I cannot remember what we used to talk about, other than Lea, who was always the focus at such gatherings.

Sometimes they went on to a party afterwards. Aware that if I went with them I would not likely come home before three a.m., I usually made my own way back to Charing Cross and took the train to Lewisham. I had a student pass so I could travel cheap and of course I never had to pay for the concerts because of Lea. Otherwise I would never have been able to afford to go out at all. Mother's contention was that I ought to get a small job in a shop to make pocket money, so what small change she gave me came only from birthdays or Christmas. I could imagine no worse scenario than going to school all week, then ringing up numbers on a till at the weekend, so I had no regular source of income. Occasionally I babysat a couple of young children who lived on Blackheath Rise, for which I was paid so poorly that it made no sense at all to seek more work of the same nature. I won a small monied prize in an essay contest at school and found a fiver on the pavement once. I was not allowed to sell my old clothes at second-hand shops because, of course, they were handed down to Isobel, but I arranged for *her* old clothes to be sold and we carried them to a shop together and split the proceeds. Otherwise I was broke, and I remember thinking on one of my innumerable trips back from Charing Cross on my own that nobody would believe I led such a varied nightlife with such a richness to it, given the money in my purse. I carried everything I had with me and it totalled seven pounds.

There is a picture taken near this time, one of those which Aunt Rose took with her box camera. It was a day in late March of unseasonable brightness and warmth, the ground had unfrozen and new sprigs of green grass pushed through the wet, dark soil on the heath. The sky was clear, with shredded tufts of clouds smearing the eggshell blue with whiteness. The sun – which we'd all but given up on through the winter – crowned the horizon and offered us a glimpse of the season to come.

'I'd love a photograph,' Rose said at breakfast. 'All of us on the porch front, just like we used to do with Father.'

It was a tradition in Rose's house that each year was marked by a spring photograph. She remembered specifically how her father had prepared for it, donning his church clothes and shaving carefully in the mirror while his daughters fretted over dresses that they'd not worn for a year and might be needing a new hem, or a collar pressed, or perhaps be judged unwearable finally. 'It served me a dozen years,' Eleanor might say, folding a favoured frock into a shopping bag to be delivered freshly laundered to one of the village charity shops. Sometimes there was some shuffling of ownership. 'Dark blue is no longer my colour,' Margaret might decide. She was the oldest, and therefore the one who pioneered the inevitable slide into old age that meant certain colours, once perfectly suitable, showed up the skin as ashen or washed out the eyes, or disagreed violently with grey hair. Eleanor would not allow such items to be pushed her way. 'Send it to the shops,' she'd insist, meaning Oxfam or Cancer Research, or even the tiny corner store that helped the aged. 'That's where it belongs.' Rose was terribly sentimental, she could not bear to give away any of her sisters' old dresses and received with a great show of appreciation whatever was handed down to her.

Perhaps for the same reason Rose was the one who tended to all the photograph albums. She tacked corner holds on to the black pages, carefully folded over the onion-skin coverlets and marked in fountain pen who the photographs were of and on what date, sometimes including a comment. 'All of us assembled with spring bonnets – except me! Mine blew off just before the picture was taken!' was one caption beneath the annual photo. I liked that one particularly, because I imagine Rose standing with her sisters in the cool, spring air, in front of the house which they knew so well they could have drawn it blind in amazing detail, not just as it was but in the various incarnations of the past – the nursery they'd had as children which later became Margaret's bedroom, the sewing room which had functioned as a kind of office (though it would never have been called this) for their mother, what was referred to as the 'old kitchen', a primitive version of what would become the 'new kitchen', that is the room that was twenty years behind the times when we lived there.

I can see, as though into a true memory and not an invented recollection, Rose standing with her sisters on that bright, breezy morning, telling them she needed another pin for her hat, which she clapped on to her head with one hand. Her father speaks now and she puts her concerns about the hat pin to one side and concentrates on his instructions. Closer together, now turn towards me. That's right. Now everyone a big smile! Rose, put your arm down by your side. She might object, but only in a mild, affable way. Had it been Eleanor or, much more, Margaret, everyone would have waited, at her insistence, for her to go back inside the house, climb two sets of stairs and find a hatpin. But Rose would never want to trouble her family in such a way. She froze, waited for a stillness in the wind, and brought her hand down to her side, looking up at the brim of her hat with mistrust and concern, as though it were a bird that had landed there. The shutter went, and the sisters sang 'Hooray!', but it was no good, the hat had flown off, captured only in the very corner of the photo in which it appears as a creamy blur. Rose's nervous smile looks like the grimace of a chimpanzee, but shown in her eyes is also a lightness of humour, for she saw anything that went awry in her small, domesticated world as slightly baffling and funny, 'Oh me,' she might have said those many years ago, 'and my silly hat!'

There were, of course, other photographs as well. Babies in enormous canopied prams set on elaborate wheels, various formations of the family sitting outside, sipping tea and looking very pleased to be there, an assortment of long-dead pets, mostly cats, and various pictures of the house in different seasons, blanketed in snow or with every window open to the summer heat. 'Granny ensuring each of her fillies are shod!' captioned an ancient photograph of a bespeckled, heavy-jowled but cheerful-looking granny (my great-great-grandmother) standing amongst a group of four girls who stare delightedly down their pale frocks at the blocky boots that were the generous gift of their grandparents. In the photograph Eleanor is smiling at her grandmother, Rose is staring straight down so that only the top of her curly-haired head can be seen, Margaret holds the baby's hand. The baby, of course, is my own grandmother, Celia. She died of breast cancer – it was never called breast cancer by my aunts. They spoke of those years as the time when 'Celia was so ill'. The tragic irony of it, that the only sister to die was the one whose loss was greatest because she left a child – my mother, who was thirteen – brought Eleanor to become the godly, fanatic Christian that I knew her as. 'She wasn't like that before,' Rose told me one night as she was sewing. 'Oh, Christian, to be sure, but not so determined a one, and *not* evangelical.'

There had been talk at that time of Mother coming to live at Dartmouth Row, and I find myself sometimes aching to reach back in time and make that so. For had she been raised among her mother's family, her path in life would have been much different, I am sure. By law, however, she was my grandfather's responsibility and he decided to keep her at home. My grandfather was, by all accounts, a stiff-natured, difficult man who understood his wife's early death to mean that his daughter would have to provide the domestic comforts that are the inheritance of women, to clean the house and cook his dinners and tend to the shopping. Nobody could have been less suitable than my mother, who even ten years later could not see fit to mop a kitchen floor. Besides, she wanted to be an actress in London, not Cinderella in Essex. Though her father was scarcely fifty when he was widowed, it would never have occurred to him to remarry. He suffered a childhood illness that left him with emphysema and he coughed and wheezed himself to an early death. 'Not early enough,' Mother sometimes joked, but you could see in her eyes the hurt he'd somehow forever carved into her heart. He was responsible for Mother's constant attempts to marry herself out of the semi-detached Essex home of which she was so unfond that she never took us once to see the house – or even the county, for that matter. If she were to trace a picture of England she most likely would have left out that particular part of the south-east entirely and slotted Suffolk right up against London. In 1960, she cheerfully bid goodbye to the whole nation and set off with my father, when she was only twenty years old. Their destination was Los Angeles, where she was sure to become an actress and he assured her there would be work.

'Are you ready? Do you need any help?' Rose called, shuffling from kitchen to hallway to Mother's room to the bathroom, where she knocked tentatively at the door, asking Isobel to please hurry because the sun was as likely to disappear as quickly as it came. It was a Saturday morning and Mother was meeting Stephen Price for lunch. On the table she used as a vanity, in front of a mirror she propped against the wall, she dabbed from various bottles and swiped at her face using facial sponges she had cut into wedges. She combed her hair up, then teased it to add 'lift'. She applied her mascara, one lash at a time, just as they say to do in the magazines, and brushed on an almost imperceivably thin powder to 'set' her make-up. All this she did while calling orders over her shoulder, 'Isobel, please take that cat off your bed. You are allergic enough without sleeping in cat hair!', 'Rebecca, can you look for my housekeys? I don't know what I've done with them. Also, my cigarettes, they've disappeared in all the clutter in this house', 'Rose, would you stop rushing around, you're going to exhaust yourself before lunchtime!'

I plopped the cat on to the floor, found Mother's keys (left in the front door, as usual), retrieved her cigarettes from the window ledge where they'd been hidden behind the curtain, and came into her room to report this. She was sitting very straight at her makeshift vanity and I remembered how back in America she'd had that special table with its winged sides and the mirror with the ring of starlet lights that dimmed and brightened for different effects. She was making an oval with her mouth and lining her lips with a berry-coloured pencil, but when I came in she stopped and looked at me cautiously. This is how it had come to be between us, the constant leery assessment, the tentative, restrained remark. It was not that I disapproved of the elaborate ritual which was her 'getting ready', but that Stephen Price was married and I found Mother's pretence that they were only 'good friends' insulting to everybody's intelligence. Good friends was what she had never been with a man, any man as far as I'd known, and anyway she was clearly in love. She spent most days thinking about, preparing for, or floating in the remembrance of her day at the office. A bad day was one in which Stephen or she had spent every working hour showing houses to prospective buyers so that they hadn't any time left over for each other. 'What a horrendous afternoon!' she might say. 'I was out all day with clients, all bloody day!'

'Those pesky people, what did they want? To buy a house?'

'Don't start, Rebecca. My feet are worn out. All day long up and down stairs.'

'Of course,' I said.

'I'm warning you!'

'All I said was "of course"!'

'I know what you're thinking!'

'No, you don't.'

A good day would be a rainy Monday when they both stayed at their desks – or somewhere within close proximity, I dared not hazard a guess where – and nothing much in the way of buying and selling transpired. On those days she breezed home wearing a look of moony happiness.

'Studying hard?' she might enquire, as Isobel and I sat at the long table with our school books propped around us. 'I'm so proud of you, my darlings. What is that chart, anyway?'

'The Periodic Table,' I said, with an even efficiency that could, I knew, be construed as hostile. Mother's high moods bothered me, not because I wished to see her unhappy, but because they seemed artificial, like the fuzzy good cheer of an alcoholic. I wanted her to be happy, but I wanted her to be happy with us, and not boosted by the temporary affections of an already wedded man.

'What does it do?' she asked, showing uncharacteristic interest in my studies, for homework was considered by her to be just one notch up from housework.

'It's a list of all the elements,' I said, and brought the chart up for her closer inspection.

'Elements!' she laughed. This was terribly funny, apparently. Isobel and I looked at each other, that knowing look that allowed us to both endure and dismiss a great deal of Mother's behaviour.

'All the *chemical* elements,' Isobel said, as though to make clear the matter. She smiled sideways at me. She had the knack, perhaps inherited from Aunt Rose, of lightening any situation.

'Well, that is wonderful! My genius daughters, you'll both be great scientists, I am sure,' she said, and whirled in the direction of her bedroom.

'Not me,' Isobel said. 'I'm going to be an actress.'

'Isobel!' Mother said, stopping dead and turning back, her mouth agape, her eyes wide as though she'd just been notified that the grand prize had been drawn and it was hers, or as though the waist-high, inefficient refrigerator which kept our food cold by slowly freezing it through layers of ice that collected at its sides, had suddenly, magically, been turned into a giant, American fridge-freezer with an icemaker. 'That is simply the best, most wonderful . . .' She was lost for words. 'News!' she concluded finally, then swept from the room.

Off she went to plan meticulously the outfit she would wear the following day. It is easy to be critical of her – and God knows that I was endlessly critical of her in those days – but the point to keep in mind is that at the time she was bringing us up, which she did entirely on her own, she was a young woman herself. She was thirty-eight when she took up with Stephen Price, and though I am willing to concede it was 'wrong' of her to intrude on that marriage, it was perhaps understandable. As she was fond of saying it wasn't *she* who promised his wife that she would love, honour and cherish until death do us part. *He* was the adulterer, she was merely a single woman. Besides, Stephen and his wife hadn't any children. How terrible could it be for a marriage to break up when there were no children to consider? Not terrible at all, was her conclusion. He had said he was going to leave his marriage in any case, and therefore it was not as though she was the cause of any specific hardship.

'Marriages break down all the time,' she told me then. 'It never surprises me when they fall apart, what surprises me is when they don't!' Such a statement, uttered with exactly the kind of flippant, easy-come-easy-go attitude that brought me inevitably to take issue, was in my view another appalling display of Mother's lack of ethics. As an adult, I have to smile and nod my head in agreement with her, however, for it has become my conclusion that marriage is as difficult and peculiar a condition as can be imposed upon a person. Despite my own marriage, which means as much to me as it would to any wife, I cannot imagine why people do it. But at the time I had elevated marriage to exactly the position the Pope would like it to have. I thought that it was sacred, final, part of what held society in balance. In my crass, inexpert estimation, divorce was in all cases a spiritual failure. My mother and me, who are on good terms now, much better than could have been expected given the inhospitable terrain of our early years, have often sat on the phone to one another talking about another couple's separation and remarking, in a way that was unfathomable to me back then, 'Well, they were together twelve years, that's a long time – but, so it goes.' What bothers us much more than the breakdown of a marriage is the prospect of spending one's life in a bad marriage. I, who silently condemned any notion that Stephen Price could ever be forgiven for cheating on his wife, have been known in recent times to say about a friend, 'Would she *leave* that horrible man! Or at least have an affair or *something* to make her happy!'

'Why are you staring at me?' Mother asked that morning as we prepared for Rose's photograph.

'I'm not staring,' I said, 'I just brought you your cigarettes.'

I laid the pack on the table beside her make-up and she tapped one end and then drew out a fresh cigarette. 'What time did you get home last night?' she asked.

'Oh, not late. About eleven.' I'd been out with James and Lea to the cinema. It was an unusual night because generally I only went with them when Lea was playing and thought it might be nice for James to have some company through the performance. But they'd been going out and asked me, in their usual manner by calling down the stairs, whether I wanted to join them. 'Are you sure?' I said, rushing to the bottom of the steps. 'Absolutely, we're a threesome, after all,' said Lea. I did not understand how it transpired that we'd become a threesome. Certainly this was an overstatement to make me feel less of a unnecessary appendage, but I dared not dwell on it for too long a time. Somehow I had been adopted by them. That was Lea's word, adopted. They did not always take me with them when they went out, and more than once I was in charge of staying home and 'listening closely' for any prowler who might steal James's parents paintings while they spent a weekend away, a responsibility I not only did not mind, but which I absolutely aspired to. But I had entered their lives truly, and taken a position that I guarded as fiercely as if they had in earnest adopted me.

'Oh, really? Where did you go?' Mother asked.

'The cinema, I told you,' I said.

'In Catford, you mean?'

'Yes,' I said. The lie was easy, easier than it ought to have been. The fact was that Lea and James never went to the cinema in Catford, but always to the West End, where they took in some 'art flick' as James called them. He pretended that he thought watching films in which you had to read the dialogue was way too much work, you might as well read a book, but never protested too much when Lea dragged him off to see something obscure, plotless and subtitled, or to one of the depressing, confusing Ingmar Bergman films that I never understood either and that she insisted upon.

'You are very lucky,' Mother began, and I wondered whether she was going to say that I was lucky to have such friends as James and Lea. For no matter how many times they came downstairs and knocked at the door, asking if I wanted to join them to go somewhere, almost always to a concert or musical recital but occasionally, as last night, to a film, I could not believe that they had chosen me, that I was suitable enough, that they found me interesting. I felt lucky, more than lucky. I felt blessed. For an instant, as Mother paused to light her cigarette, I wondered if she might agree with me how fortunate I was that people so talented and interesting, not to mention a few, important years older than me, should be so kind as to take me with them into London on a Friday evening. For certainly, I would never have gone on my own. But that is not what she said. 'You are very lucky I allow you to go merrily around the city at all hours,' is what she said. 'I can think of one or two parents who would not.'

So, there it was, a détente. I could see it as clearly as if we'd sat down with a contract and meted out all the clauses and conditions. I would be allowed to see James and Lea, but only on the condition that I did not interfere with, judge, or in any way allude to what I considered to be her disgusting connection with her boss. I would overlook the fanatical primping and preparation that went into every brief occasion she saw him, and she, in turn, would disregard how I borrowed Lea's clothes, doted on James's every word, listened with attention to the tapes of famous concerts that Lea lent me to play on my rickety mono tape player through headphones that were also borrowed from them. We would stonewall each other, tolerate each other, and silently condemn each other.

I thought I knew then why she was condemnable but I could

not imagine what she saw as wrong in what I was doing. I had friends, wasn't that normal? Wasn't that what she should want for me? But from the very beginning she had not liked Lea. I cannot tell you why, except that Mother was given to jealousy and she might easily have been jealous of Lea, who had a remarkable career, a lovely face, an adoring and handsome husband. She lived in the larger, grander part of the house and she had perfect freedom, by which I mean no children.

Isobel and I were born six years apart, me as the inevitable product of young matrimony and Isobel as an attempt to keep the marriage together. I remember very little about my father, he was around so seldom, but I doubt Mother ever knew marriage in the way that most women did. She'd been married and divorced years before a woman these days would even be likely to have a serious engagement. And all of her adult life she'd been responsible for children, whom she loved and loathed in turn. Some nights she turned up the radio and danced in the kitchen, her face tilted up as though to an imagined lover, her bare feet skirting the floor, lifting and turning. She always danced on her toes, executing dips and whirls and covering ground as though the kitchen were her stage. She was not a gifted dancer – she might twirl, knock into a chair, laugh at herself, then start again. But she had a certain elegance, she held her shoulders straight, moving with precision, unselfconsciously, her eyes half closed, her lips parted. Once I saw her pause suddenly and move her hands over her face. In the drifting, languid hopeful world of her dance, she was somewhere far beyond the reach of children. But when she opened her eyes, opened them and saw with unimpeded vision, the fact of us – in our shabby nightdresses, with our knotted hair – standing in isolation well below the ever collapsing heavenly world she occupied in her dance, and wearing expressions that told her of our need of her, our dread and love and fear of her, she ceased to dance and fell heavily upon her heels. For a moment she curled around herself, hands across her belly, chin against her chest, her back quaking. We were not meant to be there, not there while she was dancing. Who were you thinking of, Mother? we might have called to her, asking, begging, wanting always to be the one in her dreams, the one who danced with her. For surely she was too good for people such as Stephen Price or the one before who'd sent her the gold pin shaped as a pair of hands.

'Lea is going on a tour with her orchestra,' I said as Mother completed the painting of her lips. 'So I guess I won't be going out as much with them in future.'

'It isn't *her* orchestra,' she said.

'She *is* the first violinist which means—'

'I know what it means!' Mother said. 'Don't be such a snob.'

There was a light tap on the door and we both turned to see Rose there, standing with her little Brownie camera, a pink dress and open-toed white shoes. She'd been to the hairdresser's the day before and her hair was a white halo around her sweet, even-featured face. I thought her beautiful. I rushed to her and hugged her. We are not a hugging family and the moment surprised her so she exclaimed 'Ooh!' and patted my back tentatively.

Later that morning we stood outside together, the four of us, while Mr Dodd, a neighbour, took the photograph. I don't know how we got him to do it, as nobody but Rose could ever operate that rickety old camera. It was a temperamental instrument that had to be held down beside your waist as you angled it, and the lighting had to be just right. Lea was upstairs, she'd not been feeling very well and her tour was due to start any day, so she needed to rest. I don't know where James was, writing perhaps.

'Smile everyone!' Mr Dodd called, and we stood stiffly, aware of our faces, our hair, where our feet were, whether our dresses were smooth. I looked at Isobel, who was the beauty of the family, and who in profile might have passed for someone my age as she took my mother's hand. I was jealous of her then, and it was precisely at that moment, when I glanced slightly to my left and saw my younger sister clasping my mother's long fingers in her own, that Mr Dodd depressed the shutter button and the moment was captured for Rose's leather-bound album.

'Very nice!' called Mr Dodd. He was elderly, with a long, thin face which creased extravagantly when he smiled. Afterwards, Mother went to meet her man and Rose invited Mr Dodd along with the rest of us to tea at a shop in the village. When we returned James was still upstairs writing – I could hear the clacking, hammering stutter of his work across the typewriter.

I did not hear Lea's violin that night, though I woke specially to listen for it. But a silence had erupted in the house, no music was played, no arguments from upstairs, no creaking floorboards, no cascade of footsteps coming down the stairs. Lea was three days away from her tour and she'd taken to her bed. I'd noticed on the previous night, when we went to the cinema together, that she was unusually quiet, preoccupied, almost as though she were suffering an illness. I'd thought perhaps I was to blame – as I was always on the lookout for signs that she would discover, finally, that I was an unsuitable companion – and tried to be especially entertaining and jolly, but nothing could wrestle her from her dark mood. James held her arm and whispered in her ear and made funny remarks all the way to London and back, but she was so subdued it was almost as though she were half awake. I did not dwell on this behaviour, and it would not occur to me to be unduly concerned. When a few days later I saw her departing for the tour, which would mean four weeks on the road, I merely waved her away and thought selfishly how much I would miss her company, the way she dressed me and fussed over me, and included me like a girlfriend in minor but important ways.

'Bye bye, Rebecca,' she said, her voice a croaky whisper. I thought perhaps she was suffering from a cold.

'Have a wonderful time!' I said.

'Well, we'll see,' she said.

The next time I saw her she was a stone lighter and could barely talk at all.

8

Sometimes I remember my friendship with Lea and James as part of my history with James specifically, as though our eventual emergence as a married couple started all those years ago. This is not how it was, I am sure. I was not nearly so taken by James as by Lea, and had he lived alone in that house I am sure that nothing at all would have brought us together. Not that I did not like him, I adored him, but I was ten years younger than him at a time when those ten years meant a very great deal. I'd found him standoffish, if not downright rude, when we'd first met. There would have been no reason whatsoever to maintain any kind of friendship with him had I not been so entirely taken with Lea. Lea was what we had in common, for a time the only thing we had in common, and because of her we were together enough that we grew fond of one another.

This is the truth. I would swear to it.

But some other niggling, treacherous side to me wonders if it can be true. A little over a year after this time, during my first year in university, I started a romance with David (as in David who married Eleanor). I knew he did not love me – I certainly did not love him – but he wheedled his way into my bed by insisting on seeing the most innocent, even accidental, action as grounded firmly in sex. A jumper peeled off amid a group of other students was a 'display' in his eyes, regardless of the circumstances (a hot day, a spillage down the front), that drew the wearer to discard the jumper in the first place. A cup of coffee shared after dinner was always a meeting of hearts and minds. And bodies, of course, especially that. 'Why do you see every friendship as a sexual one?' I asked him once, late at night, at a wine bar. We were among the last patrons remaining. The litter of empty glasses and cigarettes, discarded ash and wadded, half-soaked napkins was testimony to the hours we'd spent staring at each other across the small, shiny brass circular table where our reflections shone as in still water. He did not answer my question, but looked at me with greedy satisfaction, his fingers tapping the underside of the table in anticipation of what would be, almost certainly, a night of sex in one or other of our shabby rooms.

'I want to know,' I said, coyly demanding, only half convinced that I had a point to make, 'why do you think every single attraction between two people must necessarily be a sexual one?'

'Because that is the case,' he said, quickly, as though the question did not require any thought at all. 'Because that is the truth.'

Such a remark would have made no sense to me back when I lived with my family, and James and Lea occupied the floor above. I believed then that the world was governed by a moral order, like a panel of judges who sat in attendance and arbitration of everyday matters, and that one had to abide by it. One had to, or the result was a messy, chaotic, desperate and finally unhappy life, a life which I saw my mother's to be. In my tidy, principled, sexless existence as a schoolgirl there was no room for anything as sullied or confusing – as *untoward*, to use Aunt Rose's expression – as attraction that went beyond the closed duality of marriage. Did I think it not possible to love a woman, Lea, and secretly covet her husband? Not ever wanting to take him away from her, but somehow dreaming, in the subconscious manner which betrays our best intentions, of a moment when he might, however briefly, cast the alluring, shadowy, irresistible net of his attention on to me? It cannot be coincidence that the next woman he loved after Lea was me. It must be that somehow I, *we*, brought this on. That from the moment we first met a tiny, dormant seed had been planted, to one day be brought inevitably to life. I would never have countenanced such a thing at the time. The very notion would have appalled me, horrified me, forced me perhaps even to give any thought of continuing to be their friend. Did I think that love was so easily controlled back then? Did I think that people fell in love only once, or only once truly, or that all love was the same, the exact same article? I don't know what I thought, but whatever it was, my ideas were well off the mark, almost comically so. Mother used to shake her head at me, close her eyes and draw a breath. 'You live in a different world,' she told me. 'And sometimes that cosy world of yours makes me so angry I could break every window in this big, ghostly house. Other times, I wish you had it in your heart to make a place for me there.'

If I was attracted to him, I did not see where that attraction went, beyond the one I held for the both of them – for they were a tremendous draw with their turbulent love, their powerful art. I could not fathom how this love could ever fall on to him specifically, exclusively, as a man I could touch, encourage, hurt, make love to. I don't think I saw him as separate from her. And if he was attracted to me, I did not know it. When I asked him many years later, he laughed and confessed that he'd not seen me as even grown-up enough to be attracted to. Stories abound of adult men falling silly for nubile young teenagers – it is one of those puzzling mismatches that makes one baulk and wonder, like when you see a cross-breed dog and the owner tells you it is a mix of Great Dane and miniature poodle – but I was a studious, slightly overweight girl with bad skin and eyeglasses. And James was very in love with his wife.

While Lea was away on tour the house fell into a lifeless silence. There was none of her music, not the albums she played during the day nor of course the nightly practice sessions which I still woke to hear, my body automatically jarring me from sleep in anticipation of a performance that no longer took place. I heard the front door opening and shutting, so I knew James went out, but to where I hadn't any idea. I heard his typewriter, the teeth of the keys popping in a burst of energy, then falling away. With Lea gone he seemed to do more work, staying up for half the night, and the typing became a soothing noise to me, a kind of soporific background sound like rain against a tin roof. I saw the glow of the lights upstairs, inviting and yet strangely off-putting. I knew he was home and also knew, somehow, that I was not to disturb him. Almost a week would go by without us exchanging more than a passing word.

Because of my friendship with Lea and James, I hadn't tried to make any new friends at school, and so my evenings and weekends seemed all at once drawn out and lonely. I tried to amuse myself with all the features of London I'd previously sought out – museums and libraries, cathedrals, and walks that would take me past the houses of famous scientists, writers, explorers, artists – but I found to my amazement that I was no longer all that interested. This struck me as a terrible corruption – what is that saying that when one tires of London one tires of life? – and I took it to mean that I was as dull as I'd suspected all along. In fact, I suppose the simple explanation was that I'd become a Londoner, and by that I mean I no longer looked with fresh eyes on the imposing architecture, the enormous wealth of history that one could observe on a simple day trip a half mile in any direction. I concentrated instead on how to get from any one point to another without being caught up in long queues down broken, unmoving escalators, or knocked down while crossing busy junctions, or left shivering for lengths of time waiting for buses that never arrived or, as often happened, arrived too full to board.

Isobel's experience of London was the mile-radius around school, and from that limited landscape she managed to extract a great deal of living. She turned out to be a joiner of teams and clubs, including the netball team, the diving team, the drama club, the forensic society and the Girl Scouts. She was forever practising, rehearsing, phoning friends for advice, or pasting leaves, beads or seeds on to card.

Rose had taken to having regular teas with Mr Dodd, which

made us all terribly curious, especially Mother, who found Rose's friendship with Mr Dodd genuinely inspirational. 'If a 76-year-old woman shaped like a box is able to attract men, there is hope for me yet,' she told us in private. To Rose she said, 'Mr Dodd is a lovely man. Well done, Rose!' Rose shook her head and claimed Mother was making things up. 'There is nothing but a pot of tea between us!' she insisted, but Mother would hear none of it. 'Am I going to have to buy a new hat?' she teased.

'And a new head to put it on,' shot back Rose, but you could tell she was pleased.

Mother herself was very busy with Stephen Price, who several times a week could be seen slumped in his car outside the house waiting for her to emerge. She never invited him in. I don't know whether that was because she feared I would make a remark that would send him flying for the exits, or whether she'd pretended to him that we owned the entire house (this was most likely) and did not want him to see that we only occupied a small portion. He always wore the same camel-coloured overcoat and his thick hair was combed into a deep side parting that made his head appear unbalanced. When I passed by, he either pretended to be reading a map or got very busy adjusting the car clock. Just to watch him twitch I sometimes tapped on the glass and waved hello, and he looked up and smiled weakly, his face heavily lined for a man of his age. I suppose the stress of conducting a clandestine affair had put years on him. I was grateful he didn't want to know any of us, or try to make conversation, because I would have no idea what to say to him. Mother left the house, a trail of perfume and hairspray in her wake, and made a great show of cheerfulness as she half walked, half jogged across the paving stones in her heels to his car. They drove away – to where I have no idea – at a speed which suggested they were being chased. Sometimes Mother hadn't even shut the car door before they were off.

Rose must have noticed my disapproval of Stephen Price because one time she said, 'You have to let your mother have a little bit of fun in life,' which cut me deeply because it had never occurred to me that I was trying to deprive her of fun. I see now that it was everyone's opinion that Mother was a martyr because she brought up two children on her own with no man and no family to support her financially. My father had never been home very much in the first place, he was in the Navy and so was often gone six months out of the year. When he finally did leave her she was pregnant with Isobel and had no idea even that she'd been left. He failed to return home from one of his postings at sea and on further investigation it was discovered that he was living in Alaska. One of Mother's jokes about marriage is that you know your marriage is in trouble when your partner lives in the wilderness and you have not yet noticed. Without children to look after, she might easily have started a new life with someone who did not live on ships or in cold, inhospitable climates where bear attacks are a regular hazard. But she was pregnant, and later had two children to look after, which, she said, was like hanging a sign on you that read, 'Beware: I'm impoverished and fertile.' For years she couldn't get a date.

I did not think that Mother was a martyr. To imagine her as such was to automatically cancel out any notion that Isobel and I were positive forces in her life. She'd gone out with lots of men, perhaps not as many as she might have liked, and definitely not The One who she dreamed of, but in all cases she'd had the good sense to keep them well away from us, which I took as proof that we hadn't driven them away. We hadn't had the chance to drive them away, she'd done that all on her own. I didn't approve of Stephen Price, no, but whatever opinion I had of him was of no consequence because in all the months she dated him we never actually said more than three words in passing.

'I think Stephen Price is a loose man,' Isobel said one evening at the dinner table.

'Loose?' I had no idea what she was talking about.

'Yes, loose. You know, *loose*.'

'Oh, I get it. Like a loose woman,' I said.

'Yeah, but he's a man,' said Isobel. 'So loose man.'

'It is not appropriate for you two girls to be discussing Mr Price in this manner,' said Rose. She couldn't possibly have known that Stephen Price was married; it would never have occurred to her even as a remote possibility. 'Especially at the dinner table.'

'We can't talk about vomit at the dinner table either,' Isobel said, and then began to laugh. It was true, one of the few rules we had in our family, one which had survived from the years when we were small, was that you couldn't discuss vomit or any other disgusting thing that would put off one's appetite at the table.

'First vomit, now Stephen Price. It's getting so restrictive around here,' I said.

'I mean it!' said Rose. 'I'll tell your mother you've been misbehaving in regard to Mr Price.'

'*She's* been misbehaving in regard to Mr Price,' I said, but very quietly, so only Isobel could hear.

'He's a Jezebel,' Isobel whispered back.

'He's a tart,' I agreed.

'What are you whispering about?' Rose said. She was hard of hearing and it made her angry, so angry she refused to wear a hearing aid, and she could not stand it when we took advantage of her disability.

'Nothing,' we said in unison. But all through dinner, and for many weeks afterwards, we referred to Stephen Price variously as a rent boy, a slut, a call boy, a gigolo, and any other debasing term we could imagine. Mother, we named 'the queen'. The queen and her fool, said Isobel. The queen and her *tool*, I quipped back.

'You know what he *really* is,' said Isobel, then twelve, one afternoon while sitting in front of the television watching *Coronation Street*. 'He's an easy lay.'

I made fun of Stephen Price but I was also aware that normal girls my age had boyfriends and I had none. No boyfriends, zero, and now with Lea gone I had lots of time to think about the fact I had no boyfriends. So I decided to do what Mother had been badgering me to do for some time now and get a job.

'I'm going to work at Lewisham Hospital,' I announced one night at dinner when, unusually, all of us were in attendance, even Mother who ate while leafing through a copy of *Harper's and Queen*.

'Lewisham Hospital. Well, that's marvellous,' said Rose, flustered and excited all at once.

'What, like in the morgue?' said Isobel, unmoved by my flight into the medical world.

'What can you do in a hospital?' Mother asked, not in a nasty way but as a serious question. 'Don't you need to have experience?'

'I'm a very good science student and have excellent reports,' I said. 'They told me I had a good chance at a number of positions. In fact, I start next weekend.'

There was a silence as everyone sat astounded and impressed by my news, a silence I enjoyed thoroughly. Then Mother asked in an emotive voice, swelling with pride, where in the hospital I would be working.

'On the wards,' I said, casually.

'With the doctors!' Mother said.

'Absolutely, when they can be bothered to show up on the wards, that is,' I said in a jokey, off-hand manner, as though I knew all sorts of things about doctors and their tendency to be self-important, preoccupied and rarely seen with patients.

'Well, Rebecca, that's marvellous news. I mean, I am so happy for you,' Mother said. 'Not that I'm all that surprised, you're so clever, after all.'

'What a tremendous responsibility for someone your age,' said Rose. 'To think, you're not yet eighteen and already a job at a hospital. It won't interfere with your studies, will it? What about your A levels?'

'I can cope,' I said in a confident, doctor-like voice.

'God, I hope,' said Isobel, who still remained slightly dubious about my claim to have a real hospital job. She wrinkled her nose and said, 'Being around all those sick people, aren't you worried you'll catch something?'

'No,' I said quickly, though the thought suddenly struck me as troubling. 'A good immune system is all I need. Plenty of orange juice.'

'Well, let's have an orange juice toast!' said Mother, getting up at once and taking from the cupboard four tall glasses. 'Except mine will have a little shot of vodka in it.'

'And mine will have a little shot of ginger ale in it,' insisted Isobel, who had the disturbing habit of taking shot glasses and filling them with ginger ale or Coca-Cola or lemonade, pretending it was alcohol. 'After all, we are celebrating,' she said in a voice that mimicked perfectly our mother.

My job *was* in Lewisham Hospital, a fifteen-minute bus ride away, and was on the wards as I had claimed. But the job, which I had presented to my family as a medical job, a serious job with all sorts of implications for my future, was so far away from anything medical, so far away from anything requiring a skill, that it was remarkable that it was a paying job at all. What it was – this job that I'd made such a fuss of to my family – was that on weekends I pushed the sweet trolley from ward to ward and made change from a change belt I wore strapped over a kitchen apron. The requirements for my position were that I had to be able to decipher squash from juice, Cadbury Eggs from Walnut Whips, milk chocolate from plain chocolate, Hobnobs from digestive biscuits, all of these subtle but important distinctions. In addition, there were a great number of newspapers I had to be able to read the names of in order to dispense them correctly to my customers – so reading came into it. And, of course, there were maths skills – I had to be able to count to one hundred.

I never saw doctors because the sweet trolley was scheduled to arrive well away from when the doctors were doing their rounds. I rarely even saw nurses, except when they asked me for a Kit-Kat or to make change for the telephone. As for the patients, I saw them in abundance, lying in beds looking perfectly well so that I could not imagine what they were doing in hospital, or much worse with drips and urine bags strapped on to iron stands, half-clothed and half-conscious, some with open wounds that were being drained and others with missing limbs or jaundiced skin. I saw them beneath oxygen tents or moaning with pain behind a curtained cubicle where they lay unaided and, it seemed, uncared for. And I saw that remarkable thing, when a person so ill cannot walk to the toilet himself, cannot sit up, cannot eat, somehow will recover to the point where one morning he wakes, dons his street clothes, and walks out into the corridor to ride the dirty, graffitied lift down to the hospital exit. The same person who I might have seen looking half-dead days earlier might be sitting on the bus next to me. I found that amazing.

Lewisham Hospital was once a factory workhouse and the wards were long, drafty rooms with grimy windows that looked out on to other hospital buildings or deep into a courtyard where a cement rectangle was littered with garbage. It did not strike me as the sort of place people were likely to emerge from in a state of health – though, more often than not, this was the case. Even in the maternity ward, one of the more cheerful sections of the hospital, though still not terribly welcoming and plainly dirty, I felt a kind of slipping away of life. The babies were mostly well, the mothers were mostly well, but there was a great deal of crying from both; one got the impression from the new mothers that they were counting the minutes before they could escape out into the world, hopefully with their babies, before some disaster in the form of strep B or pneumonia attacked them or their offspring.

'How much to lend me your trolley and your stripy shirt so I can make a break?' one woman asked me. She was about my age and was wearing a pale blue nightdress with buttons down the centre so she could feed her baby, who was clapped on to one of her nipples as she ate the chocolate I'd sold her, five

Mars bars, one after the other in succession. 'Go on, tell me. I'll pay you for it. Anything to get out of here.'

I smiled. I told her she had a sweet baby.

'What, this one? He's ugly. My baby girl, she was a beauty. But you're an ugly little mug, heh? Aren't you? Aren't you?' She smiled down at the baby and rubbed his shock of dark hair, and I thought the place really was very strange indeed.

Though it was a pretty menial job, it was not meaningless. There are few interruptions during a regular day in hospital that patients enjoy more than the sweet trolley. I was hailed and rushed towards – okay, not rushed, I was limped towards, wheeled towards, slowly but enthusiastically teetered towards – whenever I made an appearance. The newspapers and magazines were pored over with a kind of saucer-eyed wonder as though they'd been smuggled inside from a faraway, free world. The joy that an adult man in backless pyjamas can exhibit over having an entire *Times* to himself on a Sunday is quite remarkable; more and more, I began to see my role in Lewisham Hospital as a kind of soothing face aligned with that of the vicar. At night I left my trolley in a closet outside the enormous, steamy hospital kitchen and went through the heavy double doors to wait along the main road for a bus, and I felt as though I'd done some small good in the world.

The salary, which was pitifully little, I saved for when Lea came home. I imagined taking them both out for a meal or perhaps treating them to a West End play. Not a day went by when I did not dream of us sitting in a black cab together en route to a marvellous ballet for which I'd secured excellent seats, or coming home half drunk, happy from a night out. I knew then, I thought I knew, that I wanted a lifetime taking in all the beautiful things the world had to offer: art, theatre, music. I'd never been to a theatre production in my life, never waited in anticipation for the gaudy curtain to rise and the clutches of lights in their metal racks to illuminate the actors as they stood in three dimensions before the audience that would judge them. I thought about such moments so frequently that at times I'd convinced myself that they were not daydreams but memories, and that as soon as Lea came home they would be enjoyed again.

One night as I climbed out of the bus on Lewisham Road and made my way up the hill to Blackheath, I saw James in the distance. I knew it was him even though the sky was darkening and there were any number of other men in long coats making the same ascent home. I recognized his walk, which was kind of a rolling lumber. I was a good five hundred yards behind him on a steep incline, and I had to run most of the way to catch up. When finally I managed to reach him, just at the dip of the heath, carved into the land during the war from an exploding bomb, he smiled broadly and looped his arm around my shoulders.

'Hello, stranger. Your mother tells me you've joined the working world,' he said.

Breathless, I managed, 'Hospital job . . . crap . . . forget it.'

'This makes me concerned. You aren't thinking of leaving school, are you?'

'Leaving what? School?' I stopped in my tracks, swallowed, and tried to catch my breath long enough to utter, 'God, no, is that what she told you? I'm planning to go to university, so of course I'm not leaving school.'

'Don't get me wrong. She didn't say you were leaving school, just that you were working in Lewisham Hospital. She sounded very proud. Your mother is not such a horrible person, you know. You always act as though she is, but whenever I speak with her she's—'

'When have you been speaking with her?' I asked, abruptly.

'Oh, just by the by, when our paths cross. She's very pleasant—'

'But why? Why would you talk with my mother?' Even as I asked this I knew it sounded all wrong, that I sounded childish and defensive. He could never understand why I wouldn't want him talking with Mother. Lea could, she had an intuitive understanding of strained parental relations. But James, who apparently had adored his mother, who took elaborate care of the paintings he inherited from her and was never known to speak an ill word about either of his parents, could not be expected to understand what it is like to be the daughter of someone such as my mother; who had only recently ceased to try to dress both Isobel and myself in miniskirts and halter tops and whose ability to charm men through casual conversations that took place 'by the by', as James described, had been honed to a fine art.

'Well, why *shouldn't* I speak with her?' he asked, genuinely. 'I mean, she's there in the house.'

'You didn't used to talk with her,' I said. Trying to recover myself, I added quickly, 'I just wondered what made her decide to strike up a conversation with you, that's all.'

'Oh, well,' he said and shrugged. And in that gesture he seemed to shake off the pointed tone of our conversation, which floated back down to normal. We began walking up the hill again, our steps in sync. He'd long since removed his arm from my shoulder and stood a good distance away from me now, I noticed, but at least the situation was recovered. Only for a moment, as it turned out. James said, 'She asked me about Lea, that's all.'

'Have you heard from Lea?'

'That's what I was telling your mother,' he said. 'I've written her reams of letters, sending them in careful order so that they arrive at the right time at whatever hotel she is staying in and she has sent me back *one line* on the back of a card she'd also used as a coaster – obviously used as a coaster because it had a ring mark around it!'

He said this in a jolly manner, as though such behaviour from Lea was on the one hand insulting but on the other completely in character, and therefore lovable. He shook his head and looked up to the stars. But I could tell there was more to it. We walked a few more steps and then I said, 'So what did the one line say?'

'Oh, it said. Well, it said—' He stopped now and stuffed his hands deep into his coat pockets, coughed once and looked away. 'It said she wasn't feeling very well.'

Since beginning my job at the hospital I'd begun carrying with me a kind of mental encyclopedia of every imaginable illness and so instantly a catalogue of possible diseases from which Lea was suffering raced through my thoughts. Pneumonia, for some reason, featured largely, also mononucleosis. She was just the right age to get one of the terrible wasting diseases that strike young adults: multiple sclerosis or lupus. I had an image in my mind of her covered in a mask of red, raw-looking skin and my whole body shivered with the thought of it.

'Well, can't she come home?' I asked.

'She's in goddamned America, that's just it. I rang the hotel, of course, but she wasn't in.'

'Did you leave a message?' I was always so practical, even then, seven months shy of my eighteenth birthday, I had that take-charge sort of disposition that made people slightly uneasy.

'I did, yes. But . . . er . . . we don't have a phone so she can't ring back.'

'Why didn't you leave her *our* number? We have a phone. You know we have a phone.' I was so worried about Lea, who in my mind had gone from having the mask-like signature of lupus to developing enormous glands and frequent fainting spells requiring oxygen, drips, all the intravenous tubing I saw at the hospital and which, deep down inside myself, scared me half to death.

'I don't know your phone number,' James said, with an incredulous smile. 'I've never had any reason to know it, have I?'

We walked along now in silence, both of us slightly annoyed with the other. As much as anything I was angry at myself, for if James took a dislike to me now, all my grand plans of surprising them with tickets to a show or concert would never take place. Our threesome would dissolve and Lea would recede from my life permanently. The prospect of this was too terrible, and I knew I ought not to argue with James. On the other hand, I don't think I ever felt quite so grown up as when I managed to pick a fight with another woman's husband.

'Obviously, you must ring her again and, if she is not there, leave a message with our number for her to call.'

'Yes,' he said. '*Obviously*, I will do that.'

'Eight five two, double seven six. You won't forget?'

'Eight five two, double seven six,' he repeated.

'And if she's not well, then she'll just have to come home. She can't be thousands of miles away and ill, on her own, in a foreign country – *thousands* of miles away.'

'Rebecca, she may only have a head cold,' he said.

'A head cold or, you know, a form of leukaemia,' I said. James looked at me as though I'd lost my mind. 'It *happens*,' I insisted. 'I see it every day at the hospital; otherwise healthy young people besieged by a blood disease—'

'Every day? You see otherwise healthy young women dying of leukaemia *every day*? While pushing the sweet trolley?'

'I see a great deal while pushing that trolley, James, I can tell you,' I said with an appalled manner.

'Am I to believe that you are selling Cadbury's Fruit and Nut to young women clutching on to the last straws of their short lives *every day*? Let me get this straight,' he said, pausing now on the pavement and miming out my absurd job. 'Thank you, madam, that will be fifteen pence. Good to see you enjoying a nice sweet as you slide tragically into a coma. But of course I see such as you *every day*!'

I laughed, as serious an egg as I was, I could not resist James when he acted out his jokes. Something about the way he moved, the expressions on his face, the attention he gave to ordinary life. I watched him pretending to make change from a palmful of coins. He picked through the imaginary coins with a suddenly feminized finger, discarding some, setting aside others. 'Madam, you are short by tuppence, and in your condition the hospital is not prepared to extend credit—'

I laughed and begged him to stop, which he did finally with

a wink in my direction. We walked in unison, turning in at the gate to our mutual house, which he held open for me in a gentlemanly fashion. I felt happy, I felt wonderful. I'd had an argument with a man and then recovered. That seemed utterly marvellous, almost like an opportunity that I'd unexpectedly come across. Then, with a feeling in my stomach like being car sick, I realized I had never actually told James I was the sweet-trolley girl. Mother must have told him. She'd done that, she'd found out what my pitiful little job was and reported it to him in a manner, undoubtedly, that drew him to laugh in collusion with her over my adolescent seriousness, my lofty and comic claims, my pathetic attempt to seem more like a woman and less like a girl. My 'hospital' job, which was really not. I could not stand this – what was it? – undermining. I turned to James at the door, my eyes ablaze.

'What is my phone number?' I demanded.

'Eight five two, double seven—' He paused, trying to remember.

'Six,' I said.

'I was going to say six.'

'Go call her. Right now. I want to know she is all right.'

We went straight into our part of the house and I knocked on Mother's bedroom door. 'Is she in?' I asked Isobel, who was watching television on Mother's bed.

'No, and please don't use the phone because I can't hear when you—'

I picked up the receiver and turned down the volume on the television. Isobel began a protest but I cut her short with a glare that could have rendered stone to dust. James stood uneasily at the door and was persuaded to enter the bedroom only after a great deal of impatient hand-gesturing on my part. He then fished out a scrap of notepaper on which he'd written the hotel phone number and handed it to me. I dialled, made sure a connection was established, then handed him the phone. I took Isobel by the arm and led her out of the bedroom and into the kitchen.

'But that's my show!' she moaned.

'Where is she?' I asked.

'Who? Mom? She's at work, of course.'

I read the clock, it was twenty past six. Saturday night and twenty past six, a very unlikely time for an estate agent to be at work. What Isobel had meant was that she was with Stephen Price. The imbecile. I had no reason to think he was an imbecile but I'd decided he was. I cursed him briefly, then returned my obsessive thinking to the thought of Mother speaking to James. I kept imagining her and James talking, kept hearing my mother's inane giggling laugh as she described for him what my job at the hospital was and how I'd made it out to be some research or medical job, a real job of the sort I so very much wanted one day to have.

'My job is as a sweet-trolley girl,' I told Isobel, who was regarding me warily. She looked at me the way one might at a slightly deranged but momentarily friendly drunk, who may launch into violence or hug you like their best friend, but who was not to be trusted in either case.

'Okay,' she said, nodding.

'I just sell squash and newspapers and stuff.'

She stopped nodding and we stood together in silence for a moment.

'Did Mother tell you already that I was a sweet-trolley girl?' I asked.

'No.'

'What did she tell you?'

'That I was not to lock the inside door because she didn't have her keys.'

'About *me*.'

'Oh, nothing.'

I sighed and let go of Isobel's arm, which I realized I was still hanging on to. I felt tired. I felt comprehensively knackered and, more than anything else, just sad. 'Well, now you know that what I do is sell sweets and newspapers. I don't work with doctors or the nursing staff or anything like that.'

She looked up at me with new interest. 'Do you sell Smarties?' she asked.

I thought for a moment. 'No.'

'Do you sell chewing gum?'

'No.'

'Well, anything?' she said, desperately. 'Mars Bars?'

'Yeah, those.'

'Can you get me some?'

'Yes. I'll get you a whole box of them,' I promised. Of all the people in the world at that moment, I loved my little sister.

'She's not there,' James called from Mother's bedroom. He walked out to the kitchen where I was talking to Isobel. In his overcoat, with his satchel slung over his shoulder and his scarf sweeping down in front of him, he looked oversized for our small rooms, enormous and male and all wrong in the female world of our household. I had the sudden fear that Mother would walk in and find him there and that they would have further reason to talk together and – God forbid – become friendly. I suddenly wanted him back in the upstairs portion of the house that contained him much better and where he was safe from Mother's intrusion.

'I'll come get you when she rings back,' I promised. 'Whatever time of day.'

'Or night,' he said. 'She's not very good at time zones; she may ring at four in the morning.'

'I don't mind,' I said. 'We've got an extension cord. I'll put the phone in the hall and if it rings I'll come get you.'

'You're a good girl, Rebecca,' he said as we walked down the dark corridor to the door that opened out into the rest of the house. I let him out, then I returned to Mother's room and rigged the wires so that the phone could be moved out to that same hallway. I knew Mother would object – she liked the phone close to her bed so if Stephen Price called she could reach for it in slumber and talk to him with the receiver buried deep in the covers. But at that moment, I didn't care.

*

I watched the phone all evening as I sorted out equations in practice for my A levels and committed to memory the simple physical laws that govern our universe. The law of the conservation of energy, the principle of virtual work, the conservation of leptons, of baryons, the conservation of charge. I drank four cups of tea and tried to imagine the way I would answer a question about how radio broadcasts are made possible by electromagnetic waves, and how Radio 3 is one frequency and Radio 4 another, which has to do with the oscillation of these waves. After a few hours of this I gave up and went to bed, then woke with a start as though the phone had rung and I'd missed it, which was not the case. What I heard was Mother coming home. She'd put the chain across the inside door and that sound, far removed from a bell sound, was enough akin to a phone ringing that I woke, then fell back asleep, then woke again. This time I gave up and turned on a light. I decided to return to my physics but my eyes would not focus and I had to read the same sentence three or four times in order to make sense of it. I went out to the hall where the phone lay, watching it like one would a zoo tiger that you've come a long way to see and all it does is lie there and sleep.

Finally, just past midnight, the phone rang. I picked it up on the first ring, half expecting it to be James ringing to see if Lea had called, though I knew this was impossible as James didn't have a telephone. I said hello and waited a few seconds for a reply. But the caller remained silent at the other end.

'Who is this?' I asked, booming loudly into the receiver.

'Lea.'

In my mind I could picture Lea's voice and my own, sets of undulating parabolas, mine sharply rising, hers gently sloping. Sound waves across the Atlantic. 'Are you all right?' I asked. She made a noise like she was considering this, and I told her to hang on while I went upstairs and got James.

A thought struck me. 'Where are you calling from?' I asked, just in case we were disconnected. She told me Washington but

I wanted the phone number, which she didn't know or perhaps just felt was too much trouble to tell me.

I dashed upstairs and then, at the landing, stopped and wondered whether it was appropriate to search for a man in his own house at such an hour. There was a light on in the kitchen and I looked there first but found no sign of James. I looked in the music room and then, by accident, opened up a closet that housed the hoover and two broken chairs. Finally I went in the direction of the bedroom and rapped on the door. I expected James to be there instantly, to have been awaiting this moment as eagerly as I had been, but there was no reply. I knocked again, louder, and then walked in. I cannot tell you how much it was not like me to walk into a man's bedroom. I was shy about all things physical and found it difficult enough to see other women naked, let alone risk the chance of seeing a full-grown man. If I'd thought about it long enough I'd have found myself incapable, utterly paralysed at the door, willing my feet to move but finding they had fixed themselves like marble pillars into the floor. Perhaps it was all those days walking up and down wards full of men in various stages of undress, but for some reason I had no hesitancy about entering James's bedroom. Knock, knock, then walk on in. I was standing in a dark room in front of their crumpled bed when his voice startled me, coming from behind.

'Hello?' he said, standing at the threshold of his own bedroom.

I could actually feel the blood rising, a river of heat moving up my neck and across my face. 'Phone call,' I said, knowing I was blushing crimson.

'Lea?'

I nodded, relieved. First, for having managed to find James so he could speak to his wife, and second that James was fully dressed. He'd been in his office reading. His glasses, which he never wore to read, were hanging by an earpiece from his shirt pocket.

We went back downstairs and I grabbed for the phone as

though a wind might carry it away, handing it to James. Then I went to the kitchen table, which was about as far away as I could get without going into the bathroom, in order to give him some privacy. I waited a few minutes, then a few more, studying at intervals the clock on the wall. It was ten past twelve, which meant that Lea was ringing him at ten past seven in Washington. I sat at the table and tried to occupy myself. My school books were there so I concentrated on physics questions, about how all enzymes are proteins but not all proteins are enzymes. About density and pressure, velocity and force. The information went into my head in clotted, meaningless phrases I could not unravel and I gave up finally and sat quietly, chewing the back of my pencil and waiting for James. I peeked out once and saw him sitting on the floor, his back braced against the wall, his long legs bent at the knee and the telephone cord dangling at his elbow. He spoke in a low, soothing manner, with long silences connecting clusters of seemingly disjointed conversation. I went back to my table and sat there determined not to move until I heard the sound of James rising from the floor and hanging up the phone. I waited, conscious of waiting, the way one waits at a bus station, until finally I heard footsteps.

I was up immediately, stepping nimbly on my toes into the hall, where I turned and nearly collided, not with James, but with Stephen Price, who was making his way out of Mother's bedroom and down the hall, past the kitchen, where normally at this hour I would be sleeping. He was wearing his suit, but the jacket was loose over his shoulders and his necktie was in his pocket. Though we nearly ran straight into each other, he hadn't noticed or seen me. And he didn't see me now as he ambled with the quick silence of a cat burglar down the hall to where James sat on the floor. I stood still, my palm clapped over my mouth, waiting for the moment he either tripped over James's feet or noticed him there on the floor. To anyone else the meeting of these two men would have no significance at all. Mother would find it not in the least bit embarrassing, and if it weren't for the time of day, even Rose would see it as inconsequential. But to me the chance meeting of James and Stephen Price was a colossal disaster, a personal tragedy, a moment so terrible I could only stand at the top of the hall in mesmerized horror thinking, *no go back, no go back*. What would James think, seeing Mother's lover sneaking back to his wife in the middle of the night? Well, he wouldn't think anything, he'd *know*. Not that he didn't know already. But there it was. Proof! My mother's unscrupulousness, her shabby manners, her thieving lovesick heart. I watched as the moment prepared itself, then occurred. Stephen Price cleared his throat, which alerted James to his presence. And James, in a fluid movement as though he'd spent his life dodging out of the path of adulterous men on late-night calls to single mothers, moved crablike a few feet to the right, enabling Stephen to get through the door. The entire shocking, dreadful moment was over in a matter of seconds. While I stood listening to my heart pound and wondering why on earth Mother had decided to let that man in tonight, of all nights, James concluded his call.

9

James sat at the table, put his head in his hands and said Lea sounded very bad. I cleaned the table of books and notepads, leftover coffee mugs part filled with dregs and curdling milk. I wanted a clear space between us, a place bare of the clutter of my family's life, where it would be possible to concentrate on James's patient, elocutionary voice as he described the situation with Lea. She was ill; she did not know with what. She felt weak, she said; she felt confused at times. She found talking a struggle, and obsessed on small, personal objects: the razor she shaved her legs with, which she'd forgotten two hotels back and thought of every day, missing it as one might a friend; her books that she found at the moment unreadable but that she wished to accompany her everywhere she went; her violin, which she'd convinced herself would be stolen unless she watched carefully, and, more than anything else, her plane ticket home. She wept copiously, and the weeping took the form of silent tears which came with a determination that seemed entirely of their own volition.

'The tears arrive, drain from my eyes, then seem to work themselves back up to the cloud which is in my head all the time, a fuzzy dark cloud that gathers them up and hangs heavier and heavier, until I find myself crying again,' she'd described for James.

'You must come home,' he told her.

'Why? How? I cannot imagine *how* to do that. Though of course I am not playing; I've missed two concerts already. I told them I have a virus but now it's gone on too long and I'm getting looks as though nobody quite believes the virus explanation. Everyone would find it a relief if I went home. It just seems impossible somehow. I am here; you are a million miles away—'

'Get on a plane.'

'But my ticket has a date on it. I can't just fly anytime. Besides, I don't know how to get there.'

'Get where?'

'You know, to the, oh—'

There was a pause and James wondered if she'd hung up the phone. 'Lea?' he said.

'Yes?'

'Take a taxi to the airport. They have taxis in America, don't they?'

'Yes, I suppose. No, it's too much trouble. I'm exhausted. I—'

He'd had to beg her to continue the conversation. Several times she lapsed into tears, then told him she wanted to be left alone, told him to hang up the phone, told him to go.

'Well, she has to – she must – come home,' I said, pinned to my seat in fascinated anxious alarm. I wanted to hear more about Lea and at the same time dreaded every piece of James's description so much that I had to interrupt him, stop him from continuing, find a solution. 'She can't let herself be dragged along like that with no recourse. She can use the ticket anyway, even if it is for a different date, she'll just have to pay a fee. Does she have any money with her? Or a credit card?'

'Yes, of course. Yes,' James said, but he seemed preoccupied. He sat curled over himself, his back rounded at the shoulders, staring down. The moon outside the window burned with a whiteness that illuminated the clouds passing by; it was such a huge, unmoving thing, so bright it was almost intrusive, like a low-lying sun that blinds you through the window. Even while I thought of all the terrible consequences of not saving Lea, saving her *right now*, that moon struck me as an eerie, magnificent eye watching us. I pulled the shade.

I got up to make James a cup of tea, then on an impulse reached instead to the cupboard where my mother kept her Scotch. I knew nothing about alcohol, the bottles all looked the same to me: shiny, green, with embossed labels written in fine script and foiled ribbons decorating the spouts. When I pulled one or two away from the others, they made the same sound milk bottles did in the morning when collected, a particular clinking sound that I'd begun to associate with England, as we'd never had milk delivered in America. I found one marked Scotch, a very beautiful bottle, I remember, with a dark, robust base and a cork that came away with a single hollow musical note, sending up a cloud of air rich with the scent of the gold liquid within.

I'd never before drunk Scotch or any other spirit. I'd been told that whisky made a nice addition to vanilla ice cream if you added a tablespoon, and that you could set it alight to make a flambé, which seemed to me an entertaining way of having dinner, but drinking the stuff outright and deliberately had never struck me as a pleasant business, and I had no idea how much to pour. I'd seen my mother countless times preparing herself an evening drink, a ritual drink known as 'cuppy', a name I cannot remember the origins of, but which I think I had, in my toddlerhood, invented. When she got home from work cuppy was her first immediate preoccupation. It included a quick cigarette, pulled at anxiously so the ash grew long and fired red for a good half-inch, followed by another which was more casually enjoyed and spent some time in the ashtray as Mother sipped at the amber drink that she set before her like a special mystical brew. I'd seen her prepare cuppy so many times and yet, this night with James in my kitchen, the amount of whisky she poured, and how she served it to herself, escaped me entirely. I filled a tumbler with enough Scotch to make a person sick, looked at it and then added some more.

It did not occur to me to add water to the bottle in order to hide what I had done. The fact that I did not feel the need to make secret my use of Mother's liquor, and that I knew intrinsically that she trusted me – trusted me with the kind of faith one usually reserves for airline pilots and dentists – to be what I always was, sensible, earnest to a fault, unwaveringly and, to her, infuriatingly correct in all things, spoke volumes about our relationship. There was tension, yes, and a constant low-grade battle that never seemed to conclude, but there was a certain amount of mutual respect. I did not think to myself that I must concoct an explanation about the missing liquor. I suppose that in the back of my mind I knew that by stating the truth, that I'd given a bit to James who was distressed over his wife, I would be at once believed.

I closed the top on the whisky without any thought of Mother, except to wish I'd taken in exactly how she made her drinks, and brought James his glass. He laughed when he saw it; so much Scotch that he'd have had to be very foolish, or as ignorant as I was, to finish it all. I felt a moment of acute, spine-tingling embarrassment at having no idea how much whisky to give a person, but he thought I'd been making a point with the gesture, like I had handed it to him saying, 'Here, you might need this' as a kind of companionable joke.

He rose from his chair and went to the sink, where a line of clean glasses sat drying in the rack. He took one and brought it back to the table, poured some of his whisky into it and handed the glass back to me.

'You'll have to help me with this,' he said. I remember the moment he put that glass down, how it hit the table with a gentle knock, how I watched the Scotch lilt and settle, how James looked at me with a different expression than I'd seen before. There are countless stories about the rite of passage surrounding drinking, nothing different occurred on that night than when a father takes his son to the pub on his eighteenth birthday, or in college dormitories across America when a beer keg – that crude machinery that always reminds me of something between an opium pipe and a horse's water trough – is tapped by one of the wiser, experienced boys to the amazement and satisfaction of a crowd of students eager for the initiation of shared drunkenness.

James set the glass in front of me and I understood at that moment that a change had taken place. I was no longer merely his acquaintance or, say, the younger, oddly selected friend his wife had made, no longer a child, no longer one who must be cossetted or kept ignorant of all the hazards and secrets of life. I took a sip and matched his gaze, showing him, I hoped, that I was up to it, that I was worthy and capable not only of hearing whatever he had to say, but of understanding and perhaps even comforting. The controlling nature that my mother always accused me of was not really anything more than a deeply feminized need to help, to manage things in order to bring about a specific positive outcome and to be found by others to be instrumental without being showy. In other words, to be the perfect fifties housewife, a goal that has seemed to be my legacy, sewn into me from birth, and from which I never will escape. Never. No matter how far I go in the opposite direction – a career woman without children – there would always be this need to hover and soothe, to don an apron and keep clenched within my palm a hidden, incriminating dust rag that would portray my inner self in an accurate, condemning, comical manner.

'Cheers,' said James, smiling defeatedly.

'Cheers,' I said, in an even tone.

There is something wonderful about drinking. I'm very cautious now because I know what alcohol does to people in my family – my father it turns out was an alcoholic – but there is a particular beauty in that fuzzy emotion, the fog of empty joy that surrounds you when you drink. I felt something opening up inside me; I felt a shadow lift. I had long held a guarded curiosity about James and Lea, a quiet seeking ensconced in all manner of finely tuned, almost religious respect. But with each sip of Scotch that reverent inquisitiveness became ever more ferocious, so that I felt impatient for it, as though for news from a missed homeland.

'How did you meet?' I asked, directly.

'At university,' James said. He looked at me, his own curiosity brewing, not over my question – what more natural line of conversation could there be than asking how a man met his wife – but because he saw something else inside me, in a place the Scotch had etched out, and it interested him.

'I'd had this wacky idea you'd met in childhood, like she had lived next door. Or perhaps that your parents had known one another and they'd flung you together for family holidays since you were schoolchildren.'

I don't know what made me say this – I hadn't thought either of these things. Perhaps it was to hide what I really thought, what I'd imagined, which was that they'd met when they were my age. I wanted to believe that. Every day I went to school hoping that one of the loutish, really rather brutal boys from the boys' school would seek me out, transformed by the mild, domestic kindness of love, and offer me his rough hand to hold. These boys, who walked loudly through the streets in packs and wore their neckties too short, or poorly tied, or flung over their shoulders in a defiant manner to mark them as rebels, who hung about the pubs on Friday nights hoping for a pint and who regularly called from the other side of the road rude, unspeakable things to the girls, were never, of course, going to be transformed in quite the manner my imagination required. They barked at us and called us dogs, they told us how fat we were in our black, uniform skirts. Girls without breasts of any size were ridiculed for being flat-chested – flat as a board, that was the expression. And those who were fully developed from an early age were mocked even more ferociously with hand gestures and licked lips.

We girls were not without our resources. We rolled our eyes and gave them the two-fingers-up sign and generally regarded them with a disdain as flimsy and full of bravado as their own cruel defence against our unwavering femaleness. We called names back, making sure to mention spots and smegma and dicklessness. Dicklessness was my invention, no English-bred girl would have thought of it. But I never used the term myself, I was in too vulnerable a position. For the worst ridicule, the truly unbearable insults that the meanest boys saved, were for girls like me, who were plain-faced but large-breasted, with hair that twisted unfashionably into Byzantine curls. I was despised for being such an utter disappointment, for the waste of size 36D breasts beneath an ugly face. The scorn I contended with, not on occasion but with regular frequency, whenever my route to school meant I had to pass a group of these mean-spirited, pitiless boys, was a more brutal and searing experience than I'd ever faced before or since. The fact that I would sit by myself at night, with my black coffee and my diet-aid chocolate (a sweet cube with a caramel consistency that expanded in your stomach and was meant to give you the feeling of fullness), and dream of one of these horrible, grimy boys turning his attention to me with new benevolence, with *love*, is testimony to my desperation and hope, my teenage pride, and my willingness to play against the odds.

'How old were you?' I asked James. See? I could not stop myself. I wanted him to say they'd been seventeen.

'I was twenty-one,' he said. He paused and regarded me. He started to speak again but then shook his head.

'Go *on*,' I insisted. But he wouldn't say.

They'd met at York University – Lea had insisted on going to a real university and not simply a music college, which was what was expected of her – and their meeting had been something close to love at first sight. It delighted me to hear this, and immediately I regarded York as a city of infinite romantic possibilities. I had always suspected James and Lea had seen each other and instantly understood the messages of belonging and desire that make up 'real love', what I thought of as real love. When James described how they met it only further exacerbated my already absurd notion of the nature of attraction;

that it strikes suddenly, conclusively, a clean injection of what had not been before. That emotions are muddy, sometimes indecipherable magnets that lead us haphazardly in different, ruinous directions never occurred to me. My idea was that love was without the ugly complications of others – other wives or husbands, other children, other opposing forces of the heart – that coloured my mother's love life. I saw James and Lea as two free, unrestricted, almost heroic figures, whose destiny (I thought a great deal of destiny in those days) was to be together. The Scotch sent a river of fire down my throat and I almost said to James that I had always thought of them as fated in such a manner. I stopped myself. I had enough sense, I suppose, to realize that such a statement was either patently ridiculous or would sound so coming from me.

There had been a group of students at York who met on an informal basis to talk about writing. They were all studying English or languages and had dabbled in attempts at writing poetry or short stories. One or two had been working on longer pieces, a play or novel or series of linked stories, and they sat together under the guidance of a classics lecturer named Nigel Gaw to talk about how to better their craft. The majority of these students were young men. It is different now but at the time, during the seventies, it was the men who were thought to be the best candidates for the serious business of writing. I don't know how this could be as not much later writing groups would be composed almost entirely of women who seemed, for whatever reasons, far better at expressing themselves in every direction, but at the time the number of men was about three times that of women. Even if Lea had not been beautiful, with her pale, luminous skin and blonde hair which, though thin and fine, provided a soft, fluttery brightness around her face, she would definitely have been noticed. She wrote poetry, and James liked what she wrote, so much so that he found it impossible not to stare at her throughout the gathering, which occurred every Wednesday night at the dining hall. They became friendly immediately; within the first week of meeting they were lovers.

'She writes with a wonderful sense of cadence, as you would expect from a musician,' James said, then paused. 'And a spareness,' he added after a minute. 'There I was filling pages with hundreds of words and sentences, thinking that if I just wrote more and more it would become something. I had this habit of counting each day's effort. Two paragraphs or two pages or whatever, as though you can measure progress in such a way.'

Lea gave up writing eventually, as most people do. I wanted to ask if there was any of Lea's poetry around now, whether they'd kept it carefully in a place it would not be lost. That would be typical of me, to want to ensure the preservation and order of a thing, but the Scotch pushed those thoughts away and instead I came out with, 'Very male of you—'

'Yes, well.'

'—Measuring the length of everything.'

He laughed. I took another sip of Scotch. My throat burned and the stuff was foul, but I liked the effect. The thought occurred to me that if I drank Scotch on my way home from school those boys would not be able to bother me, I would be armoured. I would shoo them off like the harmless pests they were. I smiled, thinking this, and stared ahead, at a table lamp which had grown a modest halo around it like a ring from Saturn. James, who had always struck me as much older than myself, suddenly seemed like a boy my age.

'We were a couple all through university,' he said. 'You know the type who everyone assumes will get married, which of course we did. We had to. That sounds wrong. I mean, no, we didn't have to, I wanted to. Eventually, when she finished her degree and went back to her music – which she was always going to do, there was no question – she started touring again and was away for long stretches. I needed some way of being linked to her, so of course marriage, I thought. I wanted stability, a normal life, a normal *mental* life,' he said.

Mental life, that is what he said. Already he knew, even then, that there was a turbulence inside him that matched Lea's, not identically but in kind. This illness, this depression of Lea's, which carried her away like a rip tide carries a swimmer helplessly from the shore, was not the first one. She suffered from depression periodically throughout her life. Even as a child she remembered vast stretches of murky, unhappy time, a sense of darkness above her, a sense of quiet, intolerable solitude. Then she'd been thought of as slightly hysteric, sickly, but her tendency to be cast into dark, unmoving moods only further convinced her ambitious father of her musical talent. He would remind her that famous composers were often moody people. She was taken to the doctor and told she was anaemic, given tablets and made to take a molasses-based 'medication' to cure her ills.

I might have asked then what James meant by needing a normal mental life but I was too busy imagining how James – who may perhaps have been when Lea met him a more closed, more crudely thinking young man than the one before me – had softened, evolved, become humanized. All of this, the work of love. I had the simultaneous picture in my mind of one of the boys who taunted me, a lanky wide-toothed boy with wiry hair and a receding chin, not good-looking or winning in any way, but fierce, with a quick enough mind that he invented terrible, original ways of expressing his feelings for me, which seemed to centre around revulsion and disgust. I thought of him one day seeing me from across the street and beginning his calling out as he usually did, then, abruptly, pausing and looking again. Really looking and seeing me all at once in a different light. In my fantasy I was thinner than I was naturally, with a long waist and straight, narrow shoulders and hair that did not fling itself out like a bush woman's but flowed in an even, shining plane down my back. I was not hunched over my books to hide my chest or walking in the rapid shuffle that was my usual gait to transport me as quickly as possible to school, but striding forward, erect and graceful, with a grown-up confidence and a carefree air. The boy would look at me and then, with a quick glance in either direction, cross the road, asking in a chivalrous, dated fashion if he could walk with me. This boy, who I believe was named

Larry, and who had made my life a misery several mornings a week for the whole of my time at school, would apologize for his former behaviour with great humility and an obvious new respect for me, his former victim. Flatteringly, beseechingly, he would eke his way towards my forgiveness. At some point I would pause and regard him with a bashful but knowing smile, the way I imagined Judi Dench in her younger days would regard a suitor. Then – and here is where my fantasy takes a vicious relishing turn – I would kick him between the legs, a single, diabolical blow that would send him sprawling on the pavement, on the girls' side of the street, and every passing girl from the most downtrodden to the most popular, would give him a good whack as they passed by. Thus ending, for ever, the taunting of schoolgirls.

I told James this.

'You're a funny girl,' he said, shaking his head. 'Who would know that inside that prim exterior exists a violent heart?'

I laughed. I liked the image of me having a violent heart. It made me sound interesting, like a mythical figure or a queen. I did not regard myself as interesting in the slightest. Not even James could lift me from my secret knowledge of myself at that time, that there was something mysteriously wrong with me that singled me out from other girls. On good days I told myself it was only that I was American, a foreigner in a country which automatically assumed that foreigners were slightly uncouth hangers-on from villainous stock, greedy for the riches of English life. But on bad days I saw myself as specifically objectionable, for being too tall and bulky, for having a fat bottom and a suspicious, overquick mind that constantly observed everything around me, drawing unnecessary, sometimes ungenerous conclusions about the really quite innocent, unremarkable lives of others.

I often wished I were like my sister, who could be friends with any girl, even one with parents who had some distinctly insalubrious aspect to them – for example, the father of one of her best friends had once been imprisoned – without having these facts constantly nag at an insatiable imagination. Isobel was a girl who just enjoyed people for who they were, who let things ride, and who was able to instantly push aside any information that interfered with the breezy, easy nature of her friendships. I was the exact opposite. The way I calculated and observed, forever sifting through information and assessing the motives and character of people – of whom I was often very fond – had choked dead almost every friendship I'd started. Nowhere was this habit more practised than in the constant devotion I had for Lea and James, who unlike the girls in my school did not withdraw from me and my disturbing nature, or attack me in a desperate attempt to stop my silent, vigilant attention.

A violent heart. I looked at James, who was sitting more easily now, his shoulders back, his long legs splayed, and reconsidered whether I liked the idea of his finding me violent. Or heartless, or whatever it was he had said.

'I'm not that way,' I protested, finding to my surprise that my voice sounded angry. I was not angry, not in the least. I was terrified that James now saw me as menacing and nosy. That he thought what my mother did, that I was too serious. And that he was one step from rejecting me, if he had not already done so.

'Rebecca?' James said. He looked at me closely and then reached forward and for a moment – a delicate, extraordinary moment – he rested his hand on my cheek. 'I didn't mean—'

'That's okay,' I interrupted. 'I misunderstood. Forget it. I'm always getting things wrong.'

He smiled uneasily and picked up his glass, then set it down again. 'It's late. I better make a move and try to get some sleep. Thank you for the chat,' he said. 'Oh, and the use of your phone! Especially that.'

He stood up, suddenly seeming terribly large, and I walked him to the door talking nervously, frantic to make up for whatever weirdness I'd inflicted on our evening. I cannot remember what I said but it was full of condolences that Lea was ill, and reassurances that all would be well when she finally came home so we could look after her.

'I'm no cook but I can make chicken soup,' I said. I remember saying that remark which would make no sense to him anyway because chicken soup is known only to Americans as a kind of cure-all tonic for the ill. An Englishman would have no idea what I was talking about. He nodded his head – I think at that point he just wanted to leave – and said goodbye. When the door closed, placing us back in our separate parts of the house, I felt dizzy with relief that he'd gone and sick with worry about what on earth I'd babbled on about. I cupped my hands over my eyes and shook my head, really I was so uneasy about myself that an exchange with any man, even someone as well-meaning as James, took a weighty toll on my fragile ego. I rubbed my eyes and then blinked, going back down the hallway and into my kitchen/bedroom. When I turned the corner I saw perhaps the one person I'd rather not have had to contend with at just that minute, my mother, standing in the spot in which not three minutes earlier James had stood. I did not know whether she knew James had been there, whether she had counted two glasses or noticed how two opposing chairs had been pushed out from the table.

'You're up late,' she said. I nodded. She looked at me steadily, deciding something. Then she said, 'Can you tell me why the telephone was strung all the way across the house?'

'We were waiting for Lea to call. I didn't want to interrupt you in your . . .' I paused, and in this moment of ill-timed hesitation destroyed what might have otherwise been an innocuous exchange. 'Bedroom,' I said weakly.

She glanced away for a moment, her mouth dropping open ever so slightly, then looked straight into my face. 'Right,' she said, turning on her heel.

I had not mentioned Stephen Price. I would not have done so in any case, even if I'd been thinking of him, which I was not. His brief, almost spectral appearance earlier had nearly vanished from my mind, so fraught was I about Lea's distant, pleading helplessness, then James's opinon of me, the whole dream-like alcohol enhanced evening.

She marched back to her bedroom, her peach satin dressing gown pulled tight around her waist, her feathered slippers slapping against her heels. There are relics from my childhood that are laden with significance, and that satin gown ranks high among the many powerful objects, most of which belonged to my mother, that can summon up whole sections of my life more accurately than any photograph. The dressing gown with its flowing, movie-star movement, drawn tight against the hip so glimmering creases rose with every step. She was able to make bold statements in that dressing gown. She was able to shrug off the mild, victim-like quality that many women find themselves adopting in their middle years and make a mockery out of maternal self-sacrifice, which she did not believe in anyway.

'You can think what you like, Rebecca, I cannot stop you from hating me, judging me, making out everything I do is wrong,' she said, pausing long enough to lock me in a gaze that outlawed any dissension on my part. You will not judge me, the look said, and yet she claimed that is what I had already done.

'I didn't say that—'

'You didn't need to! But don't go acting snooty about my having a friend when you invite a man into your own bedroom on the very same evening.'

My *bedroom*, is that what she'd thought I'd done? Invite James into my bedroom? I'd let him sit in our dining room, which was admittedly next door to the kitchen, which was in fact my bedroom, but everyone who entered the house had no choice but to walk through what was my bedroom. I might have told her that: that everybody from the man who read the gas meter to the lady who collected for Christian Aid had at one time or another stood in my bedroom, that her own boyfriend had in fact walked through my bedroom this very night, but I was dumbstruck, humiliated. My mind worked well enough but my speech was drowsy with alcohol. I could not muster the words to fend her off as she stood scornfully on the threshold of her own bedroom, a real room with a door and a lock, and bore into me with a remark so cutting I literally reeled from it, pitching myself backwards as she spoke. 'There's something sinister about making friends with a woman you intend to replace, Rebecca. Don't you think?'

'Replace,' I repeated. 'I couldn't possibly.'

She crossed her arms and regarded me with a narrow, pitying look. 'No, you couldn't. That is correct. Because she is the first wife. It's a very definite, unmovable thing. She is the first one he wanted, so no matter what happens – no matter how loving or deserving or sexy you might be ever, *ever* – just remember you are always second! You may not think me too clever but I know that much. I *know*. That is the lesson I have learned, my life's message. I can't stop myself – can you? Or are you just as dumb as the rest of us?'

This speech, which had crescendoed midstream, came to that quiet, sad conclusion. Are you just as dumb as the rest of us, she had asked me. The rest of us women, she meant. The rest of us keepers of secret loves and morbidly hopeless dreams. Are you going to harbour an ill-spent longing, are you going to make yourself unhappy? I saw at once that to correct her with the truth – that I had no designs on James, that he did not interest me that way, that I was in any case too young, too inexpert and naive, that I had not inherited the sophisticated manner that had made her precociously successful with men – would be to push away the one hope we had for a reconciliatory conclusion to this bizarre, misguided exchange. And so for once I allowed her the privilege of being my mother, of being right for that simple reason only.

'Yes,' I said, breathing out heavily. I owed her this, my capitulation, my respect. 'I mean, yes, I can stop myself doing anything silly.'

'Good girl,' she said, and that is all she needed to say.

*

Nothing more of the incident was mentioned, but I thought I noticed my mother doing something like spying. Not spying exactly, for she did not go through my clothes and possessions; did not sit up at night waiting to see who I let through the front door, did not ask me leading questions or try to corner me in a lie. She was far too sophisticated for that sort of amateur espionage, what she did instead was lie low and wait. My mother is sure she understands all the wiles of the female heart. She had always been such a victim to her own that she'd learned to study it, to understand and accept it the way one might a long-standing enemy. And she knew, or thought she knew, that I would find it impossible not to indulge my own, secreted passion, what she thought was my passion. Not that she imagined I'd do anything deliberate – she did not blame me for any of the ways I might feel – only that once the choice of love is made, it is hard to unmake it. There is a moment early on when it is possible to walk away, clean-handed and free. Unscathed. But once you fall in love, once you let yourself fall or push yourself there, it takes you places you didn't know it would, perhaps where you did not want to go. Mother knew this and she waited.

I thought I was innocent. I thought her a fool.

Lea came home shortly after that night she spoke to James. I expected her to look slightly different, to seem tired, to cough into her fist like the people I saw every weekend at the hospital. I spent a great deal of time speaking to ill people, whole weekends wandering from one ward of them to another along the drafty corridors of Lewisham Hospital, steering my sweet trolley over dirty linoleum that smelled like a mixture of urine and antiseptic and the dank mop that the janitor whisked about. I passed people in wheelchairs and stretchers and varying degrees of inertia, lying in bed or propped up on pillows. Over the months I'd grown so used to this that it did not even disturb me all that much. Occasionally, yes, when I saw a sick child, a dying child, a baby. But that was rare. Those children were always cordoned off, behind colourful doors decorated in clowns and Winnie-the-Pooh.

I saw Lea in her black cape coat walking with James to the corner shop. She'd been home over a week and this was the first time, to my knowledge, that she'd left the house. It was a beautiful summer day and she was the only person in long sleeves, let alone a coat. Her eyes seemed sunken and dull, her cheekbones stood out and she'd developed a rash – eczema, I think – on the patch of skin between her eyebrows. But she was still Lea, still beautiful, no amount of ill health could rob her of that.

'It's wonderful to see you,' I said, and found, strangely, that my words were more than hollow, they were deceitful. It was not wonderful to see her, it was awful to see her. She seemed to have shrunk. Standing next to her, I felt myself overlarge, ebulliently and obscenely healthy. My sunburned skin, the slight moisture beneath my arms, the flush of heat in my cheeks, all the signs of movement and youth of which I would normally be completely unaware, seemed at once ostentatious and unclean. I was ashamed of myself, for my voice, which seemed overloud, my fleshy hips, my restless hands.

She made a motion with her mouth, almost like she were forming words, then gave up with the effort.

'Don't worry, you'll be better soon,' I said to fill the void that had at once opened between us. This, too, sounded remarkably wrong, patronizing, almost hostile. I wanted to see a sign she was going to be better, a glimmer of her former, wacky, animated self, but there was none. Just this shell, and it made me impatient, wanting more.

Really, all I wished to show her at that time was my love. Years later I would think of this moment and wish that I'd had the confidence to touch her, to soothe her in some small, unspoken way. I have found when James has been depressed that words are sometimes wasted, tortuous, almost dangerous. I've knelt before him and kissed his hands, pushed my palms beneath his shirt and rubbed his shoulders, curled myself around him and felt, body upon body, just exactly how he feels. Depression causes chemical changes in the brain. And that chemistry, in addition to changing the way the brain works, literally how it fires, alters every aspect of the physical self. It can make you cold, your hands, your feet, the tip of your nose, as though you were dying from the extremities inwards. It can make you sweat and your sweat smell like someone different than yourself. When James is depressed, when he is heading there, before he actually sinks down into the well, I can smell it on him. I can feel it on his skin. If I'd touched Lea there on the pavement at least I'd have known, if I were paying attention, a little more about how she felt. I ought to have touched her and then walked away. But instead I let her stand, looking at me from across the abyss of her depression, and grow anxious at her inability to speak.

I could see it was exhausting for her to look at me.

They kept to themselves. I understood, after that one encounter with Lea, that this was the right and only thing for them to do. Had she come home with a strange American flu or been diagnosed with any other malady, ME or diabetes, she would have rested and recovered. Nobody would have expected her to pull herself together and carry on. James had told me she was suffering depression but to the rest of the world he maintained the lie that Lea had become exhausted on tour and contracted chicken pox, which she'd never had in childhood. It was me who suggested chicken pox, a relatively harmless virus in childhood, it is much worse for adults. Fierce, painful, and it lasts weeks. By offering chicken pox as an excuse James could buy himself two weeks free of visitors and then, for a long while after that, he could claim Lea was too upset about her appearance to be seen. In all, he could string out the lie for at least five weeks, I told him, perhaps longer if he claimed a few of the spots had developed a streptococcal infection.

'But wouldn't she have scarring?' James asked.

I smiled cleverly. 'Not if she doesn't scratch.'

Despite my being handy for this lie, I was not otherwise included in their lives. I told myself I did not mind, that the important thing was that Lea was home and that James was looking after her. I carried on studying and working at the hospital, saving my money for when Lea was better and I could surprise them with wonderful theatre tickets, dress-circle seats at the opera, a concert. I fantasized endlessly about the day I'd come home, seeing all the lights on in the upstairs windows and hearing Lea's violin, knowing that the storm in Lea's mind had ended and now we would be like we were before. Being James and Lea's companion had been the only sign in my life that I was the least bit acceptable. Every day I went to school anticipating the inescapable torment of the boys who walked together in a large, menacing cloud, every day I faced the fact that my mother had given up on me, that my popular little sister was beginning to realize I was ever so slightly a freak. I needed James and Lea, I was determined it would all go as before.

I hoarded money. Unlike most girls my age shopping held little appeal to me. I was not proud of my figure so I saw no point in buying clothes and would not have known the best place to buy them in any case. My student travel card allowed me cheap access to the London Transport Service, many of the museums I visited were run on voluntary admission payments, and again my student status saved me where an entrance fee was required. So there was not a great deal of opportunity for me to spend my salary, as meagre as it was. Make-up, that was expensive. I spent hours examining the choices in the village pharmacy, a shop with a surprising abundance of beauty products, special lavender-scented soap and bath salts, tubes of body moisturizers and all manner of enhancers for the hair and skin. I wore make-up so infrequently that the bottle of tan liquid (ivory beige with a matt finish, designed specifically for oily skin the shopkeeper promised) seemed to last forever. As did the special kohl pencil,

I might mention, and the pressed powder blush and waterproof mascara, none of which I could bring myself to actually wear.

My hair was a different matter, its frizzy uncontrollable nature required vats of conditioner and spray. I was forever tampering with special moisture packs and hot-oil treatments, which had instructions that the plastic phials be heated in warm water, combed through wet, unwashed hair, then kept warm through the use of a plastic conditioning cap (in my case, a shower cap) which stayed on for twenty minutes near a source of heat (the oven) before being rinsed thoroughly in clean water (from the kitchen sink) and shampooed out in special expensive shampoo which required two different applications and rinsings. To undergo this ritual I needed full use of the kitchen, a sink clear of dishes, and a great deal of time. It was what I did every Friday night.

'Rebecca's beauty routine,' Isobel said, impressed by the science of my undertaking. I'd explained to her about the chambers of the hair shaft, how to keep smooth the outer layer, or cuticle, so that a shine could be achieved, about proteins and chemical damage, about the way in which split ends erupted in badly kept, dry hair. I'd even shown her an actual split end and let her pull at the edges and part a single strand of hair right up the middle. 'Remarkable,' she'd said, with a serious face.

'Perhaps you'll attract a nice intern,' said Mother, who thought that the reason I did my hair on Friday nights was because I worked in the hospital all Saturday.

I affected not to hear her and carried on with my task – I was at the heating stage – turning my chair in front of the oven so as to catch the warmth on the other side of my head.

'Well, if you don't want him, bring him home to meet me,' she sighed.

A week passed, another. I was desperate to see Lea and James. It did not seem fair that after she'd been gone all that time, and I'd helped fetch her back, that she should disappear altogether once more. I hung around the hallway, pretending to be sorting my schoolbooks into my book bag. Several times each afternoon I went to see if the post had arrived, on summer nights I stood outside and I stared up at the lights of their windows, wondering if they were home and what they were doing. They no longer went out after supper to walk across the heath to the Prince of Wales pub for a drink in the night air. They no longer knocked on the door asking me to listen for burglars when they went into town for a long evening. Lea did not appear to be going to rehearsals or playing in any concerts. There was no music resonating down the kitchen chimney, no sounds of laughter, not even the clanking rifle of James's typewriter. Surely, they must be alive up there somewhere, I thought, and yet days would pass without a trace of their existence.

Rose noticed, too. 'Where *are* those two?' she asked at dinner. 'The couple upstairs.'

'She's sick,' I said.

'Well, I *know* that,' said Rose.

'She's not sick,' Isobel corrected. She'd taken to adopting only English expressions. To her sick meant being sick, throwing up. It no longer meant not feeling well. 'She's *ill*.'

'I saw the doctor on his way in to see her. Doctor Daisley, what a nice young man. He didn't look too impressed,' Rose said.

Doctor Daisley was not young and had not been anything near young for a decade or two, but I let that pass. It was shocking enough he'd come to the house. 'When did you see him?' I asked Rose.

'Yesterday.'

'What happened?'

'I imagine he came to examine that poor girl. He spent a half hour or so, then I saw him going back out the door into his little car – he has one of those minis. I like those.'

'Left with Lea?'

'No, dear,' Rose said, shaking her head as though I'd lost my mind. 'Why would the doctor leave with Lea?'

I thought of reasons to go see them and decided one Friday

when I knew I'd have the kitchen to myself for the purpose of transforming my hair that I could bake them a cake. This was a greater undertaking than one might imagine as I had not done any cooking at all since arriving in London. The domestic tasks in our little maisonette were divided in an understood, silent agreement, and baking was very much *not* a task I ordinarily undertook. I was the one who did what Rose called 'heavy cleaning'. She was always so grateful. For though she did not dodder around like an old woman, she had what she called a 'trick' knee, which in fact had been operated on and was missing a kneecap. This knee kept her from stairs and ladders and reaching down into low, deep cupboards. She often said it was God's grace to grant her two such nimble great-nieces who could fetch vegetables from the bottom of the fridge, scrub with an abrasive agent the sticky messes that accumulated in corners and along the kitchen skirting boards, and stand on chairs to reach into the airing cupboard for extra blankets and pillows. 'I used to clean the bath while I sat right in it!' she'd once explained to us, speaking in a cheerful, robust manner as though about some shocking, delightful pastime. 'I had a system for this. When I'd finished the bath I let enough water out to show the ring around the tub. I scrubbed that ring with a clean brush, then let a little more water out, and scrubbed down deeper. Then I threw the plug over the side and let the water run out completely, sitting shivering in an empty bath with my scrubbing brush and not very comfortable, shining the surface of that silly bath. It was not a pleasant way to conclude!'

'You cleaned while naked!' Isobel said.

'I did,' confessed Rose.

'People would think you'd gone senile if they saw you like that,' declared Isobel. It always amazed me what she was willing to say to Rose. I never would have dared to mention the s-word, not since we'd really thought she had gone senile, back in America when she thought she'd left Stanley the cat at the airport or whatever. But Rose didn't mind what Isobel said. I suppose the thought had struck her as well.

'They might,' she said. 'But I don't have to do that anymore, do I, now I have you girls?'

That was undeniably true. She really did have us; we'd have done anything for her. I regularly cleaned the bathroom, carefully scrubbing off watermarks and limescale deposits. I swept and mopped the halls and made sure the mop was washed properly and wrung dry so it wouldn't smell the way the hospital mop did. Isobel liked to get on her hands and knees and clean the kitchen with a floor cloth. It made her feel like a class-one Victorian maid, which she thought was a romantic thing to be. She also liked taking down cobwebs and reordering the refrigerator, removing the garbage to the cluttered, weed-strewn alleyway beside the house, scraping grease from the roasting pan after Sunday lunch. Anything that involved the ugly side of domestic life, gooey matter, or a possible encounter with vermin.

'Look at this disgusting stuff,' she'd say, showing me the sauce pot with which Rose had made gravy. She peeled a layer of grease with the back of a desert spoon. 'You *ate* this,' she'd tell me in an accusing way, as though she hadn't.

Mother must have been relieved never to have to do any housework, for she was hopeless at it and loathed it. Our house in America had been stocked with an inordinate amount of clutter – dusty knick-knacks and piles of dirty clothes, unopened post left on the counter top, books heaped in piles against walls, magazines (hundreds of these) which Mother hadn't yet completed reading and therefore was unwilling to throw away, the toys we'd had then, stray photographs, empty Kleenex boxes – and everywhere a solid layer of dirt. I'd tried to clean, but I was a young child and not so expert then, and spent a great deal of time anyway in front of the television. But Rose made keeping the maisonette clean a kind of humane husbandry, as though the rooms were alive and needed us to care and tend to them. Indeed, the house had a spirit, it was alive to us in a manner that no house had been before or since. We polished the floors with a mixture that Rose concocted out of lemon juice, lavender and oil. We pushed mothballs into designated corners of cupboards and lined kitchen drawers with new colourful paper, used stepladders to get at the picture rail with a dusting cloth, swathed a mixture of borax and household soap on to the walls. Every so often Rose would decide a curtain needed cleaning and there would be a day spent taking the heavy pleated fabric down from its rod, removing the copper hooks and handwashing it in mild soap flakes, drying and ironing, then the hazardous task of rehanging.

But cooking we were exempt from. Rose shopped and cooked for the family, two hot meals a day and a cold tea at five o'clock. I'd never had reason even to heat a can of soup. Still, I'd decided on a cake and while Rose was out with Mr Dodd (they played Bingo on Friday nights), I fished around for the chipped mustard-coloured mixing bowl, the flour sifter, the huge, battered wooden spoons, and a set of dented measuring cups so old you could barely read the marks along the sides. I didn't understand about letting butter soften and spent a painful half an hour churning ice-cold butter in eight ounces of flour, ending up stabbing it with a serving fork to part it and bring it into a workable, malleable form. I used granulated sugar instead of caster sugar – I didn't realize that a distinction could be made between sugars – and added baking powder when I didn't need it. In order to be fancy I separated the eggs before adding them in, beating the whites into a froth which I hoped would add airiness to my cake. The recipe did not call for milk but I distinctly remembered using milk in previous cakes I'd made from packaged mixes, and so added a little in anyway. The batter was poured into a sandwich tin – it was the closest thing I could find to the round, nine-inch cake tins I remembered from America – and overflowed while it baked so that half of it ended up on the floor of the oven. The salvageable bit, which was a disappointing, scanty amount of cake, was set on a slope, crusty at one end and almost uncooked at another. I put it aside to cool and made a frosting out of icing sugar and margarine. It looked rancid and yellow, not at all like the picture on the box that showed a glassy white icing with great swirling tufts. Nevertheless I ran a dollop of it over the crumbly, thin cake and then heaped a great deal more on in an attempt to even up the sides. In the end it did look quite a bit like a cake and I decided it was good enough to present as one. I tidied the kitchen, which looked like a bomb had hit it, and went to the bathroom to scrub my arms free of flour and wash my face, which was hot from all that work and worry, and comb down with a wet brush my unruly hair. I put on a clean blouse and went out of our door, carrying the cake in one hand like it was something I did every day, and just as I turned to go up the stairs, James came in through the front door, holding an empty shopping bag.

'Hello there!' I said in a loud, over-cheerful voice. 'I was just coming upstairs to bring you this cake.'

'You were?' James said, his manner distracted, his voice taut over his words.

'Yes,' I said, instantly wishing I'd not sounded so brash and presumptuous, and wanting more than anything else to hide the lopsided, ridiculous cake. 'Of course, if it's not convenient—'

'It isn't that—'

'—I was just going to drop it off anyway, so why don't you take it now. Take it for Lea. I've got to go anyway, I was just going out to – ' I stopped for a moment and thought of a convincing lie ' – to fetch some milk.'

I held out the cake, which had been too warm when I iced it so that the icing had gone transparent in places and dripped on to the plate in a slatternly, unappetizing way. It was a terrible moment for me, holding that cake, and James made it much worse by refusing to take it. The cake remained suspended in the air between us like a hand outstretched to be clasped and shaken – but instead refused – and so I had to withdraw it. I had to pretend it hadn't been offered and go on, with whatever boldness I could muster – all this over a cake – before anything more damaging and embarrassing transpired.

'She's in hospital,' James said. His words were so disconnected from all the crowded, self-conscious thoughts that rattled in my fraught mind that I looked at him blankly at first and had no idea what he meant. She was where? In the hospital? Who was in the hospital?

'Lea?' I said, as though this was impossible even though she'd been sick for weeks, even though I had not laid eyes on her for most of that time and a doctor had visited not two days earlier. 'For what?'

He shook his head, signalling he did not want to talk about it. He turned towards the staircase and walked heavily up several steps. 'I'll speak to you in the morning,' he told me.

10

James and I visited Lea at Maudesley Hospital where she'd been admitted for 'exhaustion'. What would they call it now? A nervous breakdown. Clinical depression. Either term would have better described Lea's condition, but depression was not thought of then as a young person's disease. We are not talking of ancient times, but of the late 1970s, a time we all think of as modern. And yet depression was barely understood, in fact not understood at all. Psychotherapy had recently become the vogue, but the essential drugs to accompany it were scantily distributed and only to the worst of cases. And they were not the drugs we know now, which are finer-tuned, with fewer side effects, but great big horse pills that gave clumsy, uncomfortable side effects or knocked a person out altogether.

We did not always go together, James went every day and I suppose I accompanied him several times a week. We took the bus from Shooter's Hill to New Cross, then changed for the one to Denmark Hill. It might have been a commute we were making, as to a job, we did it so expertly, regularly, so that we hardly had to pay any attention as we went. If no Denmark Hill buses came, we took the 36 to Camberwell Green and walked. It was warm and walking was a pleasant thing to do. We knew a short cut which brought us past the Phoenix and Firkin, with all the regulars, the somewhat alcoholic middle-aged couples and the younger ones, too, out in the refreshing coolness of the evening with their arms looped around each other, or sitting on the stone wall talking intently, quietly, their foamy pints clenched between their thighs. So many people they spilled out of the pub on to the narrow street and the garden outside. It felt odd to walk by them, like walking past a party to which you were not invited, and I tried to affect an air of impatience as we wound our way through the knitted groups in conversation, the couples basking in each other's company, the men standing with their weedy, self-rolled cigarettes, watching as though from a ship. And everyone riding a tide of sexual attraction, of possibility.

Impatience and annoyance, it seemed the decent thing to do. We might have stopped and had a drink – Lea would not have suffered more if we'd have done so – but to have stopped was unthinkable. I liked that pub, the mull of voices, the steady laughter, the sounds of matches being struck and of glasses clinking, but I did not let on. Sometimes, on the way back, it might have been nice to stop and rest and feel the sense of shallow joy all around us.

On the way to the hospital we did not speak except to mention the essentials of the journey, perhaps, or to ask whether it would be a good idea to get some fresh fruit on the way. In this manner we were like a veteran couple, two people who'd weathered many years together, so joined in thought that talking had become less urgent, at times almost irrelevant. I looked older than I was, a tall girl with large, round thighs, a heavy chest, a serious, plain face. My clothes were not what the other girls wore; shops did not stock teenagers' clothes – the denim and peasant blouses and the long, billowing India cotton skirts which were in style then – in a size that would suit me. I was five foot ten, eleven stone, I had to shop in the women's department at Marks and Spencer, no junior department would stock my size and even my school uniform had to be specially ordered. But when I walked with James I felt beautiful, and safe from the kinds of teasing that accompanied my school journeys. I remember walking with James and thinking that anyone looking at us would imagine we were a steady couple, the cosy feeling that this gave me. I sometimes held my own, singular conversation with him as we went. I imagined remarks I would make and how he might respond, his grin, his laugh. I sometimes even thought of his hands, so large and expressive, touching me in a casual, reassuring manner. I did not think about anything more deliberate than that, nothing like walking arm in arm, just what it might be like to move through the city with a man, a boyfriend, a lover. It seems such an innocent, expected, almost obligatory yearning for a girl to have, and yet I have never to this day mentioned it to James. I might have done – certainly those years have been mulled over countless times between us, casual references to specific days and more studied, debated memories, when we tried to resurrect the truth from the littered facts, tried to salvage what we could from the wreckage.

'Was I devoted, do you think? I feel I was a child then. How could I have been any kind of husband?'

'You brought her clean underwear, kissed her forehead, held her hand for hours in silence—'

'Anyone would have.'

'Maybe, but it was you, specifically you.'

'There must have been more. If I'd gotten her a better doctor – I was so stupid then, trusting everyone.'

'You did the best you could.'

'She killed herself—'

'Please don't start.'

'— I must have been in on that somehow.'

'In on it? In on what?'

Piecing it through, we might have been constructing something. A fabric, a tapestry. Who could know the truth?

The greengrocer in Camberwell got to know us. He was a confident, pleasant Asian man with a wide, inviting smile and he always rushed from the back of the shop with an eager expression, wiping his hands on his apron. 'More seedless?' he'd say, meaning the grapes which we bought hoping that Lea would eat them. They were her favourite, round, translucent, succulent, James only bought them at their freshest, holding them up to the light to check there were no gritty brown patches or puckered, older fruit. He bought them for her twice a week or so, and they aged on the table beside her bed and then disappeared altogether; I never saw her eat a single one. He also brought her fresh-squeezed juice and flowers. The shopkeeper thought we were lovers and that the flowers were for me. He always handed them to me in a particular manner, as though presenting them. This happened a few times and then, one day, I saw James speak to him in a low, icy tone. I could not make out what James said but the expression on the man's face changed, became serious, anxious. He nodded and swallowed and looked away from James all at once. It was important on the way to see Lea that no festivity was made, no jokes, no conversation even, and the greengrocer had violated this code by being too friendly, too pleasant. I don't know what James said to him but he was cautious from then on, polite but no more. I felt bad for the man but it was necessary, he'd always come striding from the back of the shop welcoming us, his face beaming. We'd braced ourselves for this and the feeling had been unbearable.

Inside the hospital there was a different set of rules. Rules of attentiveness, of false good-natured cheer. James and I hovered close to Lea's bed like two statue dogs on either side of a gate, staring at her in careful attendance, seizing immoderately on any remark she might make. We moved with an unnatural quickness to fetch her water or a tissue or to fluff up the pillows on her bed. On a good day she sat in a chair and we brought over two other chairs, battered nylon ones with foam cushions, squat and unstylish, chairs that one never sees outside a hospital, and set them opposite, huddled together as though on a train. Our voices seemed to resonate too strongly, our feet in street shoes made clomping sounds across the linoleum, all wrong for this place of subtlety and silence, of steady recuperative hours. We laughed too loud when the slightest chance of humour showed itself, and we brought in foreign smells, the smells of the city. The hospital had a stagnant, permanent odour of disinfectant and paper, of alcohol and the lingering cooking smell brought in from the trays that were presented to and removed three times daily from patients who rarely ate. James and I smelled of rainwater and fresh air, of the perfumes of those who sat squashed against us on the bus, of chapstick and shampoo, and freshly laundered clothes.

We tried to bring her some of what we had. A clean nightgown and fresh toothpaste, new slippers, a kit containing scented soap, a pair of her earrings. The earrings were taken from her, we discovered later, for being 'dangerous'. The tie to her dressing gown was taken for the same reason. I gave her back the little cassette player and headphones she'd leant me months previously and then found out the headphones had been removed that night by one of the nurses. Again, dangerous. I argued for them to be returned to her but could not budge the sister.

'Wires,' she said. She said this very softly, with apology, as though telling a tiny child why it was he could not have any more chocolate.

'But she cannot be without any music. She'd feel better if she could listen to something.'

'There is a radio and television in the patients' lounge,' the sister said, and shrugged.

'She'd like to listen to her own selections,' I insisted.

'She's not mentioned that.'

I knew this was probably true. Lea seemed wholly unconcerned about the music which had once impassioned her. It was hard to fathom, but she didn't want any music. It made her even more upset, she said. She wanted silence, she wanted quiet, she wanted to hide and wait and, more than anything, to sleep.

We offered up our gifts, a different one each day, hoping it might make a difference, and we watched, half waiting for the hours to pass, for a sign that she might come back to us, to the world which missed her so. All around her were people stretched out along the wards or occupying tiny rooms just adjacent. Some talked to themselves, some sat quietly shaking or rocking. Most slept. Sometimes even Lea was asleep. The drugs made you drowsy, I was told, and anyway that is what the patients wanted, to sleep away this time in their lives. To escape. Sometimes Lea slept twenty out of twenty-four hours, other times she could not fall asleep no matter what. If we arrived and she was asleep we waited for forty minutes or so and then James wrote a note and we left. That was terrible, when we had to leave her, having come all that way and not a word spoken.

When she talked she did so in the manner of someone with a throat infection, as though it pained her. On a Bank Holiday Monday, the hospital full of visitors, we pulled the curtains around her bed and listened with difficulty as she spoke, her voice a thickened whisper. She said, 'It's like I want to run, but have no legs, like I want to scream but have no tongue.'

I had no answer to that. Around us were people looking for extra chairs and pillows, asking for the plastic vases they used for flowers. Someone pushed a chair in such a manner that it made a bulge in the curtain around Lea's bed, so that if we'd had any illusion of privacy it was instantly gone. There seemed too much intrusion in the room for Lea's confession. I looked over at James and saw he was staring at the floor.

Sometimes we arrived and it was clear – from a gift bowl of fruit on the hospital nightstand that we had not brought, or a jar of borrowed handcream – that Lea had had some other visitor. A fellow patient, a nurse who bothered to spend more than the requisite time necessary to perform a routine blood-pressure check. We never knew or asked, but it struck me as strangely inharmonious, almost alien, to see these other things, these products of friendship. Other people's love for her, their gifts or time, struck me wrongly as strangely inferior and intrusive, and I imagined that James felt the same. Once when we arrived there was a balloon floating above her bed and James looked at it with a mixture of curiosity and distaste that conveyed – I thought – the message that he did not like the idea of Lea becoming part of the hospital's social world.

'That boy over there tried to kill himself with drain cleaner. He swallowed it using Pepsi as a chaser,' Lea told me. 'Don't tell James, it will only upset him.'

James had gone to get a jug of fresh water from the kitchen. I nodded to indicate that I would not tell him about the boy, who was about my age, perhaps slightly older.

'Drain cleaner, can you imagine? What made him think of *that*?' she said.

I laughed, I thought that was what she wanted me to do. But she surprised me, her face went dark and she looked accusingly at me.

'It isn't funny,' she said.

We wanted to think every day that she might be discharged, that she might come home, but she seemed ever further entrenched in the hospital, its patients, its daily rituals, the trivial gossip and the appalling facts – the shaking, rocking, crying, screaming, and the equally dreadful long, sedated hours.

'I want her out of here,' James said.

'I'm sure it will be any day,' I told him.

But then we would arrive to see that a vase of small sprigs had been given to her by one of the other patients – one of those who had gone home and so had no further need for hospital flowers – and we felt rebuked for our scant, unfounded hope.

We rode the bus home at night, sitting together in the hard, domestic light, crowded by women carrying shopping bags, by men returning late from work, by drunken, unruly guys going to the pub. The windows fogged and I had to rub out a spot to peer through, watching to make sure we did not miss our stop. It had become such a routine, this commuting to Maudesley that soon I could not remember a time when riding these buses, sitting next to James, pressing coins and transfers into each other's palms, heading in unison down the same doors and corridors, past the nurse's station to the wooden double door with the coded lock to gain entrance to Lea's ward, all the ordinary matters that made up the journey to see her, had not been a part of my everyday life. I'd become so accustomed to it, used to Lea being ill, being frail, failing to eat. I forgot just how horrible the situation was and began, almost, to enjoy this time in my life when I had an easy focus for my energies and someone to be with.

'You weren't in love with me then, of course.'

'No, don't be ridiculous. You were just a guy, you seemed so much older than me.'

'You didn't feel anything, did you?'

'Not then, no. Not really.'

One evening a doctor came in and asked to have a word with James. We'd been sitting beside Lea's bed as she sat on top of it, cross-legged, so thin her wrist-bones seemed disproportionately large, her thighs those of a child. She was not usually a modest person – I recalled how easily she flung on and off clothes without a great deal of regard for such things as blinds or company – but here in the hospital she clung to her privacy. She pulled a blanket around her, cape-style, as soon as she figured out that I'd noticed how thin she'd become, that I was looking at her. She watched the doctor as he walked off with James to the other end of the ward. Then she said the letters 'ECT', as though spelling out a word. Then she said, 'Shock treatment.'

I knew at once what she meant, she didn't need to explain. In those days ECT was exactly what many people think it is, a treatment in which the patient is strapped on to a gurney and has electrodes strategically placed over the skull. With the flip of a switch so much electricity is coursed through the body that the patient's entire body, including his brain, is sent into convulsions. It is not what ECT is today, of course. Though still mysterious in its healing properties, the refinement of technique in ECT means that the electricity is confined to the brain only. A small amount of twitching in the fingers and toes might occur but no enormous convulsions. The brain convulses – that is the main thing – and in realigning itself somehow shorts out the depression that has taken hold.

The doctor had taken James aside to discuss it with him. Lea had only been hospitalized for three or four weeks at this point and it seemed to me a rash course of action.

'Do you want that?' I asked, trying not to sound alarmed.

She made a gesture I could not interpret, a kind of shrug with a shake of the head, as though she did not want it, but only in the same way she did not want anything. Desire had abandoned her altogether, she did not care.

On the way home that night I sat in the bus daydreaming. I don't know what I was thinking about, perhaps the way Lea had seemed not to mind what happened to her, that any outcome was equally without appeal to her, or perhaps I was thinking about nothing related to Lea at all. In such a short time it had become routine, visiting her in the hospital, seeing her ill. The school holidays had begun and every day was structured in the same manner, working at Lewisham Hospital in the mornings and visiting Maudesley at night. It isn't that I wanted her to be ill, only that I'd come to accept it, to live with it. I believed Lea would get better – as the one thing I knew about depression was that, sooner or later, it always lifted – and with that knowledge I filed away any impatience I might once have had.

I was looking out of the bus window at the lights strung along the entrance to New Cross market when I caught James's reflection. His head was bent, his hand was cupped over his eyes. He was crying. I realized then that the situation was not the same for us. I always knew this, of course, but I realized just how much different. He'd watched his vibrant, young wife sink into a dim, barely communicative state. The flowers, the bowls of fruit, the cotton-lace nightgown, the boxes of sweets surrounded her like overbright, mawkish decorations had only served further to reduce her. Lea was not entirely resigned to her depression, she was not even, in the end, a victim-type of personality, but she was so laden with it, so stuck in, and she demanded James to carry on seeing her without being able to offer him any consolation or, for that matter, any hope.

I'd seen James crying only through the reflection in the glass; it was possible to pretend that I had not, to focus my sight out to the street and to wait for the moment to pass, as surely it would. In some ways this would have been the most humane thing to so. His tears were the kind of effortless, unstoppable stream that one cannot choke back. He mopped his eyes with his cuff as though stopping a nosebleed, surprised at how wet his sleeve was becoming and yet, of course, unable to do anything more than wait for the flow to cease.

I remembered just then that I had a handkerchief in my pocket. Aunt Rose always insisted that I carry one, though of course I would never have considered using it. To pull out a cotton handkerchief in school would be instant social death – we all used wadded bits of Kleenex or nothing. But the handkerchief was there, ironed and folded as always. I took it out quietly and handed it to James. He put it to his brow and pressed his face against it.

I watched him in the reflection and he looked to me so sad and, for that instant, so boyish and young. I remembered watching a girl from our school, one like myself who was forever being teased by the boys, as she walked crying down the road, her face red and distorted, her heavy, marching step so quick I had not been able to catch up to her. She was teased for being fat. She was fat. But she had a beautiful, winning face and a goofy, fun nature, the sort of girl who was always laughing and who, you could just tell, came from a family that approved of her utterly whatever weight she was carrying. It had been terrible to see her crying and to have been able to do nothing for her. I looked at James, turned to him and looked. He was not so different from that girl, whose name was Alison. Tears reduce us all, equalize us, and make it possible for others to approach where previously it would have been impossible. I put my hand out to him and wrapped my fingers carefully around his wrist.

'I was thinking that it was time I sold one or two of my mother's paintings and bought Lea the violin she wants,' he said. It is impossible to convey how slowly and deliberately he said this, how hard he concentrated to control his voice so that it did not wander in pitch. 'But now she doesn't even want it. I asked and she said no. She said no thank you, darling, as though I'd offered her a cup of tea. I can't reach her. I can't get anywhere near her—'

He stopped, gathering himself, blinking purposefully, his entire body tense. I did not know what to say. I knew how much Lea had wanted a violin, a particular expensive model that at one time James had found extravagant. They'd argued about it – I'd heard those arguments – and even then I'd thought James ought to part with at least one of those paintings, which never saw the light of day in any case. I suppose that now he'd reached that same conclusion, sadly at a time when it didn't really matter.

'She'll be better soon.'

I waited for him to bring up the subject of ECT but he said nothing.

'She'll come home and things will be different,' I said.

Either he didn't believe me or he found it too difficult to speak. He closed his eyes and quite deliberately forced back the tears so that he was no longer crying but his eyes were fiery, his face pulled into a shape that was not quite natural. I laced my fingers through his – I will never forget this moment – and in an instant I could not have anticipated he clasped my hand and I felt something, my skin tightening around me, a lightness and a shudder as though I were getting the flu. I felt so nervous my legs began to shake and a chill, as though inside me a coldness was finally melting, crept all the way up to the base of my skull. Was he feeling this way? Of course not. One reaches a stage in which touching another person, even a person of the opposite sex, no longer brings with it the instant smoke and excitement. One grows used to it, in the same way one grows used to one's own body. Attraction is there, but is more easily directed, brought under control. But he felt something, of that I am sure. I dared not look at his face, but I felt his expression, his own taxing, shameful surprise.

And then, in a moment I calculated wrongly, I tried in a clumsy inexpert manner to hug him. What was I thinking? You read in books about people who suddenly lose their senses and throw themselves, dangerously, whimsically, almost heroically, in one or the other crazy, ill-thought-out direction. You read this and you think that nobody would be so swept up, so completely absorbed in the moment. Wouldn't some part of one's mind know full well the consequences, and prevent the humiliation, the damage? I tried to hug James – I tell myself now that it was a friendship hug, to make him feel better. The man had been crying on a public bus, the man had been desperate.

There was a line of passengers standing above us and no room at all to manoeuvre. The hug was ill-accomplished but I felt, I think I felt, a moment when his body relaxed against mine, and his muscles gathered around me. I could smell his skin, damp and fresh, a scent like fresh snow. Only a second, and then it was over. I felt him tense, and then he moved me quickly away, he all but pushed me back into my seat. This was done with such determination, such effort, what could almost be thought of as revulsion, that I knew the attraction was complicit.

We did not speak all the way home. When at last we came through the big, heavy front door, I turned abruptly to the smaller door that led into our maisonette and James darted upstairs, taking two steps at a time. We'd frightened ourselves, we'd tempted something utterly terrible and wrong and we'd wanted – I think this is true – for there to be some unprecedented reason, some force larger than ourselves and which we could not resist, which nobody could reasonably expect us to resist, so that in our minds we could alter what might have been, changing it from opportunity to fate.

You were not in love with me then, were you?

No, you were just some guy . . .

The next day we went to see Lea again and I thought I detected a change in her as well, as though she'd gleaned something had happened, that she knew. She'd acquired a sweetness which was in part due to her helplessness, her complete and utter lack of resistance, her quiet neediness, but there was a ghostly quality to her, a watchfulness, a sublime, almost lofty passivity. She looked at me differently than she ever had, I thought, lifting me into her sights with her enormous grey eyes fastened in place, her cool, opaque madness swirling quietly between us like a pool of ever-deepening water.

James did not once offer me direct eye contact. I cursed him silently, for being so stupid, for acting like a cheat, like a guilty man. He'd been distraught, I'd held his hand – if there was more than friendship linking our hearts it was too confused with all manner of other feelings to work into anything as concrete as sex. Sex. Why use made-up names for it – passion, love, need – it was sex. My mother's life had taught me as much. I'd rather have faced it outright and gotten past it, but James, with his knotted mind, his senseless guilt, his accusing, relishing blame, he would never allow for such disclosure. And now she knew. Lea knew. It was plain to her because she was too shrewd and too accomplished in the art of attraction, its rules and by-laws, its treachery and injustice.

'Why don't you two go get some dinner yourselves,' she said when her tray of hospital food arrived. The attendant insisted that Lea go and join the other patients at a makeshift dining table in the middle of the ward, a low-level picnic table, like the tables one eats from as a child at school. 'Go on,' she insisted. 'I'm sure you must be hungry.'

Was she giving permission for something or just making a suggestion for how we occupy our time?

The next day James left before our usual time and did not come downstairs to knock at my door. The following day the same thing happened. I got ready, collecting my purse, my umbrella, a bar of scented soap I had bought for Lea, and waited for him. I suppose I knew he would not come for me that evening either but I had to get ready just in case. He returned home about ten – it was impossible not to hear someone coming through the front door which required a great deal of negotiation with the heavy, ancient lock – but he did not stop in. He seemed to stay up later and later at night, I could hear him typing or walking around, banging into things from the sound of it. Sometimes he was still awake when I woke up.

After three or four days of this I decided we ought to talk. Before going to work one morning I brought him a cup of tea and knocked on his bedroom door.

'I'm leaving this for you,' I called into the wood. 'Tea.'

'Go away,' he said.

'I *am* going away. But I thought I'd finish my sentence first.'

'Go to school.'

'I've finished school,' I said. I frowned, wishing he could see that he was only annoying me with his menacing, patronizing tone, that he was not doing what he hoped to do, which was to hurt me, to make me go away now and forever. I backed away from the door and started down the steps, hoping that his bedroom door would open and he'd see me, staring back at him, unafraid. He could say what he liked, send me away or ignore me completely. It did not matter because I knew, even then, that there was an important connection between us, a link which we could not sever.

I walked down the steps then stopped, hearing his footsteps beating against the floor. He ran through a door – probably the music-room door, but perhaps just the kitchen – opening it so fast it sprang on its hinges. Then he was suddenly on the landing, staring down with his eyeglasses in his hands so that his face seemed naked, exposed. His eyes were dilated as though he were on some kind of drug. He cleared his throat to speak but made no sound. He wet his lips with his tongue, breathing as though he'd just run up a hill on a summer's day. He stared down at me, perhaps for only a second or two, but the concentrated power of those few seconds made me hold my breath. We stood like that, with an air of confusion swelling around us, and then he ducked back into the rooms which were his, and did not appear again.

The next day was Sunday. Rose conjured up a roast dinner with Yorkshire pudding and summer vegetables, new potatoes and a crumble for dessert. Such a feast always seems to me an overwrought chore for a summer's day but that is what she felt she had to do each Sunday. The thought of letting the week began with anything less casual was as unthinkable as failing to go to church. Mother had no rules regarding attendance to Sunday lunch, nor about what we wore, but out of respect for Rose, Isobel and I always put on clean blouses and combed our hair. It made a difference to Rose. She laid out a tablecloth which might have taken the better part of an hour to launder and iron, she served on dishes she warmed in a sinkful of hot water and she rubbed the cutlery with a tea cloth so that it shined. She did not insist on saying grace – she knew we were not a religious family – but paused before serving with a dignified bow of the head and sent a silent message to God.

'We must invite that poor boy upstairs,' she'd said to me several times that morning. 'He could probably use a decent meal.'

'He'd only refuse,' I insisted.

'It doesn't hurt to ask.'

'He's been in a bad mood. I don't want to go up there,' I said.

'Then *I'll* go up,' Rose said. 'I think you'd be surprised at how people take nicely to kindness.'

What concerned me was that *Rose* would be surprised. I was terrified she'd climb all those stairs only to have him be rude to her, and the thought of anyone being rude to Rose made my stomach seize up. So I told her that James might very well be asleep as he had been putting in a lot of late nights working at his typewriter. It was best not to disturb him until we were sure he was awake, I said, after all he had so much on his mind. This had the effect of quelling Rose but it was agreed I'd take him a plate of dinner later that afternoon.

I went up to see him on Sunday night. I did not knock or ask if it was all right for me to come in. I did not ask his permission in any way but simply went to where I knew he'd be and planted myself in front of him. I had the plate Rose had prepared with slivers of carefully carved roast beef, three perfectly cupped Yorkshire puddings and vegetables steeped in butter. I laid it aside, knowing he'd only find such a gift unwelcome, and he looked curiously at it before turning his attention back to me. He was exhausted and half-drunk, sitting in Lea's music room at a chair by the window. He hadn't shaved or washed in many days.

'You can't do this alone,' I said to him.

'This is nothing you can understand,' he told me.

'You're heading more or less for the same place Lea is.'

'You're just a child, you don't get it.'

I shook my head. 'I'm not such a child,' I said.

We stood, looking at each other. Then he laughed in a wretched, old-man sort of way and turned his gaze to the open window. A breeze had caught the curtain and it billowed up. From down the road someone whistled, neighbourhood kids called to one another.

'Rose made you that dinner, she's worried about you,' I said.

'Very nice of her.'

'I'm worried about you, too,'

'No need for that,' he said. 'I've run out of fags. You can go out and get me some if you want.'

'I don't want to fetch your cigarettes,' I said.

'Well, what *do* you want?'

'I'm just trying to say that—' I wasn't sure now. I paused and tried to think. 'I think you are by yourself too often,' I concluded. This seemed a reasonable remark. His job – his writing – kept him apart from people. His only interaction for weeks, months now, had been with Lea, who was a strain to be with, who ate up your energy, who left you feeling a husk, a shell, a set of bones barely walking. Sometimes when we left her I felt as though I'd taken a sleeping pill; it may have been the heat in that hospital, which hadn't any decent ventilation and depended upon mounted wall fans to circulate the air, but I always walked out feeling dozy, inert, with no more energy than a scarecrow.

James said, 'Do *you* want to be with me?'

It was such a strange, deliberate, accusing statement. It was clear what he was asking. Did I want to sleep with him. Did I want to. I was not so stupid that I did not know this. And had I answered yes, I cannot say what would have happened. He was drunk, as I have mentioned, he was acting in a crazy, self-destructive manner, a manner I grew to know very well years later. I've seen him this crazy, this reckless, I cannot say what he is capable of when he reaches the extreme, the 'periphery' as he calls it, that liminal place between sanity and madness in his own particular mental geography. Had I said to him that this was so, that I wanted exactly what he thought I did, and that my concern for Lea had dissolved into something quite different, into a lurking, desperate, bodily need, then what?

I don't wish to think of it.

'Don't be crude,' I said.

'Well, all your hanging about—' he began, and held his hands up as though to indicate that he could not help but draw his own conclusions.

'I'll go,' I said. 'I'll go now.'

'Go on, then. I don't blame you.'

'You bastard,' I said.

'That, too.'

'I thought we were friends,' I said.

'*I* thought so, too,' he said in a sly, horrid, almost affronted manner, as though it had been his impression we were friends but that I had changed all that. With my female wiles, my insistence on sexualizing what ought to be left alone.

'You fucking bastard,' I said. I was shaking. He was looking straight at me with eyes like two loaded pistols, with his smile of knives. He was laughing at me, I was sure of that, laughing at how seriously I took him, at how much he mattered to me, and at how easily I was humiliated.

'You didn't feel anything, did you?'

'Not then, no. Not really.'

I went downstairs and flew through the front door to our maisonette. It seemed suddenly so quiet in there, a tranquil, domestic, warmly lit set of rooms. I felt as though nothing of consequence could possibly happen inside such a place, where the perpetual machinery of household chores churned in a maddening continuum. This thought gave me comfort. Here I could be safe. Isobel was lying face down on her bed in her room – the room she shared with Rose. She was reading and singing while she read, a strangely impossible feat. Rose was ironing. She always ironed with great intensity, puffing while she did so. There was the smell of beef fat and leftovers, a ripe, salty smell I usually considered unappetizing, offensive even, but tonight found mildly pleasing in its familiarity. There were chopped vegetables on a cutting board, the grassy ends of spring onions pushed to one side, not yet thrown away, with some torn sections of butter lettuce set aside in a wooden bowl.

Mother had finished a bath and was standing by the kettle in her dressing gown with a towel wrapped around her head. She'd made herself a cup of tea and was standing to drink it. The teacup was nearly empty and it was positioned just next to the kettle, where she usually would put it to steep before whisking it off to her bedroom. I saw the teacup and Mother standing there and I thought that she must have stood at the kettle waiting for it to boil, poured the water and waited for it to steep, then drunk the whole thing down while standing in that one, same place in the kitchen with her hair wrapped in a towel.

You would have to know how unusual this was for my mother; you would have to know that she never left her wet hair wrapped in a towel because it took out all the curl and made it harder to style; that she always did several things at a time and so to remain in one place to drink a cup of tea was unthinkable, and in any case she normally took a hot drink to her bedroom after a bath where she applied various creams and oils to her skin while it was still plump with moisture from the bath. I knew all this – the habits of my mother were so ingrained in my mind – and so I knew that she'd been standing in the kitchen doing what I had done for almost a year now, which is listening to the cascade of voices that filtered down the flue. She'd heard everything that James and I had said, and she hadn't even had the decency to pretend she hadn't, to leave the kitchen before I arrived back downstairs, which would have been much kinder to me.

The knowledge that she'd heard James's and my conversation caused a fluttering in my chest and I could feel a place inside my solar plexus grow warm and spread, rising to my neck, my face. I felt breathless and jittery, the walls of the room seemed suddenly askew. Without my mother even having said one word I was launched into a panic attack. Was it visible, this agony? I looked at my mother, at her expectant, concerned, fascinated expression. She disapproved of James – of my being his friend, of my visiting Lea for that matter. She thought the two of them were spoiled and odd and she imagined – I thought she imagined – all sorts of goings-on that never took place. Drug-taking or open sex, the sort of thing that was supposed to be happening all around us in the permissive seventies but that I never saw or even heard about, although the innuendo was there, on television, in the tabloids, in the lyrics of all the pop songs. Mother was very permissive herself, it has to be said, but she was also a mother, with a mother's disapproval and agitated worry. She must have been appalled at what she'd heard during her eavesdropping, but there was another aspect to it, and it was this that made me squirm. It was her interest, her almost voyeuristic curiosity. I found the idea of her listening to my conversation with anyone, but particularly with James, with a man, disgusting, because I knew it gave her satisfaction, some modicum of wrongly derived pleasure. With the towel tied on her head she looked immeasurably tall, and seemed to peer down at me from a great height, studying me, calculating, imagining. How I dreaded her imagination.

I thought perhaps I might faint and so without even saying hello I made my way clumsily down the hall to the bathroom, which still smelled faintly of shampoo and bath foam, and yanked the light cord, closing the door behind me. The room was tiled in pink with a fuzzy rubber-backed mat on the floor and a pink pedestal sink. It was brightly lit and still a bit steamy from Mother's bath. The mirror was fogged in the centre and the walls damp. It was hot, I stood in the bath and reached up to open the window. I turned on a tap in the sink and put my face in the cool water, then found there weren't any towels at hand. I closed the toilet seat and sat down, drying my face on my sleeve. I must have been there a good ten minutes before I found the courage to rise again and go out.

I opened the door and fell back as though struck, for there, standing before me, still in her bathrobe and towel turban, was my mother.

'Excuse me,' I said, trying to pass her.

'Rebecca, we need to talk.'

'I'm in a hurry. I'm late for something.'

'You're not going back up there to him, are you?' she said, more of a statement than a question. 'Because I can tell you right now that would be a very bad plan.'

'Him, who? What are you talking about? I'm going to the library.'

I managed to get by her and back down the hall to the kitchen – my bedroom – then realized that this gave me no privacy at all and would need to be escaped just as the hallway had been. I grabbed my rucksack and purse, then my mind did a very strange thing indeed and I thought, as though I really were going to the library, which I was not (the library was of course closed on a Sunday night), that I ought to return my overdue books.

'I heard what he said to you, and I think you have to consider just how strange those people are. It isn't your fault, you weren't to have known. But now that you do know, don't you think it would be a good idea to avoid all contact with them in the future? Rebecca, I happen to have a little expertise in this area and I can tell you now—'

I tried to block out my mother's words. I thought, if I can just get out of the house. Out of the house and perhaps on a bus, on a bus anywhere, tonight still may be survivable. I may not have to go through any further, excruciating examinations. I went back through the door, fleeing from the maisonette with the same urgency with which I'd left James, thinking that once I got outside I would finally be alone, which is really all I wanted. I hadn't done anything so wrong; I didn't see why I had to stand around and argue my case to anyone, and I just wanted to get out of this crazy house and go somewhere I might be anonymous.

Mother, of course, would not easily allow this. She walked right out into the street in her dressing gown, wagering, I suppose, that even if she did not mind displaying to the neighbourhood every minute detail of her life, from her dressing garments to her arguments with her daughter, that I would be mortified enough to stop and insist we go back inside the house to continue our discussion behind closed doors. I am sure this is what she thought would happen, that I would tackle my own shame in the face of such an exhibition, she could count on it. Count on me to always do the decent thing.

I heard her voice behind me. 'Would you stop running away,' she said, with considerable annoyance. 'You're acting like a child.'

I was heading for the railway station in Lewisham. Two blocks along Dartmouth Row, then straight down Lewisham Hill. I could not believe Mother would follow me, dressed as she was. It bothered me, just as she knew it would. I thought of the couple of homeless drunken men who always sat along the walkway that led to the station. What would they make of my mother, marching behind me in only a scanty gown?

Oh well, that was her problem. I walked, wishing mother would have had sense enough to put on some clothes before coming out, but determined to get to the railway station in any case. I could just imagine the spectacle we were making of ourselves.

'Honestly, Rebecca, stop. Stop right there. *Stop*!'

I had no intention whatsoever of stopping, and might not have but her voice suddenly changed in tenor and volume. I'd reached the end of Dartmouth Row and was just on the incline that led down into Lewisham. I could tell from the sound of Mother's voice that she had stopped walking and was now standing in the same place on the pavement, unwilling to continue into Lewisham where such a show would likely be enjoyed, if not celebrated. This surprised me, it was the first time my mother had given up on anything, though I suppose even she knew she could not walk into a railway station dressed as she was.

'Why is it that I'm not even allowed to talk to you?' she asked plaintively from fifteen feet behind me. 'You don't understand that no matter how much you reject me as your mother, I *am* your mother. I cannot help it. And I cannot help but feel like a mother, and worry about you.'

'You worry about *me*. You ought to be plenty busy worrying about yourself,' I said. I hadn't turned around. I didn't dare. I spoke into the air in front of me. I closed my eyes.

'Oh, I worry about myself as well. Of course. Offer me a chance to ruin things for myself and I'll take it, that's just how it's always been. But I cannot stand to see you make the same mistakes—'

'I could never make the same mistakes.'

'Perhaps not, but this James—'

'He is not an issue!'

'Oh, Rebecca, you think he isn't. But he is. *He is.* I don't know what will happen, I'm not a gypsy with a crystal ball, but I can tell you that you'd be better off if you walked away from this one. My god, you're so young, you can't defend yourself against a man like James. He'll eat you alive.'

'They're my friends.'

'They're *not* your friends,' she said. Her voice was frustrated, desperate, sounding like someone whose fists were clenched, whose brow was furrowed in despair. 'That girl, half-crazy and looking to die. And don't think she won't know what is going on. They're married, Rebecca. *Leave them be.*'

And that is when it hit me, that she thought I was sleeping with James. Four months before my eighteenth birthday and without so much as having kissed a boy – I was not just a virgin but a relic – and she thought I was having a full-blown affair with a married man. Not just that, but Aunt Rose and Isobel thought the same. Thinking back now on the moment I walked into the house and saw, through the crack where the door meets the wall, Rose ironing, I suddenly realized that the effort she was putting in, the huffs and little wheezes, her direct, concentrated gaze on the collar of a shirt, was because she was attempting to occupy herself. To avoid me, to keep silent and by her silence quell any talk of sex, of adultery, of marital duty and hazardous, stray women. Thinking this, my heart sank. I could talk to Isobel, convince her of the truth. She would believe me. But Rose I would have to leave to her own conclusions, no matter how wrongly derived.

'You could have *other* friends,' Mother was saying now. I wasn't listening to her. My mind was crowded with thoughts of how Mother had concocted this extraordinary tale of my affair. All those times we went off to the hospital together, she must have thought that we were on our way somewhere else entirely. To a hotel or a friend's vacant apartment, somewhere dark and unwholesome, somewhere we had no business. But why would we need to find someplace, when there was a whole empty upstairs we could use? And how could she think such a thing in the first place? Had she discussed it with Rose? The thought of the two of them talking about such a thing made me feel quite sick. It was all so absurd, could they not see that James and Lea were my friends, my only friends, and that I cared as much for Lea as James?

'How can you even talk about James when all you do night and day is figure out how to get beside that Stephen Price?' I said.

'Oh, I knew you'd pull that one out,' was all she said.

'Well, how can you?'

'Because I'm not seventeen, that's why. I wish I were, because if I were seventeen I wouldn't be carrying on with Stephen, I can tell you that.'

'*Carrying on*, you said it, not me.'

'I'm not going to stand and be lectured by my own daughter.'

'Are you going to marry him?' I asked. I don't know what made me ask her this, except that it felt a lot easier to talk about her and Stephen Price's real affair than my supposed one with James. Even the thought that I was having an affair with James, that I would have sex with him and then go visit his wife in hospital, hung on me with such shame I almost felt crippled by it. I needed another way to go, attacking Mother for her involvement with Stephen Price was infinitely easier than talking about James, who I probably was in love with, it was all so mingled with guilt and curiosity and another love, for Lea, that I could never tell.

I turned to Mother, intending to give her a look of utter disdain, and felt another great boom inside my chest, and all my warring anger dissolve. Her slip strap was showing through her dressing gown and her hair had come loose from the towel, which was now draped around her neck like a boxer's face towel. Without make-up her skin was shiny, with patches of purple on the inside corners of her eyes. She looked haggard, spent. All my life I'd had a young, glamorous mother and suddenly, through my own ill-use of her, she'd been plucked from me and replaced with this much older, exhausted version.

'Oh, Rebecca, please. Am I going to marry him? *Marry him?* What do you want me to say? That I deserve what I get? That I don't deserve anything at all? For fifteen years I've thought that loneliness was a temporary matter, that I was still beautiful and everything was just on the verge of changing. Well, I'll be forty next month. I'm now coming to some certain conclusions. That I won't ever be able to stop work, or even to work part-time. That I might never get married again. That certainly there won't be any more children.'

This last bit struck me. 'You want more children?' I said incredulously.

'I'd like to raise you properly next time.'

'Next time?'

'I didn't mean that the way it sounded. I realize you cannot raise the same child twice,' she said, looking sad.

She shook her wet hair and ran her fingers through it. The moment had passed when she was so full of emotion she didn't mind standing in the street exposed, and now she was doing what she could to appear less dishevelled. I was wearing a summer jumper – I'd never left the house without a jumper and even in my mad escape I'd managed to pull it on – and I took it off now, tugging one sleeve then another. 'I just wanted to know because I don't want to live with him, that's all,' I said, handing her the jumper. 'He gives me the creeps.'

'Well, I don't think you have to worry about that. He's still married, as you know, and he's not mentioned getting unmarried, let alone *re*married.'

She said this brusquely, as though describing a particularly aggravating real-estate transaction. She might have been saying, *the sellers aren't prepared to take an offer and the buyers don't have the money in any case*, so matter-of-fact was her voice. She put on my jumper and I was surprised to see it hang on her, much larger than I would have guessed. A breeze had picked up and her arms had gone goosefleshy, so she wrapped the jumper around her and huddled into it to keep warm. We started walking back to the house, not speaking. Then she paused for a moment and dug into the pocket of her dressing gown, coming out with a small tube of lipstick, the sort you get as a 'gift' when you buy an excess of cosmetics. She checked the colour, shrugged, and put it expertly to her lips. In that one act I felt immeasurably reassured.

We did not get all the way home before I thought that perhaps it would be better if she went back into the house herself and I went on as I had originally planned. Just outside the house I looked up at the windows where, in what felt like a very long time ago, I had sat and smoked experimental cigarettes and listened to Lea's violin. The curtain was still pushed in, just as it had been an hour previously, for all I knew James was still sitting in the same chair nursing his heartache and his drink. I told Mother that I thought I'd go to see a film, that it was the best thing to do to clear my head, and showed her my house keys. 'Don't worry,' I said, when she suggested I come inside and see if she had any spare money in her purse. She'd just been paid and was sure there was a stray tenner that nobody had claim to. 'Let me,' she offered, but I explained it was unnecessary.

'You want to know the irony of all this?' she said, just before we parted. 'One of the reasons I thought perhaps we ought to come to England and look after Rose instead of staying in California was that I looked around at all those druggy, rich, sex-starved southern Californian teenagers and I thought, "Rebecca will be safer in England." I thought by bringing you here I could preserve your childhood for just a little bit longer.'

I didn't know what to say to that.

'Don't be late, darling,' she said, and went inside the gate.

I left that night. I took the train to London Bridge, changed for King's Cross and bought a ticket bound for York. I had a university place there for the autumn term and had planned anyway to leave in August. I'd chosen York because of Lea and James. I'd applied to medical school and been rejected, but York was strong in sciences and I was bound there. Mother was going to drive me up in her big, expensive car. She'd been aching to drive her daughter to university, to settle me into university halls, to go with me to second-hand stores in search of table lamps and bookcases. Did it make such a difference that I left eight weeks earlier, alone, and without so much as a pocket comb or a single book? I had all that money I'd been saving from my hospital job, enough to pay for a bedsit and to buy whatever I might need. Mother had run away from her own father when she was younger than me, though he'd deserved it.

'We get what's coming to us,' Mother liked to say whenever hardship fell. But I'm sure she didn't deserve me leaving like that, like an outlaw in the middle of the night, for it was ten o'clock by the time I got the York train and two in the morning before I phoned Mother and told her I wasn't coming home. I said what I had to and she hung on the phone in silence. When I asked if she were still there her voice cracked. 'Yes!' she said in an alert, alarmed manner. I could not think of what to say next. The train journey had been tedious and long. I'd drunk a can of lager to try to fall asleep but all it had done was make me feel queasy from so many miles in the jerky, draughty car. I wanted to say something grateful and loving, to leave Mother with the certain knowledge that I had not felt driven out of my home, that she had not raised me so badly as she imagined, that I had indeed loved it there.

11

One day, during my second term at university, I got a phone call. This was unusual because the house I shared with several other students only had one telephone and it belonged to another girl who did not allow the rest of us to use it except in cases of dire emergency. To call an ambulance was what she meant, though occasionally we finagled it for lesser reasons, to ring a professor's office to make an appointment, perhaps, or in case of illness to cancel a date so that some poor guy didn't think he'd been stood up. Even then she turned the phone over with begrudging, stubborn reluctance, as though giving you money she didn't think you'd earned. We weren't supposed to give out her phone number either, as though it were a house phone, but I'd told Mother the number anyway. Rose had been ill – she'd contracted pneumonia and it had adversely affected her heart; there had been talk about her never fully recovering. Mother had been nursing her at home but she was always in peril of returning to the hospital, where she did not want to go as she was sure she would die there. A reasonable suspicion, Mother had said in front of a whole crew of hospital doctors, we'll keep her with us while we can.

That was Christmas. We'd all stood around her bed in the geriatrics ward, a terrible, depressing place to be, made worse by cheap tinsel decorations and a large paper banner over the nurse's station that read 'Happy Christmas!' in chunky, red and white lettering. What a dreadful place, I'd said in the car, the only thing you *could* do is die there. Rose is not going to die, Mother had said as though this were an obvious fact, like saying yellow is a primary colour. Lea was out of the hospital by then but they weren't living in the house at Dartmouth Row. She'd gone back to her parents in Somerset and James seemed in between the two residences. I'd convinced myself I didn't care where they were, that they did not matter so much to me anymore. I had a boyfriend, David, and university life had swallowed me up so that, for a time, the whole ordeal with James and Lea seemed some fragmentary inconsequential vision of long ago, irrelevant to me now or, at any rate, over.

It was eight o'clock at night, I was in my room forcing myself to read a chemistry book, goaded on by a full pot of black coffee and a box of cheap chocolates, one of which I rewarded myself with for each turned page. Despite the coffee, I felt sleepy. I turned the radio on and off, on to keep me awake and get me revved up for studying, off because the lyrics distracted me, all that hollow desire and love, all those male voices so full of longing. No football lyrics, I noticed. No songs about how much a guy loves football; how he craves to play it and to watch it and to worship the better players; how he cannot wait to get back on the pitch if only the pitch would have him and to snuggle up close to his fellow drinkers at the pub afterwards. A song like that would be more accurately descriptive about male longing, at least what I'd seen of it at university.

I entertained myself with this thought and filed it away to reveal later to David, who I knew would be amused. What I'd discovered at university was a lot of young men with sport in their hearts and no idea how to talk to a girl, except for David, of course, who saw no appeal in competitive sports. Or rather, who considered sex a competitive sport and was devoted to the subject. I'd kicked him out earlier that night for being yet another distraction from studying. When my housemate came upstairs and said the phone was for me I thought for a moment that it might be him, trying to convince me to give up on chemistry and go see him. Then I remembered Rose and my heart dropped in my chest. I walked downstairs, seeing myself as though from above, taking each step carefully down. I was at a stage when I sometimes thought of my life as though it were a movie – I'd say this was a result of too much television except that I never watched television – and I saw the house as a kind of backdrop for my own drama. I saw the rickety staircase with the poached, torn runner rug and the wallpaper with its watermarks and uneven, sunbleached hues, the dark furniture, cheap, over-varnished stuff that had been set down without proper care, the skinny lightcord, the dangling unshaded bulb, all these artefacts of everyday student life. I'd never really noticed before the physical side to my life, the actual things I touched and saw every day. Now, suddenly, they took on the quality of props, of unreal instruments which did nothing but fill space. What had been my entire existence for two terms, the house with its shared conveniences, the boyfriend, the books upstairs, suddenly seemed a makeshift stand-in for something much more important. Everything with any meaning was at the other end of the telephone, a kind of umbilicus that connected me to my real life.

'Well, she surprised us all and went in her sleep,' Mother said. I remember this as the first thing she said – the way she'd spoken was as though the conversation started in the middle – but she must have said hello first and prepared me in some small way, through a hesitation in speech, an ellipsis suggesting she was sorry to deliver bad news. It would be the decent thing to do, but I don't remember any such pause. What I remember is that statement, said without apology or any obvious sentiment, but like an item of curious, unexpected news.

Went, that was the word she used. I knew what she meant was that Rose was dead. But what she'd said was went, like she went off to the market to get a joint for Sunday, and for a moment I felt relieved as though this was actually what had happened. I asked Mother to repeat what she'd said, which she did, adding that she'd had an easy passage – passage, like a voyage out to sea. I thought of Rose sailing away, lying helplessly on a lone raft, the kind of mattress raft people float in their swimming pools. Rose on a raft in the middle of a wide ocean. It was an absurd, surreal image but it disturbed me enough that I found myself shaking. The whole, roiling sadness of it hit me like a hard wave of icy sea water. I heard a cry, a wail, a long steady howl like a dog and realized the noise came from myself. I sat down on the floor, pulling the cord of the phone by mistake so that it all collapsed on top of me in a hard knock of plastic and loopy cord. My head smarted from where it had crashed and, strangely, I found this minor, localized pain soothing, a reassuring focus for my other pain which was inescapable and boundless.

'Darling, she was seventy-eight,' I heard Mother say. 'I know that doesn't help but I want to tell you now that if I get to seventy-eight and die peacefully in my own house with my loved ones sleeping near me and never so much as call out in pain, I will expect you all to throw a party for me, dance naked in the street and thank the Lord, because that is surely how we all would like to go.'

I kept thinking of Rose on that lonely, inadequate raft. I hadn't believed she was going to die. I'd returned to university feeling with certainty that she had plenty of time, plenty. There were much older people than Rose doing all sorts of things with their lives, caravanning in Wales, taking cruise trips to Scandinavia. People get pneumonia all the time, newborn babies get it and recover, I'd seen a case just that week at the hospital in York (I was a weekend volunteer) and that baby had recovered like a shot after the very first injection of antibiotics. Heart attack, stroke, malignant cancer, those are the things that kill you. But pneumonia?

'I wasn't there,' I said, my voice quaking.

'She'd been reading your letter last night. It was probably the last thing she read in this world.'

'She was well enough to read?'

'Isobel read it to her. But actually, yes, I think she was well enough. She'd been looking at the paper earlier in the day.'

My housemate – the keeper of the phone – came out and glared at me as though to give me a scolding. But when she saw me there, slobbering and tearful, she visibly shuddered and then she retreated from the room.

'Why didn't you call me until now?' I asked in an accusing voice.

'There's been just one or two things to do around here.'

'Where is she?' I said, and then immediately wished I hadn't. It sounded wrong and disrespectful and curiously macabre. 'I'd like to see her again,' I added quickly.

'The funeral is on Friday.'

I went upstairs and closed my chemistry book, stacked it on the table with my other books and then tidied my desk so that it looked like a perfectly maintained, never-used bit of decorative furniture. I put away all the stray paper and brought down the bin full of orange peels and cigarette ash, and polystyrene cups that David had brought in filled with chips. I opened each of my dresser drawers and took what I needed, trying to maintain an orderly presence of mind, trying not to become morbid or overly sentimental, there would be time for all of that but it would be better now if I just concentrated on what I had to do, which was pack and purchase a train ticket. There was no point in hurrying – she was not dying but dead – and I tried not to picture her lying in her bed, the same narrow, iron bed she'd had since her girlhood. The mattress she still called her 'new mattress', even though it was over twenty years old, was always dressed in a flannelette 'protector' and a coarse woollen underblanket over which she put the rest of the linens. She had a cotton throw in the summer and a heavier bedspread for the winter, both of which had been made from extra curtain fabric and sewn by her own hand. One of the blankets had been sewn together, too, concocted of several lap rugs which had collected uselessly in a wooden box and Rose felt were wasted. It was heavy work to piece together woollen rugs, but she'd done it in her gradual manner, the way she went about all things, as though the task at hand – sewing blankets or stewing a beef bone or rolling out royal icing for a cake – were the only thing she had to do and that no more important, later chore were occupying her mind. I thought of that hand-sewn blanket, one pink square and one tartan, a black hairy rectangle and a more cheerful white one splashed with timid, unspecific flowers. She'd offered it to me when she'd first finished it, explaining that if I were to tuck it underneath another blanket nobody would see it, and that it really was very warm. She'd worked for weeks but I didn't consider that when I turned it down. I only thought it was typical of her to put to use every little tattered bit of cloth she found around the house and that I didn't want the blanket in any case.

That's the kind of thing you shouldn't hurl at yourself late at night when you've received news of a loss. It sent me down, that memory, so that my room went blurry and I had to sit on my bed and cry. I thought that I ought to go over to David's and spend the night there rather than be alone, but just as this thought struck me, I felt an opposing, forbidding judgement inside myself, and knew immediately that I could not. He shared with a number of other boys and though there was no obvious thing wrong with them – they were not foul-mouthed, they did not leer – there was something about them, a disturbing, silent, stalking sexuality, that I found awkward and raw. The fact of a female in the house brought them out, lurking and inquisitive, their long legs and heavy shoulders strangely juxtaposed with their still boyish, somewhat immature faces. They seemed over-large in the small confines of the flat they shared, not a single room or piece of furniture seemed big enough to contain any one of them. They all three had bicycles, pinned up on walls or lining an empty, dimly lit section of the hall, and these bicycles, too, had that same sleek angularity, the same sinewy power, as their owners. I could not go to that house, with its sink of crusted, dirty dishes, and everywhere you looked an unfinished, many-days-old beer bottle or, draped on a doorhandle or over a radiator, some kind of sweat-stained, slightly damp sports jersey with an earthy, not altogether unappealing smell. It wasn't the mess that bothered me – such casual sloppiness was almost reassuring in that place of concentrated, sexual awakening. But David's housemates were forever lingering, their heavy footsteps, their muscular, independent energy, their ripe newly acquired masculinity, impossible to escape.

I could not go there feeling the way I did about Rose. I thought about fetching David back to stay with me in my own room, but even that seemed wrong, a violation of the code of grief that does not make allowances for frivolous relationships, especially those of a sexual nature. And though it might have been nice to have company, David was not really a friend, he became a friend years later, but at the time he was a kind of menacing, slightly unreliable partner in an unspoken mission to bust open the gates to adulthood. It was with him that I felt most grown-up, even though all we did was talk philosophy and see how much sex we could cram into a night. It was rotten, marathon sex, the kind that leaves you sore later. I thought because we did it so frequently and for so long, that we must be good at it. I thought about getting David, telling him what had happened and instructing him to stay the night with me, sleeping in my armchair if that suited me or on the floor or anywhere I chose and not necessarily in my bed. But then I thought he would think that I was crazy. Anyway, I did not want him here with his dreamy, philosophizing mind, his perpetual state of semi-arousal, his ever-analytic disposition. He'd have some fancy, unbearable theory on why I felt like I did. I got mad just thinking about this. Why should he judge me so.

Of course he'd done nothing to deserve my confused, unfriendly mood, but I could not help but fix upon him and all his typical, expected inadequacies, the same failings one would find in any nineteen-year-old boy. Suddenly I thought of him as an unnecessary, sordid pastime, a bad habit I'd gotten into. Within minutes of considering the need to see him, I'd decided to break up with him. Break up, as though there'd been anything so solid that it needed breaking.

My suitcase was packed now and I had a canvas bag of books,

including my address book so I could make whatever phone calls were necessary from home. To the hospital where I worked, to various classmates who could tape lectures for me while I was gone, to the tutor I met up with on Thursdays. I imagined myself making such calls, speaking in a measured, thickened tone of the nature of my absence, my personal grief. With these things I left the house and on my way to the railway station I stopped at David's house, breathless and dishevelled, and knocked wildly at the door.

He answered looking bored and sleepy, his shaggy head bent to one side, squinting because he wasn't wearing his glasses. His feet were bare and his jeans were torn at the knees and too tight at the waistband, so that they hugged him in a prissy way. He'd been reading a music magazine – one of those that features stereo equipment, comparing the sound quality of different speakers and amplifiers – the boy equivalent of a fashion magazine, I suppose, and exactly the sort of thing which, when I saw it, revitalized my feeling that there was too great a gulf between the sexes. We could never bridge this gap and to attempt to do so was to breach every known and unknown natural law.

'I'm going home,' I said. 'My great-aunt died.'

'Died,' he said, shaking his head, considering this. 'That's terrible.'

'Yes, for her that would be just about as bad as it gets,' I said, impatiently. 'I am going to the station now. You could go with me, and stay with me until the train came.'

'Yeah,' he said. But he didn't move. He seemed fixed in a dreamy, half-awake state. Perhaps I'd woke him, or maybe his head was so flooded with facts about hi-fis that it was taking him a while to digest the non-autonomous world in which people live and die.

'You sure there are trains?' he said. 'I mean, it's kind of late for—'

'I have tickets,' I said, which was, of course, not true. I hadn't considered the likely situation, which was that there were no trains to London at this hour.

'I have to get my keys,' he said and stepped back inside the house. He'd left the door open, but had not invited me inside. I did not have to wait for an invitation, he undoubtedly meant for me to come in and find a place to sit among all the amassed clutter, the stacks of folders, the record albums set leaning against the skirting board, the textbooks, the discarded ruck-sacks, all the debris of university life. But I preferred to stay outside. The hallway was lit by an ugly copper-coloured plastic table lamp, beneath which a whole pile of newspapers and junk mail threatened to set itself alight against the unprotected, shadeless bulb. I waited for David and the thought crossed my mind that it was exactly this sort of thing, papers piled so that they might at any moment be set alight by a light bulb, which would never happen in a house inhabited by women. First, a table lamp would always have a shade (it was impossible to imagine otherwise in a house with women in it), and also we would automatically recognize a fire hazard when we saw one. I was never a great reader of feminist studies, but something about being at university made me think in terms which could vaguely be thought of as feminist. I'd look at the actions of my male colleagues around me and question, how on earth has this evolved?

I waited five minutes and David did not show up. Then I called for him and heard a noise from somewhere upstairs. Finally he emerged, holding his shoes in one hand and in the other the music magazine and a hardback book. It was an anthology of Frankfurt school theorists, a great big book filled with tiny text. I wondered why he thought he needed so much reading material. Was the thought of sitting, talking with me as I waited for the train so terrible? It wasn't as though I did not have plenty to talk about. A woman I loved, who I'd known all my life and lived with for two years, a woman central to my sense of myself and my family, had died. I had plenty to talk about. I looked at the book and told David I'd changed my mind.

'I'd rather be alone,' I said, rather unconvincingly.

'I don't mind coming,' he said. 'Anyway, I'm ready now.'

'No, thank you. I think it would be better if you didn't come.'

'Why not? I mean, how long can it be? When does the train leave?'

He thought I didn't want him to be bored, that is why I'd demurred all of a sudden. He caught my sharp glance at his book and that dumb magazine and he'd decided that I imagined him to have better things to do than see me off at the railway station.

'I'll go now,' I said. 'I don't think I'll be back.'

'What are you talking about?' he said, concerned. 'You can't drop out of university over a *death*. That's ridiculous.'

This made me laugh. I wondered what reason he thought might be adequate for dropping out. Not that I planned to. What I'd meant, of course, was that I wouldn't be back to his house again. But in his typical David manner – he was always amazed when women broke up with him – this thought did not occur to him.

What I longed for, as I sat in the railway station by myself that night, was a girlfriend. My childhood had been filled with the received wisdom that girls form fierce, lifelong alliances with each other and that there was for every girl a single other who would be her best friend. Best friends took advice from one another on important clothes purchases, on which boys were worth 'going for' and which were best left alone. They borrowed each other's make-up and a real best friend trusted the other to trim the front of her hair or curl the back where she could not see. More daring, better friends allowed the other to use a crochet needle to pull strands of her hair through a plastic cap, coat the hair with coloured bleach, and then shampoo it out after a set time. In fact, most friendships could be judged by what they let each other do to their hair. That was my understanding at least. I knew of a girl who let her best friend lop her shoulder-length hair off into a layered, sporty look, just above her ears. That was pretty stiff devotion, I'd thought. But I'd never myself had a best friend. I'd been temporary best friends with girls who were engaged in one of the momentary battles with their real best friends – temporary alliances born through the need to make another girl jealous – but I'd never had a real best friend of my own.

If I'd had one now, I could call her and she would sneak away from whatever lesser demand occupied her at the time – a library job, babysitting duties, a date – and come to me. I thought of that all the way back home on the train, about how if I were a different sort of person I'd have a best friend and that girl would find a way of coming to my house and staying with me, of holding my hand through Rose's funeral, of listening as I confessed all my secrets: how even though I loved my aunt I was revolted by her dead body, how it looked like her but was not her. How during the funeral itself my mind had wandered, I'd not been paying full attention the entire time, and had thought of trivial things, like I wanted to use the bath that night before Isobel because she always left such a ring and got every towel in the place soaked. I thought how wonderful it would be to hide somewhere dark and secret and safe and tell my best friend these sorts of silly, slightly shameful truths. And of course about David, how I'd hooked up with him and how we'd worn each other out so much we had to stop seeing each other. That is what I'd tell her, my pretend best friend. I'd say the sex was so constant and unrelenting we had to cool off. That would make her laugh! I would not tell her I'd given up on him because he'd brought books to read while waiting with me at the station. Not even a best friend could understand such a strange, inappropriate sensitivity. After all, what difference did it make what a man did – bringing books or not – when he was a man and could never, no matter how well intentioned, be a best friend?

There'd been a football game so they were running extra trains that night. I was lucky – or unlucky, depending on how you looked at it. I managed to get a train to London but I was surrounded for most of the journey by raucous, drunken fans who – when they weren't swearing across the cars at each other – burst into patriotic, demented football songs or collapsed in alcoholic sickness, groaning miserably into the corners of their seats. The journey took a crazy, illogical route through Leeds, involving a change at Milton Keynes and a long delay somewhere else. It was an old train that travelled slowly and made tremendous clanging sounds and ear-piercing, metal-upon-metal squeals. I found a place near a couple of businessmen who looked reassuringly boring, preoccupied with such matters as the *Financial Times* and corporate reports that they produced from leather cases. When one of the football fans passed by, falling about and loudly calling to another, the businessmen angled their disapproval so that it subtly, but determinedly, drove the menacing character away. This gave me great confidence. Somehow, miraculously, I fell asleep.

I woke to the smell of vomit and stale beer. Someone had been sick in the compartment where the businessmen had been, but now weren't, and I was nearly sick myself when I woke and saw this. I left the compartment and went down the narrow passage, searching for a clean spot to sit down. The train was less crowded now, but every compartment had been trashed by the football fans, with worrisome, stained seats and mysterious puddles on the floor. I decided the best thing was to stand in the area between cars, where if you could endure the constant jolting and the crashing noise around you, you could enjoy the open window and the swiftly moving spring air. I smelled silage and diesel and the comforting smell of cow dung.

I closed my eyes, breathing all these things, savouring them, enjoying the movement of the train with its singular purpose. I heard a noise behind to my right as the doors to one of the cars opened. Fearing football fans I braced myself for some kind of half-disclosed verbal assault, a comment made just out of earshot which would turn me red with anger. To my relief it was only two off-duty conductors. They were talking about an accident in which a person had thrown themselves on to the tracks in London. The driver hadn't had a chance to brake and the person was dead – gruesomely so, from what I gathered. How anyone could choose such a way to kill themselves was beyond me. I always stood well back from the platform, fearing that some minor loss of balance or an unexpected, accidental shove from behind might cause me to fall on to the tracks. I'd heard of this happening, or perhaps it was only a story my mother told me to keep me from taking any risks. At any rate, the idea of deliberately throwing oneself on to tracks sickened me, even more than the horrible, vomit-soaked seat in the compartment where I'd slept. I thought, *what other diabolical thing will transpire before the night is out*? I'd had news of the death of a beloved aunt, broken up with my boyfriend, shared close quarters, while sleeping, with a stranger who was sick all over his seat, and now I'd heard that somewhere out in the world a person had chosen to end his life in the most terrible of ways.

'She was only young,' the conductor said, which surprised me as I'd imagined from the beginning that he'd been talking about a man. In my mind I'd pictured some down-and-out middle-aged man with a grey beard and ill-fitting, tattered clothes, finishing off the last of a can of triple X and hurling himself into the windy, treacherous space in front of an oncoming train. Just at that moment a train on the adjacent track passed in the opposite direction and I jumped back from the window, dazzled by its speed: a startling unforgiving speed which, for the first time ever, struck me as potentially lethal, almost innately evil, like a handgun or a switchblade knife, or the shackles you see as proof of some terrible deed. The speed, the grave heavy armour of the train's engine, the endless rotation of the undercarriage. When the conductor spoke again he said the woman who had killed herself did it just outside Waterloo Station – and I nearly collapsed right there.

Of course it had been Lea. I only needed to hear it had happened near Waterloo. We'd always gotten off there to walk to the South Bank for concerts. The pedestrian bridge allowed for extensive views of the immense, many-tracked passage for trains going to and from South London. She'd been fascinated by this particular section of track, studded with signal boxes and meaningful flags, signs of warning and tall banks the trains rounded, inches from one another.

'It just looks so ominous,' she'd said once, a casual, passing remark. Had she thought about it then? Had she thought that if her life ever got too unbearable she might end it here in a conclusive way that left no doubt of her intention? This was no call for help, from what I gathered. The body, once it was recovered, was scarcely identifiable.

'What was her name?' I asked the conductor. The words were out faster than I could reel them in. I had to know, then suddenly couldn't stand to know. The conductor looked at me blankly, noticing for the first time that I was there. Then he shrugged, shaking his head with a reticent indifference.

'Dunno,' he said with a Northern accent. 'Some sorry lass.'

12

The person who died outside Waterloo was not Lea. I was convinced at the time it had been her, but it was not. It was a much older woman who drank a great deal and fell on to the tracks only half deliberately. Lea killed herself much later with an overdose of prescriptive pills, the very ones which were meant to make her better. James went to North London to see a special solicitor about selling one of his mother's paintings (apparently the selling of fine art has its own special legal requirements) and was due to have lunch with his editor in Kensington afterwards. She told him she was going to the Chelsea Flower Show and to meet her at a pub in Kensington, just around the corner from his publisher's, when it opened at six-thirty. Perhaps she planned to do all that, go to the flower show then on to the pub, or perhaps she told him this knowing all the while that she was lying and that by the time he figured out she'd lied, it would be too late to save her.

The thought that she deliberately created an opportunity for her suicide seems so cold-blooded and gruesomely practical. Had she been in a state of deep depression at the time she would never have been able to carry off such a plan. But she was sinking back into a depression, not quite there yet but on her way. She knew this, and her fear was such that she would do anything, anything at all, to limit the pain, to avoid the crisis she saw coming. Anything. People with Lea's sort of depression often lapse in and out of it with increasing frequency throughout their lives. Sometimes there is a gap between cycles and sometimes one bout of depression rolls into another. One learns the signs. Had James been more practised he'd have known not to leave Lea alone. But she'd been all right for a couple of months and he had business to attend to. The sale of the painting was in order to buy her a violin, something he was anxious to do. He left her alone for eleven hours and she was dead when he returned. He found her. There was not one suicide note but several attempts which she'd discarded: wadded bits of looseleaf paper marked in her vaulted, strangely overfeminized script.

James and I do not talk about the time following Rose and Lea's deaths – which were spaced apart by less than a year. We used to, of course. For a time it was the only thing we talked about at all, first deliberately, as a subject that needed to be constantly attended to, recaptured and worked over, and later as a kind of painful touchstone, a raw and lonely place which had become so familiar that it felt necessary to remind ourselves of it every so often. Not of Rose, so much, though we thought of her fondly, and with a certain brightness that she had always brought with her. I could accept Rose's dying and therefore felt less need to mull it over, to explain it to myself. Mother had been right that in the scheme of things she'd gotten off lightly. She'd lived almost eighty years in relative comfort, with her own sisters or with us, her end-of-life ersatz family. True, she'd never had much of a career, the part-time teaching she'd done was the sort of makeshift piecework that never amounted to a great deal, but she'd never had to worry about money. She'd never had children, this is perhaps the only real loss she'd felt in her life. She often said she wished she'd had a child (or two, she was among the generation that would assume an only child to be miserable and lonely). But Isobel had still been very much a child when Rose came to live with us. So that left the fact she was a spinster, that there had been no husband.

Later in my life I began to envision spinsterhood differently than I had as a young woman. Then I'd imagined it as a kind of tragic solitary imprisonment, and most certainly as a failure; but later I saw it as a kind of wonderful alternative, a rather grand freedom that required more guts than I had. Down the road from where James and I lived was a woman named Dorothy. She was about forty-five and she drove the school runs in her reliable, sluggish Ford wagon twice daily and in all weathers; she kept the house in immaculate condition, cooked economic nutritionally balanced meals from recipes she cut from the Sunday papers. She saw me walking the dog one morning and asked what that was like, to walk a dog every morning. Pleasant, I told her. He's good company. I'd like a dog, she said, but my husband won't agree. Too much of a bind, he says, too much work. We talked about the possibilities, a small dog, a dog that had already been housetrained but needed a new home, a dog that did not shed hair, but she shook her head after a few minutes and laughed. Oh, no, he would never agree. Laughing as though about some grumpy, best-avoided boss, an amiable authority who needed to be got around. I'd seen her husband on occasion, in the garden raking leaves or up on a ladder trying to resolve some minor guttering problem. He hadn't struck me as such a bully, why had she allowed him to become a barrier to her pleasure? Just tell him you are getting a dog, I said. And that you will assume full responsibility for it. This made her laugh more. Oh, God, no. I couldn't, she said, her face red, her smile becoming less amused, more urgent and pained. No, she said, anyway we don't really want a dog. She'd turned away then, quickly adding goodbye in her light voice. I saw her many times after that, watching through the window as I walked the dog, but she never came out again, not after that one time.

But that's a loss, isn't it? Not having a husband, or a wife, say.

Perhaps, but then she'd have had to cook for him and clean for him and do what he wanted. Spend money the way he wanted, you know.

No, I don't know.

Well, it's a lot of work, constant negotiation with a man.

And women are easier? Is that what you are claiming?

By comparison, yes.

Then what about Lea?

Lea. The conversation would always return to her, the cycle of our feelings like those of the seasons. After a long drift elsewhere, after a surprisingly pleasant interlude that felt like summer, after many turns and distractions; but eventually, always. At the bottom of every exchange there was that history, that demon, that common denominator that fixed us to each other and held us captive, though never struggling.

It was two in the morning when I arrived back at the house on Dartmouth Row. The trains had long since stopped running and I'd had to show the taxi driver at King's Cross that I had cash before he'd journey across the river to Blackheath. He'd grumbled anyway; even if he were being paid for it he didn't see why he had to drive across the city. In the world of students, two in the morning is not so late but Mother was not expecting me and it was a bit unfair to arrive at such an hour when she no doubt was exhausted if not suitably drugged with one of her rich, timely administered sleeping pills that she came to depend upon. I expected to sneak into the house as best I could without disturbing anybody, without disturbing Isobel and Mother, and go directly to bed. But when the taxi drew up outside the house I saw that there were lights on everywhere and when I went inside I found Mother furiously engaged in housekeeping chores. She was dressed in a hideous pink shellsuit and was polishing one of Rose's silver candelabra with a blackened J-cloth. The house was terribly clean, much cleaner than a house ought to be, overtidy, fussy, immaculate. Rose's eyesight was not perfect and there'd been plenty of areas of mounting dust, splattered, tea-coloured stains, yellowing porcelain, filmy glass. She was slightly prone to collectables and had way too many table ornaments and figurines, all of which required some small measure of cleaning that was impossible to administer after she'd become ill.

But now the house was unusually spotless. The floor had been handwashed, someone (Mother) had gotten down on her hands and knees with a scouring pad and brought up all the gummy residue that accrued in dark, overlooked corners. The windows had been shined, just beneath the stink of the silver polish I detected the lemon ammonia smell of Windolene, which only Mother used. Rose preferred a simple vinegar mixture. She always felt that modern cleaning agents were over the top, crazy to fill your house with those chemicals when a little soda or borax or regular house soap – big blocks of waxy soap that came wrapped in plain paper from the chemist – did the job just as well. But Mother liked the spray bottles, the caustic limescale removing creams, the vivid, violet-coloured goopy mixtures and powders with a fair burning power. To the right of the hob, next to a shiny newly purchased toaster was a cardboard box filled with bottles of such things. Toilet duck and Dettol, steel wool coated with a foul-smelling pink dust, bleach in a tall white bottle.

'The funeral will not be too small. That is the important thing,' she said. She must have said something else before this, some kind of nominal greeting, but this is what I remember. I walked into the house at an incredible time of day and she launched straight into the subject of Rose's funeral. 'I can't bear the thought of some sparsely attended, depressing little gathering for her,' she said. 'But it won't be like that. I called the vicar and told him to go to every pensioner in the area who knew Rose and personally invite them to the funeral. Nobody over sixty would dare not show up if a vicar asked them to. He's the new vicar, young and involved in all sorts of missions and foreign aid, all the trendy causes, you know. He's not the sort who goes out of his way when some old lady in his parish dies, but I said to him, "Do it. Here's a list of names."'

There was a time when I would have felt a kind of shrinking embarrassment and, something else, almost a revulsion at the idea of my mother approaching anyone, especially a man of God, with her overly controlling, almost hostile instructions. But I was worn out, shocked, with my mind reeling in an obsessional, crazy manner about Lea. I had to know, I had to know right then if it had been her on those tracks. Ever since I'd overheard the conductor I'd thought what an absurd, unlikely coincidence it would be that she died the same week as Rose. How doubtful it was that of all the people in the world it would be Lea, how silly I was to assume. But I also had an intuitive, doomed feeling about it. In my mind I saw her standing at the rim of the platform, the wind a stiff current pushing her light hair up around her head like the leafy branches of a tree. I saw the train coming, I heard the hard mechanical grinding that deafened the other sound, the thud which arrives with unspectacular simplicity. Then the train is gone and there is nothing but silence.

'I won't talk about that. It is too painful, and completely unnecessary.'

'Of course it is necessary. That is the whole point – you need some help getting through this, getting over it.'

'I won't ever get over it. I don't even want to get over it. Anyway, what happened is a known fact. The shrink can fill in the blanks himself.'

'Herself.'

'Her bloody self, then. I won't talk about it.'

We were in my mother's car, the one Rose had bought her and which, once upon a time, I had detested and sworn never to drive. Funny how old passions of resistance become so familiar they lose their fire. The car was no longer a symbol of my mother's spoiltness, her greedy vanity, but a thing with wheels that took us where we wanted to go.

James's cheeks dappled, his heart beat uproariously in a mixture of fear, anger and advanced shame. The psychologist was only a few miles away but the trip seemed to take forever and there were moments, at traffic lights, when I thought James would just step out of the car and disappear into the city.

'I cannot go in there and talk about it.'

'Then don't talk about it. Just go in.'

That was 1980, three months after Lea's death.

But a year earlier, when I saw my mother in the kitchen

working furiously on the house and speaking in a steady rattle about the vicar and the flowers and who is likely to come and who we must still notify, I took it as a sign that it had not been Lea who died. That she would live on to be a grand old woman. It did not occur to me that I could know a fact before my mother, she was still in some way the omnipotent creature of my childhood, and my relief that it had not been Lea was so great it was as though a whole furnace of worry had suddenly been removed from my body. Finally, I could rest. I listened to Mother, who prattled on about the mundane details of Rose's funeral – the flowers, the catering, the music. I made her a cup of tea, which she accepted gratefully but did not drink, then I got into my bed in the kitchen and lay down – I was suddenly so tired – and nodded occasionally as she lulled me to sleep with her voice, full of responsibility and concern. A dignified end, she kept saying, is what that good woman deserves.

I went to the funeral in a suit my mother chose for me and that I have never worn since. I stood in stunned silence as the whole congregation breathed together and coughed at intervals and spoke in solemn, heavy voices of God and devotion, of gratefulness and forgiveness. Not a bad-sized congregation. My mother's success with the vicar was evident from the crowd, though I like to think that the memory of Rose herself drew much of it. I went to the wake, which I thought was too much like a party and sulked through, then endured the next few particularly quiet days, which felt very much like those long grey days following Christmas, when the holiday is over and yet nobody has quite returned to their regular lives. Except that in this case there was no feeling of joy or plenitude. The house had turned suddenly into a kind of mausoleum, every corner held some small article infused with Rose's memory – a pad of her notepaper, a book she was reading, a pair of her wide, low-heeled practical shoes with worn soles and the soft, round indentation of her heel at the instep. There was nothing nice about those days at home. We were steeped in sorrow, even the house seemed to sag with her loss. But there was also the strange freedom that mourning allots you. I had a sense that all the petty aspects of life were suddenly well beneath me. As my mind was constantly occupied with greater matters, minor aggravations held no purchase with me. I could not care if somebody's dog ran barking at my heels; if I were delayed by a late bus, or found myself drenched in a sudden rainstorm without my umbrella; what Mother said or did not say, the fact that I was steadily losing ground with my studies. None of these things mattered.

We skulked around guiltily, we talked about Rose, drifting off into other subjects, the coming spring and how we would have to tend to the garden ourselves, hack down last season's raspberry canes, rake the leaves from the flower beds, rekindle all the flowerpots, the hanging baskets in which ivy now grew in abundance, spilling messily over the edges. Oh, we could ignore these things – there is no chore in a garden that is truly required – but our allegiance to Rose would never allow us to neglect what she found precious so we set to work on these tasks. I found repetitive, physical work in which the body is worn out and the mind able to satisfactorily switch off, both necessary and satisfying. It was early March, the days were lengthening.

'You're a natural gardener,' Mother said, watching me as I weeded. 'I can't tell what is meant to be there and what isn't.'

Shortly after that, in a burst of ill-directed sentimentality, Mother bought a rose tree, a rare and difficult to grow specimen which she wanted to plant in memory of Rose. A nice idea except the garden already had an abundance of roses, a few tidy, yellow-flowering bushes and several more wild-looking shrub roses that bloomed luxuriously no matter what the weather. The tree was pernickety, it needed mulching and feeding and specialized pruning – in Mother's care its survival was unlikely.

'Well, we'll plant it anyway,' she said, knowing herself how low its prospects were, it was a particularly spindly, fragile-looking tree that seemed nothing like the photograph on a tag tied to one branch.

'I don't think we should plant it,' Isobel said. 'It might die and then we'll be even sadder.'

'All right, we'll give it away,' Mother said.

'To whom?' I asked.

'To James and Lea,' Mother said. 'They can plant it and if it lives then we'll know it was Rose's tree and if it dies then it was just some silly plant I bought at a garden centre.'

It was late afternoon on a Sunday, the sky was pale blue in some places, with dark violet clouds in others. The trees, just beginning to get their buds, were still darkly skeletal, waiting. The wet ground, slushy with topsoil, hid a lower, frozen ledge of earth that would not yield easily to a trowel. I squatted by a flower bed, my hands caked in dirt and Mother towered above in a pea coat and watch cap, not Mother's usual dress at all but in our united misery we'd grown practical, miserly with our luxuries. None of us, willing yet to venture down familiar avenues of comfort, the long baths or special meals or the heady momentary intoxication of sex. Stephen Price was banished from the house at this time. They were breaking up, Mother said. The wife was pregnant. 'Will I grow old alone?' Mother had asked, almost giggling, the night before. The punishment of poor decisions, she concluded, when we did not answer immediately. Now she stood above me as I pulled weeds, the cup of tea she'd brought out funnelled steam into the crisp air. Isobel squinted up to see the moon, which was so thinly sliced it looked like a tiny nick in the sky, and I concluded, for no reason at all, that Lea must be alive. How ignorant I was, I decided, to imagine such coincidence, to occupy myself with a tragedy so unlikely. It was almost folly to punish oneself so.

I am guilty, I told myself, my hands sunk in blackness, the weeds giving themselves over finally to my greedy, implacable pull. To imagine her dead was a sort of horrid wish. I was in love with James, wasn't he the one I wanted to see now? Did I have any genuine desire to see Lea? No, it was all as Mother had said almost a year ago. She'd known because she'd been plagued by the same menacing characteristic, a selfishness, a need, and she'd seen it in me, her virginal daughter with all the good marks.

Thinking this, knowing this, I almost cried out. All my alibis, all my certain denial, became broken buckets shedding water, everything leaking. James's face bore itself on my mind, it had always been there anyway. I looked up to the windows where he lived, and to where he would shortly return – I assumed this, I did not truly know what had become of him – and wished him there. Despite death, despite loss and guilt, I still felt it. I will not seek him out, I had told myself, and he will notice this and respect me. At Rose's funeral I had thought how she had lived for so many years without a husband, without any known lover, and how she had gone to her grave without the sin of wanting, of coveting, and yet I could not live twenty years cleanly. Sometimes when David and I made our frantic love, I'd thought deliberately of James, confronting for that brief moment the fact of my desire. I'd done it several times, but banished it from my thoughts afterwards. *Well, you won't be so quick to judge people now, will you?* I thought, and then shivered and looked up at Mother and Isobel's confused, surprised expressions. It would seem I had spoken out loud.

13

He did not diminish in my mind. I did not picture him deliberately or in a particular pose, as in a photograph, he simply existed inside me. A phantom limb, a recurring dream. Walking down the crowded streets of York I would think I saw him, the back of his head, his profile in the distance. Why such concentration, such preoccupation, with a man who was not particularly kind to me? At the library I was drawn to the area of contemporary fiction in which one of his novels – the first one, which was the only big success he had – seemed to leap at me from the shelf. Inside the yellowing pages I turned to the dedication to Lea as a way of waking up, of throwing water on my face, of concluding yet again that the man was taken. Not taken, *given over*.

I had any number of ways of punishing myself for my feelings, but no way of stopping them. I worked at my tiny desk, a relic from the junk shop with thick veneer and fake brass handles, writing equations on the insides of my fingers, and special codes to help me remember physics laws. I thought how not long ago nothing had seemed so complicated that I could not commit it to memory. Now my mind worked normally, except it was unable to store information. My memory had become reluctant, unreliable, like a cranky old car in deep winter. This I blamed on my preoccupation, my guilt. Why was I guilty? No one had suffered, how could I appoint blame when no injury had occurred? I wrote mathematical formulas on my kneecaps and stared at them in the bath, I decorated my ankles with bits of information, linking them with chains of ink. I thought that this was probably fairly crazy, and with a small fragment of wonder considered that many of the people I'd seen at the Maudesley in the course of visiting Lea had ended up there for acts less nutty than drawing biro tattoos over significant portions of their body. There'd been one patient who had driven to a traffic light and failed to accelerate when it turned green. She'd sat in her car and let the stream of traffic hoot behind her; people passed her with irate expressions, some of them using violent language and threats of all kinds. But she could not move. A police officer appeared on a motorcycle and asked, in a routine manner, if she was having car trouble. Could you put on your hazard lights and move off the road? he'd asked. She burst into tears and did not respond. He took her to the local hospital and she was eventually transferred to the Maudesley. Later, sitting on the narrow iron bed which was hers for the week she underwent treatment, she remarked that she'd been admitted for a traffic violation. She'd meant it as a joke and I'd taken it as one, but now, with my biro in my hand and my feet blackened in ink I thought it was not so much a joke.

I decided to be sane and not to draw (overmuch) on myself. There was really no reason to be so anxious anyway. Unless James told Lea what had occurred between us – what had almost occurred, what had never occurred – then it might as well not have happened. Nothing *did* happen, that was the point. We'd had some feelings: *I'd* had some feelings, all he'd done was make an unwise remark or two. How in this age of highly charged sex, of wife-swapping and mile-high clubs and celebrity porn stars, could these non-actions even register?

'I'm going to stop this,' I vowed to my new best friend Claire. I'd finally gotten one, yes. And though I'd waited a long time for such a friend, she remained my best friend for life. 'I mean, why am I still bound up with these people?'

We shared a mews house. I'd seen an ad for it in the paper and took it immediately, hoping to get a housemate to share the expense. It was a tiny place but nicely furnished and non-studenty. The wallpaper was not ripped, the bathtub was not stained yellow and rusted. There were new carpets upstairs and smooth, wide-planked oak floors in the sitting room and kitchen. Only the size of it, and the rather dismal brown-coloured suite in the bathroom made it less than ideal. An academic couple owned it and he'd been given a year teaching in Italy, so they let it out. Claire was in my physiology class, and she and I'd become friends. The first night she moved in I told her all about James, then worried I'd scare her off with my obsession. But she was not scared. She understood the house was part of a plan to get better, to get through this snarled segment of my life and on to flatter ground.

'Fantasy men', she said, with a wise look, 'are the best kind.'

'Oh, no, he's plenty real,' I said. 'I mean he exists.'

'But you never actually had an affair, right?'

'Right.'

'Just my point, then, fantasy,' she said. 'God, I wish I had one like that. All my daydreams are marred by reality.'

She made me feel better and I convinced myself there was no reason to feel uneasy, let alone guilty. But alone, later, I would always turn the whole issue over in my mind like an hourglass and let the thoughts fall again in one continuous flow. I drew to remember and to keep myself busy. I'd stopped drawing on myself but taken up doodling on a legal pad, a yellow one with faint, green lines. I was waiting for something, but I did not know what, occupying my hands by tearing pieces off the legal pad, the bits I'd drawn on, into confetti. I thought about my mother, and that old, finger-pointing saying that the apple does not fall far from the tree.

I had ways of banishing James from my mind. Whenever I thought of him, when his face popped into my mind or a comment he might have made presented itself in memory, I imagined him and Lea at their wedding. A big church service, Lea in a white silk, blossoming dress with rolled shoulders and a sweetheart neckline. An elaborate, flowery white wedding with bridesmaids and rings on a velvet pillow. This is not at all what they'd had, they'd been married in a registry office, but in my imagination there was an ancient stone church, a choir of children, their scrubbed faces shining, their mouths open in song, and the final crucial detail, the vows. I made myself imagine James taking his vows, and Lea's beautiful face tilted upwards to receive them.

If this did not work I thought about what he would look like as an old man, with long earlobes like turkey wattles and a neck creased like unironed cotton, a belly that ballooned over spindly, unmuscular legs. I imagined his hands blue-veined with thick skin, his wedding band cutting deep into his flesh. I imagined all the lovely things he whispered in Lea's ear, and how he'd been cruel to me just because he'd had some moment of attraction.

That I did not deny myself, the fact of his attraction. I allowed myself to believe he'd felt it because if I did not, I could figure no reason for my feelings. If he hadn't felt something, too, then I was just crazy. And that scared me a little.

To keep myself busy, too, I embarked on a headstrong sex life. I stopped sleeping with David (who was already sleeping with someone else by the time I arrived back at university anyway) and instead busied myself with another boy, who then went off to study in Germany, and so I had to find a new one. My studies went to ruin. At the end of the term I hardly recognized myself. I, who had been so studious and careful, did not bother to finish my course material, or even sometimes to purchase the necessary books. I, who had been so little drawn to the pleasure of sex, could not find a way of curbing an ever-increasing, almost predatorial obsession with my male classmates. This, even though what went on in bed still seemed to me somewhat appalling, alien and strange. Sex seemed to me an act made for people other than myself, more an accessory to ordinary life than an act that consummated an emotion. I had a long chat with David about this. Since our affair had ended we'd begun an unusual friendship. It was as though now that the sex was out of the way it was easier to talk. I discovered there was much we agreed about, including that we both felt that sex seemed to be a distancing activity. Neither one of us felt quite as capable of being close to a person after we had gone to bed with them.

'I liked you so much better before we were sleeping together,' he confessed. 'I liked what you said, how your mind worked. I liked how big you were, when you walked in the door you filled up the room. I was obsessed, I was frantic for you,' he said.

'Then afterwards—' I forced myself to speak, even though I felt something welling up inside me, an anger about being spoken to like this, as though sex with me had been a funeral for his admiration and desire. He'd never said anything so lovely as that he'd been frantic for me back then. He'd only looked a little moony and made jokes, half of them at my own expense, and shoved himself as near to me as possible. 'What happened after we were, you know, together? What went wrong?'

He gave a little shrug and smiled mischievously. 'That's just what happens. Maybe just to guys. It might be different for girls. You lot are far better at all this than we are.'

I let his stupidity on this point stand. I could not have begun to explain to him the nature of female desire and, in any case, I didn't know for sure that he was wrong. 'But surely this is the opposite of what sex is supposed to do,' I pleaded with him, hoping that if I could convince him I might convince myself.

'Yes, obviously, but I am telling you what happens, not what is meant to happen.'

'Perhaps it is different when you fall in love,' I said.

'You let me know,' he shot back, and laughed in a way that I thought pretentious, as though falling in love were beside the point anyway.

One day around this time I was walking around the man-made lake at the centre of the campus, my unread books clutched in front of me. I often walked, it had become a pastime for me. It was summer, or near summer. The days had grown so long the sun hardly had time to set before it was up in the sky again. I wore jean cut-offs, quite short, and black tights and a lycra top that snapped together at the crotch and made you feel you were wearing a swimsuit all day. Like this I walked around the lake, sweating uncomfortably in the tights and the nylon top – which was really inappropriate for such hot weather – and holding my books in the hope I might sit down and read, or perhaps because I knew I wouldn't. I must have walked around that lake for over an hour in the sun because I began to feel weak, sun spots floated on my vision. I touched the top of my bare head and felt my hair, hot like the bonnet of a car after a long journey, and knew that I was getting heat exhaustion and must stop walking and come out of the sun. But why should I leave the sunshine? It is so rare in England, after all, and I had been a Californian girl before. I should be easily capable of coping with whatever sun dared present itself in Britain. I walked, mourning that girl I'd been, and thinking how silly I looked in my outfit, one that many girls wore but which I felt was too deliberately sexy to be the least bit alluring. Why did I need to costume myself so? Why couldn't I go back to the way I'd been, in my plain skirts and boxy blazers, always working or reading or studying, always doing something useful with my time? I'd worked so hard to get myself a place at university. And now I was blowing it and, worse than that, I could not even feel that upset about blowing it. Failure was inevitable, I was sure of it. For most of my life I'd held the arrogant conviction that I would be a doctor, then I'd accepted that I would not be a doctor but might, with a little luck, manage a career in the sciences. Now it was becoming quite apparent that I'd be lucky to get a degree at all, in any field. I felt hot and terribly thirsty. Finally, in an almost dream-like state, I sank down on to a bench just outside the dining hall.

It was then that I saw him. My vision, hazy in the heat and sun, took in the landscape of the university, the burnt grass and blistering walkways, the flat concrete bed of water that formed the lake, and then settled on this one man in the distance and focused until it became clear. James. There had been all those times I imagined I saw him – at a stall in the crowded market on Thursdays or through the window on a bus, and these imagined sightings all seemed grossly unfounded when finally he was there. He was standing by himself squinting out over the lake in the direction from which I'd just come. He looked almost like he could be a student; he could easily have been a lecturer or even a PhD candidate. But he was dressed not like a student but like a member of the 'real world', which in student parlance meant everyone outside university. I cannot tell you what specifically made him so – perhaps it was his leather shoes – but there was an air about him as though he didn't quite belong. He was standing by himself surveying the campus the way one might look at a foreign city.

It did not seem so strange a thing to see him there, four hours from London, on a university campus he had not visited since graduating many years earlier. In a way, I'd always expected him to turn up, always known that one day when I was not searching for him in a crowd or imagining his face on a stranger, he'd show. Part of me reckoned that my preoccupation with him was only a silly, half-mad invented love, an unrequited and wholly inappropriate set of silly emotions, but part of me felt also that our lives had just pressed together, naturally, and that he was there because it had become impossible not to be. The old pain still existed, the pain of his rejection and his anger, the pain of my guilt. I thought how easy it would be to leave now, to drift away without it ever needing to be known that I saw him there by the lake. Then it occurred to me that he could only have been there to see me. Why else would he be on campus? He'd come looking and by chance I'd seen him first.

Without thinking about what I was doing I gathered my books. I stood, a twitching, energized nerve coursing through me, and turned around so he would not see my face. I knew that if he did not see me from the front he would not recognize me. The girl he was searching for wore cotton summer skirts and loafers, crisp blouses and pullovers, not the clothes I wore now. I walked away, imagining his eyes burning on to my back. If he saw my hair, of which I had a great deal and wore in the same way I always had, he might come after me despite the clothes. Hadn't I crossed busy streets and gone into stores after men whose resemblance to James was so vague as to be laughable? Twice his age or half his height or younger than myself. And now I was walking deliberately away, avoiding him as he stood so close that if I shouted he would hear me.

He did not see me. When I chanced a backwards glance he'd left the lake and was walking the opposite way down a hill. I stood on a mound of grass, what might be considered a hill in the city of York, though like the lake it was man-made and divided by beds of tulips and shaggy daisies, and watched him walk away. I practised my habit of imagining him getting married or imagining him very old, thin and brittle, with a halo of white hair. I found I could not concentrate on these thoughts, however, so busy was I watching his every step, his real hair, curly and dark, caught in the sunlight, his shoulders that rolled with his gait. I watched him walk away and I felt better for having let him go.

Lea died less than a year later. I did not know about it for some time. They'd had a bad year together. He was coming unstrung from the constant stress. She vacillated between despair and anger at her illness. She became pregnant and lost the baby almost immediately. Eight per cent of women who miscarry try to kill themselves, according to one of the studies I read in the *Lancet*. My mother had moved in with somebody named Michael, he was younger than her and had a little bit of money; she called him her toy boy and let him buy her clothes. Isobel, now fifteen, objected to Michael and spent most of her time staying with friends who lived in a room over a dry-cleaning shop on Southampton Road. Mother had rented out the house on Dartmouth Row, our part of it anyway. She couldn't quite bring herself to sell it. 'I think I ought to sell,' she said, in her serious estate agent's-tone, 'and then I imagine some horrible couple ripping out the fireplaces and putting in a ready-made kitchen from B&Q and I just *cannot*.' I didn't know what James and Lea had been doing, they'd vanished in every practical way from our lives and we didn't discuss them. If I returned to London I had to stay with Mother with her new beau in Chislehurst, which I couldn't quite bring myself to do, so I tended to stay in York. I had this feeling if I just stayed in the North that my life would begin again, begin afresh, and that is what I needed. A new start. I was sure that if I managed not to fail university this would all happen. I'd already decided to be a Northerner, or as near enough as someone who'd grown up in California could be, to wear wellies and drive rusted-out cars and to treat the south of the country with a certain pious disdain. I had a plan, a complete life plan that I'd discussed with David who called it quaint and misguided, complete rubbish and embarrassing to hear about.

'I suppose that in your little scenario you settle down with a farmer and raise four kids?' he said, his eyebrows raised in disdain.

'Two kids,' I corrected. 'And he doesn't have to be a farmer, though I admit a farm sounds nice.'

Then I remembered that James's parents had had a farm in Derbyshire, a very strange farm, of course, because they'd concentrated all their efforts on that one rare and relatively unspectacular sheep and knew nothing at all of farming generally. Nevertheless they'd lived on a farm.

'Actually, I've changed my mind,' I said. 'I think I'll move to Edinburgh and be an urban girl, but up there. That might suit me better.'

'At least that's slightly more realistic,' David said.

Isobel vowed never to leave London.

'Why on earth would I leave such a great city?' she often said on her marathon phone conversations with me, during which we talked about truly senseless things like skin care and Isobel's boyfriends and what we would do if Mother had a baby with this new guy she was living with. The telephone had become a crucial part of my life, another way to fritter away my time, but at least I wasn't drawing on myself anymore.

'Mother says you won't go home and that you live in a dump,' I told Isobel. 'She says you are underage and it's against the law.'

'There's nothing so wrong with this place,' Isobel insisted. 'I get to see all the attempted break-ins from the front-room window. I'm a most useful tool for Southwark police, who don't seem to have noticed I'm breaking any laws.'

'Are her locks any good?' I asked Mother. Another useful aspect of the telephone was how it could be used as a means of prying indirectly. 'The chain on the door looked flimsy. It looked like something you'd wear around your neck.'

'Her friends from school would scare away any prospective criminals. And she lives with a huge black guy who knows judo,' Mother said.

'Do you have a black martial artist for a boyfriend?' I asked Isobel.

'Gay,' she said. 'Him not me. Otherwise I would, *definitely*.'

'When are you coming to see us?' Mother asked me.

'When are you going to see them?' I asked Isobel. I could not, for some reason, stomach going to visit Mother and her boyfriend in their newly built Berkeley home in Chislehurst, at least not on my own. Isobel had to be there for me to even contemplate a visit.

'I'm there all the time,' said Isobel. 'Mother is exaggerating. I *have* to go home whether I like it or not. For money and, you know, clean clothes.'

One day Mother rang to say that the tenants at Dartmouth Row had given notice. They were leaving because of an incident that occurred on the property. An incident, Mother said.

'Oh,' I said. I didn't know what this had to do with me.

'They left because of a reason that will have a great deal of meaning to you. You might want to sit down,' she said.

'I am sitting down,' I told her. 'When they invent visually

aided telephones – which I cannot wait for – you won't need me to tell you this.'

Mother laughed in a fake way, her tone going up a whole octave. 'That's very funny, dear, but there really was an incident.'

'What? An *incident*. Like a wall collapsed and they found a skeleton? Why are you being so weird?'

'Because Lea died in the house, I'm afraid. They'd been living there again for some time and she died. I'm sorry. I know how fond of her you were, how fond you used to be.' Usually when Mother had something terrible to tell me she spoke in a voice that did not sound like her own at all but like some practised version of it, a jumble of sentences all clinging together, not spontaneous, not directly communicative, but like she was reading aloud and not taking in the content. That is what it had sounded like when she told me of Rose's death, like a script she was reading. It was her way of coping, it was not meant to be offensive, and I'd grown used to this manner and felt almost reassured by it. But when she told me about Lea she did not sound this way, she sounded all at ends, unsure of herself. She said, 'I hope it isn't a terrible shock. She killed herself, I don't know if she meant to, with pills. Rebecca, I'm sorry. I always told you that girl was troubled. And now the tenants don't want to stay, and frankly I think it is time to sell it. Don't you think, Rebecca? You don't want Rosie's old house, do you? No need to keep it going, is there?'

'I'll come home,' I said, my head swimming, my mind suddenly numb.

'No, darling, there's no need. You mustn't be interrupted in the middle of term. It all happened a few weeks ago, anyway, I only found out now because of the tenant, because they don't want to keep the lease. They're paying the two months they owe and leaving now, won't even stay in the house another night. It's the woman, actually, she's pregnant and a little hysterical. It's like that when you're pregnant, you get very superstitious. She doesn't want to stay and the husband has to do what she wants.'

'I'm going to come. I need to,' I said.

'I wish you wouldn't,' Mother insisted. 'I think the further away you stay from this the better.'

'I'm on my way.'

'Honey,' she said.

But I did not leave. Something stopped me – I don't know what. I stayed in York and got used to the idea of Lea dying, dying in our house in Blackheath, and of the world going on as it did, with its preoccupations and momentary pleasures, with ruddy-faced young lovers banking the river, market merchants calling to a crowd, jugglers and unicyclists and preachers standing on tea crates and talking about God. I got used to the idea of James alone, disconnected from his wife, of his grief and his failure. He hadn't any parents himself, and now no wife. I could not imagine what it might be like to be so alone in the world, but I tried to enact it. To see nobody, to hear only the expressions of sadness and bewilderment which rang in my head.

I thought at first to write to him, and began several letters that never got past the third sentence. I thought I ought to ring him – that would be the wisest thing – but when I rang the number the operator gave me there was no answer. Even at five in the morning there was no answer, so I figured he either had pulled it from the wall or had moved. Of course, he'd have had to move. Nobody could stay in the house after such a thing had occurred. I thought of the house, Rose's old house, and how once it had been a shrine to cleanliness and order, to the bustling chores that busied three spinster sisters the whole of their lives. They'd had a sewing room to make their own tablecloths and hem their own linen. They knew how to do ordinary tasks that young women today do not know how to do: darn socks and mend rugs, knit, cut cloth correctly on the bias, make a simple dress from a pattern. They made up their own cleaning solutions of vinegar and soda crystals, of lemon and wax for the furniture, and stored these concoctions in glass jars. It was not that they were spartan or martyrs to hard work, they believed themselves to be doing what was required, that is all. They bought the newest most up-to-date washing machine in 1956 and discussed at length which concentrated powder cleanser was best used with it, but they never upgraded the model and so, until the drum started leaking and the heating mechanism went awry, they did not indulge in another machine. That washing machine had lasted for almost twenty years. Well, why not? They only ran it once a week. Underwear was always hand washed in their day and much of their winter wear was wool and therefore unsuitable for machine washing.

'We used it mostly for the bedclothes,' Rose admitted, 'and for Father's shirts. Everyone was wearing drip-dry dresses back then but they didn't shape quite right if you let them stay in a machine. The nylon wasn't so good in those days, you had to be careful. It was wonderful for dustrags and floorcloths. And for towels.'

Floorcloths. You see, I don't think I could even identify a floorcloth. She lived in a different world and that house on Dartmouth Row was, for a long time, part of that world. But now it was orphaned, an empty echoing place where a girl killed herself in despair. Rose was dead and the house was to be sold. The era had ended. As much as I wanted to go back to London, I could not bring myself to do so. As often as I'd planned the right thing to say to James, or how I might approach him, in the end I did nothing at all even to recognize Lea's death.

Is this forgivable? Not a week goes by even now when I do not think of her. So I cannot pretend that I was not among the grieved. And yet I did nothing, not even write a note to her parents.

Many months later I came home on an ordinary Monday afternoon and glanced over to the place in the hall where Claire and I kept the answering machine and saw that the red light was on, which meant there was a message waiting. I thought at first to leave it, messages were usually for Claire, who was involved in a great number of student activities inlcuding a dramatic production which required lots of detailed work and impromptu meetings about such things as backdrops and props. Usually, if I played the messages I ended up scrambling for a piece of paper and trying to write as fast as possible the details of who was meeting where and over what subject – for Claire of course. But that afternoon I had a feeling, I cannot say why, that the red light had particular significance. I pressed a button and the tape rewound; I listened as a voice came on which I realized, all at once, I had not heard for almost two years. James's voice, slow and precise with a slightly Northern sound to certain of his vowels. I listened to him speak, not at first, taking in the message at all but just hearing the sound of him, then rewound the message and listened again. He was in town, at a hotel near the city centre, he'd like to meet up if that was possible. He gave a time and an address, and said if he didn't hear from me he'd try to ring again.

I went to your hotel. It was one of the hundreds of tiny hotels in York, in a street I'd passed many times but never had reason to walk down. I hesitated at the reception area, just a desk in a lobby not wide enough to hold more than two people, which was vacant at this time of afternoon. It was decorated with the usual array of travel information, colourful brochures of the minster, tastefully drawn maps of the city done on heavy woven paper, not white, of course, but a dull beige to look old, like the city, to look quaint. In a wire rack were folded leaflets of other nearby areas, Knaresborough and Harrogate, National Trust properties and open gardens. I stood looking at these, not touching them, but just staring for something to do. For some reason I thought of hundreds of colourful kites flying in the air. It was October and the weather was much colder already. The cherry tree outside my house had beautiful golden and red leaves the size of dinner plates, and the wind had picked up so that my lips had chapped from all the long walks I'd been taking lately, to clear my mind, to concentrate my thoughts, to breathe easy for a while. All the students were flying kites, it had suddenly become a big sport: box kites and stunt kites, some of them tied together so that they flew as one. The array of brochures had made me think of that, and of the fact you were here only temporarily, travelling through. Perhaps you had places to go afterwards, destinations I could not imagine.

You appeared, coming through a fire door to my right, and saved me from the dilemma, the embarrassment even, of having to track down the owner to find you. You were wearing a cloth jacket and jeans with a nick on the thigh, a black T-shirt, shoes that needed polishing. I noticed you'd changed your glasses, from the plain gold frames I'd known so well to a heavier tortoiseshell pair, simple ovals with a gold bridge across the nose. You smiled weakly when you saw me and sat down on the step. The way you sat, all at once so your limbs went akimbo, made me start. For a moment I thought you'd collapsed.

'You look so much older,' you said. 'I looked through the glass on the door and thought at first it wasn't you, just some nice-looking young woman who was checking in.'

I was going to say to you that the situation was true in reverse for me, that you did not seem older at all. In fact, much younger. You were young then of course, awfully young to be a widower, how old were you – thirty? Certainly no more. You rose and kissed me on the cheek, so quick. I tried to speak but couldn't. I must have looked ridiculous, standing there, overcome with gratitude at having at last seen you again. You, who linked me back to my past, to my girlhood, to the place I lived and to my family who I did not see for reasons that were impossible to pinpoint. I watched you in amazement and in fear: for as soon as I saw you I thought simultaneously about how terrible it would be when you left and you went back to whatever eerie, far-off, mysterious place it was you now occupied and I went back to my house at the edge of town. All this – the rustic hotel with its smell of varnish, rose oil and ink, you standing in a lobby that was almost too small for you, the step at the fire door, the lightning fast kiss, the yellow lights clicking alight from a timer – all this would be a thing that happened and would never happen again. A past, a bit of history, another recollection to slide into oblivion in my shabby memory. But see how I remember it? How I remember it so well? What was wrong with me in university was that I was in love – from the beginning.

You asked me if I wanted to go somewhere for coffee or wait a bit and have a drink at a pub. I looked out the window, at a sky smeared in red and orange with big, balding trees acting like a wall around us.

'Pub,' I said, barely audible, my voice deeper than normal, sounding almost like it was coming from someone else entirely, someone standing directly behind me, a woman I did not know.

'Oh, good, you're feeling the same as me,' you said, meaning about the drink, of course. I don't think you were feeling the same as me – not at all. You seemed jolly, like some gentle, half-remembered uncle paying a family visit. Only your hands gave you away, they were restless, you shoved them in your pockets to keep them still.

We walked for a good while and came across a pub which had opened early and was already bustling with students. We liked it because it was noisy, frenetic, with a row of gaudy one-armed bandits, a poolroom that gave rise to loud bursts of male voices, and a juke box that played slightly dated hits. I apologized for this, for the noise, as it had been my suggestion that we went there and now every exchange had to be shouted, but we secretly (not so secretly) enjoyed not having to say much. We sat at a table, our knees almost touching, and you said we'd have a glass and then go on a walk. That was good, a walk, something to do, a destination. I liked looking at you in the pub and I liked the comfort of not having to enact conversation. I liked drinking. A few minutes after I finished my pint you took my hand and rose up, pulling me out of my seat in a gentle fashion, almost gallantly, I thought, and we got out.

I don't know how far we walked that night; I've never been any good at judging distance. We headed for the outskirts of the city and found a footpath through a field. The day had faded entirely now and we picked our way across a cow pasture, unsteadily. We thought we might not be able to make it – the grass was long and we couldn't see at all – until I remembered a penlight attached to my key ring, a present from Mother, which put out a surprising amount of light. On the other side was a stile and a single-lane road, but it was flat and seemed luxurious and easy after the hike through the field. We switched off the penlight to save the batteries and focused instead on the stars, which seemed very low that night with a brightness that dazzled the eyes. The road ended and we headed back into fields. We took the fields because that was what was available to us, though our shoes were wrong, and we could hardly see. But we wanted the preoccupation of walking, the repeating fields, always one more. We read the sky, the hedgerows kept us straight. After a couple of hours I was hungry and you reached into your jacket and fished out a packet of KP peanuts you'd bought at the pub. We sat on a stile and ate. As far as we'd walked the minster was still easy to see, we could have walked another twenty miles and still seen it, lit up against the sky, so we never felt lost though we had no idea where we were.

I still don't know. Later Claire and I got in her car and tried to figure it out; she drove and I navigated, an ordnance survey map across my lap, but it was impossible to determine. The cow fields were identical, all the stiles looked alike.

You told me about Lea. I told you I'd found out from my mother, how sorry I was.

'Yup,' you said, and nodded your head. You wouldn't talk about it, not then, not right away.

You said, 'It's the practical decisions which are the worst. To bury or cremate. She had nothing like a will, we'd never even discussed it. I did not sleep for three nights trying to decide. In the end I let her parents make the decision. They chose everything, which was perfectly suitable I now see. Of course, they ought to have. Their child. Their little girl.'

'You found her?' I said, then instantly wished to withdraw the question.

'Yes.'

'She had such faith in you,' I said. 'Utter trust.'

'I think so.'

'I'm sure whatever you did was the right thing.'

'Oh, no,' you said, shaking your head violently. You'd hardly showed any emotion at all until then. I'd hit a nerve. I'd hit that nerve, the same one that would hamper you for the rest of your life. Then, in a staccatoed mantra, 'Not at all, not at all, not at all,' you said. A stream of words which pushed it all away for a time. 'Let's go.'

*

We did not know where to go. Turning around and going back the way we came seemed unduly wasteful, for surely there must be an easier means of circling back, and anyway we could never have retraced our journey. We looked towards the minster and headed there, the stem of light from my penlight fading by the minute. We were lucky, a full moon, a clear sky, a flat land drenched in starlight. You talked about what we would eat when we got back, for now we were famished. The tree branches made clattering sounds in the wind, the cows looked like tables set out on the horizon. We planted our steps, backs bent. When we reached a line of hedgerow I started, thinking we'd come across an electric wire, still alive, somewhere near, but it was only a strand of barbed wire ringing with the striking wind.

When the street lamps began we followed the road into town, feeling like dwarves in a big land, or like foxes coming in from the night to thieve. We entered the city again near the minster, passing beneath the ancient gates like good pilgrims.

'Four and a half hours,' I said, finally able to read the watch face on my wrist.

'I'm sorry,' you said, smiling as one who pulls, by accident, a practical joke. 'I'll buy you dinner if there's any place open.'

A pizza place I knew of, and a fish and chip shop. We went that direction, along towards the high street, but there was a queue for a place to sit, so we ordered two large pizzas and carried them back to my house. The warmth from the pizza and the smell of it was a lure that kept us walking. You couldn't stand it anymore and grabbed a slice from the box, holding it up to your mouth as you walked.

'You'll burn your tongue,' I said, envying you. I'd have liked to have done the same thing but did not dare. Being near you brought out a little more of the part of me that existed long ago, a part that would never have considered eating on the street or wolfing down pizza without a knife and fork.

My feet were sore, as though I'd worn the flesh away and was stepping on the bone rock of my heels; you had blisters because you wore your good new shoes. In my kitchen, your feet denuded, white, broad as fins, you showed me where the leather had rubbed neat holes, one on the back of each heel. I inspected like a good nurse and went upstairs for bandages and salve. I hardly heard you coming after me. After so many miles your steps were practised glides, but when you caught me, searching through a cabinet of face creams and old medicines, I did not bother to feign surprise. We worked all night trying to find each other beneath so many years and memories; the harboured sentiments, the connotations were all of them like further layers of concealing clothes. Even with you inside me, I did not think really that we'd shed everything. We dared not speak. To attach words to it all would be like slicing at a jungle with a dull sickle. Our voices became dangerous; we did not trust them. The hours diminished until birdsong woke us, still entwined, our passion not completed, nothing at all finished between us. We woke as partners labouring, and who had been labouring a long time, unravelling, loosening a knot that had been tied tight long ago.

He did not stay long that visit, I let him go as one might a cat that had ventured in for milk inside a comfortable, lighted kitchen but was anxious to set off again for other places. He explained to me that he was not well: nothing specific, only that he got headaches and found sleeping difficult, the normal sort of thing one would expect after a loss, though this had gone on a long time. I thought that even then; that it seemed an extreme reaction to have such preoccupation, insomnia, and basic dysfunction almost a year after her death. But I let him tell me about it without trying to rush in and care for him. He sat in bed with his mug of tea, smoking steadily, a mark from the bed sheets across his cheek like a tribal scar. The morning was so bright outside and of course we'd not drawn the curtains the night before. He told me the reason for his trip to York was to come to some kind of resolution, some kind of closure with his relationship with Lea. After all, this is where they'd met. He said it just like that, as though she were still alive somewhere but leading another life now, separate from him, and I thought at first that his statement sounded a little naive. He was still wearing his wedding ring, I noticed, and he was still so obviously caught up with what had happened.

'I think this was the right thing to do, coming here, seeing you. Last night was the first time I've slept in a long time.'

'That was only a few hours, hardly what I would call a rest. I'm exhausted,' I said. Then I added quickly, 'This is not a complaint.'

He laughed. He could not sleep at all some nights, he said, but lay awake in a kind of waking dream state, which rested him enough to carry on, but not enough to ever fully recover himself. A few hours, no more, sometimes in trains he might nod off, or while reading at his desk, but these were only brief naps. He always woke with a start as though slapped.

'You need a doctor,' I said.

He looked at me. 'Perhaps I have one.'

'I'll never be a doctor, nothing like it. I'd like to be a researcher or work for a drug company, or *something*, except that I haven't a chance in hell of passing an exam.'

'I cannot believe that,' he said, almost laughing. His recollection was still of a studious, academically successful girl. A girl I had not been for years.

'It's true. Anyway, you need someone with a medical licence who can prescribe.'

'No,' he said sternly. 'I don't like pills. I won't have anything like that.'

Of course not. No pills. Her legacy – part of her legacy – was that he no longer trusted doctors. He saw the whole of the psychiatric world as a kind of distorted, funny house full of odd people and wrongly contrived tonics no better than leeches for curing. No doctors, I would be his medic. His mother, his wife. I assigned myself all of these roles without thinking, without knowing. I tried not to, but this is what happened. It was inevitable, once he'd found me.

He speed-trained from London to York, from York to London. Having him in my bed became familiar, expected; all the little things about him that I'd half-forgotten, turns of phrase, the way he raised his eyebrows to make a simple declaration into a question, the way he walked, his handwriting, reasserted themselves in my mind once more. One night the central heating failed and he wore that same disgraceful wool cap that Lea had often threatened to burn. In the morning his hair was flattened sideways and I thought of what Lea would have said if she'd seen it. Hedge hair, that had been her expression.

I thought of Lea often; I did not always feel that I'd betrayed her. Sometimes I did. But I had not always been in love with James and certainly if Lea still existed I would not be with him now. We'd have drifted apart, me from him and Lea. We'd have forgotten all about one another. But that is not what happened. Would I have been in love with James now if I'd not had the feelings I did so many years ago? This was the question I grappled with. The question for James, if he entertained any such issue and I'm sure that he did not, was different. Would he love me had it not been for Lea's death?

I don't think so. He loved me because I linked him back to Lea, to his home with her, and I substantiated the fact that she had existed at all. For here was the point he made, over and again: there was nothing to remember her by, no children, no sign of their marriage. With her death, the sense of a family, of his family of two with Lea, dissolved to ash and floated weightless into the air.

'We ought to have had a child,' he said, much later when he spoke openly of her, of the event of her suicide, of his whole doomed world now that she was gone. 'Not that we didn't try.'

'That would have been awful,' I said.

'I know, but it feels like there ought to have been a child.'

I sighed. I pretended to understand. 'Perhaps, but it would have been worse for her, leaving a child behind. That would have been terrible for her.'

His response was quick, he'd obviously thought of this before. 'She wouldn't have done it. That's just it.'

'Don't be silly. There is no evidence that having a child reduces one's chances of suiciding.'

'No *medical* evidence.'

'Well, what other kind could there be?'

We were adversaries, and we were lovers. Lovers in the deepest sense. I'd have died for him. I'd die for him now. We embarked on a romance, unique I think, but wouldn't everybody say that of their own love? I think it is safe to say that we were beyond the normal hoped-for love. We just wanted to survive. We had been, both of us, drowning for a long time. In each other's company we could make sense of our stuttering lives. I would not say it felt good to be together, only that it felt right.

A couple of months later we were sitting in the kitchen at my house. Claire, who had trained briefly as a hairdresser before getting a place at university, was giving James one of her at-home haircuts. She was a 'mature' student, though she wasn't much older than myself, a short muscular woman, gypsyish, with dark eyes and a mouth that seemed tiny until she smiled. Such a big, open grin, she was grinning like that when Mother rang me. She'd tucked a towel beneath James's shirt collar and wetted his hair with a houseplant mister she kept by the window, and in a good-natured, bossy kind of way was instructing him: chin down, now to the left, look straight ahead, now down again.

The phone rang, I should have let it go. But like a dog to a whistle, I set out for it immediately.

'Do that once more and you'll lose an earlobe,' Claire was saying to James. He was jotting notes into his desk diary as she worked above him, snipping at the ends of his hair with a delicate lightness that reminded me of the way a butterfly flutters around a sweet-smelling plant. 'You think I like doing this? It's a favour for you, don't you forget,' she said. 'Act grateful.'

'Shall I grovel?'

'Just be a little more cooperative. Hold still, for example.'

I think she was amazed by him. She always said there was something chivalric about him, something chaste and abiding, something violent that he kept to himself. It is important with that man, she told me once, never to let him get too serious.

'Quiet everybody,' I said, holding up a finger. I should have known it would be my mother; she always rang on a Sunday.

Claire said, 'If it's for me I'm not home.'

My mother hardly said hello before launching into a story about an art show at Blackheath Library that she'd gone to in which Isobel had sold two paintings. 'Right there, on the spot,' Mother said. 'I kept hauling Isobel away from all those other artist types – an untidy lot, not at all like Isobel who is so vain, really, classically vain, it took her as long to dress for the event as it did to paint those paintings, I can tell you. Anyway, I kept pulling at her sleeve and sending her over to the people who wanted to buy her paintings. I told her, go and talk with them. Isobel is so daft, she says to me, "What will I talk about? I don't know what to say." About the work, you silly cow, I told her. They wanted to give her a hundred quid each, these people. One was an older couple, the sort of rich, retired sort. The other was a young man with an immense beard and fat as a house, but loaded, you could tell. He was practically begging Isobel for another painting – that is, once I finally got her to deign to introduce herself. I had to go shortly after that so I don't know what happened. I think we're talking a couple of hundred quid, perhaps more, but it's a damned good start, don't you think? Who is that? That man in the background? Who is he?'

James had made a remark to Claire; he'd only spoken for a moment and not very loudly at that, but Mother had heard it. It had registered.

'Who was that?' she asked again, sharply.

Should I have lied? Probably. We could have gone years without her knowing. But I told her it was James; I felt I hadn't any choice. Until that moment I hadn't given much thought to what to say to Mother about him. Despite the constancy of my affection for him, and the slavish way he came every weekend to York, I'd always thought that each of James's visits might be his last. I hadn't any expectations, really, though that is not the same thing as having no hopes.

Mother was horrified.

'Oh, please,' she said. 'Please, *no*.'

The chatty, jocular quality of her voice while telling the story about Isobel was gone, replaced by a stark, contracted groan, a forbidding silence.

'We'll talk about it another time,' I said, evenly.

'We'll talk about it now!' she insisted.

I tried to disguise this conversation from James. He was so sure of his unworthiness. He often looked at me with a longing that suggested he was, or part of him was, occupied far away. He had his demons – I knew that – and his young wife's ghost to contend with. Every night we talked about her, in slow-moving conversations that seemed to fill the room with a heavy unbreathable air. Her ghost hovered around us, pressing against the closed glass of the window, rising with the smoke of his cigarette, tunnelling through the easy darkness, to find us, naked and alive.

'Are you out of your *mind*?' my mother was saying to me now.

'I'm very happy,' I said, remembering what she herself had taught me. That to be happy was itself a form of defence.

'Well, I can't imagine how,' she said.

Last weekend, before returning to London, James looked at me as at a bird soaring overhead and pushed his hand towards me as though trying to feel for the place where I became unattainable. Could I explain that to my mother? Could I explain how, one night, I woke to find him staring at me with opaque, dark eyes. I imagined his thoughts, the ones I could never reach, and as easily as if we were of one body, entered them into my dreams.

'This is special,' I said, quietly.

'Don't be ridiculous,' she said.

James made love to me as though the act were nothing more than a lullaby. It was not the sort of crashing, desperate sex of the newly enchanted. Sex came later, sex. For now it was a gathering pleasure, not even all that often.

My mother could never understand that. Oh no.

'I must go now,' I said.

'He will ruin you,' Mother hissed into the phone. 'He was always one for taking others down.'

If he heard this or gleaned this I wasn't sure. I'd moved as far away as the phone cord allowed and cupped the receiver in my palm, but still I felt like the conversation were taking place aloud, right in the centre of the room.

'Stop it,' I whispered.

'Listen to me, Rebecca, listen to me now. You have a chance at life, right now, you have a real chance. Don't let that man ruin it for you. Because that is what he'll do. He'll suck up whatever you'll let him. He'll—'

I hung up and turned around, the phone behind me, an unnaturally large smile across my face. I wished more than anything else to protect him; a desire that bore into me so deeply it lasted a lifetime. He was trying very hard not to appear upset. His face was very still, you could hardly detect a change, but a change was there. His features had softened, and he had a distracted, urgent look in his eyes. He did not seem so much hurt as disgraced. I could tell he knew. He was suddenly remote, serious, darkly quiet.

'Don't drop your head like that,' Claire said, her scissors poised above him.

'Should we stop, then?' he asked later, almost matter-of-factly, while standing in the bathroom. He ducked his head down and rinsed his newly shorn hair out in the sink. The cut ends came away, fixing themselves in the creases of his hands. He took up his razor and dragged it slowly across one cheek. 'What I mean is, would you like me to go? Because she is right, you know. You would do better without me. I don't imagine I was ever such a good deal for any woman—' He laughed, looking at himself in the mirror, observing himself as a kind of specimen. An oddity, a fairytale beast.

The idea that he might leave one day and never return, that I might be set back into my life without him for the second time, gave me a feeling of physical fear, a primitive simple terror, like I was about to fall from a great height. I knew how easily he could accomplish the simple task of disengaging himself from me. Because although he was dependant on me, on the one hand, and utterly reliant on the solid weight of my affection, he did not look after himself. He often made decisions that were directly opposite to what behoved him. He could easily leave me and absorb the hurt, the way a very large animal can absorb a bullet and run with it for miles. What had happened to him meant that he was able to do almost anything.

'Of course not,' I said, my voice shaking.

'She's right, you know.'

'She's not right.'

'You could get along without me, that's for sure.'

'Don't go.'

He slammed his wrists against the porcelain and threw his razor against the mirrored glass. There was a moment – how long could it have lasted? ten seconds, perhaps – when my fear found a new focus and I was scared of James himself. Then he smiled, a strange, austere smile, his fury melting. He held his hands out, palms up, as though to show me these puzzling weapons that misfire so easily. He came towards me, his pulse beating in his neck, and plucked me from the floor as though I were weightless. In the dark of the bedroom he locked his arms around me and spoke directly, no slurred whispers, nothing easily denied later. And I felt, here it is, the place I have been travelling towards, the end of the awful thirst. Here is the love story, already dreamed up, dreamt a million times in my fraught uneasy sleep. We made promises and bartered for each other's love, and in the morning there was no retraction, only a sense of renewal. He had decided on something, I saw it in him, and I suppose that was our real beginning.

14

I am not a young girl anymore, not a university student – I haven't been that girl for a long time – but a woman like I am now. Heavier with a few grey streaks in my auburn hair, still young, of course, but with a fading quality to my eyes. I look tired most days. I am nobody you would pick out of a crowd, but once singled out I still hold an attraction to some men – fewer every year, I presume.

At David and Eleanor's wedding I was sitting in a middle pew, on what would traditionally be the groom's side of the church. Even in my best dress, my red lipstick, my hat, you would not have noticed me. Except when James made such a noise about his headache. He was sitting close to me, emanating a heat that is peculiar, a raging aura, a fiery madness. It is as though he has a fever or has come from some exotic, faraway place in which a sun radiates brightly against an arid soil. His heat is not the nourishing warmth of the sun but the magnification of that warmth to an intolerable fire. It is uncomfortable to sit close to him. And he smells in a manner that is soupy, liquid, not altogether bad but not correct either, not for the formality of a wedding or the proximity of the guests, lined up in pews.

One of the facts I remember from my previous studies, my medical studies, is that our bodies carry with them more bacteria cells than cells that make up our own selves. We are a vast mixture of chemicals and of other organisms. Our brain, taking in clearly all that surrounds us, is like a clear window in a muddied hut. The organic body is subject to chemical change. And this change, in James's case, for example, can become palpable, available to the naked eye. Imagine how much one's body must alter in order to become visibly different in kind. When James's mania erupts it becomes obvious, manifest.

'Am I okay?' he whispered to me, in a voice so low that even Claire could not hear.

'Just stay still,' I told him. 'You're fine.'

He pushed close against me, like a child – almost, because unlike a child he communicated a small measure of aggression even as he hung close to me for comfort. He did not like to be so needy, he was not ready to give up his pride. These moments, when his discomfort was brought public, when the threat of humiliation loomed, made him uneasy, angry, helpless. And he was never a man who suffered well.

'I wish I could just go away, away, away,' he whispered.

I want to tell a story about how we were as a couple, just a simple example of how we functioned, but as I try to conjure one up, to remember, the days blur and all I can remember is the feeling I've held for decades of wanting and hoping. I cannot think what exactly these feelings are connected to, what specific thing, but there they are like dominant colours in a decorating scheme, found in some small way everywhere I turn.

James is not timid about love – he is phobic about untold hundreds of other things, refuses, for example, to go through long tunnels or up in small aeroplanes, will not take any drug strong enough to require a prescription, cannot bear television – but he is brave in love. He is sure. In love he is stealthy and knows how to wait. He is cunning. When we married he was still sometimes shy in small ways. He would not disturb me when taking a bath, or presume how I might spend my time on weekends. In bed he would act as though there was something forbidden in his touching me and would wait for a signal that it would be all right. That I wanted him to. He kissed me in a tentative manner, he assumed nothing. Perhaps this was because I was younger than him, or maybe he realized the great range of behaviour in sex and chose to go about a sexual relationship with a pace that assumed everything would be gotten to in time, eventually. Certainly, as I look back on it, the nature of our sexual relationship was unusual in its development. While most of my friends exhausted themselves in highly charged sexual relations, which withered over time, the spark in our relationship seemed to come from elsewhere, almost from an assumed fate.

After James and I were married he introduced me to a number of publishing people and I managed to get a job editing science books, which turned out to be exactly the sort of thing I was good at. By this time I'd given up on ever working even remotely in medicine, and pretty much on everything else as well except making a life with James. But I surprised myself by being good at my job. Within a few years I was promoted, then I moved to another house. By this time I had a number of authors and I came to be friendly with one in particular, a woman named Mimi Azad, an ethologist who has written several books on brain chemistry, two of which we'd published. I think of Mimi, because it was through her that I finally came to understand how it was that James and I were a couple, and how we appeared to the outside world.

We'd been married for six years; by then, it was a veteran marriage. We owned our small house, drove a sky-blue Astra, had insurance policies and wills. Few wives question the basis of their marriage to a particular man after six years. Or rather, many wives question their marriage, but not in quite the same way. I was sure I loved James. I had always loved him and my feelings were not so different than any other woman who falls in love and eventually marries. What made me feel different than other women was that I was never sure I understood James's love for me or, indeed, the basis of our attraction, our sense of belonging to one another. This is a small but fundamental distinction, one that would never occur to most people in the first place. I am sure most people simply marry somebody because they think they love them sufficiently to do so, then make the most of it over a period of years. There is not this question of why, this need to understand more than the simple declaration of love that precedes a marriage proposal. But even here James and I are different. We do not say I love you to one another. I cannot recall more than one single time. I am sure he has felt it, as I have, and I am almost as sure that the reason he does not say as much is the same reason that I do not. The redundancy of such a message, the lack of any necessity, the feeling – and this is critical – of having a better and more fundamental reason for being together.

I came to know Mimi very slowly. First through her manuscripts, which were highly technical and impersonal, but required a measure of revision which meant that we met a few times to discuss changes. She was a small, graceful woman, unbelievably beautiful, and she was as likely to wear clothes from Mark and Spencer as she was one of the many traditional saris that hung in her wardrobe in her house in Primrose Hill. I always found this strange, her ability to switch like that, to be Indian and look Indian, and then to change altogether and assume the standard dress of any middle-class Englishwoman. It was like at her many dinner parties, when she spoke in rushed, beautifully accented English to all the guests and then turned to her husband Raj and uttered some small, domestic instruction – please open a window or find another bottle of wine – in her native Urdu. Seamless, without a need to think about the switch.

I don't know why this should have surprised me, I felt as comfortable in 'American clothes', in what is thought of as American clothes, that is Levis' and sweatshirts, as I did in Laura Ashley or any other English manufacturer. I could still speak with a perfect American accent. But whenever I looked for Mimi at a restaurant I was always looking for the wrong thing – either for a dark, exotic-looking woman in the bright folds of a sari, only to find her wearing leggings and a tunic top, or the reverse. I'd search the room for a tiny woman in dark trousers only to find myself surprised to see her in the opulent folds of some lurid, exciting fabric.

We saw each other often. There is an on-going social season in publishing and we continued to run into each other, or find ourselves invited to the same event, or arrange for a lunch. More often than not it was without our husbands. I knew little about Raj, only that he was the managing director of a string of highly successful restaurants (English food, not Indian) and that his work enthralled and exhausted him.

'He works all the time,' she said, flipping the back of her hand into the air, in a gesture that meant, I suppose, that she accepted that he worked non-stop and that it did not bother her. 'He arrives home looking like he's been blown through a high-powered vacuum, his hair standing on end, his shirt rumpled as though he's used it as a washrag. My son calls him Action Dad, like he's out of a comic strip. My daughter – she's fifteen – she calls him Moneybags, because he's always talking about how much money this or that restaurant might make us, someday, always in the future, I might add. We laugh at him, at how hard he works. But if he didn't work that hard, if he were home with us all the time, we'd have to sedate him. Really, he's that keyed up. My mother once accused him of being a drug user. Of course, my mother thinks everyone who lives in a big city is a drug user.'

She told me this at a club in Soho. I cannot remember the reason we were both there. As she spoke she looked away, through the small, slightly dirty windows that faced the street. I remember thinking that she had a point to make, a subtle but important one.

'Your husband,' she began again, and here the conversation took a different tone, 'he is very unusual as well, I gather.'

I wondered if she'd heard gossip or if, somehow, she had guessed there was something not quite right through my own admissions or possibly from James's behaviour. I could not recall him ever doing much to cause her to think him 'unusual' as she'd said. He liked to socialize and was usually very good at parties or dinners or what have you. Witty, but not verbose. Quietly amusing.

'Well, he's a writer,' I said, ducking out of an answer.

'I haven't read his work. Please don't tell him that. It's just that I have so little time to read for leisure,' she said. She turned towards me. She had a long, slightly pointed nose and large, doe eyes. Her lips were unpainted tonight and I saw that they rose in the centre in a curious, appealing angle which I had not noticed before. She wore her glossy hair up, folded around her head in a manner that exaggerated her slim neck. She'd said exactly the sort of thing that would make James furious. This idea that fiction was of so frivolous a nature that it was not the sort of pursuit a serious thinker such as Mimi Azad, a scientist, would undertake. But I also knew that her appearance, her beauty, would keep him from being angry with her. He'd be hurt, but not angry. He would look into the warm brown of her eyes and protest that she must make time, that is all. And he would make a gift to her of one of his books.

She continued. 'What I meant was something else entirely. I sense from him a kind of spirit, a belonging only half to this world.'

I felt I should be shocked, such a bizarre thing to say. 'That is not the sort of statement I am used to hearing from science writers.' I smiled.

'I cannot help but be curious about you two,' she said. 'I have lain in bed and tried to pinpoint what it is. I have badgered Raj, who tells me to stop making things up and go to sleep. I have imagined unspeakable secrets, like that he has some whole other family in another country, or that you were partners in a covert, glamorous criminal act – a diamond heist, for instance. When you are around him, the way you watch him, it is not like a wife looks at her husband, but as a lover does. A secret lover.'

When she finished speaking I discovered that I had, without knowing it, lifted myself up from the barstool where I sat so that I was standing. And that my position was not straight, but slightly inclined. Falling slowly, I caught myself and leaned against the wall.

'It even occurred to me that somehow this was an arranged marriage, that you had not meant to love each other quite as you do. Is this absurd? I know a little about arranged marriages,' she added, laughing slightly.

If I'd ever believed that James and I were like other people, like other couples, I did no longer.

'Are you all right?' Mimi asked. How could she have known how this would affect me? All this time I'd imagined that to other people we seemed normal enough, and now I knew that this was not the case.

'James and I have never done anything to be ashamed of,' I said. 'There is no secret.'

'I'm sorry,' she began, 'I had no business.'

None of the furniture from Rose's house remains. Mother sold it all at auction after her death. I have no photos of my kitchen bedroom, of my boxes of clothing stored under the bed, of my stacks of books arranged against walls. I cannot recall exactly what towels we used, the pattern to the wallpaper, the way the light hung across the room in the afternoon. All of that is lost to me. I have Rose's old picnic-making things, her flask and biscuit tin, a canvas bag she always carried, and her album of the yearly spring photographs that spans the better part of a century. I have a pin she wore at Christmas, a silver wreath studded with a few small sapphires. I have the blanket she sewed out of lap rugs. The auction took place without my knowing about it, or perhaps I did know about it but did not have sufficient energy to combat Mother on the subject. Anyway, I haven't the space – James and I haven't the space – for all those big pieces that require the sort of house Rose had, not the cottage James and I live in.

There are, of course, James's mother's paintings, arranged in the dark corners of our house. In the hallway, along the staircase away from windows. Light is the enemy and must be kept away.

'I should sell these,' James has said. 'I think they bring bad luck.'

'They are your mother's,' I reminded him. 'And all you have of her.'

'Lea wanted me to sell them; she was always asking.'

'Oh, well, then sell them if that is what you want to do,' I said, and my voice was suddenly angry.

Our garden is what James calls a 'wildlife garden', which means he lets the grass grow long except where he's carved out a little, tidy green in which to park the picnic table and chairs, his hammock, the shed where he examines spiders and insects in his strange, boyish way. On the day that he left, the day he disappeared, the house seemed a vessel that had lost its contents. The garden suddenly took on the feeling of a public place that people might pass through on the way elsewhere, but not a place to enjoy. I could not sleep in the house because of its emptiness, I found sitting in the garden impossible because it felt like a cemetery plot. So I went to my car and curled up in the back seat. There I could sleep, the smallness of the car, the purpose of it – to transport, to deliver one to another place – made this possible. I knew he had left before I found his note just from the feeling of the house, its certain abandonment.

I discovered his note and the phone number which he had written for me to call. The way the note was written, so informally on the back of a delivery note, in small, almost indecipherable handwriting, made me think that leaving a note was an afterthought and that he'd nearly left without any explanation at all. Or perhaps it had all happened quite suddenly; this evacuation of his life with me may just be another whimsical half-mad act inspired by nothing. Should I take it seriously? Part of me believed that if I just ignored him the episode would draw to an easy close. He would return, life would continue as before. When he did not come back I was surprised. I went back to his desk and picked up the note with the phone number. I realized all at once, from the exchange and the first several digits in the number, that it was from Blackheath, from somewhere near where we used to live, if not actually on Dartmouth Row, and felt a sinking inside my chest. It hollowed me out so I sat down suddenly in a chair.

The past is not lost with James and myself, but resurrected again and again.

15

All love stories end unhappily. Why is this?

I walked down the street which I had thought of so many times that it had begun to feel like a dream place, an imaginary place. But there it was, just another London road, ordinary in its way. I'd meant to leave the car just outside the house in the spot where Mother used to park her Rover, but a sign indicated that a residents' permit was required for the spaces along that side of the street so I parked opposite, in a place marked 'Visitors'. We hadn't such a sign when I lived here, the road had been bare, without the parking signs or the single yellow line along the kerb. I parked and walked back to the beginning of Dartmouth Row, without allowing myself anything more than a cursory glance at the house which had once been my home. I wanted to come upon it as I had hundreds of times before, in my youth, panting up the hill with my school books in all weathers or marching down from the Shooter's Hill bus stop.

I noticed changes immediately. The fussy parking restrictions, first, but also that many of the houses, particularly the tiny terraced cottages at the end which had been quite ordinary, nothing grand about them at all, were 'done up', decorated to emphasize the trim, the sash windows, the heavy wooden doors. They seemed almost gaudy with fresh paint and scrubbed windows, potted plants and elaborately blooming window boxes. Mr Dodd had lived in one of those houses and I remembered his was a dull grey with a stark iron railing and a plain lawn in front with a bird table. Now his cottage bore expensive awnings on the ground-floor windows, an outdoor lamp, a security lamp, and a flowery number sign beside the door. Some sort of romanesque stone cherub held up a bird bath, which did not seem to be attracting too many birds at present.

Many of the houses had been named – Yew Cottage, Holly Cottage, Heathside. I could see down into their cellar kitchens, modern with matching units and fired-earth floors, ceiling spot lamps and French copper pans hanging along a wall or over a showy, completely spotless butcher block. Where the road met Blackheath Rise there was a patch of grass that had been glorified by some garden committee's attention. I could imagine the sort of women, their coiffed iron-coloured hair, their home-county accents, who had decided one day that for the good of the community they would beautify the spot with careful selections of bulbs and small, flowering heather. At one end of the road a cement slab blocked off its union with Shooter's Hill. I had discovered this in an abrupt fashion, when I tried to drive in from that direction. And I had no doubt this was also the work of those same women, who would not want the nuisance of commuter traffic.

But these were only superficial changes, essentially the place was the same. Teenagers still gathered at the heath end, I saw their cigarette butts lying in heaped, grey piles, like rotting nests. And the church with its notices and times of service beneath the same glass-framed sign. When I stood outside the house, Rose's house, James's and Lea's house, my house, I felt strangely that I'd never left it at all but could walk right in and find them all there, on the other side of those solid walls, sitting around the kitchen table in idle conversation. They would lift their eyes as I walked in, not surprised at all to see me there among them. Where have you been all this time? my mother might ask. We've been waiting for you.

James had been to the house many times. He never told me when he went, perhaps because he knew I would argue for him not to go, and remind him that we had agreed to sell it and that we really *ought* to sell it. There had been many minor catastrophes – broken pipes, mouse infestations, some dry rot in the attic – which we'd had to take care of at great expense. We could not afford to keep up two homes and we hardly used it. Wasn't that right, I'd insisted?

'We never go near the place, James,' I'd said.

'I go.'

'Well, you ought to stop.'

'*Ought to stop*. And why might this be?'

There was no point in arguing with him. He visited, solemnly and alone, the way one visits a grave. Once, during the year after Lea's death, he managed a brief stay there. Ten days, during which he felt assaulted by the morning's post bearing letters with her name on them, as though insistent on her continuing existence. He was driven out by this, as by so many other things; a purse left behind the sofa, a lipstick still marked with the print from her lips, a book with a dog-eared page where she had meant to return to it. A small group of friends had come to relieve him of the burden of moving her things on his own, but there had been these random, stray items left behind, exactly the ones that would do the damage.

'That sort of thing', he told me later in my bedroom in York, 'will burn a place in your chest.'

Even then I'd been amazed and slightly impatient by such action. What sort of man goes to stay in the house where his wife has killed herself? Perhaps I'd been jealous. It was early enough in our relationship that I might have been jealous. I pretended not to care too much. 'I'm surprised you lasted ten days,' I said to him.

He went, he explained, to be with her. He could not bring himself to visit her grave. He'd lasted ten days, and during that time, he said, he felt himself going mad. At first, it is not an unpleasant sensation, he said, a quiet unravelling, a softening, almost like a comfortable drunkenness. Later, when things progress, it is fierce and terrifying, a beast at the door.

'But you keep me steady,' he said, coaxing my arm from across my bare chest.

'You're foolish to go there at all,' I'd said, pulling my arm back and looking among the bedclothes for my nightshirt. I didn't think it was nice to be so stern, but I had a feeling – vague but present – that he might try the same again. It was that self-punishing aspect of him, that negligence he showed towards his own welfare. I had to protect him from that, I thought, even if it meant rebuking him, sometimes painfully, for the things he thought and did.

'Haven't you ever gone somewhere you shouldn't have?' he asked, genuinely curious.

'There's never been anywhere I ought not to have been,' I shot back.

Until now. I stood at the gate. The small front garden had been mildly attended to. The grass cut, the rosebushes brought back so they did not poke over the iron railings and hook people with their thorns as they passed. A retired widower had bought our little end of the house and this amount of gardening, a sort of general tidying, was probably his handiwork. But he would never be able to manage the back garden on his own. That must be a meadow by now, with foxes and hedgehogs and generations of rabbits. I imagined it, resplendent with flowering grasses, the bane of the ladies who beautified the street corners and planned hanging baskets for the village each spring. It had been a big garden, and quite wild even when we'd lived there, much too much for a single, elderly man. Mother was lucky to sell it at all, the part she'd owned that is. People talked about the house, telling how there had been a death in it, rumouring the possibility of a ghost. It had been on the market for over a year. I imagined the schoolchildren holding their breath as they passed it, running. The dares to enter through the gate, the stories of what happened if you were caught. The gossip would grow every year, embellished preposterously so that the story about the empty house grew more interesting and bloody. Lea's gentle descent to death through pills would be reworked so that it involved all sorts of props: butcher's knives, a fire rope, blood everywhere. Perhaps they'd made it into a murder. James, the suspicious young husband, would invite all manner of speculation. Some would say he'd been broken-hearted, but others would claim he'd had a mistress all the time. A young girl who lived below him in the garden flat, which was all the divorcee mother could afford.

I watched the house as one watches some exotic zoo animal that sleeps away its hours of boredom. I would like to have walked inside and toured the rooms, but that would be impossible. I'd long since lost my key and who was to say whether the locks were the same anyway? I'd have to break in and then I would be arrested for burglary. No, not arrested. James still owned his part of the house so I, by extension, was also an owner. The key, the proper key, I realized with a sudden jolt, would be in the drawer where we kept the cutlery at home. I thought about it there, a simple reminder of our connection to this house, to this past. Why hadn't I brought it with me? Why hadn't I thrown it away? I didn't know the answer to either question. But it wasn't the house I had intended to visit.

The address I was heading for was several blocks away on Morden Hill, across from the doctor's surgery. My appointment was for 10.30 and I was already a minute late. By the time I got down the hill I would be ten minutes late, perfectly on time as these things go. I turned away from the house and headed down the hill. I knew which house it would be, next to the house of a girl I went to school with. We'd been friendly, but never close enough for her to invite me over. Still, I knew the house.

What sort of woman would James have an affair with? I had various pictures in my mind, one of a pretty European woman with dark hair and strong, almost masculine eyebrows. She would have wide, heavy features and a full, womanly body. Her voice would bear the accent of her native country, and she would speak in a deliberate and unhurried manner, most seductively. What sort of profession? A curator for a museum, perhaps. Then there was another possibility: a youthful, slightly tomboyish woman, not necessarily younger than myself but more outdoorsy. She would have round, muscular thighs, a wide chest, hair which ran the length of her back that she tied back in an elastic band. Her face would be freckled, the crow's feet around her eyes giving the appearance of a squinting smile, a quirky habit to her speech, perhaps a slight whistle to her s's. I could picture him with her, watching as she hoisted a saddle on to her horse in a casual, effortless manner that suggested she'd done this hundreds, thousands, of times. I could imagine her long fingers, bare of rings or perhaps adorned with a half-dozen rings, artsy but not expensive. A functional, plain watch. She would be a riding instructor with a simple, undecorated name. Sue, perhaps. Or something slightly masculine – Toni. The other woman would have an ugly but interesting name, and unmistakedly feminine. Svetlana. Greta.

I did not believe that I had been left for some younger, more exciting, youthful girl, not a dewy, smiling, friendly sexpot who could carelessly, without meaning to, end a marriage cold. I believed this woman to be someone slightly older than myself, someone with whom James had very little in common. Attractive but mature. Perhaps she would have children. I could imagine the children, watching television in a back room, the curtains drawn against the sun, their big eyes darting from the TV screen to me, guessing; why is this stranger here? But of course they would not be there, the children, they would be at school. This must be why the woman – whose name I knew perfectly well, it was Charlotte – made the appointment for mid-morning.

I stopped imagining. When I reached the house she was there, outside on her knees fixing a plastic barrow that had come away from its frame. There was duct tape around the rusted corner of the frame and she had worked the barrow back on, but it still wobbled. I stopped and looked up at her. The front garden formed a hill and there were cement steps leading up to the door. Above me she seemed bigger than she was, with long legs encased in close-fitting denim. She turned out not to be tall at all, merely fine-boned and light. Later, when we stood awkwardly in her small entrance hall, it was me who seemed by comparison enormous. Five foot ten to her flat five feet.

She hardly glanced at me before making an introduction.

'Charlotte,' she said, bracing her lip over her teeth in a small, uncomfortable looking smile. She put her hand out then apologized for the garden soil smeared on her wrist, despite the wearing of gloves. 'I've been tinkering with this thing all morning but it's knackered,' she said about the wheelbarrow. 'Please come in. Would you like a coffee? Or something cold? Lemonade?'

She'd been a light blonde but her hair was mixed now. There were still soft, wispy bits, but where it had greyed the texture had changed. It was a bit woolly, dry, lopped off just below the ear. Her neck was slender and tanned, with certain giveaway crease marks that we all get in our late thirties or forties. She was perhaps a half-dozen years older than me, but she had delicate skin that could not take sun. Small spidery lines edged up from her lip. She was faded but still pretty with light eyes and scanty blonde brows that she filled in with a pencil. A full mouth, her beauty point, and fine teeth that she could not help but show even when only half smiling.

'I'll get us something. I won't be a minute,' she said, and left me in her living room, seated on a chair that had been recently re-covered in a stripy silk, and was perhaps her best. The rest of the room was more ordinary, a squat green couch, slightly dated wallpaper, grey carpet, a bookshelf that seemed scantily stocked, with ornaments of various sorts taking space where the books ought to have been. On a glass coffee table were a number of magazines about gardening and a vase of fresh flowers that were undoubtedly plucked this morning in anticipation of a visitor.

Ordinary, I thought. Was this terribly unkind of me? What an ordinary house and ordinary woman. I could not picture James with her. I felt almost as though Charlotte had been plucked off the street randomly. I watched through the open door as she made the tea and I thought this was the most shocking aspect of the whole situation – how very unlikely Charlotte was to have been the one. I almost felt like asking her if she was sure, if she was quite sure, that she was the woman I telephoned a few days ago asking after my husband.

Charlotte brought the tea out on a National Trust tea tray stocked with blue and white crockery. She was elfish, tiny; she'd swapped her garden shoes for a pair of flat ballet slippers so small I doubt I could have gotten more than my big toe inside one.

'I'm surprised you are here,' Charlotte was saying now. 'I don't really know why James wanted us to meet like this, I have to admit. Though it is like him to come up with something totally unusual. This can't be what most people do.'

I agreed with her. I might have said so. But the words did not come. Instead I said, rather icily, in a voice that at first I did not recognize as my own, '*Most* people? I'm not sure most people find themselves in such a situation in the first place.'

'Well, if you believe what you read. Or watch on television,' she said casually, as though it didn't mean very much to her. 'It has stopped being unusual, extramarital relationships.'

I glanced sharply at her at the word 'relationships'. Was that how she saw it? Not as an affair – too tatty, too scandalous – but as a *relationship*? She busied herself arranging the cups and saucers and so didn't notice the way I looked at her, with a certain degree of disdain and incredulity. I supposed she thought that I had known all along, even consented. This was something Mother had once said – at least I thought I remembered her saying it – that the wives always knew. They put it out of their minds, she'd claimed, but they know. How couldn't they? They only care when it becomes a problem, when the marriage might end or the affair itself gets known. But until then they are happy to let things go. To let their husbands go. It's pride, mostly, and vanity that makes them angry. Not that I blame them, she'd admitted, I'd be furious.

But I did not feel proud or angry. Looking at Charlotte, at the face that my husband had kissed, at the body he had connected himself to, made love to, at the woman whom he had no doubt promised all sorts of things, I did not feel much more than curious, even bewildered, at his choice. There was a bloating in my stomach, a kind of queasy heaviness that I attributed to nerves, and a sense of being overlarge for Charlotte's house. She was such a nimble woman, with her small legs tucked up beneath her, her knees making diamond shapes against the taut denim of her jeans, her slim fingers, her face so tiny I could have covered it with the span of my palm. Not angry, no, but baffled. I could not imagine anything as interesting as an affair happening inside Charlotte's home, which was furnished in flowery overstuffed sofas and flimsy desk lamps and 1960s style nesting tables. The kitchen was wallpapered in a textured woodchip paper to hide the rough plaster. There were tiles in a muddy colour along the lower halves of the walls and a fluorescent strip light that ran along the ceiling. The rooms were small and low-ceilinged, with the sort of framed prints – of orchards and fishing villages – that one finds in hotel rooms. Charmless, and somehow cold. I could not imagine James sitting with her in front of the electric fire and speaking meaningfully of anything at all. I could not imagine him even making Charlotte's acquaintance, let alone falling in love with her. Of course, nobody had mentioned love. That was my invention.

'I have to say I admire you for coming. It's very brave of you, but nothing I would not expect from a wife of James's,' Charlotte said.

'There wasn't any bravery in it. On the contrary, it is you who would need to be brave.'

She seemed unsettled by this remark and for a moment – a very brief moment – I almost felt sorry for her. First, because I could not imagine that my husband could love her in the slightest, but also because she wasn't terribly bright and was no match for me. I supposed she was the sort of older, still sexy woman who some men might find attractive. She would not want to start a family or get any money out of the situation, or even expect a great deal. The affair would be enough of an entertainment, the giddy triumphant sex a goal in itself. I'd been wrong to imagine children in a back room. Her grown children smiled down from school photos of many years ago. Judging from a desk frame in which there was a photograph of a tiny week-old baby, Charlotte might even be a new grandmother.

'Is that your baby?' I asked, nodding at the photograph. I could not ask if it was her grandchild, to do so would seem impolite, even hostile.

'Good heavens, no,' she said, clearly amused at the thought. 'My youngest niece. My children are all at university now. My husband is older, it would not do at all to have another child at this stage in our lives.'

'While you are having an affair with another man, you mean?' I said.

'In *any* case,' she sniffed. And then with a certain amount of relish, I thought, she said, 'I am not surprised that you reproach me.'

'Was that a reproach?'

'My husband and I have been separated for nearly three years now. He's known about James all the while. We do not lie to each other. After twenty-three years you don't lie.' She smiled, and looked at me as though I were a journalist and she a glamorous, minor celebrity. A well-known clothes designer or the wife of a politician. I resented this. Was this feeling, this resentment, what my mother meant when she said the wives were vain? If anything it was the adulterers who were vain for thinking they could borrow a woman's husband for a while, cut in as one might at a dance and just waltz away.

'Is that how long it has lasted? Three years?' Now I was upset, though desperate not to show it. Three years, perhaps she had every reason to look at me with that wise, smug expression.

'Oh, no. No!' she said, cheerfully. 'James and I have only been seeing each other a few months.'

'Oh, I see.' I was greatly relieved, though again I hoped that this did not show.

'Since early spring,' she said. 'Hasn't he told you?'

I shook my head. 'My mother used to have affairs with married men,' I said. Charlotte's smile lost a bit of its bloom at this comment. I got the feeling I'd confused her, shooting off on such a tangent. She clearly had an idea of how the conversation would run, she had an efficient, take-charge aspect to her – if I were to pin a profession on her it would be as a personal assistant to a pushy, male executive for whom she was always arranging conference calls and working overtime – and this aspect of my mother's history had not figured in how she'd envisaged the conversation. 'Does that surprise you?'

'It surprises me to hear you talk of it. Anyway, I don't have affairs with married men. I have a connection to James, who happens to be married. That's different.'

'Of course.' I decided to let her have her point. I needed to dig deeper. There was something fundamental at stake. Not just in knowing why James had chosen Charlotte. I mean, maybe there wasn't much to discover on that front. Why *not* Charlotte, after all? These things are probably much more random than I imagined. She might be looking at me wondering how it was that James came to make me his wife. In point of fact, if I did not know the history between us I might very well ask the same question. I had never quite shed the slightly librarian aspect of my appearance. I'd tried, by giving my hair a permanent wave and swapping my eyeglasses for contact lenses, dressing in expensive, slightly off-beat clothing, hiding my legs in dark, opaque tights and never, ever wearing anything with a waistband, but I was still very much the same. Big busted, big hipped, big in general. And bookish. My job as a science editor was perfectly suited to me. Whenever anybody at work met James – who never seemed to age and who was, if not spectacularly handsome, nonetheless attractive – they always regarded me slightly differently. Perhaps they were trying to discover the very thing I was trying to discern in Charlotte's case, the answer to the question *why her*?

'What made you decide to take on James?' I asked.

'Take on?' she said, and again that smile. 'You make him sound like a job.'

'He is,' I said, and laughed. 'Exactly that. A job. Not an unpleasant one, however.'

'He doesn't need management,' Charlotte said, and again the coy, almost sanctimonious smirk.

I raised my eyebrows.

'He needs understanding.'

'Oh, well, I'm sure he needs that,' I said.

'You may have just been with him too long. That's often what happens, you know. My husband and I were classic. Married young, a couple of children. We both worked, well, he worked more than I did but I had a part-time job and he had very late hours. The kids grew up and one day I looked at him standing in my kitchen and I thought, "Who is this man?"'

'I see.'

'We'd just been together out of habit. Told each other I love you out of habit. I think I felt a hundred years old by the time we split – amicably, I assure you. The repetition, the lack of pleasure, was so heavy, so aging.'

She paused and sipped from her teacup, looking at me all the while.

'I'm sure you know what I mean,' she said. 'The history becomes like a leaden thing, the relationship utterly stagnant.'

'James and I have a rather colourful history, as I'm sure he's told you.'

She nodded enthusiastically. 'Oh, good God, yes. The fights!' she said, wagging a finger in the air and swallowing all at once a mouthful of tea. 'He's described them to me! And his descriptions are always so funny! I'm sure they aren't funny at the time, the fights, I mean, but you have to admit there is some amusement in each one. You're probably thinking I am awful for saying so, but really you must count yourself lucky, at least they are life affirming. I mean, you cannot be indifferent to someone who fights like James. Or like you. I don't mean to insult you, much the opposite. I admire you. Both of you. But of course, it could not go on. Not like that.'

This was hard to hear. He'd described our fights to this woman and she'd found them amusing, 'life affirming'. This ordinary soul in her cream-coloured blouse and ribbed low-necked vest, her denim trousers, her girlish slippers. He'd told her how we argued and suggested, it would seem, that we ought to separate. I considered this and felt, for the first time since learning of Charlotte's existence, that perhaps it was me who had been foolish, foolish for having taken for granted the bond between James and myself, for believing that everything about us, about our love, our history, meant that we would always be together. Together regardless.

'I'm sorry. I've upset you,' Charlotte said. 'Well, I suppose that was inevitable this morning, wasn't it?' She let out a fluttery little laugh. 'But nevertheless, I am sorry.'

'Well,' I began, but could not think of what to say.

'Sometimes these things run their course. And then one or the other – usually the man, it has to be said – finds a way out.'

I found myself nodding, despite feeling very much like throwing my tea at Charlotte, who had a moment ago seemed a bizarre and ridiculous choice and now did not at all. Her ordinariness was exactly what James was seeking. A normal, ordinary woman who had not witnessed the other part of his life, the painful part with Lea. And who did not know him as a difficult, somewhat unstable man, but as something as simple and single dimensional as a lover.

'I think you ought to know that it isn't just because of me, he really is a complicated, difficult person,' I said. 'I haven't made that up.'

'He's creative. He's a *writer*,' she said, as though this word carried with it a descriptive quality I ought to understand immediately.

'Writers are not much different to anybody else,' I said, automatically. This idea that writers, fiction writers in particular, are a breed apart, that they deserve special attention, has always bothered me. The authors I dealt with on a daily basis at work were very accomplished, often quite brilliant, and they seldom demanded a great deal of special massaging.

'Well, James is certainly different,' Charlotte said. And then, in a slightly sorrowful, utterly patronizing voice, she added, 'Oh, I see, you've lost that. Between you, I mean.'

If James had been there I could imagine what he'd say. What a load of perfumed bollocks, he'd say. Save it for *Oprah*.

But then he *had* been there, and she must have uttered similarly repellent remarks from time to time. Maybe at those moments, when she issued some platitudinous statement, he insulted her to her face. Maybe she found that 'life affirming' as well.

'He's got a mild mood disorder. I mean, he's got a mood disorder and fortunately, at this time, it is not as acute as it might be, but there is—' I felt suddenly the need to describe to her exactly James's condition, and this feeling, I realized, was as though I were handing him over to her to care for and wanted to be quite sure she was able to do so adequately. It was pathetic, really, to want to ensure this. What would you call it? His continuing comfort.

'I think I realize his complexity,' Charlotte interrupted. 'There is no need to label him with a "mood disorder". Is that something you made up, a *mood* disorder? Honestly, I've never heard of such a thing.'

I smiled. I decided she was a moron and that I could not bear to be in her presence for another minute. 'Yes,' I said. 'I made it up.'

She smiled uneasily, knowing I was lying about something but not sure what, and began to pour me another cup of tea.

'No, thank you,' I said. 'I best be going.'

'Are you sure?' she said, but rose immediately, turning towards the front door.

I was flustered, slightly giddy, and with that sick feeling in my stomach. I did not know why I had to meet this woman.

Why James had felt it necessary to bring us together. Maybe he was just too cowardly to confront me on his own, though he must have realized that at some point he would have to. He could not go on hiding from me, that would be impossible. Did he think it best to have the women meet to negotiate a settlement of some sort? Did he honestly believe bringing us together would do any good?

Then, a thought occurred, a terrible thought that stopped me in my tracks.

'He's not here, is he?' I said, gently. 'I mean, somewhere in the house?'

'Oh, no,' Charlotte said, shaking her head. 'Absolutely not. I wouldn't have allowed you to come here and for him to duck out into a closet somewhere. That would be absurd. No. James is in the country, with his parents. I'm surprised he didn't tell you himself. I'm sorry to keep insisting like this but, after all, we are all adults undergoing what is really just a normal part of life in this age. There is no need for any of us to lie.'

'Of course not,' I said, struck by this news. In the country, in Derbyshire, with his parents? His parents, who after all had been dead for many years? I looked at Charlotte again and for a moment I thought I recognized someone else, someone at once familiar and strange. As we rose and walked to the hall I felt a sense of revisiting, of having been in just this place or perhaps with this same woman before. And then, as we went into the entrance hall, I saw it and it seemed to jump out at me like a live thing. In a corner behind the door, set against the wall, was a violin case.

Certain things fell in place all at once. Charlotte's appearance, her wispy blonde-grey hair, her thinness, her prominent mouth. It was only a faint resemblance to Lea, not a striking one, but it was there.

'That is a violin,' I said, in what I hoped was a neutral tone. 'You are a musician.'

'Yes. Yes, it is,' Charlotte said, sliding open the bolt on her front door as she spoke. She couldn't wait to get me out, that was clear, though now I stood well back from her, pinned in place by the sight of the violin case.

'Are you musical at all?' she asked. 'Never mind. You can tell me about it another time.'

'James loves music,' I said. I looked at her. 'You must have noticed that,' I said.

'Oh, yes.' She smiled. 'He loves to sit and read as I practise.'

'Do you play every day?' I asked.

'Oh, no.'

'I mean every day that James is here.'

She looked at me quizzically. She held the front door open and her smile changed, becoming impatient, more a baring of teeth than a true smile. 'I've never thought about it before. I suppose I do. Why do you ask?'

Why did I ask. It was almost impossible for me to believe that she did not already know.

'I just wondered. Because Lea, of course, was a violinist. You must know that.'

'Lea. I'm not sure I know who she is. I don't know all of James's relations. Is Lea his sister?'

The sunlight was pouring through the open door and a couple of young mothers, making their way up the hill with babies in pushchairs, peered up curiously at Charlotte and me as they passed. Still, I could not quite make myself move.

'I know you are upset, of course you are,' said Charlotte. 'But we'll talk again. And more importantly, James will talk to you. He really needs to, I can see that now. I ought to have insisted on it from the beginning. I'm sorry. You really must go.'

'Yes,' I said, my eyes still latched on to the violin case. I could imagine her playing, him watching, listening.

Poor James. He must have known that by coming here I would see it. Looking at Charlotte now, with the sunlight catching her hair, she was really very much like Lea. If I'd been searching for the resemblance from the beginning I'd have seen it. I would not even have had to spot that violin.

I said, 'Why is the violin near the front door?'

'I don't know—' she began.

'Perhaps James put it there,' I said.

'Certainly not, he'd have no reason,' she said, sharply. She was annoyed, troubled. She realized, I suppose, that I had gleaned some new insight and that I would not divulge it. This made her uncomfortable and she all but kicked the violin case out of the way with her foot. 'Why on earth does it matter where it is? A violin in a case. So what? It's usually in my spare room upstairs. The neighbours complain if they hear it so I can't even play in my own living room, which is a shame—'

'So it is usually upstairs?'

'I—' She opened the door wider. 'I must ask you to leave.'

'I'm sure you play very well,' I said.

'Thank you for coming this morning—' she said.

'Don't worry, I'm going now,' I said, making my way out of the house. I thought I heard a sigh of relief behind me as I went. Charlotte was not as stupid as I first thought; she'd figured out where she stood with regard to James and myself and that it was not a comfortable place. This annoyed her. Everything about me would in time annoy her, I was sure, but this especially: how I knew instinctively more about the man in her life than she could ever come to know, and how she'd been used in some way that she could never guess.

I walked heavily up the hill. He was so ill, I thought to myself, so sadly ill. I felt – how exactly? – defeated. Not only because I'd just met Charlotte. That did not bother me nearly so much as I'd thought it would. I felt defeated because I knew now that however I'd tried, however I'd steered a course in life for James, so that he might reasonably enjoy himself and experience a more or less happy, healthy life, I had failed. He was still so stuck on Lea, so stuck. Not in love. No. I don't think one can be said to be in love with a dead woman for more than a decade. But it was as though his life, or part of his life, had been left behind with her death. And he could not help but go fishing for it, searching for it, feeling it at times as though it were still there like some phantom limb abruptly severed. He'd wanted me to see this about him, to present it in as shocking and detailed a manner as possible so that I might understand and leave him to it. Leave him.

Is that what he wanted me to do?

I reached my car and saw that despite my heeding the parking restrictions I had still received a ticket. How ridiculous, I thought. How perfect. I did not even bother to remove it from the windscreen. I got in and took several deep breaths, wondering how I was going to drive an hour and a half back across London with my mind so cluttered, my spirit so low. I put the keys in the ignition and looked up, seeing at the bottom of my windscreen handwriting that was so very familiar. James's handwriting. What I'd thought was a ticket was in fact a note from him. In capital letters, in a faded black marker pen was his unequivocable request:

HELP ME

I felt the bottom slide from my stomach. I jumped from the car and tore the paper from beneath the wiper blade. The saddest thing about living with James, the part which I'd found at times almost unbearable, was how he understood fully how ill he was and yet could do nothing to allay the cycles of mania, the crushing black moods, the frenetic energy, the past which was never very far from his thoughts. He'd always relied on me, needed me. He needed me now.

Help me.

I looked up. I knew exactly where to look. The other side of the road, the tall iron gate, the wide, paved, mossy flagstones, the worn stairs. Over there, through all those glassy windows. So he was in the house, living for the time on Dartmouth Row. He'd known I would come this morning, that I would park the car near my old home, would stroll the length of the street and eventually head down the hill to Charlotte's house. He'd watched me. He'd waited and written his note, knowing that when I returned up the hill I would understand his plea.

I got into the car again. I switched on the ignition and put it into gear and forced myself to drive away. When early on at Charlotte's house I'd thought for a moment that he was making a fresh start with this new woman, a fresh start in his life, I'd felt jealous. Not just lovesick, but jealous of his having given himself such an opportunity. I'd wanted the same. A new beginning. I drove down the street and said out loud to myself, *You are only thirty-eight. Nothing is out of your grasp. You could find another life, have a baby even. You are not so old. Not so old at all. Young, this is your youth.*

A baby. We'd always meant to have children but it was just impossible. I'd thought it impossible. With a different man, someone other than James, it did not seem impossible in the slightest.

I reached the end of the road and realized I'd forgotten about the road closure, so had to back up a hundred yards and execute a three-point turn. As I drove past the house a second time I looked up, half expecting to see James. Then I did see him, not at the window but standing in the middle of the road in front of me, his hands in his jeans pockets, his chin bent towards his chest, his body relaxed in front of my moving car. He was just a figure in the road, standing on a slope, looking too sad to be capable of movement. How had he gotten there? I could not imagine him walking. He expected me to stop. He knew with certainty that I would. Or perhaps he thought I might run him down and was offering his body to be broken at my whim, as a means of apology.

Suffering, he once told me, was not such a bad feeling as long as you accepted it and did not yearn for release.

But I did want release. I wanted not to run him down but to skirt niftily around him and leave him standing in the road. This was impossible and so I had to brake. I stopped not much more than a foot from him. I'd let him think I might very well run him over; I'd watched his face carefully as I came at him nearer and nearer – and no, he did not flinch.

'Come inside,' he said.

'I won't,' I said. 'I'll never enter that house again.'

He opened the car door.

I held up his note. 'This frightens me.' My voice, I realized, sounded tremulous and unusually loud.

He nodded. The area beneath his eyes was purplish and swollen. He'd not been sleeping, I could see that. The way he held his head clamped down upon his shoulders told me why. Headache. Terrible migraine. If I'd cared at all about his physical pain at that moment I might have wondered how he could bear standing outside on such a bright, sunny day.

'I can't endure it,' I said, quickly. 'There is no peace, there is no end.'

He smiled, painfully, a wincing smile. I did not dare look into his eyes, knowing what I would see there. The panic, the desperate, trapped intelligence.

'Get out of the way of the car', I said, 'or I will run you down.'

Afterwards there is so much that is merely logistic. I answer the telephone, explaining that he is not there. A wedding ring is removed, a bed remade with only one pillow so that it seems fitting that it sleeps only one. Things are stacked, then boxed, then stored. Mail is divided. Certain areas of the house are neglected – his office, his closet full of sports gear and clothes. Then one day, not so far along, a door is opened and the objects are no longer infused with quite so much meaning. The museum of his love is dismantled, stock removed, thrown out or sent away to an address I know so well, Dartmouth Row, which I've decided is indeed a haunted place. It haunts me now.

The living room is rearranged, several times. The first time I think he will be surprised to see this and perhaps critical of the arrangement of lamps, which no longer shed quite as much light near his favourite reading chair. The second time I rearrange the furniture I don't imagine his comment. Then I give away the furniture to a man who buys your old when he sells you new.

First days, then weeks, then months are counted. Two months. I consider changing the phone number so that I am not aware that he does not try to call.

I am more competent at work and have more time to deal with the small, personal managerial problems that befall those in the world of publishing. My secretary is the only one who knows something is wrong. James no longer calls, and when she mentions that in an innocent, teasing manner, I do not hide my pain quickly enough. In that fraction of a second, before I cover up my feelings, she sees and knows.

'I'll tell you about that another time,' I promise.

How do I cope otherwise? I tell myself I am lucky: I am not dying. It only feels like it, and is a meek imitation at that.

My friends still invite me to their houses. Without him, they claim, I am better company.

'Better how?' I ask. I insist on being told.

'You are more fun,' Claire says.

'You are more honest,' David claims. David and Eleanor are a happy and very new married couple, so they think that the break-up of a marriage must be the worst, most dreaded thing.

'How do you *survive*?' asks Eleanor, her eyebrows pitched up, her dreamy beautiful face in shocked amazement.

Claire and I crack up at this.

At home there is no laughter. No fighting either, but the silence, so complete it is like living underwater, moves me at times to tears.

'Why are you crying?' asks Isobel. She knows him so well, knows the story as completely as it is possible for someone other than myself to know. 'You should be happy.'

'Would *you* be happy?' I ask her. She says nothing, but considers the question.

'I would be relieved,' she says, finally.

I admit that at times I am strangely relieved.

'Well, that's a start,' she says.

One day Charlotte rings me and without saying hello says, 'I hope you're satisfied. You got what you want!'

'What do you mean?'

'You *know* what I mean!' she hisses.

'No.'

'He's ended it with me.'

'He has?'

'I'm sure of it now. I never hear from him.'

This confuses me. It sounds like some kind of email romance. One day, after a stream of unanswered messages, one party realizes that the other has disappeared into cyberspace. I offer Charlotte my condolences and she tells me to fuck off.

At night I dream of him. In my dreams we argue. Or we make love. Or we sit side by side reading a newspaper. Or we do nothing particular at all. Then there is the dream in which his presence is casual but there, a figure in the background. This latter dream seems so familiar, and I realize one day why. Because it is the sort of dream I had when we were together.

The worst part of it all is knowing that one day he will come back and a decision will have to be made. I know, you see, that what I am doing now, with all my reorganization and redecoration, all my adjustments and new trials, is only a rehearsal. A mock-up for the future. For when he comes back through the door I will realize there were things I did not take into account, things I'd forgotten. James has not passed from my life. To believe that he has would be a trick, a dangerous one. He is a clever player, devious in a way that is strangely alluring. When he returns it will be with new hats and machinations, a gimmick or two, a show of bravado. I may give into him, I may not. He will show up when I stop looking for him, looking the way I did long ago and the way I find myself doing now. In trains, along busy streets, through shop windows and across the fields where I still walk every morning with the dog, and where he knows I walk.

What will he say when he approaches me? How will he look? I must stop imagining these things. It may be years before I stop and turn, thinking that I've heard his voice behind me, that my longing and judgement have betrayed me once more, and find him suddenly there.